The Arben Bridge

Ellie Rees

For Nan & Bamp

PART ONE

Ellie Rees

CHAPTER ONE

The gate was locked, she knew that. But this fact did nothing to calm her. Instead, her hand tightened on the jeweled hilt of her sword and she forced herself to take in a long, deep breath.

She gave herself the indulgence of glimpsing towards the intricate locks that were set within the gate before her eyes flitted back to the forecourt. Nothing moved besides the flames in the lamps.

The night air was not cold yet Tarley's skin felt like it was covered in a sheet of ice that would never thaw. Even under the layers of her uniform her body seemed unable to retain warmth and her free hand was starting to tap against her sword, seemingly of its own accord. As soon as she realised what she was doing she silently chastised herself and stopped. Regardless of her status she felt that she should be above such nervousness.

She glanced at Macklyn, standing tall in his uniform as if nothing could scare him, and wished she knew what he was thinking. She wanted to know what all the guards were thinking as they stood in front of their gates, waiting either for something to happen or nothing at all. She was certain that they all feared one as much as the other.

"I didn't use to mind working nights," said Macklyn, smirking.

"Me neither," said Tarley.

"At least it's not raining," said Macklyn.

Tarley smirked and turned her attention back to the forecourt; it was just as quiet as it had been thirty seconds ago.

Ainsley, the commander that Tarley and Macklyn had been assigned to that night, had gone to the toilet fifteen minutes ago and had still not returned. Tarley would have usually called him a lazy arse but not anymore. If a guard was away from his or her post for longer than five minutes everyone started to worry, whether they said it or not. Another commander had gone missing the night before, which only caused more people to give weight to the current theory that a Senior Guard was looking for promotion. But she knew that couldn't be true.

Despite the fact that just as many guards as commanders had gone missing, everyone who worked for The Arben Bridge understood the value of their oaths and the hard work it would take to go from a Junior Guard to a Senior Commander. Tarley very much doubted that anyone would go to such extremes just to secure a promotion; simply the idea of taking such a pathetically idle route sickened her. Nevertheless, there had been a clear shift in the way the commanders were talking to the guards since the disappearances began. Tarley had always admired the stern yet polite manner in which the guards and commanders had always conducted themselves. They all knew who was ranked higher and yet there was never animosity, everyone seemed determined to do their job and keep Miraylia safe.

She would often think back to when her father used to take her and her brothers on visits to the bridge. The guards had so much respect for Commander Hillis that chatting to his children seemed like no problem at all. Tarley and Macklyn quickly became enamored with the bridge and would spend years training and studying in the desperate hope that they would be accepted into the academy.

Despite her love for the bridge, it had always been a mixture of beauty and eeriness for Tarley. The five gates to the mile-long bridge were all magnificent in their own right; each one completely different in design and demanding to tell their own story.

Tarley's favourite was The Queen's Gate because it was the most ornate and intricate design that the bridge had to offer. She would always allow herself a small smile when she was assigned to guard it. The gate was made of black wrought iron that had been twisted into so many different shapes that it was impossible to follow the lines that had been created. At its centre was the face of a woman with such delicate features that Tarley often wondered how the sculptor could capture a beauty of that kind in simple pieces of metal. But it wasn't her face that amazed Tarley the most; it was her hair. Jewels of every kind exploded from The Queen's head to create a dazzling mane that flowed down to her waist and, even after hundreds of years, still left plenty of tourists trying to break on to the bridge to view her for themselves.

Macklyn spotted Tarley gazing up at The Queen and shook his head whilst smirking to himself.

"Someone could attack the bridge right now and you would be of no help in defending it," he said.

"You underestimate my response times," said Tarley before casting another glance over the forecourt.

The cobbled bricks and wrought iron fence at the bottom seemed so nondescript but Tarley had studied them for so long that she was certain that if even the tiniest crack appeared, she would be able to report it straight away. She could feel herself teetering into the realms of paranoia but she was content to be so if it meant that the bridge and the city were safe.

"How's your head? Have you been to the doctor's yet?"

"Fine and no," said Tarley, "stop fretting."

Even though she had chastised Macklyn, Tarley secretly

appreciated the thought; she had always been grateful for having two older brothers who cared so much about her but she would never tell them that. She hated being the baby of the family even as an adult.

Macklyn looked down at his watch and sighed. "It's one minute to ten," he said, "Ainsley should be back by now." Tarley desperately wanted to say that he would and that Macklyn had nothing to worry about but the words refused to form on her lips. She briefly contemplated searching for him but Darvin had always instilled in them that the bridge's protection came first. Everyone took their oaths knowing that although every guard would aim to protect their comrades, if it was at the detriment of the bridge then they were bound to the bridge.

Tarley could see beads of sweat forming just above Macklyn's brow, even though the rest of his face appeared calm and unperturbed. She wondered if anyone else would be able to tell how uneasy he felt or if she instinctively knew what signs to look for.

A few minutes passed and Tarley looked back at Macklyn, whose eyes were now darting from side to side. She was worried about Ainsley too, but if he had gone missing what good would it do for them to go looking for him? No one had been found yet and leaving the gate unguarded incurred severe consequences.

The sound of footsteps broke Tarley's ponderings and her gaze shifted from Macklyn to the dark figure that was slowly approaching the gate. The Cloaks had always made Tarley feel on edge. She could be feeling at her most calm and then at exactly ten o'clock, if she was guarding The Queen's Gate, a Cloak would appear and she would want to retreat from their presence. They all moved so steadily, as if there wasn't an actual person beneath their black capes but a light breeze that glided across the cobbles and their heads were always bowed so that no one ever saw their faces. No one was supposed to discuss the Cloaks, it broke every kind of confidentiality law, but Tarley had been on the bridge long enough to hear whispers from those who dared to comment. Some thought they were from outside the city, others thought they were an elite clandestine group of guards that not even the commanders knew about. Tarley, however, tried her very best to pretend that they didn't even exist.

Only commanders were supposed to open the gate to Cloaks but if for any reason they had to leave their post it was vital that they give their keys to the most senior guard on the gate until they returned. It was one of the many rules ingrained into the guards' memories during their time at the academy but lately Darvin had even began patrolling the bridge himself to ensure that everyone knew the protocol.

Macklyn took the keys from his belt and unlocked the four locks that spread across the gate. Both he and Tarley kept their heads bowed as the Cloak walked through the gate and made his or her journey to the end of the mile-long bridge. Tarley didn't dare to lift her head until she saw the golden trim of the Cloak's cape disappear and Macklyn closing the gate.

A lot of the guards would sneakily watch as the Cloak walked down the bridge towards the small building at the end but not Tarley. She had no fascination with them and it was the only thing she disliked about her job. She'd happily fight a crazed extremist that wanted to find out what the bridge guarded but remaining in the presence of a Cloak for five minutes made her shudder. The feeling eventually passed and she continued to guard in another half an hour of complete silence before the sound of gasping cut through the air.

Ainsley, his red face looking even more scarlet in the glows of the lamps, ran towards the gate before coming to an abrupt halt and panting like a dog.

"What's happened? Are you okay?" asked Tarley, grabbing his arm to help keep him upright.

"I'm…fine," gasped Ainsley. "I only went to the toilet….and then…ended up falling asleep…for an hour!"

"You're serious?" said Macklyn.

Ainsley nodded as he pushed Tarley away.

Macklyn rolled his eyes. "And *you're* meant to be our commander. For fuck's sake."

* * *

The following evening Tarley decided to play the role of the dutiful daughter and visit her parents. She regretted it as soon as her mother opened the door. Tarley could hear the raucous laughter from the living room and it was the kind of laughter that only occurred when her father and uncle sat down with a strong beer. Or several.

Her mother and aunt would often join in but soon faltered due to their smaller frames. They could only maintain control of their bodies for so long before they began to feel queasy and decide it would be best to go to bed and leave the Hillis brothers to their bonding.

Tarley thought their relationship was very special in that even after fifty-seven years neither her father nor her Uncle Emlyn had ever had a catastrophic falling out. She doubted that she had ever seen two brothers who were closer and that included her own. However, that evening she would have appreciated it if the alcohol currently running through their bodies had had a more calming effect. She had not got much sleep after finishing her shift the night before and had spent most of the day feeling quite ratty.

Carida tentatively led her daughter through the house and into the living room where Gwyl and Emlyn were sitting side by side with a firm grip on their drinks whilst Tarley's Aunt Tulis sat opposite them, half paying attention to the soap opera that was currently playing via the image crystals. As soon as Tarley entered the room her aunt jumped to her feet and wrapped her arms around her, squeezing tightly.

"It's so lovely to see you, Tarley!" said Tulis. "How are you?"

"I'm good," lied Tarley as she sat down next to her aunt.

Carida picked up the image crystals, causing the soap opera to disappear, and placed them on the shelf before offering Tarley her obligatory food and drink.

"I'm fine, thanks, Mum. I've already eaten," said Tarley.

"I don't care. With everything that's going on with that bridge you need to keep your strength up! I've got some left-over pie that will only waste if you don't eat it."

Tarley rolled her eyes as her mother rushed out of the room but she couldn't help but let a small smile appear on her face. *This* was comforting, even if she felt like everyone around her was slightly manic.

"In all seriousness," said Emlyn after another swig of beer, "don't you worry that you're going to disappear, Gwyl?"

Tarley's stomach tightened at the words. Of course she'd thought about it, she'd thought about it more times than she would ever admit but she would never talk about her worries. She kept telling herself her father wasn't like the others, whatever it was that was claiming those innocent guards and commanders, Gwyl was a hundred times stronger. He could fight them off. And so could she and Macklyn.

"No, I can't possibly imagine why someone would want to kidnap me," said Gwyl.

A hum of laughter went across the room as Carida re-entered with a large helping of pork pie and a glass of cranberry juice. She placed the tray firmly on Tarley's lap and glared at her in a way that suggested that if Tarley didn't eat it all she would be disowned as a daughter.

"I still think The Inquiry is involved," said Carida as she sat down in one of the low arm chairs. "Especially after those records they stole from Jobern. They're clearly after the guards."

"I don't know why they don't just round the lot of them up and-" began Gwyl before his eyes landed on Tulis. He stopped talking and took another swig of his drink, averting his gaze to the corner of the room. Tulis turned her head away but everyone had already seen the faint tears welling in her eyes.

Tarley continued to eat; she never knew how to react in those situations and always felt like no matter what she said it was the incorrect response.

"Well, there are still many theories, I'm confident that Darvin will get to the bottom of it," said Gwyl.

Emlyn guffawed, "Someone better had."

Tarley quickly finished her food as the conversation progressed to other goings on in Liliath, including the recent drug raids in Cornlake and whether Yanto's half-sister's cousin's boy was still thinking of applying to the academy.

Twenty minutes later and Tarley was finally out of the door and strolling through Miraylia. It was a fairly warm night with just enough of the sun's glow left that people weren't hurrying to get to the believed safety of home. Tarley could feel the infection of panic spreading across the people and the days of denying it were starting to come to an end. The people were scared and they didn't want to pretend otherwise for any longer.

No one knew why the bridge needed guards but it had been that way for centuries and now they were disappearing from their homes or even while they were on duty without a single clue left behind. That was what the public were told, anyway. Tarley knew of several guards who had been present during a disappearance but they were bound by the bridge's confidentiality laws never to speak of it unless given direct orders from Darvin. Even family members couldn't discuss their shifts with each other and there had been so many times when Tarley had wanted to ask Gwyl about something peculiar on her shift. Had she really seen The Fire Gate open by itself? Why was there a group of civilians being escorted from the bridge in shackles? What was the blue smoke emanating from The Arben Tower? But if Gwyl had not been there with her she would have been committing treason as soon as she uttered the words.

The bridge had always been the most secure location in

all of Liliath but for centuries even the Head Commanders had allowed tourists to come up to the entrance gate to see if they could get a peek at the guards in their famous uniforms. But those times now felt like a passage in a storybook. The only people who could ever step foot on that bridge were its guards and the Cloaks. Tarley was certain that no guard of The Arben Bridge would ever commit such treason and, despite the chill that the Cloaks brought, she very much doubted that they were responsible for the disappearances. Even so, the people of Miraylia, especially The Inquiry, wanted answers. Tarley used to wear her uniform with pride through the city but now she did her best to hide any evidence of her job and she hated herself for it.

She reached Gracefalls Park and stopped for a moment. It had long been her favourite place in the city and it saddened her that so many people were now in a rush to leave before it got dark. The crystals in the trees would soon be alight and the whole park would be bathed in a dim, golden glow that made it look like it was bursting with life, refusing to quieten even as the night drew in.

"*Do not follow me, my dark mistress, for only sorrow you will bring. I am but a man, who can do nothing but fall, when you begin to sing,*" a weak voice sang from behind Tarley.

She turned around to find a thin man sat on the pavement, covered in dirt and clutching his knees like a scared child. He had a threadbare blanket hanging over his limp shoulders and before him sat a tatty hat with a pitiful amount of coins lying inside it.

"*If you do not leave now I know that my soul will be yours forever more. A dazed shadow of a body, failing at hope, which we can never restore.*" The man looked up at Tarley and gave her a melancholic smile. "Do you like the *Songs of Night*, young haf?"

"Not really," said Tarley, fearing she had offended him. The way he had sung the start of the song had somehow saddened Tarley and she wondered if he could sense it. The weakness and fragility of his voice made her unsure if she should comfort him or run as far away as she could.

"That surprises me," said the man but his lips did not seem to move. Tarley felt like his words had thundered around and enveloped her without a sound even leaving his mouth.

She stepped back as he smiled at her, revealing his yellowed and decaying teeth. His eyes also seemed brighter, as if a sudden flare of light had risen behind them.

"Am I a surprise to you, haf?" his voice echoed across Tarley's mind but, once again, he didn't seem to be speaking.

She turned and ran, her hand flying towards where her sword usually hung. She could hear him cackling in the background as she sped along the cobbled streets and her heart continued to race along with her. She finally slowed down as she reached Battle Close but she still glanced behind her to see if she had been followed. However, all she was met with was bemused stares from the few people that dared to be on the street at that time of night.

She took a deep breath and walked into the pub where the sound of laughter and chatter was verging on overwhelming. Tarley almost felt bewildered at the contrast between the pub and the near perfect silence of the streets.

She tried not to dwell on the homeless man as she scanned the small pub for her friends but his ominous tone and deep laugh were still repeating themselves in her mind. She tried to picture his lips moving as he spoke but the image never materialised, all she remembered was a perfectly still man taunting her with his eyes.

Small white light crystals were dotted around the dark room and gave it a serene radiance that went someway to pulling Tarley's mind from her recent encounter and into the pub. The landlady was renowned for providing a homely and comforting atmosphere that very few other pubs offered in the city. Tarley and her friends had all had their first glass of beer there and had no intentions of ever turning their backs on The Tulip.

Tarley pushed her way through the small crowd that was gathered at the bar until she was at the centre of the pub and could finally see a glimpse of spiky brown hair that belonged to Ada. She walked towards the table, which was surrounded by her friends and a few faces that she didn't recognise, but that didn't bother her. She could feel her chest relax somewhat at the sight of them and unclenched the fist she had unconsciously formed.

"Hello!" beamed Ada, pulling her friend close. "You're just in time; it's Mitch's round."

Mitch, a fairly tall man with dark stubble and thick hair, shook his head as he got to his feet. "What do you want, Tarley?" he asked.

"A white wine would be perfect, thank you," said Tarley before turning her attention to everyone sat around the table. "So what are we talking about?"

"Just work, I've been commissioned to redesign Visolette Park," said Ada.

"That's fantastic!" said Tarley and gave her friend another hug. She couldn't remember a time when Visolette Park hadn't been in a state of ruin, no plant attempted to grow there and it was an infamous hotspot for drug dealing. Tarley knew that if anyone could turn it into a beautiful haven it would be Ada.

For as long as Tarley had known Ada she had found her friend squinting her eyes at a part of Miraylia and saying which plants and flowers could drastically improve it. Of course, Tarley never had a clue what Ada was talking about but she smiled and nodded just the same.

"What about you? How is the bridge?" asked Ada.

The talk around the table seemed to mellow slightly as Ada finished her question but Tarley answered with the same 'Fine, thanks' that she always did. Mitch soon returned and placed a glass of white wine in front of Tarley, which she quickly took a huge sip from as Ada told her more about her commission. However, Ada's words seemed superfluous as Tarley's mind was wandering and at the forefront of it was the homeless man from the street. There had been words for people like him a long time ago but no one really believed in those anymore and those that did were met with smirks and sniggers. Tarley believed the history books to be true and was confident that anyone who possessed those supposed abilities died out centuries ago. Even so, there were those who still thought that they could prey on people's uncertainties with little tricks.

That must have been all it was, a trick, thought Tarley.

"So then I took all of my clothes off and gave Neb Figmore a lap dance," said Ada.

"What?!" said Tarley, her mind suddenly thrust from the streets outside and back towards her friend.

"So you *are* listening," said Ada with a large smirk on her face.

"Sorry."

Ada leaned in and lowered her voice so that only Tarley could hear her speak. "Rough day?"

"Sort of. I'm just going to pop to the loo."

Tarley left the main room of the pub and walked into one of the empty cubicles in the women's toilets. She locked the door behind her and leaned against the wall, closing her eyes.

Am I a surprise to you, haf?

The question was replaying in her head as if someone had pressed the repeat button on a music player. What had he meant? Why had he said it? Maybe if she'd just tossed him a few coins and walked away he wouldn't have tried to agitate her. She tried to imagine how she would have reacted if she was living on the street and saw hundreds of people walking past her without so much as a glance in her direction; she had no doubt that she would snap sooner or later. But how had he done it? He must have just thrown his voice but his lips were perfectly still, a man like that could make millions. He wouldn't be living on the streets.

"Get a grip," Tarley said to herself and left the toilet. She washed her hands in the sink, splashed her face with the water and made her way back into the pub.

"Excuse me," said a middle-aged man as Tarley walked past. "But did I hear you mention that you work on the bridge?"

"Only if you were eavesdropping," said Tarley and the man answered her with a toothy grin. "But yes, I'm a guard."

"And how does it make you feel knowing that one of your own has turned against you? Those poor people disappearing without a trace, it has to be an inside job."

"I can assure you it's not."

"Pull the other one! Somebody is killing those guards, I'm convinced of it, and if it isn't one of your scummy pals, then who is it?"

Tarley reacted before she gave herself a chance to think and pushed the man so hard that he fell backwards against a nearby wall. She could hear the gasps but part of her didn't care, she knew that guards of the bridge were meant to be in control of themselves at all times but she had felt the tension building inside of her all night, waiting for a time when it could be released.

"See?! Fucking scum!" yelled the man as he got to his feet. "You all act like you're so much better than us but you're not!"

Tarley lurched forward but Ada was already in front of her, blocking her path and glaring at her friend. Despite her small frame Tarley suddenly saw Ada as one of the large guards on the bridge who was always desperate for an excuse to punch someone.

"Stop it, Tarley!" she shouted. "I think maybe you should go home."

"Why should I? He was-"

"-just go home," Ada interrupted. "Do you really think that a volatile guard is the kind of publicity that the bridge needs right now?"

Tarley didn't respond but marched through the pub towards her friends and grabbed her bag in one fell swoop before striding back out on to the street. She could sense everyone staring at her and as she closed the door behind her the chatter began in earnest.

Let them talk; they obviously have nothing better to do.

As she walked home all she could think about were Ada's words. She wondered if Darvin would find out, or anybody on the bridge for that matter. The number of guards on the bridge may have been dwindling but she felt she knew the commanders well enough to know that they would have little problem dismissing a Junior Guard for improper behaviour.

She was furious with herself. She had never behaved like that and would never dream of hurting someone unless they were attacking the bridge. A few nasty words from a drunken fool shouldn't have affected her so much, she knew that. She was meant to be better than the average person on the street.

By the time she reached her house her mind was no less calm than it had been at The Tulip. She headed straight for the kitchen and poured herself a large wine with shaking hands. She took a large gulp before going into the living room and placing three image crystals into three slots which were carved into a pane of wood with a numeric keyboard at its top. She placed the controller on the floor and a slim woman in her thirties soon appeared via the hologram. She was walking through a field in Paxia explaining why it was so important for local residents to support their farmers; Tarley couldn't care less but she was far too content to sit with her wine than to trawl through all the channels. Besides, there was rarely anything decent to watch at that time of night.

Twenty minutes later the front door opened and Mabli, an athletic woman with blonde, wavy hair walked into the lounge. Tarley was a little surprised to see her as she had assumed that she was already in bed.

"You're back early," said Mabli.

"Yeah, no one turned up," replied Tarley. "I thought you

weren't on a shift tonight?"

"I wasn't, I just fancied a walk."

Tarley nodded. She often found it hard to make conversation with Mabli, not because she outright disliked her but because she had taken a room after one of her house mates had disappeared from the bridge. Tarley didn't understand why they couldn't keep the room empty considering that the rent was paid for by the Bureau but Darvin had been adamant that it should be filled. There were still another two empty rooms in the house but every guard that was now left had a home.

Tarley used to relish coming home to such a full house, there would always be someone at home to talk to after a shift and, luckily, everyone got on really well but now she was growing to hate it.

Not one of the people who lived at number twenty Fray Avenue had ever thought that they would go missing. They were all young and strong; the perfect examples of Arben Bridge guards. Even the two commanders who had lived there had only left the academy five years previously. But none of it mattered. The commanders disappeared within two weeks of each other and then Brecon had gone a month later. Mabli seemed to sweep in out of nowhere with her constantly upbeat attitude and total ignorance as to how Tarley was feeling. She didn't want a new friend; she just wanted her old ones back.

No one had prepared Tarley for the silence that came when they left. She didn't just miss them but missed the *noise* that they brought the most. She no longer came home to the sound of laughter or the clatter of pans as someone experimented in the kitchen. There were no arguments or pointless drunken debates, just Mabli and Tarley plodding through the day.

"I don't think I can be bothered with this," Tarley finally said after a long silence. "I'm going to bed. Night."

"Good night," said Mabli as she watched Tarley leave the room, wishing more than anything she could make her trust her.

CHAPTER TWO

Tarley felt restless as she walked to work the following morning and seemed to be finding fault in every little detail of her journey. The pavement was too narrow, the market sellers were too loud and the sky was far too blue. In truth, she had not slept well at all the night before and she had never been the kind of person to function well on just a few hours of sleep. Not only did she have a dull headache the entire night but the homeless man had seeped into her thoughts and clung on tight, forcing her to analyse every aspect of what had happened. If he hadn't unnerved her so much she would never have got into that row in the pub. Maybe.

She still couldn't figure out how he had managed to talk without moving his lips and she was failing to think of a time when she had felt more frustrated. She hated being made to feel like a fool, she was certain that there was an unbelievably simple reason as to how he managed it and not figuring it out was embarrassing.

Just try to forget about it. It was nothing.

Tarley turned on to Delyth Avenue, a hugely popular area of the city because of the quirky shops and cafes it was home to, before joining Victory Road. The road ran directly through the centre of Miraylia with almost every other street, alleyway and avenue being an offshoot from its twenty-mile stretch. It was also the most direct road to the bridge.

As the bridge came into view she could feel her anxieties slowly disappearing and being replaced by a sense of purpose. Most people she knew dreaded going to their jobs but she found that hers brought her a sense of determination that she found unusually calming.

On the rare occasions Darvin had visited during her times at the academy he had always commented on how focused Tarley was, whether that was on her fighting technique or on her study of the bridge. She had never shown the pride that his comments had given her but she always secretly wanted to squeal with happiness. When she felt under pressure she would often think back to those moments in a bid to remind herself that this was the perfect job for her. After all, being a guard was in her blood and she reveled in that feeling of heritage.

As she neared the first entrance gate to the bridge she was grateful that there were only a handful of tourists that she had to push through. As the day wore on she knew that the surrounding area would be brimming with people taking photos and trying their best to trick the guards into revealing the secrets of the bridge. Even the disappearances had not deterred them; some had arrived with the sole purpose of solving the mystery and making a name for themselves in the process.

Tarley walked up to one of the guards and flashed him her pass before he carefully opened the gate for her, which caused several of the tourists to point and whisper.

Tarley nodded and headed towards the second entrance gate where she could see Ryder standing firmly in front of the black wrought iron bars. She felt silly for thinking it but just seeing his jolly face would make her smile. She had known Ryder for years as he was a close friend of her father's and had fond memories of him playing tricks on her as a child. His impression of a drunken walrus still made her howl with laughter.

"Hello, Tarley," said Ryder as she approached the gate.

"Hi, how are you?" she replied and placed her right hand on top of a large crystal that rested on a wooden podium.

The crystal was more jagged than most and every dent in it was a different colour. It was extremely rare, especially in Miraylia, and Tarley knew from her father that Darvin would have to get a replacement shipped in from Andice if it were to ever go missing. However, only the best guards got placed on the entrance gate and the last time it had been stolen was over fifty years ago and even then the thief only got as far as Delyth Avenue.

As soon as her hand touched the crystal it began to change to blue and then fade into purple before turning every colour imaginable. Tarley had found it quite distracting the first time she visited the bridge but now it felt as natural as guarding the bridge itself.

"I'm well," said Ryder but his eyes were looking over Tarley's head.

"How's Colt? Does retirement suit him?"

"He's fine."

Tarley felt a shift in the air; Ryder would usually be making jokes about her father or Darvin by now, leaving Tarley with tears in her eyes. But that morning it was as if he was addressing the Premier herself.

She waited in silence until the crystal finally turned clear and the words 'Tarley Anwen Hillis, twenty-five and three months' appeared on the crystal in bold black letters.

Ryder glanced at the crystal before retrieving a set of keys from his belt and unlocking the gate.

"Darvin has requested your presence in The Arben Tower immediately," said Ryder once Tarley had stepped through.

"Why?" said Tarley.

"I can't tell you, love. But I'm very sorry," Ryder softly placed his arm on Tarley's and looked into her eyes for the briefest of moments.

She didn't push the subject anymore; she knew that Ryder would never disobey orders from Darvin. She turned on her heel and almost ran towards the tower, a place where guards rarely went. The commanders would often meet there but it was made quite clear to the guards throughout their training if they were ever asked to go there it would either be for a promotion or to be dismissed. Tarley had not applied for a promotion.

Shit! I bet it's about what happened at the pub!

She slowed her pace down as she neared the old grey bricked building, suddenly not wanting to get any closer to it. If she got sacked she had no idea what she would do, she didn't have the skills to do anything else. There was a sword fighting center near her house that always seemed to be advertising for new tutors, she was sure they'd relish the chance to hire an ex-guard. She would bring a gravitas to the entire community. Or would they just turn their backs on her for disgracing her profession? Maybe her mother would finally help her master sewing and she could work in the shop but after twenty-five years of attempts Tarley was still hopeless with a needle and thread.

Shit, shit, shit.

If she was no longer a guard, what would she be?

She entered the tower to find a woman in a commander's uniform standing in front of an old door. She had not come across her before and Tarley could only assume that she was constantly assigned to the tower.

"Tarley Hillis?" she asked in a stern voice.

"Yes, haf," replied Tarley.

"Follow me."

The commander opened the door and gestured for Tarley to follow. They both walked into the small and cold room which gave Tarley a sudden shiver. There were numbered buttons on the wall and the commander pressed fifteen; the highest floor.

Tarley hated the lifts in old buildings, the crystals that they used to make them move were often inefficient and so the ascent to the correct floor was painfully slow. Eventually the lift came to a halt and the commander pushed open the door to reveal a large room with several Senior Commanders gathered around a holograph that Tarley was struggling to see.

"Head Commander Wavers," said the commander as she walked into the room. "I have brought you Tarley Hillis."

"Thank you, you may return to your post," said Darvin.

The commander saluted and turned on her heel before re-entering the lift.

Tarley looked up at Darvin, who seemed taller than ever, and waited for him to speak. She could feel her hands clenching into fists at her side and silently prayed that he would give her another chance to be worthy of the bridge.

"Tarley, I'm afraid I have some bad news for you," began Darvin, walking back towards the holograph and indicating that Tarley should do the same. As they drew closer Tarley could finally see a tall building made of dark brick with a reporter standing outside and the words '*The Inquiry Infiltrates the Harkon Building*' scrolling underneath her.

"Shit!" shouted Tarley. "My brother works there!" Several heads turned towards her and Tarley could feel her cheeks flushing red. "Sorry, hyd, I just-"

"-I understand, Tarley," said Darvin. "Several Inquiry members infiltrated the building about an hour ago, we're unsure as to their motives right now but I think it's safe to assume that they were after Neb Figmore. Baodor was one of the workers who tried to apprehend them."

Tarley's heartbeat had increased with every word that came out of Darvin's mouth and she found her hands tightening into fists. She only hoped that her efforts to keep an expressionless face were working.

"I'm afraid that Baodor has been taken to hospital," Darvin continued, "but that's all I know. I've arranged for a car to take you there straight away and you must take as much time off as you need."

"Thank you, hyd." Tarley saluted, as did Darvin, before

running out of the room.

She raced towards the entrance gate where she could see the black car waiting for her on the other side of the bars. It was clearly a car meant for Senior Commanders because there wasn't a single mark on it and there was no sound as it hovered slightly above the ground.

Without speaking Ryder opened the gate for Tarley and she briefly nodded at him before jumping into the back of the car. She allowed herself to finally let out the breath she had been holding in for the past five minutes.

"I'm very sorry to hear about your brother," said the driver, a middle-aged man who Tarley had only ever seen on the rare occasions that Darvin required a car.

"Thank you," said Tarley, softly, wondering why they weren't currently speeding towards the hospital.

The driver quickly checked his mirrors before pulling off and they were soon on their way, with the entire journey being made in complete silence.

Tarley would have been in awe of the car had she not been so shocked. Her parents' car, although it wasn't in a state of disrepair, still made a ghastly chugging noise now and again when the crystals needed replacing but this car made no noise whatsoever. She gratefully accepted the silence as a million thoughts fought for precedence in her head.

She could feel the sweat building up across her body and a dull ache began to form across her head as she tried to imagine what state Baodor would be in when she saw him. She could have asked Darvin for more details of the attack but her main concern was getting to the hospital as fast as she could.

Tarley admired Boador for trying to stop The Inquiry but he was not a fighter in the same way that the other Hillises were. He could handle a sword and throw a punch but those that joined The Inquiry were taught to fight as well as the guards and to be a hundred times more ruthless.

Tarley had always been prepared for such things happening to her, it had been part of her training, but not for Baodor. She and her brothers had been inseparable growing up but one of the only ways in which they differed was what career paths they chose. Having grown up in a family that had guarded the bridge for decades, they all felt a strong tie to it but Baodor was never one to play fight and when their father placed a sword in his hand he would stare at it like it was a dead animal that he didn't know how to dispose of. Baodor wasn't prepared for the unpredictability of the bridge, he just handled its admin, and now all Tarley could see was Baodor lying in a hospital bed covered in bruises and cuts. Or with blood pouring out of him. Or his face mutilated in a million different ways.

She hated The Inquiry. She always would.

The driver finally pulled up outside the hospital and wished Tarley all the best as she scrambled out of the car and into the small crowds gathered outside the hospital. Tarley felt no guilt as she pushed through them to get to the door; most of them were just there for the gossip, anyway. She elbowed her way through the reception area until she reached the desk and demanded to know where her brother was.

"Fifth floor," said the receptionist, curtly. "Room six."

Tarley gave her an insincere smile before heading to the nearest lift and punching the button for the fifth floor. As the door reopened she could see her mother, father and Macklyn standing in the corridor talking to a very tired looking doctor.

"Mum!" shouted Tarley as she ran towards them.

Carida turned around, her face red and puffy from crying, and opened her arms to her daughter. She felt oddly reassured that all her children were in the same place at least.

"Is he okay? Where is he?" asked Tarley, pulling away.

"He's stable," said the doctor, extending his hand to Tarley. "I'm Doctor Orling; I've been treating your brother. He tried to take on two of The Inquiry members and sustained a minor head injury and some cuts and bruises in the process."

Tarley grabbed Carida's hand without realising and squeezed tight.

"Can we see him?" asked Macklyn.

"Of course; his fiancée is already with him. Follow me, please," said Dr. Orling.

He led the four of them down the long corridor and pushed open the door with a number six painted on it to reveal Baodor sitting up in bed with white bandages covering his head. Ivy sat next to him, clutching his hand with hers, the last remnants of tears in her eyes.

Baodor turned towards his family and gave them a small smile. Carida instantly ran towards him and wrapped her arms around him, sobbing into his shoulder.

"Mum, I can't breathe," said Baodor.

"Sorry," said Carida, eventually letting go. "We've just been so worried. How are you?"

"Well I've been better."

Gwyl quietly chuckled and arranged a group of chairs so that they could all sit either side of the bed. Tarley sat down next to Ivy, grabbing a nearby box of tissues as she did so.

"So, what happened?" asked Tarley.

"Tarley!" shouted Gwyl with an almost growl like quality to his voice.

His daughter gave the slightest of jumps before laying her eyes on Baodor and presenting him with the smallest of smiles. Tarley had been told before that she tended to employ her guard training at inappropriate times.

"It's okay, dad," said Baodor before taking a breath and relaying the events.

Baodor said that they still weren't sure how many Inquiry members were in the building, or even how they got in, but the current estimate was twelve. Baodor had gone into work early to plan an upcoming press conference for Darvin when he heard a scream from outside his office. He ran outside to find two men standing over an unconscious co-worker. They both immediately tried to knock out Baodor but he fought back as best he could until one of them withdrew a knife and sloppily sliced open his forehead as they tried to pin Baodor down. His head smacked the floor and he woke up in the ambulance half an hour later.

Ivy lifted Baodor's hand to her mouth and kissed it while everyone else in the room was grateful that the sinking feeling in their stomachs wasn't visible to the young man lying in the bed.

"If I ever see Penn Heath or his bloody followers I swear I'll remove their heads from their shoulders!" yelled Gwyl.

"Even Lenna?" snapped Tarley, unsure where this sudden surge in anger had come from. She hated The Inquiry just as much as her father did.

"You know your father didn't mean that," said Carida, her eyes shooting from Tarley to Gwyl. "Anyway, Baodor is our priority right now."

"Yes, the most important thing is that Baodor is safe and that he gets better," said Ivy, glaring from Tarley to Gwyl.

"Yeah, we can't have that pretty little head of yours falling apart," said Macklyn, lightly tapping the top of Baodor's bandages.

Tarley remained silent for the following hour while the others talked about every subject other than the attack. She could tell that her mother and father were in no mood to discuss anything more serious than which vegetables were in season and Tarley hated it. She hated being made to feel like the youngest child with nothing valuable to say. She adored her family but their ability to bury their heads in the sand was sometimes second to none. A possible attack on Delegate Neb Figmore's life had been made and no one was acting like it scared them, even though Tarley knew it did. Her whole family was tied up in the government somehow and if The Inquiry were finally positioning themselves as the criminal organisation that they had been deemed then that didn't bode well for anyone with the Hillis name.

Dr. Orling finally returned and suggested that they all go home to rest; he needed to run some more tests on Baodor and it wouldn't do him any harm to get some sleep. Nobody argued, although Gwyl had to almost pull Carida off Baodor as they left the room.

As they waited for the lift Tarley glanced back down the corridor to see a man just slightly older than her lurking around Baodor's room. He had a white coat on but his shoddy clothes and stubble stirred a doubt within Tarley.

She took a step forward to go back to her brother's room but the man caught her glance and smirked. The action made Tarley feel incredibly uncomfortable; it was too knowing, too presumptuous for a stranger. He gave her a small nod, turned on his heel and disappeared into the flood of people that were crowding the corridor.

CHAPTER THREE

Tarley, Gwyl and Carida sat either side of Baodor on his third day in hospital as Gwyl retold his famous story of how as a young cadet he had drunkenly broken into the gym and spent the night cuddling a punching bag. Ever since Baodor had been admitted to the hospital he had always had a family member by his side and it seemed to be an unwritten rule that only the quaintest and lightest of conversation topics were to be employed. Any mention of the attack and Gwyl or Carida would shoot a look that could silence a lion.

Tarley thought about the many death threats she had been sent, the numerous tourists she had fought off and even a Senior Commander who had gone rogue on a shift. She had battled all of these things and had never been as injured as Baodor, the worst wound she had received had been a deep cut in her right arm. She almost felt guilty that he had suffered so much more in comparison.

"Why don't I get us some coffee?" said Tarley midway through her father's anecdote.

He simply nodded as she stood, he was too enthralled by his own story and Tarley had no intention of breaking him out of his cocoon. She walked down the corridor and into a waiting room where almost everyone seemed to be watching the holograph at its centre.

Neb Figmore and Henya Quinn were standing on a stage as reporters all shouted questions at them. There wasn't a single bruise on Neb Figmore's balding head and Tarley couldn't help but feel slightly outraged. She had nothing against the man, he came across well, but the attack was meant for him and, instead, it was her brother and his brave co-workers who became its victims.

"I am, of course, incredibly grateful to be alive," said Figmore, "and utterly devastated that three people died as a result of this attack. Following on from the attack in Jobern last month we can only conclude that The Inquiry is more dangerous than ever. Henya and I will continue to work hard to ensure that all of their members are brought to justice."

"Haf Quinn, do you now feel that it is time to tell Liliath what it is that the bridge is guarding? Three people have died as a direct result of its secrecy; do you not owe it to them to at least consider releasing that information?" shouted a plucky reporter.

Suddenly all the reporters in front of the stage fell silent as Henya Quinn approached the microphone. There wasn't even a hint of a smile on her face.

"Government policy has always been to let the public know exactly what it needs to know and my stance on this has not changed. As Neb has said, we will both be working closely to ensure that we find The Inquiry and punish them for their crimes."

In all her years as Premier she had never spoken about the bridge and, for the most part, the journalists didn't ask. Tarley was sure that it was an unspoken agreement between the government and the press but every now and then someone would try their luck and it would always end the same way. Henya would give a vague yet polite response and then the interview would end.

Everyone in the room immediately began to respond to

what they had just seen as Tarley walked towards the coffee machine, still frustrated that there was no news on those responsible for the attack.

"Doesn't she think those poor families have the right to know why those people died?"

"How hard can it be to find The Inquiry?"

"They're scum."

"They do have a point, though. Why can't we know?"

Tarley joined the queue for the machine, her eyes barely focusing on the rest of the press conference. Suddenly, she saw a flash of dark hair moving towards her brother's room and instantly recognised the man. She'd been waiting for him to return and although she felt annoyed at the intrusion she also felt gratified that her instincts were right. She treaded softly towards him, using her years of training to ensure that she weaved through the bodies that cluttered the hallway almost soundlessly. By the time she reached him he was trying to peep into Baodor's room, despite the frosted glass on the door.

"I know who you are," she whispered into his ear.

His whole body jerked at her words and he quickly snapped around to face Tarley. His eyes were dark and boring into Tarley's with such aggression that Tarley felt like he was begging her to fight him.

"I'm a doctor," he said, smirking and shoving Tarley out of the way before hastily walking down the corridor.

Tarley began to follow him, his pace quickening as he walked further away. Every turn he took he tried to get lost in the throng of the hospital but Tarley's eyes were fixed on him as her legs gained speed.

He soon broke out into a sprint, breaking through the walls of people to get to the stairs and knocking over anyone who dithered for too long. Tarley was only metres behind him and ignoring every shout and scream that was hurled in her direction.

"Just wait for a moment!" yelled Tarley but the man continued to run and so she continued to chase.

Insults and threats followed them both as they ran but neither stopped to take any notice. Tarley loved to run; the feeling of rushing past everything in sight was always liberating but this was far more intense. She had no regard for the people around her and didn't feel any guilt for it but the idea that this man could get away and almost disappear into thin air made her chest tighten.

He veered left and ran straight across the busy road, loud horns following his path. A large car was heading towards Tarley but she didn't stop, she sped up just as the car clipped her ankle.

"You stupid bitch!" shouted the driver but Tarley didn't care as she raced down the cobbled street. She'd been called worse.

She glimpsed his dark hair disappear down an alley and she followed, screaming at him to stop. She could tell that he was getting tired, his pace slowed as he ran through the grubby alleyway but Tarley used this moment to put all of her energy into her body and push on despite the fatigue that was creeping over her. She pushed her legs forwards and when she was close enough she threw her whole body on top of his, forcing him on to the dirty, cold ground.

He groaned as he hit the floor and Tarley quickly pulled his arms behind his back. With her free arm she pushed it against the back of his neck and pressed down hard so that he was unable to move his head. To her surprise he didn't even try to push her off.

"I know you're with The Inquiry," said Tarley.

He laughed but the sound was distorted as Tarley pushed his head against the ground. "You're sure of that, are you?" he spat.

"Why else would you want to check up on a victim of the attack?"

"I told you, I'm a doctor. I have an interest in medical dramas."

Tarley twisted his arm, causing him to wince, and pushed further down on his neck. She had learnt the maneuver as a teenager during her fighting classes and had always been able to overthrow her opponent but employing it now seemed to have a whole new level of satisfaction.

"Do you know Lenna Hillis?" she said but he remained silent. "Do you know her?!"

"For fuck's sake, why-"

"-do you know her or not?!" shouted Tarley, twisting his arm again.

He let out a groan as he tried to free himself but Tarley's strength was too much for him. He knew the guards were trained to the highest caliber, he had even seen it first hand, but he hadn't expected this. He had never lost a real fight in his life.

"Yes, I know her," he eventually said.

"Then I want you to give her a message from me. I'll be at Gracefalls Park a week from today at five pm. I want to see her."

"Well I know for a fact that she doesn't want to see you."

Tarley let go of his arms and neck and stood up, breathing fast and deep. "Just tell her."

Tarley walked out of the alley without once looking back at the breathless man lying face down amongst the rubbish of the nearby streets. In any other circumstances she would have stayed to help but, then again, in any other circumstances she doubted she would have had to attack a lone member of The Inquiry. She was still pretty certain that she hated them but she needed to see Lenna, even if it really was for the very last time.

Tarley made her way back to the hospital, ignoring the stares and whispers from those who had just seen her tear through the building after an unknown man. She quickly wiped off some of the dirt from her clothes and readjusted her hair before walking into Baodor's room, trying to act as composed as she could.

"Where's the coffee?" asked Carida.

The fake smile that Tarley was wearing disappeared in an instant.

"The machine's broken," she spat. The words came a little too quickly than she had expected and she could sense her mother preparing to chastise her. "I got to the front of the queue and then the stupid thing conked out."

Gwyl tutted. "Typical," he said, turning to Baodor. "Anyway, what is it you were saying about the potato industry?"

* * *

Tarley was glad to be back in work that evening. The inane conversations that inundated her at the hospital were starting to drive her mad. She had huge respect for her family's intellect but it had been nowhere in sight over the last few days. She understood why they were doing it but, even so, she had to wonder if Baodor was sick of it, too.

They had always been protective parents and since the disappearances had begun their innate drive to care for Tarley was at an all-time high. Gwyl had even requested that he join Macklyn and Tarley on all of their shifts but Darvin had promptly said that it was not feasible. Tarley had tried not to show her relief too much to her father.

Tarley's eagerness to get to work was only increased by the fact that on her way there yet more whispers followed her. She had walked the same route to work almost every day for four years and so most of the locals knew who she was. The same people who once smiled at her and asked her how she was. The same people who proudly told their children that she was a guard of The Arben Bridge.

"Look at that lovely uniform."

"That could be you one day".

"Say hello to the nice lady."

But now they would hide their faces as soon as they saw her or turn to a nearby friend to gossip. Tarley could hear the fear in their voices, even if their sounds were muffled. The terror was like a disease spreading through the city and even if you weren't infected you still felt its danger lurking behind you.

The guard families who had lost a loved one had quickly become pariahs as more people disappeared. On the rare occasions they were seen on the streets they seemed to unconsciously dispel anyone around them and the friends that dared to visit were seen as being far more honourable than they had been just months before. Tarley was sure she would never understand how or why people could be so fickle.

Ryder was keen to ask after Baodor as she entered the bridge and, as much as she respected him, the last thing she wanted to do was talk about her brother. She was desperate to get into her uniform and guard her gate.

As she walked towards the small grey bricked building that contained changing rooms for the guards, Tarley could see Darvin heading her way at his usual slow and assured pace. She was still waiting for him to sack her over the attack in the pub and so her palms quickly became hot and clammy.

"Good evening, Tarley. How are you?" said Darvin.

"As well as I can be," she replied.

"If you're not feeling up to it I can get someone to cover your shift. I'm sure that your family-"

"-with respect, hyd, I'd rather work. I've already missed two shifts."

"I understand. I've put you on The Cloud Gate with Sarva, Pep's your commander."

Tarley saluted and walked into the changing rooms, doing her best not to scream out in rage. Why was everyone treating her like a child? She was yet to have a mental breakdown and until that happened she just wanted everyone to treat her like they normally did. Once she was changed she took a deep breath and examined her sword.

She had been awarded it four years ago at her graduation ceremony, as was every other graduate of the academy, by Darvin himself and she still liked to take a moment to appreciate its beauty.

The silver hilt was an intricate design with the guard

crossing at numerous places in a semi-globed shape. On top of the pommel was a sapphire, which many may have deemed impractical but an Arben Bridge guard sword was meant to inspire in its look as much as in its use and Tarley had never doubted that the sapphire would fall. Finally, the words 'The Arben Bridge' were inscribed at the top of the blade in a cursive font that Tarley had selected herself.

Tarley sliced the sword through the air several times before placing it in her scabbard. She looked in the mirror one last time to ensure that her uniform fell perfectly around her body before finally heading back out on to the bridge.

Sarva was already waiting at the gate by the time Tarley arrived and after asking how Baodor was the two remained silent for a long time, only bidding Pep good evening when she arrived.

Tarley had nothing in common with either of them other than the bridge. Sarva was a man in his late thirties who kept himself to himself and Pep was a grumpy woman on the verge of retirement who had always loathed Gwyl. Tarley constantly had to practice her best fake smile when she was around Pep simply because she knew it would drive her crazy.

Tarley looked up at The Cloud Gate, the least impressive of the gates in her eyes, and wished she could be in front of the Queen again. The metal of The Cloud Gate was painted in a pale grey at the top that gradually darkened into a deep blue at the bottom. At its head there were three small houses and a large cloud residing over them that was filled with swirls and intricate patterns. Tarley thought it was pretty enough but it didn't have the overwhelming sense of grandeur and beauty that The Queen's Gate did.

The bridge had always felt like a second home to Tarley. When she was in school she would be desperate to finish so that she could see Gwyl and his colleagues as they finished their shifts. And when she joined the academy she was always the first one at the entry gate on their sanctioned trips, eager to be rewarded with her visitor pass.

After Lenna had left the first place that Tarley went to was the bridge; she wasn't even booked on to a shift for another two days but she knew it would be the only place that could calm her. Its old cobble stones had been tread by generations of Hillises and Tarley was certain she could feel every one of them walking next to her whenever she stepped out on to the forecourt.

Lenna.

Even after two years she still felt a tightening on her heart when she thought about her. Tarley still wasn't sure that she regretted everything she said to her when they said goodbye and that made her feel uneasy. She should hate herself for the way she acted but she didn't. Lenna always knew that Tarley felt an affinity to the bridge and anyone who sought to destroy it could not exist in Tarley's life. Their familial bond had made no difference to Tarley once the insults began pouring out of her mouth. Once she knew who Lenna really was Tarley would never be able to care for her in the same way. It was Lenna who had severed their tie and did so in the most devastating way that she could.

And yet Tarley never stopped thinking about her. She never stopped worrying that she was safe nor wondering where she was hiding. Was she even in Miraylia anymore? She could have scaled the world ten times over and Tarley wouldn't know. Tarley couldn't even talk to anyone about it; Emlyn and Tulis refused to acknowledge that they even had a daughter and Tarley's own family would try to quieten her whenever she mentioned Lenna. All of the memories they had made together had just been expected to disappear and condemned to nothingness.

She looked through the gate and down the bridge where that evening's group of commanders lined the walkway. She would be in their ranks one day and then years in the future she would have Darvin's job. She only hoped that Lenna saw sense by that point.

Before she realised what was happening, Tarley had instinctively raised an arm to cover her eyes as a flash of blue light erupted at the end of the bridge and up into the blackness of the sky. It seemed to last for less than a second but it was so vibrant and defined that it was impossible to miss.

What felt like an electric shock hit Tarley's chest as she gasped, her free hand flying towards the hilt of her sword and clumsily attempting to remove it from its scabbard.

She looked around but neither the guards nor the commanders seemed perturbed, they were as still as they ever were.

"You okay?" asked Pep.

Tarley's eyes shot from Pep to Sarva, who both looked at her with what she supposed passed as concern and pushed her sword back into its resting place. The tightness in her chest disappeared but she felt like her uniform was soaked through with sweat.

"Yeah, fine, just a headache," said Tarley.

She turned her back to them and massaged her temples, doubting that they were stupid enough to believe her performance but nevertheless hoping that they were.

She'd seen the light before. It had been just over a month ago as she was walking to her locker to change; it was just as bright and lasted just as long. But the pain had not been as intense. She didn't tell anyone; she just assumed that she was exhausted and her brain was playing tricks on her. Maybe that's all it was. Baodor had just been seriously injured; of course she wasn't going to feel normal. If no one else could see the light how could it be anything to worry about?

CHAPTER FOUR

Five o'clock finally arrived and the sun slowly began to make an appearance. Tarley had never been so glad to finish a shift as she had been that morning. Her body always ached after a shift but that night had been different. She had spent the whole nine hours trying to work out if she was going mad and by the time she was ready to change out of her uniform every part of her mind and body was exhausted.

She didn't see the blue light again but she had seen a Cloak approach The Queen's Gate out of the corner of her eye, which had only increased her anxiety. She wondered if they had seen the light, too, but she wouldn't dare to ask. Tarley couldn't help but wonder what it was he or she would be doing in the building that night.

Sarva and Pep had been their usual quiet selves for the rest of the night and so Tarley was forced to pretend that nothing unusual had occurred. Until Darvin asked to see her, the events of the night would not exist in any other form other than Tarley's memory.

However, as she placed her uniform and sword in her locker all she could continue to think about was the light, despite her best efforts to remind herself that it was best that she didn't know what it meant. She had been trained to protect, not to ask questions. Curiosity would only bring her harm. She didn't need to know. She didn't want to know. But she had been trying to reprimand herself all night and the questions still circled in her head like vultures. How bright must the light have been for her to see it a mile away? Was it a signal? And who was it meant for? Most importantly, why did everyone on the bridge appear as though they had not seen it?

She slammed her locker shut and threw her bag over her shoulder. What she really needed was to get to bed and have a few hours of sleep; she obviously wasn't coping as well with the stress as she thought she was.

Baodor was meant to be leaving the hospital later that morning and Tarley hoped that this thought would ease her nerves, but it didn't. Her hands were beginning to shake and it wasn't until she took in several deep breaths did they steady themselves.

She finally pulled on her jacket and tied it tightly around her waist before leaving the changing rooms, only mumbling goodbye to the few guards that were there.

"Oh no," said a voice as Tarley walked away from the building. "Korla is never late."

Tarley turned around the corner to find Darvin and one of the commanders facing each other with looks of equal distress upon their faces. They seemed to jump apart at the sight of Tarley.

"Is everything all right, hyd?" asked Tarley.

"Of course. Nothing for you to worry about," said Darvin. "Go home, please, Tarley."

"Hyd, if Korla has gone missing I believe I have a right to know."

"Do not talk to your Head Commander in such a way!" snapped the commander, moving in front of Darvin so that she was mere inches away from Tarley. Her hand was already resting on her sword and there was a small part of Tarley that was strangely desperate for the commander to try and fight her. Tarley only had a small knife in her pocket but she didn't doubt that she could beat the commander.

"I'm sorry, hyd, but as a guard of the bridge I feel that it's only fair that we are *all* made aware of what is happening regarding the disappearances," said Tarley.

"As a *guard* you are made aware of exactly what it is you need to know," said the commander, moving silently towards Tarley. She was a good four inches shorter than Tarley and with the angry look on her face she looked almost comical to the young guard.

"Thank you, Commander," said Darvin. "Tarley, I appreciate your concern but *please* just go home."

Darvin's face was not stern like it usually was, although there was an intensity to his eyes that never seemed to truly fade. Tarley felt that they were pleading with her rather than trying to aggravate. Even so, she still felt frustrated; every minute of her life seemed to entail more questions than answers right now.

Tarley turned on her heel and marched out of the building, leaving the commander yelling at her for not saluting. She was tempted to throw her another gesture but decided against it; losing her job over a stupid commander would be its own special kind of embarrassment.

When she got home she almost knocked Mabli over as she pushed past her to go up the stairs. All she felt was anger and it was continuing to grow at a rate that she had never experienced before. She wanted to protect the people of Miraylia, it was her job, and yet she felt as if the one thing she had waited her whole life for was now slipping away from her. If the guards couldn't even protect themselves how were they meant to protect the people of their city? Over fifty guards and commanders had gone missing and no one from the administration would reveal what it was they were doing to find them or even what their thoughts were on the situation. Yes, they were sad, yes, they were doing all they could but what *was* that exactly?

Tarley looked out of her window towards the bridge and

sighed. The eerie, imposing, beautiful fortress always had and always would be synonymous with danger for her but not like this. She always thought it would be a tangible danger; something she could see and, hopefully, control. The Arben Bridge was the most frustrating and addictive place that she had ever graced and she was determined to protect it no matter what.

* * *

The Tulip was quiet that evening and so Tarley felt more relaxed than she had done on her previous visit. The wine was flowing, her friends were laughing and everyone seemed glad to have her there. For the briefest of moments, she could pretend that nothing was troubling her.

"How is Baodor?" Mitch asked Tarley.

"Better," said Tarley, quietly lamenting being pulled away from her fantasy. "He went home today so Ivy is obviously spoiling him."

Everyone around the table voiced their relief, many of them had known Baodor since they were children and respected his kind nature immensely. He had never been the kind of older brother to mock Tarley and her friends as if they were beneath him simply because they were younger. Tarley would never admit how smug that had made her feel.

"He was so brave to face those Inquiry members," said Ada, shivering slightly.

A gentle hum of agreement went around the group as they all imagined how they thought the scene had played out. Baodor, understandably nervous, facing off against two towering monsters from The Inquiry, equipped with the most vicious weapons ever to have been made in Liliath. He would have stood his ground and attacked bravely but he wasn't a guard like his siblings and father, The Inquiry wouldn't have taken long to disarm and injure him.

"The whole thing just shows how determined The Inquiry is, I suppose," said Wyatt.

Every pair of his friends' eyes were soon set upon him; a mixture of confusion and apprehension.

"What do you mean?" asked Tarley.

"Just that they will do anything it takes to find out what the bridge is guarding. I mean, in a way it's sort of admirable."

"And so attacking government buildings and injuring innocent people is justifiable?"

Ada's hand rested on Tarley's arm but she shook it away, her gaze was now fixed on Wyatt as he calmly took another sip of his drink.

"Obviously not…but their willpower *is* making me start to see their general argument, especially with more guards and commanders disappearing into the unknown every day. Isn't there even a small part of you that thinks the world has a right to know what the bridge is guarding?"

"No. Whatever it is, we're not meant to know."

"You can't really believe that, Tarley. The thing is centuries old, whatever's in that building can't harm us now."

Tarley had heard all the arguments against the bridge a million and one times before, of course, and usually tried not to enter into an argument as she was comfortable enough in her beliefs not to enforce them on other people. But Wyatt's belittling of the attack on Baodor felt like a punch to the chest.

Tarley glared at him as her hand tightened around the stand of her wine glass.

"You don't know that. When I was training to become a guard we were taught to prepare ourselves for anything-"

"-oh get off your high horse! All of you guards are the same! You walk around thinking you're better than everyone but you're not actually protecting us from any great threat."

Tarley stood up without thinking, ready to launch herself at Wyatt. A man she had spent so many of her days with and had so much admiration for was demeaning her whole life and from the way he was speaking these were not the spontaneous ramblings of a drunkard. Tarley wondered when he had decided that they were no longer friends because how could they be when he despised her livelihood so much?

"Are you all right, haf?" A middle-aged man in a middle-aged suit asked, seemingly appearing out of thin air. His brown hair was receding and small crow's feet outlined his eyes. "Is this man bothering you?"

"I'm fine, thank you," she said before glaring back at Wyatt.

"Stop being a prat, Tarley. Sit down," said Wyatt.

"Shut up, Wyatt. You're only making it worse," said Ada. "Come on, Tarl, let's just have a drink and forget about it, yeah?"

"No, thanks. I know where I'm not wanted."

"Let me give you money for a taxi, haf. No young lady should be walking home alone at night," said the middle-aged man, following Tarley out of the door.

"Oh, fuck off," shouted Tarley as she left the pub and headed for home.

* * *

Over the next week Tarley made numerous attempts to get in touch with Ada but every time she called or knocked on her door she was greeted by silence. She even found herself beginning to loathe Wyatt the least out of all her friends, at least he spoke his mind. She knew that they probably all agreed with him but didn't have the courage to be open about it. Even Ada, her oldest friend, merely tried to quieten Wyatt rather than challenge him at the pub.

She soon fell into a monotonous routine whereby she'd go to work, remain silent during her shift, come home and get quizzed by Mabli. How was work? Was she feeling okay? How was Baodor? She was even offering to cook her meals for her and clean her room.

She guessed that it was Mabli's way of trying to bond, in fairness to her Tarley hadn't exactly been welcoming when she moved in, but all her attempts were futile. Not only was she too zealous in her approach but Tarley was starting to think that keeping friends was a waste of time, especially if they were a guard. Tarley only partly felt guilty for wondering if Mabli would disappear soon.

When the day she had been counting down to eventually arrived, Tarley found herself sitting by the central fountain in Gracefalls Park an hour earlier than planned. She was almost shaking with nerves as she sat on the pristine bench and watched the water fall from the top of the fountain to the bottom.

They had come here as children with their families and created some of Tarley's favourite memories, many of which involved the fountain. It was made of white marble and at its centre were five warriors, each standing tall and proud with their swords and shields. Beneath them was a slain dragon, its eyes shut and its body limp.

One day I'm going to make a sword that can slay ALL the dragons in the land. Even the super massive ones!

And I'll use it to slay them!

Tarley smiled. She could see the two little girls that they had once been running around the fountain, pretending to be in the middle of a great battle. They would always win and the imaginary king would bestow great honours upon the both of them. Tarley would be rewarded for her impeccable fighting technique and Lenna for her excellent craftsmanship that helped them win the long and arduous war. Both were applauded for their gallant bravery and both accepted the gratitude of their kingdom, including a few gold coins as a way of saying thank you. Macklyn and Baodor were strictly banned from such games; they became too strategic and wanted everything planned to a tee whereas Lenna and Tarley just wanted to be wild.

There was hardly anyone roaming the park at that time, it would soon be dark and the park would fall into silence until the morning. There was an invisible and evil person at work on the bridge and until they were found the only reaction the people of the city had was to hide. Even those who claimed that the bridge was nothing more than bricks and concrete fell victim to the fearfulness that the sunset brought.

"You're early," said a voice.

Tarley's head shot up to look at her. She hadn't changed. Her dark brown hair was still tied back in a neat ponytail and her physique was as athletic as ever. Her blue eyes bore into Tarley's, looking neither angry nor happy to see her cousin.

"I didn't know if you'd turn up," said Tarley.

"How could you?" asked Lenna, sitting down on the bench but leaving a wide gap between the two of them.

Tarley noticed that her leg had started jerking at some point and so she forced herself to place her foot flat on the ground to steady it. She opened her mouth to speak but quickly shut it again. The sound of birds chirping and flapping through the trees seemed to be louder than normal, making Tarley feel inadequate in comparison to their ease at communicating.

She shuffled slightly and dared to glance at Lenna. She had been wrong; Lenna had changed. There were faint bags under her eyes and her lips were pursed rather than in their relaxed, almost smug, smile. Lenna was also sitting more upright than Tarley was used to, she felt like any small movement could cause her cousin to reach for the knife that was almost definitely hidden in her jacket and place it against Tarley's throat.

"Were you involved in that attack?" asked Tarley.

Lenna's eyes remained on the fountain, staring at the smallest of the warriors. They'd nicknamed him 'Hairy' as children because of his large beard.

"Baodor could have died," continued Tarley, her voice shaking. "One of your closest cousins could have been killed by some manic-"

"-he's fine, isn't he?!" Lenna yelled, causing Tarley to jump slightly.

"Yes. And three people died," said Tarley, turning her head away from Lenna.

They both sat in silence for a moment, staring at the fountain and wondering if the other woman was also lost in the past. Neither of them asked.

"You wanted to meet. So tell me why I'm here," said Lenna.

Tarley turned her head back towards Lenna and looked her straight in the eye as she had done many times. But this time she experienced a hesitation that made her hate herself for even contemplating what she was about to say. Words used to flow so freely between them and now Tarley felt like she had to analyse every syllable she wanted to voice before she even dared to speak.

"I want an honest answer, Lenna. Forget all the politics and hatred, just tell me. Are The Inquiry involved in the disappearances?"

Lenna smiled and began to laugh, shaking her head at Tarley. "And here's me thinking that after two years you might actually want to apologise for how you spoke to me. But no, you just want to use me for information and then never see me again. Have I got that right?"

"I just want answers," Tarley replied.

"Well the answer is no! Do you seriously think we have the man power and resources to abduct that many people without anyone figuring out how?"

"What about the attack in Jobern? Why did The Inquiry steal the guard files?"

Lenna let out a low scream as she jumped on to her feet. "Use your head, Tarley!" she yelled. "That's just a lie from the government! We have no interest in who *works* on the fucking bridge!"

"Then why were you all there?"

Lenna sighed and sat back down on the bench, still keeping the same distance from Tarley. "I'm not going to risk my life telling you that and, before you ask, I'm not telling you about the Harkon mission, either."

"You're as much use as Darvin," mumbled Tarley, instantly regretting her words. Thankfully, Lenna didn't deliver her usual snide remark about the Head Commander.

"We have theories," said Lenna, "that's all I'll say. More informed theories than the rubbish on the street."

"Then you're legally obligated to share them."

Lenna turned away and could see him waiting behind the trees. It was time to go. Part of her wanted to stay longer and have the melodramatic argument that had been two years in the making and another part was desperate to run away.

"Come with me," said Lenna. "There's hardly any of you left, you could be next. Or Macklyn, or Uncle Gwyl. Do you really want to risk that?"

"I'm not joining The Inquiry," said Tarley, unable to look at Lenna.

"It's the safest place for you! Maybe you can help us find out who's behind the disappearances."

Tarley snapped her head back around and looked straight into Lenna's eyes. "I took an oath to protect that bridge until I can no longer protect it and I still have a chance to do that."

Lenna screamed in frustration. "Fucking hell, Tarley!" She stood up and looked down on her cousin. "I hope your pride doesn't trip you up one day. See you in another two years."

CHAPTER FIVE

Carida poured Tarley another mug of tea, her hands shaking slightly as she did so. Tarley had been forced to watch over the past seven months as her mother grew increasingly worried over her family when she couldn't see them and Tarley hated herself for not feeling guilty enough over it. Despite their declining numbers, Tarley felt that she would never be ready to leave the guard, even if she were allowed.

Carida had always been supportive of her family's decision to be part of the bridge. After all, she had married into an old guard family and had always said that she fell for Gwyl as soon as he walked into her shop in his navy blue uniform. She could not be prouder of any of them and had instilled a strong sense of discipline in all their children as they grew up. No matter what they wanted to do, whether that was to become a guard or something else entirely, they should do it to the best of their ability and always be the person that other people relied upon.

The bridge had never appealed to Carida, she couldn't keep still for hours on end, never mind the danger that it brought. She tried not to dwell upon the many mysterious scrapes that her family had fallen into on the bridge over the years, as she knew it would send her stress levels into the stratosphere but, even so, she never wanted to be the person who stopped them doing exactly what they wanted to do. However, since the disappearances began it was becoming increasingly difficult to keep her opinions to herself. She longed to have all her family, Baodor included, back under her roof where she could see them and spoil them every day. She just wanted her husband and her babies to be safe.

Neither of them had spoken for a while, Carida had been watching the old clock on the wall tick away and Tarley knew that her mother was in a place where she could not be reached. Her mind was focused on one thing and until that was resolved any words that were uttered would be lost on her.

"I think you should move back home," Carida said, finally averting her gaze from the wall. "Just until all of this is sorted."

Tarley rolled her eyes. "I'm not going to do that, mum."

"Please, Tarley. It would just put my mind at rest knowing where you are."

"I'm not a child, I don't need babysitting."

Carida opened her mouth to reply but was interrupted by the front door creaking open to reveal a weary Gwyl and a tired Macklyn returning from their day on the bridge.

"Thank the sunset," said Carida under her breath as her lips curled into a smile. Carida and Gwyl had never been overly affectionate to each other in front of their children but whatever primness they possessed was soon forgotten as Carida wrapped her arms around Gwyl and kissed him on the lips. Gwyl smiled and pulled Carida closer.

"There's no need for all this," he said but there was a softness and joviality to his voice that contradicted his words.

Macklyn poured himself a glass of cranberry juice and sat next to Tarley at the table, his legs were still aching from the long shift and he had no intention of moving from that spot until he had to. This was usually when Carida shouted at him to get off his arse and clean something.

"Darvin has called a meeting for all the guards and commanders tomorrow. He wants to talk about our safety, apparently," said Macklyn.

Tarley rolled her eyes. "Well, he hasn't done a great deal so far, has he? It seems to me that if we're going to disappear then we've-"

"-Tarley!" Carida chastised, "please don't talk like that."

Carida's hands were shaking as she crossed her arms but both Tarley and Macklyn had already seen. Macklyn glared at his sister, condemning her with his eyes and making Tarley feel like a small child. She wanted to get better at talking tactfully but it was still a skill that continued to evade her.

"I suppose I may as well stay tonight, then, if we've all got to go in tomorrow," said Tarley.

Carida's haunted face soon transformed and a smile spread across it. "Excellent!" she said, "I'll make a nice big lamb pie and *you*," she turned to Gwyl and pointed her finger at him, "can make the gravy."

"Of course, my love," said Gwyl with a chuckle and kissed the top of Carida's head before washing his hands and rummaging around in the cupboards.

Tarley found herself enjoying the evening a lot more than she had expected, Carida invited Baodor and Ivy over and they brought an instant comfort that Tarley happily bathed in. Baodor's cuts were healing well and Tarley couldn't help but smile at the way he would grab Ivy's hand whenever he could. The couple's wedding took up most of the conversation, which in turn led to Carida asking Macklyn about a nice young man he was supposed to be "courting", which in turn led to Macklyn turning a shade of red and refusing to elaborate.

"What about you, Tarley?" asked Ivy, "is there anyone we should know about?"

"I am currently in a very committed relationship with myself. It's going very well so far," said Tarley, causing everyone to laugh.

"I don't think our Tarley is the relationship type, are you, love?" said Gwyl.

"That's not true!" exclaimed Carida, "she went out with Norwin's son for over a year!"

"Did you?!" said Gwyl, turning to Tarley in shock. The look of bemusement he was now wearing sent Tarley into fits of giggles that spread across the table. She remembered at the time that he had failed to make the connection between Tarley and Norwin's son but the whole situation had been so entertaining that she wanted to see if he would ever figure it out.

"What did I do to deserve such a family?" said Gwyl to the ceiling, which only resulted in more laughter.

Tarley loved to see them all smiling; Macklyn and Carida both had the faintest of dimples whenever they broke into laughter whereas Baodor and Gwyl shared the same jerk of the shoulders that Tarley was certain only she could recognise.

Her whole life it had been a running joke that she looked so different to the four of them that she couldn't possibly be their daughter. She shared the same nutty brown hair colour as the tufts that were left on Gwyl's head but there were no other similarities between her and her family. Lenna had always looked more like Carida and Gwyl's daughter than Tarley ever did.

Lenna, as well as Baodor and Macklyn, had a long oval face like Gwyl that had been passed down the generations ever since the first Hillis decided to reproduce. She also had faint blue eyes that were just a few shades lighter than her uncle and father's. Tarley, however, had a much rounder face and was the only one in her family to have dark brown eyes.

Tarley smirked to herself as she watched them all, grateful that regardless of their appearances there was no other group of people she felt more connected to or more loved by.

* * *

That night Tarley enjoyed a deep sleep that she had not experienced for a very long time. When she woke up there was no queasiness in the pit of her stomach or feelings of fatigue, just pure relaxation. But as soon as she realised how calm she felt, she knew that it wouldn't last and instantly mourned the passing sensation.

Gwyl, Macklyn and Tarley were some of the first people to arrive at the tower later that morning and as the others trickled in all Tarley could think about was how downtrodden everyone looked. Guards were meant to be excellent specimens of the human physique but the worry and exhaustion was now set deep within them and visible across their bodies. The majority of them would have usually marched into the room but on that day Tarley was more aware than ever at how many guards were dragging themselves towards their chairs.

Meetings for all the guards and commanders were rare but Tarley still knew that if everyone was there the room would be brimming with bodies. That day it was just over half full. Darvin finally entered the room and was greeted by everyone jumping to their feet and watching him as he walked to the podium that was stood before them. He saluted his guards and commanders and they instantly returned the gesture.

"Please sit," he said and everyone obeyed. "It brings me great sadness that I have had to call you all here today but I fear that unless we do something soon these disappearances will only escalate."

Nods of agreement spread across the room, particularly from the commanders who seemed to be nodding so furiously it looked like their heads might fall off.

"We had just over two hundred Senior Commanders, Junior Commanders, Senior Guards and Junior Guards in our ranks," Darvin continued, "but now only one hundred and thirty-eight of us remain."

Tarley inadvertently took in a deep breath and felt for her father's hand, which he gladly gave with a small squeeze.

"This means that action must be taken. I have been in talks with the Premier, the Delegate for Miraylia and the Bureau of Liliath for weeks in order to come up with preventative solutions to this problem. As of today, guards will no longer man their gates in threes but in groups of five; four guards and one Junior Commander, to ensure that no one is ever left alone. Due to this increase in security we will be forced to take on new recruits, which means that the best cadets at the academy will be graduating a lot earlier than expected."

Although a small sense of shock went around the room, this manoeuvre was not entirely unusual. Tarley remembered in her second month of joining the academy several guards had been poisoned by a small terrorist group who wanted to slowly infiltrate the bridge. The Head Commander recruited several third years before they finished training and Tarley had silently wished that she had been three years older.

"Unfortunately, until these new recruits are selected commanders and guards alike are going to have to take on even more hours," said Darvin.

A few guards dared to groan but were soon shot venomous looks from various commanders that forced them to look away, embarrassed.

"I appreciate that this is a huge ask," Darvin continued, "but all overtime will be double pay. Finally, I would like to say that anyone who wishes to leave their employment at The Arben Bridge is free to do so. I firmly believe that everyone in this room took their oaths with the full intention of protecting the bridge until such a time came when they were unable to do so. However, I also understand that in our wildest imaginations we could never have expected to face such an unknown yet very real and very scary threat. If anyone wishes to leave they may do so without judgement."

Tarley looked around the room to see people shifting in their seats, turning their heads away from their friends and closing their eyes in thought. Would anyone actually do it? Every single person in that room had sworn their lives to the bridge until their bodies no longer permitted them to guard it effectively. Most guards died before they even thought of retirement.

Tarley looked at Darvin, who always stood upright and with a composure that never seemed to falter. She had long dreamt of having his job one day but she wondered if she, too, would be able to come across so stoic when the situation was a million different kinds of messy.

A man in his early thirties, who Tarley had only worked with a handful of times, stood up and looked Darvin straight in the eyes.

"It has been an honour to serve the bridge," he said before saluting the Head Commander.

Darvin nodded his head before saluting. "Thank you, Rorden. You will be missed," he said.

Rorden marched out of the room, not once meeting the eyes of his colleagues. Within ten minutes five other people had followed him out of the room, going back on their oaths and saying goodbye to life on The Arben Bridge.

Every time someone stood up to leave Tarley felt a small twinge in her stomach. She understood why they were leaving but the only thought that was flying through her head was that they had all made a lifelong promise. A single vow that joined them all forever. It was an oath that they were never meant to break. An oath that tied them to centuries of men and women who all believed in the same thing and wanted to protect their city. How could they disregard it so easily?

Tarley had been trained to think of such people as traitors but she knew all of them to varying extents. She knew that they all had families; people that they loved and who loved them back. Tarley was certain that if Carida had been in the room she would be begging Tarley, Gwyl and Macklyn to take Darvin's offer.

Tarley looked at Gwyl, who met her eyes and shook his head. She looked at Macklyn, his eyes soft and confused.

"Are you-" she whispered.

"-no," interrupted Macklyn. He turned his head away from her, "No."

"Okay," said Darvin after another moment's silence. "Thank you all for electing to stay, it won't be forgotten. If you could now all stand, I'd like us to recite the oath."

Everyone in the room got to their feet, straightened their backs and looked straight ahead.

"I swear," began Darvin and the rest of the room soon joined him, "to protect The Arben Bridge from all beings who mean it harm. I will do everything I can to keep it safe until the day that I am no longer able to do so. I understand the responsibilities of a guard and willingly accept them. From this day on I declare myself a guard of The Arben Bridge."

Silence fell and Tarley was almost certain that she could see a tear welling up in Darvin's eye. Nevertheless, he cleared his throat and began to speak again.

"Thank you all. For now, I recommend that those of you who are not on shift to go home and get as much rest as you can."

He stepped down from the podium and was immediately greeted by a mob of guards and commanders, desperate to talk to him. The guards were known for their deep respect of tradition and protocol but in that moment all anyone wanted to do was pose their questions to Darvin before he left.

"I'd better get to my gate, then," said Gwyl.

"I'll come with you," said Tarley. "It's my day off, anyway."

"No, Tarley, you heard the man. You need to go home and rest." He placed his hands on her shoulders and kissed the top of her head. "Love you."

"You too," she mumbled before leaving the room with Macklyn.

As they left the tower Tarley could hear Mabli shouting after her. She stopped and waited for her housemate to catch up but she could have happily continued to walk without acknowledging that Mabli was even there. Macklyn smirked at Tarley as Mabli drew closer, causing his sister to lightly punch him on the arm.

"I thought we could walk back together," said Mabli.

"Sure," said Tarley without really looking at her.

Macklyn left after five minutes, claiming that he had to shop for food but Tarley wasn't convinced, especially as he was still smirking at her as he walked away.

"So what do you think about Darvin's plan?" asked Mabli.

"I'm not sure. At least he has a plan, I suppose. I just hope the new recruits know what they're doing," said Tarley.

"Don't be too hard on them. We were all cadets once."

Tarley only nodded, wondering why Mabli continued this façade of being friends. Surely it would be easier for the both of them if they just maintained an ambivalent relationship? As long as the dishes were cleaned and the house was tidy there was no need for them to have any more meaning to the other.

Tarley avoided Mabli as much as possible for the rest of the day, listening out for her footsteps so that they didn't happen upon each other in the hall or the lounge. She tried to call Ada several times but the crystals wouldn't connect to Ada's; Tarley liked to think that they needed replacing but she knew it was more likely that Ada was rejecting her call. They had not fallen out a great deal during their friendship but when they had Ada had never ignored Tarley, she would much rather shout and scream and so the cocoon of silence she found herself in was a worryingly unfamiliar experience.

As Tarley settled into bed later that night she was suddenly blinded by a blazing light. She quickly raised her hands to guard herself from it but the brightness approached her window nonetheless. As the light began to fade she looked into the distance to locate its source and found that it seemed to be emanating from the bridge.

But that's a mile and a half away…

The light finally faded and she wondered if she should tell Mabli; was it breaking protocol if she wasn't actually on the bridge? She couldn't even say for definite that the two were entwined.

Tarley had to remind herself that the most likely explanation was just pure exhaustion; she was well versed in the kinds of tricks the mind could play on someone who is drained and stressed. Darvin would be stratospheric if she came to him with a problem that didn't really exist; he had enough to worry about. Instead, she lay back down in her bed and pulled the sheets up high, hoping that she could hide away for just a moment.

CHAPTER SIX

"Tarley," a shaky but firm voice spoke into the darkness. "Tarley, wake up. Please, wake up."

Tarley could feel her arm being shook slightly as her groggy eyes opened. The room was blurry for a couple of seconds and it took her a few moments to remember that she was in her own bed in her own room. With the little energy she had she propped herself up against the headboard to see Mabli moving away from her so that she was sat at the end of the bed. Mabli looked up to the ceiling and her right leg shook so violently that it looked like it was possessed.

"Why are you in my room?" asked Tarley, feeling that it was too early in the day to be polite.

Mabli's head snapped round to Tarley's but she didn't answer. She stood up and walked closer towards Tarley, looking down on her with pained eyes.

"What's going on?" said Tarley, her palms suddenly becoming quite sweaty.

"I'm really sorry, Tarley. Darvin came in the night with some bad news. It's your father…he's…" she turned her head away before speaking. "He's disappeared."

Tarley threw her duvet off her body and leapt out of the

bed so that she was face to face with Mabli. "What?! Why didn't you wake me earlier?"

"Darvin said to wait until the morning! I'm sorry, Tarley, I didn't know what to do!"

"You could have used your brain! He wasn't even meant to be working last night! What the hell was he doing there?!"

"I don't know; all Darvin told me was that he disappeared on the bridge last night and that I shouldn't tell you until the morning. I think maybe he wanted you to have a good sleep before…you know, having to deal with it all?"

Tarley was pacing the room, not knowing where to place her energies. She wanted to cry, scream, run and hit something hard in equal measure but she wasn't sure which one she should do first.

It had finally happened. She was now one of the families that the other guards would look upon with both sympathy and fear. They would pretend to feel sorry for her and her family and simultaneously try to avoid being put on a shift with her.

"It's really very sad."

"Yes, but if he's gone, maybe one of the kids will be next."

"Better not get too close. Who knows what could happen to us?"

"I need to see my mother," said Tarley, softly. "I need you to get out of my room and I need to go and visit my mother."

Mabli left immediately so that Tarley could grab whatever clothes were nearest to her, get changed and run out of the door. She made it to her parents' house in record time, not once stopping for breath. By the time she let herself into the house she was panting and dripping in sweat.

As soon as she walked in she could see her mother and Macklyn sat on the sofa; the latter cradling the former. They both had puffy eyes with red circles enveloping Carida's which made Tarley's heart curl up inside her chest.

She sat on the other side of her mother and rested her head on Carida's shoulder, unsure of what to say. Carida kissed the top of Tarley's head and softly stroked the side of her daughter's face. She would never say it but out of Gwyl, Macklyn and Tarley, Carida had always thought that if any of them were to go missing it would be her beautiful, reckless daughter.

"I can't believe this has happened," sobbed Carida.

She was answered with silence. Both her children agreed to some extent but, even with their training and faith in the bridge, the faintest fear of disappearing had always been lurking in their minds. They'd only hoped that if it had to be someone from their family it would have been themselves.

Tarley felt like she had regressed into a child; all she wanted was to be close to her mother and to sob into her embrace. She wanted them all to cling together and never leave the sofa; if there was a way to protect and elongate the moment they would be safe forever.

The front door swung open to reveal Baodor and Ivy. They walked into the living room, seemingly holding on to each other for support and with the last remnants of tears in their eyes.

"I'm so sorry," said Ivy, her eyes darting between every saddened face in the room.

Carida managed a faint smile and a quiet "thank you, lovely," but even Tarley could tell that it felt like an automatic response.

"Why was he even there?" asked Tarley, "I thought his shift finished at three."

"It did," said Macklyn with a sigh. "But someone called in sick on my shift and dad was the first to volunteer to stay on."

"Stupid, stupid man," uttered Carida whilst she dabbed her eyes with a tissue.

Ivy and Baodor sat down on the sofa opposite, their hands clutching each other. Ever since the attack on Baodor, Ivy had been wearing an almost constant worried expression which didn't look like it would be fading any time soon. Even on the occasions when she did smile she didn't completely look like the happy version of herself.

"So…what happened?" asked Tarley, tentatively. As much as she felt anger and heartbreak she also had an overwhelming feeling of curiosity. No one had seen a disappearance occur and those that were privy to the events leading up to it had been sworn to secrecy. Darvin had made it quite clear that anyone who appeared to be causing unnecessary unease amongst the ranks would be dismissed on the spot.

"You don't have to say if you don't want to," said Baodor. "We know it's breaking the law." There was no chastisement in his tone towards Tarley, only a softness that he reserved for his brother on rare occasions.

"It's okay," said Macklyn. "We were on guard as usual but about an hour in a huge wind came along. It was so strong that it almost knocked us over; all I could see were four people desperately trying to cling on to their swords and helmets. Then all the lights on the bridge went out. Within two seconds every gate and walkway was in complete darkness." His voice began to quiver as he spoke, "I was calling out for dad but no one was answering. I'm not even sure if my own voice was making any noise, I know that sounds ridiculous but I felt like I was shouting and shouting and nothing was coming out." Macklyn was now staring at the empty fireplace; his eyes fixated on the ashes that were left from last night's fire. "And then I heard a voice. I don't know if it was a man's or a woman's; it was just about audible."

"What did the voice say?" asked Ivy.

"'It's time'," said Macklyn. "That's all it said, over and over again until the lights came back on. 'It's time, it's time.' I turned around and dad was gone. I found Darvin straight away and he had every guard on the gates searching for dad for over two hours but you know what it's like there, Tarl, there are only so many places he could have been."

Tarley nodded, the area in front of the gates was an open courtyard with nowhere to hide. The only buildings that sat there were The Arben Tower and the staff changing rooms.

"Darvin told me not to tell you," continued Macklyn, "he didn't want you to freak out and come to the bridge unnecessarily. He thought it would be best if Mabli told you in the morning."

Tarley snorted. "Because she's exactly the person I'd want to deliver that kind of news."

"I know; I did try to change his mind but you know how stern he can be."

Tarley finally felt like she was beginning to understand why Darvin and the commanders had been so secretive about the disappearances; clearly they were no ordinary kidnappings. Whoever was behind them had a love of the theatrical and in Tarley's mind any criminal who liked to make a show was only going to cause more problems the longer they were left undiscovered. The more they made the authorities look feckless and weak, the further they would want to push the boundaries. How much psychological damage could they cause before they were caught? How many tricks could they play? How many people could they hurt?

If the circumstances surrounding her father's disappearance had been the same for the others, then why weren't there any preventative measures put in place? Darvin could have been doing more to find the perpetrator. Tarley wondered if he had even bothered to ask the guards in charge of the light crystals why they had gone out or talked to the city's meteorology department to discover why a sudden gust of wind appeared on the bridge.

"This doesn't make any sense!" Tarley said, "how is it humanly possible to create an isolated wind? Never mind one that is strong enough to almost knock over five guards!"

"Maybe it isn't human," said Carida, staring at the wall opposite her. "We all know the stories. I've heard people on the streets. Some think it's a Sovran."

Her hands began to shake as she spoke and even with Macklyn's arms around her she was still sobbing uncontrollably. Tarley was terrified that her mother was going to have a heart attack but she had no idea how to calm her down. She had spent years learning how to diffuse hostile situations, especially involving anxious or unpredictable individuals, but in that moment she couldn't apply any of those techniques to her mother. Tarley could usually separate emotions and break them down but she felt like she was being flooded by it. There was no room to breathe or speak, all she could do was allow her mother to howl and hopelessly wish that she knew how to stop it.

"Enough of that," said Ivy, walking over to Carida and kneeling down in front of her. She grabbed her hands and looked straight into Carida's eyes. "All the Sovrans are gone, there haven't been any for centuries."

"But-"

"-but nothing. *Whoever* has taken Gwyl will be found and revealed as the evil, egotistical bastard that they really are."

Carida gave a soft nod but Tarley could see that her mother's eyes weren't really in the room. There was no attentiveness behind them and Tarley was certain that a million different scenarios were racing through her mother's mind. No matter what Ivy said to Carida, she wouldn't be able to contend with the uncertainty of possibilities.

"Mum, I hate to bring this up," said Baodor, "but Darvin asked if we would like to attend the press conference. I told him I didn't want to put any of us through that but I'm still going to go if that's okay. And not just because it's part of my job, I want to make sure it's done right."

"Thank you, Baodor," said Carida.

She gestured for him to come closer and when he did she stood up and wrapped her arms around his waist. He was at least a foot taller than her and so he could easily rest his head on top of his mother's and kiss her hair.

"I'll come back as soon as it's over," said Baodor before giving her a final kiss and heading off.

As soon as he left Ivy was in the kitchen and brewing a pot of blue leaf tea; everyone declined her offer of food but she was adamant that they all drink something.

Tarley had never felt so useless or confused in all her life. Should she be crying like her mother? Helping with the tea? Following Baodor to the press conference? She felt lost even though she was surrounded by her family. And numb. She felt a numbness that eradicated the pain and loss that she was sure she should be feeling by now. She thought back to her time at the academy and during her medical training her teacher had said that after witnessing or experiencing something horrific a lot of people will go into shock before their emotions kick in. Perhaps Tarley was experiencing shock and soon the tears and the screaming would begin.

Your father is gone.

Tarley repeated the words in her head and, despite understanding them, their meaning was futile. They were just words; Gwyl could still come home.

Why aren't you crying? You should be crying. You're a horrible daughter.

Carida was still wiping away tears and even Macklyn had blotchy skin from his own and yet Tarley was still sitting calmly in her chair drinking her tea.

The press conference took place in the early afternoon but Carida decided she'd rather attempt to have a nap than sit through it. Besides, most people in Miraylia had now sat through countless numbers of the same performance.

Henya Quinn took to the stage first, as she always did, and delivered her sympathies towards the family, this time looking towards Baodor who was stood just a few feet behind her. Everyone in the Hillis house was used to seeing Baodor standing in the background but this time they all silently reprimanded themselves for allowing him to be there alone, even if none of them could bare to leave Carida by herself.

After she had finished her speech, which Tarley could almost recite word for word, Henya stepped down from her podium and was replaced by Neb Figmore.

"I can only reiterate the heartfelt words that Henya has

expressed," he began. "And, although I do not wish to turn this press conference into a political debate, I *must* encourage anyone who knows the whereabouts of Penn Heath or any Inquiry member to come forward."

"Do you now have reason to believe that The Inquiry are involved, Mr. Figmore?" asked a reporter.

"You know I can't divulge explicit details but, nevertheless, I cannot stand up here and not ask the people of Miraylia to help protect their city."

Tarley glanced over at Macklyn and he returned her look of bewilderment, even if Macklyn didn't know what Lenna had told Tarley it was still clear to everyone in the room that Neb Figmore didn't know as much about the disappearances as they had first thought. The Inquiry were a group of people constantly on the run, stealing weapons and anything else that they couldn't afford, how could they possibly pull off what Macklyn had witnessed?

After the questions died down Darvin gave the final speech; the only section of the conference that ever differed. As frustrated as she was with him, Tarley admired that Darvin took the time to know each and every guard that was in his employment and Gwyl was no exception.

Darvin spoke about what a respected commander Gwyl was and how he was one of the first guards that he ever worked with. He also spoke of the three wonderful children that he was father to and that he was certain they could all work together to bring him and the other guards home.

"I need something stronger than tea," said Macklyn and left his chair to pour himself a glass of whiskey.

The cameras then cut to Darvin, Henya, Neb and Baodor walking into a room of The Arben Tower that was now covered in photographs of the missing guards, each one with a burning candle underneath it. Tarley wondered if it was Darvin himself who ensured that the flames never died or a commander who no doubt thought they were better than that.

Darvin hung a picture of Gwyl on the wall and stepped

back while Baodor lit a candle. The cameras promptly cut back to a news reporter in a studio who led straight into a story debating whether the bridge still had a place in Miraylia.

Tarley let out a low groan and followed her brother into the kitchen where a glass of whiskey was already waiting for her on the counter.

CHAPTER SEVEN

The following evening Macklyn and Tarley were on the same shift but as soon as they arrived Ryder sent them to the tower to see Darvin. Neither of them had left their mother's house all day and although Macklyn didn't want to leave Tarley was grateful for the distraction. She was still waiting for someone to shout at her for not crying but if she was on the bridge at least she had the excuse that she had a duty to remain emotionless.

"I wonder what he wants," said Tarley.

"Maybe he wants us to take some compassionate leave," suggested Macklyn as they stood in the lift.

"With only a hundred and thirty-seven guards left? I don't think so."

The lift opened and Darvin was already standing there waiting for them with a rare smile on his face. Tarley wasn't sure why she suddenly felt so nervous.

"Hello," said Darvin. "Macklyn, if you'd like to come with me. Tarley, could you please wait in the meeting room?"

Macklyn gave Tarley a confused look as Darvin ushered him down the corridor and into his office. Tarley had assumed that Darvin had wanted to talk to them together so she reluctantly told Macklyn she'd see him later.

Tarley sat down in the large meeting room but its stillness and memories gave her a chill. The last time she had been in there the room was filled with people and the holograph of the Harkon Building where Baodor had just been attacked.

Her foot started to twitch and her eyes were darting around the room so she quickly got to her feet and began to pace the room.

The large window that took up most of the furthest wall presented an astonishing view of the bridge, especially at night when it was lit up by the lamps. Tarley looked down at the five guards standing in front of The Fire Gate. It was the gate furthest left on the bridge and although the design was of a simple fire it always looked magnificent. Jewels and gemstones that were centuries old intertwined in varying shades of yellow, orange and red against the black iron. Even in the height of summer when the sun was blazing down on Miraylia the stones still managed to dazzle.

The guards all looked shattered, there was no denying it. Each of them had bags under their eyes and Tarley noticed that the commander didn't even have his open. She couldn't help but worry that if an attack were to take place in the next minute the bridge would be more susceptible than ever.

Tarley had fiercely denied that anyone who worked for the bridge could be behind the disappearances but now that she knew that The Inquiry wasn't involved she couldn't completely dispel the theory. The public only ever got to see the entry gates on the news or official images of the other gates that had been heavily altered and even those were a rarity. It would have to be someone senior; guards only had access to the bridge and changing rooms. Whoever this person was Tarley assumed they would need to know every aspect of the bridge inside out. And why take guards one at a time? Wouldn't it be more efficient to round them all up and kill them?

She shook her head; Gwyl was now on the list of missing and she didn't want to dwell on the horrid scenarios that could play out wherever he was. Most daughters would refuse to focus on anything other than their grief.

"Tarley, we're ready for you now," said Darvin as he re-entered the room. Tarley hadn't even heard the door open.

"That was quick," she said, following him down the corridor. "Is Macklyn okay?"

"He's fine. I've sent him straight home, there's no point in him waiting around."

Tarley knotted her eyebrows, Darvin could be cryptic at the best of times but he seemed to be extra peculiar that day. He opened the door to his office where Tarley was greeted by two smiles, both of which made her feel uncomfortable.

The first one belonged to Henya Quinn and despite appearing soft Tarley could clearly see a flutter of fear in her eyes. The way she held her hands in her lap seemed conservative but to Tarley there was something odd and unnatural in the gesture. Henya was holding her hands too tightly, as if she had to stop herself from reaching out for something.

The second smile belonged to Neb Figmore and was the same large and toothy grin she had seen numerous times via image crystals, especially when he was on his latest campaign to remain as Delegate for Miraylia. Unlike Henya, Neb looked very happy to be sat in his large and comfy chair, resting back in it as if he were a judge presiding over proceedings.

"Hello, Tarley," said Henya. "Please. Sit." She gestured towards a small sofa that was in between her and Neb.

Tarley crossed over to the sofa while Darvin sat down on the edge of the chair next to Neb. Only one out of the four of them seemed to be glad to be there.

"There's no need to look so scared!" bellowed Neb, "we just want to ask you a few questions!"

"About what?" said Tarley.

"About your father," said Henya. "We've had these chats with all of the families of the missing guards, we just want to make sure that everyone is coping."

Tarley glanced at Darvin. His face was as plain as ever.

"Are you going to visit my mother, then? And my eldest brother?" asked Tarley.

Henya's hands briefly broke apart as she shifted in her chair. The movement would have perhaps been too quick to notice if Tarley had not been looking but she could see Henya flex her hands before placing them back in her lap.

She's a bag of nerves, thought Tarley, trying not to smirk.

Thousands of people dreamed of meeting the Premier and now that Tarley was in her presence she had never felt less enthused towards her.

"Of course," said Neb, finally breaking the silence and greeting Tarley with one of his infamous grins. "But today we're concerned with how you're doing."

"I'm fine," said Tarley. "But my mother is in bits."

"Understandably. I do hope you realise, Tarley, that you don't need to play the strong guard of The Arben Bridge character with us. If you're feeling overwhelmed, we're here to help."

"I don't need any help."

"You're quite sure? You don't feel at all upset or angry? You don't think that more could be done to help find the missing guards?"

Tarley's eyes fell to the floor. "I think that Head Commander Wavers and his team are doing their best," replied Tarley.

"Do you really believe that? Are you telling us the *absolute* truth?" Neb pressed.

"How much longer do I have to stay for?" Tarley asked Darvin, turning her head away from Neb.

"Until you start speaking your mind!" Neb interjected. "We're not fools, Haf Hillis! If you have an agenda with the bridge just come out and say it!"

Neb was on his feet now and almost red in the face as he shouted at Tarley. She had always been ambivalent towards the Delegate but right then she wanted to repeatedly kick him in his special place.

"I *am* speaking my mind!" shouted Tarley, also getting to her feet. "Don't you worry about that, Hyd Figmore!"

She was the same height as him and so any attempt to intimidate had been lost as soon as Tarley had stood up. She glared at him, not blinking once as if she were a child again and having a staring competition with Macklyn.

Tarley didn't know if she hated the way he had questioned her or the idea that he knew her doubts more. The only person she'd dared speak to was Lenna but if she ever shared that information with the Bureau she would be surrendering herself to prison.

Anger was aiming for her at all angles and she didn't know how to contain it; Henya and Darvin looked like they barely cared while Neb looked ready to attack her. She felt like there were hundreds of words and emotions hanging in the air but no one was brave enough to give them a voice.

"Thank you for coming in, Tarley," said Henya, softly. She crossed the room and placed one hand on Tarley's shoulder and held out the other for Tarley to shake. "Just let Darvin know if you ever want to talk."

Tarley finally removed her gaze from Neb and quickly shook Henya's hand before turning to Darvin. "What gate am I on?" she asked.

"I think it's probably best if you go home tonight, Tarley," Darvin replied.

Tarley scowled, "Fine." She limply saluted and marched out of the room.

How could Darvin just stand there and barely speak? Neb had been goading her and neither Darvin nor the Premier did anything to stop him.

Well I'm never voting for her again! Tarley thought as she stepped into the lift.

They had hardly spoken about her father, never mind discussing the efforts that were being made to find him and the other guards. The whole meeting had been odd from start to finish but Tarley had no idea why. But she would, she was determined to find out.

She knew that the next logical thing to do was to find Macklyn and see what he had said to them but all Tarley wanted in that moment was a large drink, or possibly seven. Ada was only a fifteen-minute walk from the bridge but at the pace Tarley was stomping through the city at she made it there in ten before knocking on the door. Ada opened it to meet Tarley with a faint expression of surprise upon seeing her.

"Oh. Hello," said Ada. "I'm sorry I haven't called about your dad-"

"-don't worry about that. Fancy a drink?" asked Tarley.

Ada was not looking at Tarley; her eyes were flitting up and down the street. "I'm actually a bit bogged down in planning for Visolette, I was going to spend the evening putting the final touches on it."

"Can't you do it tomorrow?"

"It's quite urgent," replied Ada, still avoiding Tarley's gaze.

Tarley sighed, she had known Ada long enough to know when she was trying to keep something to herself. She was notoriously bad at keeping secrets.

"What's really going on?" asked Tarley as Ada became fixated on a couple walking down the street. "Ada!" shouted Tarley.

Ada's eyes instantly fell upon her old friend's. "I'm sorry, Tarley. I just think maybe we should keep our distance until all of this has blown over."

"Until *what* has blown over, exactly?" asked Tarley through gritted teeth.

"Look, I'm really sorry about Gwyl, Tarley but....," Ada's eyes fell to the floor, "I think it's for the best, that's all."

Tarley didn't reply. She marched back down the street and cut through a small park until she reached Victory Road. The shopkeepers were locking up, the pubs were starting to fill and those too scared to stay out into the darkness were hurrying home.

She had no friends. She had been catapulted into a chaos that she did not cause or understand and yet her friends could not stand by her. She was beginning to feel like a leper, like the homeless man she had encountered two weeks ago.

The thought of him made her pace slow down. So much had happened to her since their meeting that she had not dwelled on his mind trick the way she thought she would.

"*As the darkness falls, our friends will go,*" Tarley began to sing to herself as she walked. "*For this is a horror that we did not know.*"

She found herself smirking. She hated *The Songs of Night* but it seemed that *The Fall* was mirroring her life right now. She hummed the melancholic tune as she struggled to remember the words, she had not sung it since school and even then she didn't enjoy the practice.

"*The flames will rise and the city will cry,*" she finally sang. What was the next part? Something about old lives? "*The flames will rise and the city will cry,*" repeated Tarley. "To our old life, we must bid goodbye! *As the darkness falls, our friends will go. For this is a horror that we did not know. The flames will rise and the city will cry. To our old life, we must bid goodbye.*"

When Tarley arrived at the pub it was only half full so she could order herself a large glass of wine and hide away in a snug corner by herself. She very rarely went to the pub by herself, she'd always seen it as a place to go with friends, but she supposed that she should start getting used to drinking alone.

She hated herself for even contemplating the idea but one day either her or Macklyn would disappear, too. They would join their father wherever he was and leave the rest of their family in further torment. Who could handle it the best? Tarley had done well in her hostage training at the academy but Macklyn was excellent at keeping calm when faced with crazed individuals. Tarley remembered being terrified during her second year on the bridge when she saw an old man holding a knife to Macklyn's throat. The attacker had come in with some government officials and pickpocketed a guard during a tour. He waited until the group was being led out and then sprinted towards The Queen's Gate where

Macklyn had been standing. Tarley still couldn't fathom how Macklyn managed to talk the man out of slicing his throat open. Macklyn didn't even attempt to move, all he used to free himself were his words.

Tarley glugged the rest of her wine. She should disappear next. Darvin would probably be glad to get rid of her and at least then she would have some answers to her questions. If only she knew how to get herself abducted.

Tarley marched back to the bar and ordered a bottle, which didn't even raise an eyebrow from the barman. He had been there during Tarley's argument with Wyatt and happened to agree with him. He'd never been a fan of the guards.

Two women on the table opposite her were whispering as Tarley sat down.

"I think she's a guard."

"A whole bottle to herself!"

"Well, whatever it takes to get them through, I suppose."

"Drink, ladies?!" shouted Tarley, holding up her glass to them. They both grimaced as they looked at her. "No? More for me then!"

Tarley poured the bottle into her glass, only stopping when the wine threatened to spill over the top. It wasn't long before she felt refreshingly woozy and content with the swaying feeling that overcame her.

She wasn't sure how much time had passed until she finished the bottle but when she stood up to head back to the bar she could see Mabli pushing through the pub towards her, pestering the locals to move out of her way.

"What the fuck are you doing here?" said Tarley, impressed at how little she was slurring her words.

"I've come to take you home," said Mabli. "The last thing the bridge needs is a drunken guard causing trouble in the streets."

"But I'm not in the streets! I'm in the pub!"

A group of men nearby snickered, which in turn gave Tarley an inflated sense of pride that only occurs in the depths of intoxication.

"Don't make me drag you all the way down Victory Road," warned Mabli.

"Fine," said Tarley and edged her way out of her corner. She stumbled slightly as they left the pub so Mabli threw Tarley's arm over her shoulder to support her body. "I didn't realise how stern you could be."

Mabli groaned in response and tried to move as quickly as she could down the street. The trams were still running but she didn't want to risk Tarley coming into contact with too many people, she'd never seen her like this and was worried about what she was capable of.

"I don't like you that much, you know," said Tarley. "You can be quite…stuck up. And the thing…the thing is…if Brecon hadn't disappeared I would never *ever* have had to live with you!"

"And who would be dragging you home, then?" said Mabli.

"Hmmm. That is a good point, Haf Fellor!"

It took them almost an hour to get home as Tarley kept stumbling or refusing to move. Mabli had to coax her like a small child to even take one step forward and the process only got more difficult as the evening went on. Mabli was already well aware that Tarley had little respect for her so when she finally managed to wedge open her housemate's door and lay her down on her bed she couldn't help but feel a small sense of achievement. Even so, she was sure she would be letting out a frustrated scream at some point.

Tarley woke up the next afternoon with her face buried into her pillow and aches all over her body, particularly her feet. She looked down to see that she was still wearing her tight boots which had always been slightly too small but she had liked them too much to get rid of them.

She ever so slowly turned on to her back and pushed herself up so that she was sitting against her headboard. She wasn't immune to hangovers but she'd never felt one like this before; it was squeezing at every part of her body as if it was preparing to completely shut down.

"Fucking hell," Tarley mumbled to herself.

She noticed a full glass of water on her bedside table with a note from Mabli telling her to drink it all. Tarley grabbed the glass and downed its contents within seconds. Her raw throat felt a little more soothed but she knew she would need gallons of fluids that day if she was going to be able to function at work. What worried her, though, was that she didn't even care. She felt disgusting but she didn't regret or resent one thing that happened the night before. She enjoyed getting drunk and she especially enjoyed annoying the punters in the pub with their looks of disdain. She was even glad that Mabli finally knew how she felt about her.

You're losing control and you don't seem to care, Tarley thought. *You should be more worried.*

She stumbled down to the kitchen to pour herself another glass of water before calling Carida. Tarley's chest tightened at the sight of her mother; she had dark circles under her eyes and was clutching a scrunched-up tissue. Carida tried to assure Tarley that she was okay but her daughter only guffawed in response.

"Well you don't exactly look fresh, either," said Carida.

"Hmm," said Tarley. "Have the Premier and Delegate been in touch, yet?"

"No, why would they?"

"Apparently they speak to all of the families after...you know."

"I'm sure they've got far more important things to worry about," said Carida.

By the time she was heading to work her headache had subsided somewhat after taking several doses of a pain relief tonic but the majority of her thoughts were about food and gorging herself until she couldn't move. She would have visited her mother and raided her cupboards but she'd already lectured her on her supposedly "destructive behaviour" and she didn't want to endure that again. The phrase *"Have I not got enough to deal with?"* repeated itself in

Tarley's mind during the entire walk to the bridge.

Ryder asked after her family as he opened the gate for Tarley but she quickly dismissed him with a smile and a "we're getting by." Talking about Gwyl to anyone just made her feel guilty, confused and frustrated.

She had always thought that she had been fairly understanding towards the families of the missing guards when she encountered them; a lot of guards had family on the bridge. But it wasn't until Gwyl had disappeared that she realised how futile her words must have been. No matter how kind or caring peoples' words were they could not bring any comfort, they knew no more than Tarley and she would just prefer it if nobody said anything at all.

"I don't appreciate you just turning up like this, Neb! You have to go!" a voice hissed as Tarley walked towards the changing rooms. Her body instantly froze. She could see Darvin and Neb Figmore coming towards her, their eyes locked on to each other as if they were having a rather heated discussion. Tarley had seconds to decide whether she should make her presence known or not. The bridge had been deliberately designed so that there were no hiding places for potential attackers but if Tarley was swift enough she could get to the other side of the changing rooms without either of them seeing her, she was sure. Her tread was almost silent, despite the quickness of her feet as she moved to the other side of the changing rooms.

"You need to get the situation under control Darvin or I will," said Neb.

"And how are you going to do that, Neb?" asked Darvin, "try to continue pinning this on The Inquiry?"

"We all know that they need to be brought in, anyway."

"Yes but if and when we finally achieve that the disappearances are still going to continue, aren't they? What do we tell the public, then?"

"We'll think of something!" shouted Neb, "we both know that if…*things*…escalate even further, it's not only the bridge that will be in danger. Miraylia will burn to the ground!"

"I'm well aware of that, Neb, but if you don't leave right now I will personally drag you across this courtyard!"

Tarley would have laughed if her heart had not been racing so much.

Those bastards knew it wasn't The Inquiry and they kept it to themselves!

Although she was glad that she could finally rule out one set of suspects, fear began to crawl across her body because if Darvin knew who was to blame and he was struggling to stop them, what chance did any of the guards have of surviving?

CHAPTER EIGHT

Tarley sat opposite the fountain in Gracefalls Park for the sixth time that week. The time was exactly five o'clock, as always. Darvin had insisted on putting her only on day shifts recently and so she had plenty of time to stroll through the park before it got dark. She had specifically told Darvin that she didn't want any preferential treatment because of her father's disappearance; night shifts were part of the job and she didn't want to be a source of resentment for the rest of the guards. But Darvin just smiled and said not to worry, he was doing this more for his own peace of mind than for hers.

Tarley had wanted to confront him there and then and ask him what the fuck had been going on with Neb. Who was responsible for the abductions and why wasn't he hunting them down? But there had been something in his voice when he spoke to Neb that had scared her; a threatening tone that demanded to be listened to. She couldn't even tell anybody; it would only be her word against the Head Commander of The Arben Bridge and the Delegate for Miraylia. Who would believe a Junior Guard against two of the most powerful people in the city?

She didn't even want to contemplate what would happen

to her if she spoke out. Who wasn't to say that Darvin was in some way connected to the disappearances? The thought had been looming over her for weeks and she was sure it was the same for many people in Miraylia, including the guards. She could resign but would face a prison sentence for abandoning her oath and, most likely, a lifetime of guilt.

Tarley wondered what Rorden and the other guards who had left were doing now. All those years of training at the academy followed by the years on the bridge only made you into one thing: a guard of The Arben Bridge. Tarley was certain that she wouldn't be able to do anything else. What would she do if the government finally decided, after centuries of debate, that the bridge no longer needed guards? All she had ever dreamed of doing was mastering the art of the sword and standing guard on that beautiful old bridge. As soon as her father had declared that she was old enough to begin practising she spent every day wielding a wooden sword, gripping it tight and swiping it through the air. Carida had made Tarley a smaller version of the guards' uniform with leftover material from the dressmaker's shop and she had been certain that she had never seen as big a grin on Tarley's face as on the day she finally finished it. The whole outfit fitted perfectly, which it was bound to if her mother had made it, and gave Tarley a sense of pride that she had not experienced until then and would not experience again until she was accepted into the academy. She still kept it in her wardrobe, pressed between her cadet uniform and her current one.

Maybe Rorden and the others were retraining as something else. A quaint little job at the edge of the city. Or, perhaps, some sort of clerical job. Or maybe not.

And where was her dear father right now? This was the only time of the day that she allowed herself to think about him; when there was no one around to talk to. When she wasn't sat on her own on her favourite bench, she busied herself with as many different tasks as she could and with as many different thoughts as she could. Sometimes this worked and sometimes the image of Gwyl would quietly work its way into her mind.

Standing on the bridge. Cooking dinner with Carida. Drinking in the pub with Emlyn. Mocking his children. Ironing his uniform. His headstone. The eulogy she would write.

Tarley wondered about a lot of things when she sat opposite the fountain.

She looked down at her watch to see that half an hour had passed; Lenna was not coming today. She had not noticed Tarley's attempt to see her again.

As Tarley walked through the park she contemplated visiting her mother; she had hardly seen her over the past fortnight because it broke her heart to see her mother so upset. Macklyn had moved back in with their mother but Tarley still wanted her own place, despite her dislike towards Mabli. Tarley knew that if she moved back home there would be constant reminders of her father that would slowly chip away at her resilience whereas staying in her house meant that she could focus her efforts more concisely on finding out who was behind the disappearances. And it was far easier to be angry with Mabli than to be saddened by her mother.

"Tarley! Tarley!" someone shouted behind her.

Tarley found herself reaching for her sword as she turned around, even though it was safe in a locker on the bridge. Her chest relaxed as soon as she saw Lenna running towards her. Her hood was down but Tarley could still recognise the shape of her cousin's face.

"You got my message, then," said Tarley as Lenna drew closer.

"I watch over you more than you realise," said Lenna. "What's going on? I didn't think you'd want to meet again."

Tarley led Lenna towards the nearest bench, which was hidden behind hordes of beautiful flowers.

"I want to join The Inquiry," said Tarley.

"What?! If I remember correctly, you hate us. You called

us-"

"-I know what I called you! But I also know that you're not behind the disappearances!" Tarley glanced around at the empty park and lowered her voice, leaning in towards Lenna. "Look, I have some information that I *know* The Inquiry will want. If you get me in, I'll share it with whoever wants to hear it."

"What kind of information?"

"Information about Darvin and Neb Figmore." Even now Tarley felt like she had betrayed her Head Commander just by saying his name.

Lenna was trying hard to remain composed. In all the guilty and confused moments in which she'd imagined Tarley joining her, it had never been like this. Was Tarley really turning her back on the bridge?

If Tarley did leave the bridge Lenna knew that The Inquiry would immediately hate her, even if she did have useful intel. That would be something else Tarley would have to reconcile with herself.

"Once you do this…that's it. No more Aunt Carida, no Macklyn-"

"-I know. But if we can work together we might be able to find out what the fuck is going on with the bridge and then it won't matter."

"I hope you're right. Go home and pack whatever you can, including weapons, into one bag and then meet me on Atella Road at nine. If I'm not there then you aren't in, okay?"

Tarley nodded.

Lenna lingered for a moment; she leaned in towards Tarley as if she was going to hug her but at the last minute she backed away and gave a quick nod of her head before walking out of the park.

Tarley ran home and bounded up the stairs to her room. Thankfully, Mabli was on the bridge so she could be as loud as she wanted. She grabbed two knives that they used to train with, there was nothing special about them but they did the job, and packed a rucksack full of clothes and snacks. She had hours to kill but she knew that if she didn't pack and get out of the house before Mabli got home she was likely to lose her nerve.

She hated herself for what she was about to do to her family but the only way she could join The Inquiry without anyone searching for her was to make it look like she had disappeared like the other guards.

She grabbed the small amount of cash she had in her room and left the house, deciding to walk to the edge of the city and buy some dinner before she headed to Atella Road. Part of her contemplated telling her mother before she left so that she wouldn't worry but she knew Carida too well. She would tell Darvin where Tarley had gone straight away and the whole city would end up searching for her.

No. No one must know.

She walked until she found a dingy little café two miles away from where she was due to meet Lenna and ordered a bowl of chicken stew before settling down at a table in the corner of the room. She wondered if it would be her last hot meal for a long time. Who knew how The Inquiry lived? Did they even have time for basic things like meals in between planning various attacks?

Tarley's head began to spin. She couldn't lose her nerve now.

She wanted her guard sword by her side but she couldn't risk visiting the bridge and part of her wondered if she would change her mind once she was there. Trying to act like she didn't hate The Inquiry was possibly going to be one of the hardest things she would ever do. She excelled in her training at the academy, even the modules she hated that involved building trust between a criminal, but that was only for short amounts of time. She didn't even want to think about how long she would have to keep the pretense up for this time.

As she ate her stew her mind wandered to what Gwyl would say to her if he was there. She was trying to join the very organisation that could have killed her brother. But her father was one of the best commanders the bridge had ever seen; she had grown up with stories about his infamous fights and how he went undercover in some of the deadliest guerrilla groups in the country before he became a father. He'd even suggested on numerous occasions that The Inquiry should be deemed a criminal organisation before it finally was. Tarley was just conducting herself the same way he did, wasn't she?

She finished her food but her stomach felt so tight that she was worried she was going to throw up.

This is for the bridge. This is for Miraylia. This is for the bridge. This is for Miraylia.

She repeated the words over and over in her head until it was finally time to leave and head for Atella Road. She pulled the hood of her jacket over her head, took a deep breath and stepped out on to the dark street.

She only passed a handful of people as she weaved in and out of narrow alleyways and turned down dingy streets. Very few people went out by themselves now; everyone seemed to move in small groups if they dared to go out. Tarley didn't understand their mentality; the disappearances happened at all times of the day and all over the city. Husbands and wives had woken up to find that their partners were no longer lying next to them as well as those that went missing whilst guarding the bridge. Nothing about the abductions made sense but that didn't stop the fear of the night creeping into the city's mind.

Within half an hour Tarley was turning on to Atella Road and could see Lenna leaning against a wall, twirling a knife in her hand. As soon as she spotted Tarley she slipped it back into her jacket pocket and stood up straight.

"Am I in, then?" Tarley asked.

"You having a place in The Inquiry is conditional."

"Okay, what's the condition?"

"You have to come with me right now and do exactly as you're told. No questions."

Tarley nodded and Lenna immediately began to walk down the street. Tarley followed her as they curved through the city until The Arben Bridge Academy started to come into view. The massive, teal coloured building loomed over the Northern area of Miraylia, standing out amongst the little red brick shops and worn-down pubs.

Tarley and Lenna walked along the fence that surrounded the academy and Tarley couldn't help but look into the courtyard. There were weights and obstacles left on the ground from that day's training session and a large track to the right that Tarley had spent many a morning running around. She wondered if any of the cadets were having doubts about what they had signed up for. They should have all been getting ready for bed right now and talking about anything and everything that concerned the young people of the city. Or maybe the talk was less frivolous these days.

Tarley and her fellow cadets had been so sure of their futures and why they were there that when they weren't in training they didn't need to concern themselves with talk of the bridge. It was very rare that a cadet didn't graduate and take up a position on the bridge; after all, the academy only took on average twenty cadets from across the country each year.

She was craving that kind of security and certainty right now as she followed Lenna towards the back entrance. They stopped by the gate and Lenna withdrew her knife once more, instructing Tarley to do the same.

"I doubt you'll need it but it's always best to be prepared," said Lenna.

"Can you tell me what we're doing?" asked Tarley.

"We've got a spy in the academy and we've come to collect him," said Lenna. "There aren't many Inquiry members left in the city now but those that remain are leaving tonight before this manhunt gets out of control."

For the second time that night Tarley thought she was going to be sick; how had The Inquiry managed to get a spy into the academy? And how long had they been there?

She hoped more than anything that it wasn't one of the trainers; most of them were retired or injured guards that had been there for years. She could still reel off their names and their classes.

"Shit, what's that?" shouted Tarley, pointing to a window on the highest floor.

Lenna looked up to see flames rising through the room but rather than seeing the fiery oranges and reds that she was used to she instead saw deep purples and blues chasing each other through the darkness.

"Fuck knows," said Lenna softly.

The door to the academy flew open and a man not much older than Tarley came running out, sweat dripping down his face and neck. He placed a jagged crystal into an indent in the gate that fitted perfectly causing the gate to creek open.

"West!" said Lenna, "are you okay?"

"No, we have to run!" said West.

"What about those flames? They're going to spread!" said Tarley.

West paused for a moment to stare at Tarley. He could feel a flicker of power almost radiating from her body but there was a sense of uncertainty about her, too. Did she even know?

"They can deal with it. We can't risk being exposed," West replied.

"Agreed," said Lenna, "come on, Ash is waiting for us on Kidcrook street."

Lenna and West immediately broke out into a run with Tarley being a little slower to get off the mark. All three of them had the city's streets memorised and so they instinctively took the same turns and dashed down the same alleyways.

After ten minutes they only had to take a few more turns down some cobbled, eerie alleys before they reached Kidcrook Street. The street itself was renowned for being the embarrassment of the city; there were no beautiful parks, the buildings were ancient and the only people who lived there seemed to be those who had condemned themselves to a life of monotony without the release of ambition.

Neb Figmore had managed to secure funding to reinvigorate the area but the building site had lain dormant for six years. It was fenced off and some of the foundations had been dug but it wasn't long before the project was suspended owing to financial issues. Everyone in Miraylia knew that those houses were never going to be built.

The three of them slowed down as a very old and clunky brown car drew up beside them. Tarley could see the man from the hospital sitting in the driver's seat, smirking at Lenna and West.

"You took your time," he said.

"Fuck off," said Lenna, opening the door to the passenger's side.

West and Tarley climbed into the back, the latter's heart still pumping ferociously. All she could see was groups of people clamoring out of the academy, coughing through the smoke and hoping that they would escape before the flames took them.

"That wasn't ordinary fire, was it?" said Tarley to West. "What have you done to those poor people?"

"I haven't done anything," said West. "And I know exactly who you are so don't you dare think you have the right to lecture me on right and wrong."

"I'm not-"

"-for fuck's sake, shut up! We've got a long drive and I'd prefer it if we all made it one piece!" shouted Lenna.

Ash chuckled as he grabbed Lenna's right hand and lifted it to his mouth. She didn't object but neither did she return the gesture. Instead, she lowered her hand and looked out of the window as they began to leave Miraylia once again.

Tarley glared at the back of Lenna's head but out of the corner of her eye she was trying to observe West and make her assumptions about him. She already loathed him, she was positive about that, but she also felt that there was a faint expression of pain etched across his face. She could see that his fists were clenched by his side and he was looking straight ahead; his eyes seemingly focused on nothing in particular. He was definitely older than the average cadet, although it was not unheard of for people to have a sudden urge to join the bridge as they grew older, but it was unlikely that they would be accepted. Tarley had so many questions to ask as to how The Inquiry managed to conceal West and remain in contact with him; she could remember all the security checks and protocol a cadet had to go through just to submit their application. Tarley's had been fairly straightforward as they could easily trace her whole family's history back to the bridge, but for someone like West The Inquiry must have spent a fortune on faking his identity and ensuring that his crimes never came to light.

Tarley turned her head away so that she could bid her city goodbye and before she knew it the whole of Miraylia was becoming a blur. The buildings and streets that she had grown up with and lived among seemed to fade into the background as they headed down Victory Road and out into the wild.

CHAPTER NINE

Tarley sat on the lumpy sofa next to Lenna as they watched the news reporter prattle on about the redevelopment of a hospital just outside of Miraylia. Tarley thought that she and Lenna would have had more of a chance to speak to each other over the past three days but Lenna had spent most of her time with Ash trying to convince him that Tarley could be trusted. They would never discuss this when Tarley was close by but she could hear them through the walls, even if they were trying to keep their voices low.

The house they were staying in was out in the countryside and belonged to an elderly Inquiry member named Portas. He had been part of the organisation for most of his life before finally deciding to live in the middle of nowhere so that no one could find him. Ash took great pride in telling Tarley that Portas and Ash's mother were very good friends when Ash was young.

Portas had been friendly enough to Tarley, refraining from insulting the bridge while she was around but every now and then he couldn't help but drop his hate towards her job into conversation.

Her old job, she must remind herself. Darvin would never

have her back after this, even if she left at that very moment and returned home. His job was hard enough without having to worry about stray guards who abandon their oaths. Tarley thought about Rorden and how she had silently condemned him for being a traitor. She was no better.

No, she thought. She was doing this to find her father. To solve the disappearances. That was more than any of the other bloody guards or commanders were doing, if anything they weren't being completely true to their oath by simply turning up to the bridge every day. They should all be actively searching for answers, Tarley was just the only one brave enough to do it. If she could just continue to think like that then, maybe, she wouldn't hate herself so much.

She tried not to allow herself to think about her mother and her brothers. They had probably assumed that she, too, had disappeared into the unknown. She only hoped that they didn't think that Macklyn would be next when there was no real evidence to suggest that he would be.

She had been watching the news almost every day since they had arrived but there had been no mention of her name or a press conference. She wondered if they were no longer releasing the names of those who vanished from the bridge; the whole government was already being criticised in the press every day, maybe now Henya Quinn had decided that an embargo was finally needed.

"The fire at The Arben Bridge Academy, which caused the death of eight cadets and one trainer has claimed another victim as its Head of Physical Activity has passed away in hospital," said the reporter before the holograph switched to the now infamous images of the rubble that was once the academy.

The morning that they had all arrived at Portas' house Tarley instantly begged to set the image crystals to see if there had been any news of the fire. At that point five people had been declared dead at the scene as they failed to leave the building in time. She had tried not to burst into tears but she couldn't stop her eyes from welling up. What had those people ever done to The Inquiry? Lenna had had to take her into a separate room when Tarley had reached the height of her hysterics in an attempt to calm her down but it only worked for a few hours. Ever since she had felt disgusted and nauseated every time she saw West.

The news report showed various pictures of Hunter Bell, a former guard who became a trainer after an attack on the bridge had left him blind in one eye.

"Did you know him?" Lenna asked Tarley.

"Yes," Tarley replied. "He was a good man and now he's dead." She spat her last sentence towards West who burrowed his brows in response.

"Good men die every day," said West.

"And that makes you feel better about killing them, does it?!" shouted Tarley. "Why don't you tell us what really happened that night? It's obvious it was you who started the fire!"

"Why are you even here? You keep saying you have information yet you refuse to share it. How do we know that you're not spying on us for the bridge?"

Tarley leapt on to her feet, raising her arm, but before she could bring it down on West, Lenna was already in front of her and pushing her back towards the sofa.

"That's enough!" yelled Lenna, "Tarley, you *chose* to come to us and that means abiding by our rules. Our mission was to get West out of the academy, whatever happened inside is a matter for Penn."

"I'm going to train outside," said West, standing up and grabbing a nearby sword. "There's a nasty smell in here."

"I think I'll join you," said Ash.

As he walked out of the house he shot Tarley a disgruntled look but she was past caring; she just had to remind herself that she only had to stay with them until they worked out who was abducting the guards.

"You're not going to get very far if you don't make any allies," said Lenna.

"I've got you," said Tarley.

"Maybe. Sit down; I want to go over the plan for tomorrow, again."

Tarley did as she was told and nodded as Lenna relayed the plan for the hundredth time. Tomorrow she was finally going to meet Penn Heath, the current leader of The Inquiry and one of the biggest discussion points for people across Liliath. Like most of the members who joined after The Inquiry became an illegal organisation not much was known about him other than that he was a tall dark-haired man in his early thirties. The media believed that he had been in charge for the last three to five years but reports were murky at best.

"Got it?" said Lenna once she had finished.

"I got it the first time, Len," said Tarley.

Lenna rolled her eyes and sat back down next to her cousin. Even now, she felt like a woman with a kid sister.

"I want you to be honest with me," said Tarley, "do you think Penn will let me in?"

"That depends. Maybe if you told me your information I would be able to make an informed guess."

Lenna had a playful smile on her face but Tarley knew her well enough to know that she was being serious. After all, she had been begging Tarley to tell her everything ever since they left Miraylia.

"And you promise you won't tell Ash or West?" said Tarley.

"I promise. I know you don't trust them but you should trust me."

"I do," said Tarley and proceeded to relay the conversation she had heard between Neb and Darvin as well as what Macklyn had told her about Gwyl's disappearance.

Lenna didn't seem phased by anything that Tarley was saying, even the mysterious way in which her father was taken. She simply sat there and nodded as Tarley tried not to trip over her own words.

"I can't say too much," began Lenna once Tarley had

finished speaking, "but what you're saying is definitely in line with the information we've gathered so far. I'm sure that Penn will want to know what you've just told me."

Tarley felt a small sense of relief but she was still terrified that she would meet Penn, he would reject her straight away and she would be forced to go back to Miraylia as a traitor. She knew it was still a possibility but she hoped that there had been enough of a shift in her relationship with Lenna that she would at least try and fight for Tarley to join The Inquiry.

Portas and West cooked for everyone that evening and they all spent dinner in absolute silence, save for the sound of cutlery against crockery. Every time Tarley looked at her companions their eyes were down and focusing purely on their plates, even Lenna seemed more interested in her potatoes than in Tarley or Ash.

Tarley wondered if there was any way of getting a message back to her family just so that they knew she was safe but that would only cause more problems for her. She thought of her mother, blotchy with tears after her father had disappeared, and what pain Tarley must be putting her through, now. The prospect made her chest tighten and very nearly tempted her to put down her fork and run through the countryside until she reached home.

I swear to protect The Arben Bridge, she reminded herself. Her vow did little to comfort her but it brought her mind back to the present if nothing more. Darvin might not be doing anything to save the bridge but Tarley was, she had to be certain of that.

They all went to bed soon after, knowing that the next day would bring fatigue and require them to be more vigilant than ever. Tarley, to her great relief the next morning, fell asleep almost as soon as she laid down her head.

She was jolted awake by Lenna shaking her and telling her that she needed to have eaten breakfast and be ready to leave within the next hour. Tarley did as she said and was soon dressed and taking her pick of the small knives and swords that the group had managed to escape Miraylia with.

Tarley had always admired weapons and the craftsmanship behind them but gearing up as if she were going into battle made her feel queasy, especially as their plan was to blend into the crowd around the Durnos Fountain as if they were tourists. Tarley doubted that there were many tourists who got ready for their travels by deciding which pocket knife looked the deadliest. She prayed that she didn't have to use it.

"I miss my sword," said Tarley, absentmindedly.

"I'll make you a better one," said Lenna, giving Tarley a reassuring smile.

"Come on," groaned Ash, "we're going to be late."

Tarley zipped up her jacket and followed the others out of the door. They each thanked Portas as they left before heading through a nearby field and towards an old tram station. There were only three other people on the platform, which made Tarley feel a little less anxious as none of them looked anything other than ordinary.

They only had to wait five minutes before a battered looking tram stopped next to the platform. The four of them stepped on in silence and huddled in a corner of the carriage. It was easy to see that this was not a city tram; there were far less people crammed into a carriage and only a few had to stand.

Despite most of Miraylia hating the tram system Tarley had always secretly loved it. The noise and the busyness had always given her a strange sort of buzz that she didn't understand but adored nonetheless. She supposed that it was because she had grown up in that city, every street it housed was a part of her body somehow and they would always be connected. She had only been apart from it for four days and yet it felt like years, she had a yearning to see its cobbled roads as if it would be the last chance she would ever get to visit them again.

"You okay?" whispered Lenna, snapping Tarley out of her thoughts.

Tarley nodded. "Yes," she said.

Lenna found Tarley's hand and gave it a small squeeze, which did nothing to ease Tarley's nerves but she smiled at her, anyway. In that moment Tarley wondered why she had ever been so horrid to Lenna but the memory of her brother lying in a hospital bed and images of cadets fleeing a burning building soon appeared in her mind and her hand fell away.

Fifteen minutes later they arrived in the centre of Rhedos and were shuffling off the tram with the hundreds of other passengers. Tarley found that she kept looking around to see if she recognised anyone, friend or foe, as they made their way towards the exit but she didn't recognise a single face.

"Try not to look so bloody nervous," said Ash angrily but also quietly enough so that only Tarley could hear.

Tarley didn't respond but she immediately straightened up and tried to imagine herself patrolling the bridge; it was the only way she could pretend to feel confident.

Once they were out of the building they began the short walk to the Durnos Fountain but due to the amount of people that were flocking towards it they found themselves barely shuffling forward.

Tarley had seen pictures of the fountain when she was younger and knew that it was the largest fountain in Liliath but standing just mere metres away from it had made her feel so small and insignificant in a way that no photograph could ever achieve.

The fountain itself was made of white marble and towered so high that only a strip of blue sky was visible over the top. The design featured two figures, one male and one female, standing at its centre and holding hands as they looked down on the water below. Both were dressed in flowing robes and where their hair should have been they had beautifully carved flowers and leaves. Fairies and wild animals looked at them with adoration as they hid behind the intricately carved fauna, seemingly wondering if their masters would be aware of their presence.

Tarley, like the rest of the country, knew the Durnos story off by heart. Coedwig, the creator of nature and all its beauty was strolling through Rhedos one morning when his eyes fell upon a young woman standing by a still pond. He asked the woman, Effor, what she was doing and she replied that the pond lacked the beauty that it deserved. She stood back and transformed the pond into a glistening lagoon surrounded by flowers and a huge waterfall that splashed into the water below.

Coedwig was so mesmerised by the woman's gift that he immediately asked her to marry him and together they rule over the countryside of Rhedos, ensuring its beauty never dies.

The lagoon that Effor was said to have transformed was also a popular tourist destination but after seeing the fountain Tarley wondered how anything could ever be as beautiful as what she was currently looking at.

"Take our picture," demanded Ash, handing Tarley a small camera. "We need to look like tourists."

Ash, West and Lenna all huddled in front of the fountain as Tarley took the picture and for just a second Tarley almost believed that they were just four people enjoying a morning at the fountain.

"Ash, I can see your mum!" said Lenna, pointing to the other side of the fountain where a group of four people stood, seemingly having a normal conversation with each other.

Ash pushed past the crowd, much to Lenna's annoyance, and almost ran into a short woman with dark brown hair, wrapping his arms around her. As she finally pulled away from her son Tarley couldn't help but gasp a little.

"You didn't tell me that Ash is Rhoswen Florrie's son!" said Tarley, grabbing Lenna's arm.

Lenna chuckled as she joined the group and kissed Rhoswen's cheek, leaving Tarley standing on the outskirts looking on in awe.

Rhoswen Florrie was infamous all over the world for

being a champion swordswoman before she and her equally infamous partner founded The Inquiry and were forced to leave the championship. Tarley had secretly admired her for years because even though no one was supposed to support Rhoswen, holographs of her tournaments were still shown to students learning to master the sword. She was commended for being as graceful as she was lethal and so it was no surprise that she continuously won medals throughout her career. But no one had seen her for decades and Tarley was just as shocked to see that she was alive as she was to see her at all.

A taller woman who looked just a little older than Tarley stepped forward and handed each of them a small piece of folded paper.

"*Don't* open them," she demanded. "They're directions to an old safe house in the middle of nowhere. You need to take two trams and then it's a mile walk, okay?" They all nodded in response. "I'm going to leave now, wait half an hour and then go."

"Where's everyone else?" asked Ash.

"We're travelling in small groups. Someone else will be along in an hour to direct the next lot. I'll see you this evening."

The woman promptly walked away while the rest of group remained for another half an hour as instructed pretending to be any other group of tourists.

As she clicked her camera and gave fake smiles to Lenna part of Tarley was convinced that they would be caught. The idea of standing still when they could be moving unnerved her but no one else seemed to share her anxieties.

The journey took them several hours and Tarley pretended to be asleep for most of it, she still wasn't sure how to talk to these people. She could hear them whispering to each other about her, discussing how Lenna must have lost her mind to open her arms to her cousin, again. Some even asked Lenna if she wanted them to get rid of Tarley for her but, thankfully, Lenna had told them to shut the fuck up.

The Inquiry had been in existence since before Tarley was born and so she had never known a time without them dominating newspaper headlines or being the topic of conversation in nearly every pub she walked into. But they had always seemed like a group of people whose sole purpose was to cause trouble and destroy the city that she loved, she had never thought of them as being people with loyalties to each other. Or even families. Lenna had only been with them for two years and yet they seemed fiercely protective over her.

"She's always missed her, that's the problem."

"Penn has lost his mind. We should just throw her off the tram."

"She's going to betray us, I know it."

They eventually reached Bluewood Station, thankfully without losing anyone, and all Tarley could see was green fields. From where she stood to beyond the horizon was nothing but varying shades of green, outlined with hedgerows and dotted with cows.

But it was the quiet that shocked her. There were no car horns, no low hums from the trams and no shouting from passers-by on the streets. All she could hear was the sound of shoes shuffling off the platform.

"This really is the middle of nowhere," said Ash as he unfolded his piece of paper. The whole group followed suit and were soon walking into the nearest overgrown field. Tarley wondered just how big The Inquiry's network stretched if they had a safe house this far out in the country, she'd always assumed that they were only based in Miraylia.

They had to climb over a rickety fence and walk through another field filled with cows and their muck, which was harder to avoid than Tarley had anticipated, before they finally saw the safe house in the distance. As she drew closer Tarley could see that it was a narrow, dark grey building with many of its windows boarded up with wood and those that had glass in them were covered in grime. Weeds grew around it and two men were outside attempting to cut them down.

Penn Heath emerged from the house, fiercely striding towards Rhoswen and pulling her into a hug. She kissed his cheek and he returned the gesture.

"West!" he shouted as he drew away from Rhoswen, "it's good to see you, again!"

"Yeah," said West with half a smile as he allowed Penn to pat him on the back.

Penn then turned to the rest of the group and reminded Tarley of the way Neb Figmore would straighten up before he gave a speech to the Bureau. "I'm afraid that there are only five bedrooms and two bathrooms and, including those already here, our numbers reach almost forty. Therefore, it's a case of sleeping where you drop. There are no luxuries here; you'll just have to grin and bear it." He said the last sentence while looking directly at Tarley. "Or buy a tent."

Ash and West greeted the two men who were hacking away at the weeds while the others walked into a narrow hallway. There was a small table by the door that was covered in dust and Tarley couldn't help but start to cough.

"You two," said Penn to Tarley and Lenna. "Come with me."

He led them down the hall and into the kitchen at the back of the house, which looked like it had had a decent clean, making it seem somewhat respectable. Although Tarley could still see a cockroach scuttling across the floor. She wasn't sure that 'safe house' was the best term for the place.

"You," Penn said to Tarley. "Tell me what your information is now or I'll bundle you into a van and drive you to the other side of the country."

Tarley's eyebrows shot up. "Don't I even get a cup of tea, first?" Neither Penn nor Lenna said a word. "I'm happy to tell you but I want you to guarantee that I have a place in The Inquiry."

"If I believe your information is valuable then you will be allowed to join," said Penn. "You have my word."

Tarley glanced at Lenna who nodded for her to continue

before she spoke.

"Darvin and Figmore know exactly who's behind the disappearances but neither of them can catch the suspect, whoever they are, but Figmore still wants to pin it all on you guys," said Tarley.

Penn sighed and folded his arms, "That's not really anything we didn't already know."

"Perhaps but I also know what happens when a guard disappears from the bridge," said Tarley before describing the events of her father's disappearance. She wished she felt uneasy about talking to Penn regarding something so personal but she had relayed the scenario so many times in her head that she felt she had some distance from it now. She had pictured the scene with every other guard in Gwyl's place and, somehow, it had caused the pain to lessen.

Once Tarley had finished Penn raised his eyebrows at Lenna who nodded in return, causing Tarley to feel like she was being left out of a secret childlike code.

"Thank you, Tarley," said Penn, "that pretty much confirms our suspicions."

"What suspicions?" said Tarley.

"Never mind that," said Lenna. "Is she in, Penn?"

"I suppose that if the cousin you turned your back on is happy enough for you to join our ranks then I should let you," said Penn to Tarley with a streak of disdain across his face. "And your guard training may come in use. But you have to do everything that is asked of you, even if that means scrubbing the toilets for twelve hours straight."

"Of course," said Tarley.

"Then welcome to The Inquiry," said Penn.

CHAPTER TEN

Tarley did not sleep well that night. After they had eaten a meagre dinner of stew and bread everyone was so tired that they all agreed to get some sleep. Tarley and Lenna joined Ash in the front room of the house with four other people that Tarley didn't know and slept on thin roll mats with just an old sheet to cover them.

Liliath was not known for its scorching heat but as they approached summer the temperature was becoming more comfortable. Nevertheless, Tarley spent most of the night wishing that she could light a fire.

She had woken up with heavy and sore eyes and an aching body. She could feel a twinge in her lower back but didn't say a word to anyone; she thought it would be best to keep her ailments to herself.

As soon as everyone had eaten breakfast Penn had announced that there would be a meeting that evening and until then everyone was free to do as they pleased, apart from Tarley who had been handed a toothbrush and told to clean the entire house.

There were quiet giggles throughout the room but Tarley ignored them as she took the toothbrush and went in search of a bucket to fill with water and cleaning tonic. Lenna had opened her mouth to object but before she could speak Penn informed her that it would be best if she began an inventory of all their weapons.

Once everyone had cleared out of the kitchen Tarley began to scrub the sink, which took her well over an hour as it was so grimy. Several members would walk in intermittently to snigger at her but she tried her best not to make eye contact with them. Instead, she found comfort imagining what it would be like to humiliate them during a duel. She was confident that she could disarm every one of them within minutes and every time they laughed at her she just imagined them cowering away from her as she knocked their swords out of their hands.

Cramp was spreading through her hand as she began to clean the counters but she didn't stop; giving The Inquiry even more of an excuse to mock her was enough motivation to keep cleaning.

"You look like you could do with a hand," said Rhoswen, walking into the kitchen and grabbing a sponge.

"I don't think Penn would be too happy about that," said Tarley.

"Ha! Penn may be the leader but I founded this organisation, I'll do what I like. Besides, I have huge respect for anyone who dares to leave the bridge."

Rhoswen gave Tarley a smile that had just enough of a hint of mischievousness to cause Tarley to do the same, despite Rhoswen's dig towards the bridge. Rhoswen plunged her sponge into the water and quickly began to wipe down the counter in front of her.

"So Lenna tells me you're an excellent swordswoman," said Rhoswen.

Tarley could feel herself blushing, "I hope so. I'm obviously not as good as you."

Rhoswen laughed, "I doubt that, I haven't competed for decades."

"So you've never had to use a sword since founding The Inquiry?"

"Fair point. I take it back; I *am* excellent with a sword."

Tarley found herself giggling as the two of them continued to chat and for a moment the anger she had felt earlier in the day was slowly beginning to lift. Neither of the women spoke about The Inquiry nor why Tarley was there. Instead Tarley was more than happy to hear Rhoswen's stories about competing in the championships and how she met Ash's father, Parry. He had been well known for being the rebel of the championship, always turning up late for tournaments and staying out a lot later than he should, so when he and Rhoswen became a couple their faces were constantly in the media. Even though they had seemingly disappeared years before Tarley was born even she knew their story and the legacy they had created.

As Tarley finished cleaning the floor Lenna sauntered into the room with a sword in each hand.

"Come on, I know you're probably itching to get your hands on one of these," said Lenna.

"But Penn-"

"-leave Penn to me," said Rhoswen.

Tarley didn't require any further encouragement and immediately stood up offering her hand to Lenna. Her cousin threw her the sword in her left hand and Tarley effortlessly caught it by the handle.

The weight felt comforting in her hands and as she brought it close to her face to examine she was surprised by its beauty. It had a curved silver handle that was too big for Tarley with three black gemstones laid across it. There were also birds mid-flight chiseled into the metal and the words 'The Arben Bridge' in beautiful writing underneath.

"This is a guard sword!" said Tarley, desperately trying to remember if she knew who owned it. Every guard's sword was individual to them and so it was difficult to match the sword to the owner from memory.

"We've had a few guards join over the years but it's all kept hush hush," said Lenna as she led Tarley through the house and out into the garden. "Ever wondered why a perfectly healthy guard suddenly has an incurable disease that means no one can ever see them again?"

Tarley only knew three people who had left the bridge for reasons other than retirement and she had never thought to question that they weren't genuinely ill. A feeling of betrayal and stupidity seemed to suddenly overcome her and when she looked at the guard sword again she almost felt as if its allure had been lost.

"Anyway, I thought you might be missing yours so I swiped that one for you until I can make you an absolutely glorious one," said Lenna. She stopped halfway down the garden and turned to Tarley, tightening the grip on her own sword. "So are we training or what?"

Tarley smiled, "If you think you can keep up."

Lenna laughed and gave an exaggerated bow, twirling her free hand as if she thought Tarley was the Premier. Once she stood up she darted forward, her sword outstretched but Tarley had already raised her arm and her sword locked with Lenna's.

Tarley pushed Lenna's sword away and the two began again, lunging and retreating as the sound of blade upon blade increased and they were running through the garden, each with a look of ecstasy on their faces. Lenna ducked as Tarley swung her sword over her head and Tarley jumped as Lenna jabbed hers in Tarley's direction. Every step that one took was perfectly imitated by the other in reverse. As their arms seamlessly moved from one position to another Tarley couldn't help but think of those two little girls in Gracefalls Park, running around frantically with wooden swords, trying to put into practice what they had learnt from that day's swordswork class. There was a wildness to their fight and yet they were both perfectly in control of their weapons. They could run, jump and duck without feeling like they were being too easy or too hard on the other. The sound of their blades coming into contact perfectly scored the dance they were performing. They locked swords one final time before Tarley put all her force behind her arm and knocked Lenna's sword out of her hand and on to the ground below.

"Nicely done," said Lenna, panting slightly.

"I have to agree. Can I have my sword back now, please?" said a voice with a hint of a country accent that Tarley instantly recognised.

She snapped her head towards the back door of the house to see a man several inches taller than her with the darkest hair she'd ever known staring back at her. He couldn't stop himself from grinning as he walked into the garden with the kind of subtle arrogance that Tarley was all too familiar with.

"Brecon," said Tarley. It was not a question; she knew exactly who he was. She had lived in the same house as him for almost a year before he disappeared and was replaced by Mabli.

They walked towards each other and promptly pulled the other into an embrace. He still smelt like the soft musty aftershave he used to douse himself in everyday and she still smelt like the floral incense she would light to relax after a day on the bridge.

"I didn't realise you guards were so touchy feely," said Lenna.

Tarley pulled away and laughed, "We used to live together."

"Oh! You never told me that!" exclaimed Lenna, pushing Brecon's shoulder.

"I didn't want to upset you," said Brecon.

Lenna rolled her eyes and said, "I'll leave you to it, then," before going back into the house.

Brecon turned back to Tarley and took the sword out of her hand. She couldn't help but flinch slightly at his touch.

"I was serious," he said, "I want this back."

"I'm surprised you'd want to hold on to it after leaving the bridge," said Tarley, sitting down on the grass.

Brecon sat down next to her, gently placing the sword on the ground and unable to hide his smirk.

"You can talk; I bet you're pining after your guard sword."

Tarley didn't reply, she was too occupied taking in his face again. His features were exactly the same; the deep green eyes and square face that were inherently confident yet his demeanor seemed somewhat different. The straight back and stiff movements that came with being a guard had softened; he was slightly hunched and his hands were loosely held together.

They had been so close once, no one else in the house seemed to have as much in common as the two of them did, and when he had left all Tarley could think about were the jokes or conversations that she hadn't had the chance to have with him.

"I can't believe you're okay," said Tarley, smiling.

"You're not mad then? It's just that I had wanted to leave the bridge for ages and the disappearances…they were the perfect foil to escape without repercussions."

"No, I'm not mad but you could have told me. I thought we were friends."

"We were. We are. I just didn't want to you to carry that burden, wondering if you should tell Darvin or not." He reached out and grabbed her hands, they were still as strong as he'd remembered them.

"My dad went missing, my mother has been a mess ever since and now I've no doubt pushed her to the edge…," Tarley's voice trailed off as she thought of her family, gathered around her mother in her childhood home. "What about your family? Do they know you're okay?"

"Yes, they don't keep up with the goings on of the bridge, anyway, living in Wedley. But they know I'm okay." He looked Tarley in the eyes and his smile grew slightly. "I have to admit that I was shocked when Penn told me you'd joined us. I never thought you'd leave the bridge."

"I'm doing this *for* the bridge," said Tarley, sounding fiercer than she had anticipated. "Anyway, where have you been? I didn't see you at dinner last night or breakfast this morning."

"I was with a group in Jobern monitoring Quinn. We've

only just got back."

Tarley remained silent; she was enjoying their reunion too much to ask exactly what it was Brecon had been doing in Jobern. She was sure that she would find out soon enough, anyway.

Ash and West walked out of the house, both carrying bottles of beer and laughing in a way that made Tarley's stomach feel queasy. They looked as if they were heading to a barbecue and not in the midst of being on the run from the government.

"Brecon!" said Ash, "I didn't know you were back! Fancy a beer?"

"Not right now, thanks. I'm just catching up with Tarley," Brecon replied.

West sniggered. "Haven't you got any more cleaning to do?" he asked Tarley.

"Just fuck off and drink your beer," snapped Tarley.

West looked as though he was about to launch himself at her but Ash placed his hand on his friend's chest and suggested that they sit outside the front of the house, instead.

"I don't know how he can live with himself after killing all those people. He doesn't even have the decency to admit that it was him," said Tarley.

Brecon moved in closer to her and lowered his voice as he spoke. "Tarley, you need to be careful what you say around here. West and Ash have a lot of respect among everyone here and you've pissed off both of them."

Tarley sighed and got to her feet. "I'm going to have a shower; I'll see you around."

* * *

Later that evening, after everyone had eaten dinner and the plates and dishes had been washed, every member of The Inquiry gathered in the garden. Penn would have preferred to have stayed inside but there wasn't a room big enough for everyone to stand in and, thankfully, the nearest people to them were probably over a mile away.

Tarley managed to push her way through the crowd so that she was near to the front next to Lenna. She could see West standing opposite them but he wasn't looking in her direction which suited her perfectly.

"First of all," shouted Penn, "can we please welcome back West and thank him for the excellent work he has done over the past three years?"

The whole crowd roared and applauded as West allowed a small smile to creep across his face. Tarley thought of her earlier conversation with Brecon and lamely clapped as the cheers went on. She still couldn't understand why no one was desperate to find out what had happened at the academy; The Inquiry outwardly hated the bridge and yet they seemed to behave just like the guards. Do what is asked of you and don't ask any questions.

"Now, I think we should recap what it is we've been building up to over these past few years for the benefit of our latest recruit," continued Penn as the applause died down.

Tarley could feel every single pair of eyes boring into her with various levels of judgement. Most of them had no issues in showing their disdain as they smirked and whispered to the person next to them.

"What is Penn up to?"

"Maybe we should give her a chance. She did come to us, after all."

"I bet we're going to dump her somewhere when she's no longer needed."

"Every attack that we've engaged in recently has been with the sole purpose to gain intel on the Sovrans that live in Liliath," continued Penn. "We infiltrated the security offices in Jobern and the Harkon Building as we believed that they have been monitoring Sovranic activity for centuries."

"Sovrans?! You think that Sovrans are still alive?" shouted Tarley, too overwhelmed by frustration to think about her manners. She'd left her family and the job she'd worked her whole life for to join a group that was seemingly hunting fossils!

"We *know* that Sovrans are still alive," said Penn and nodded towards a young woman who was stood just a few feet away from him.

Within seconds the wooden table in front of her had caught fire but the flames were twisting into the shapes of stars, moons and suns before they finally disappeared and the table stood there seemingly untouched.

A gentle hum of laughter went through the group as they saw the shock spread across Tarley's face.

That can't be real. It's a trick.

The homeless man…

Tarley was still staring at the table, looking for burns in the wood or anything that suggested that it had been set alight but there was nothing. And everyone had seen it, she was certain. Glorious, beautiful flames that disappeared into nothingness.

Her eyes soon fell upon West who was now glaring at her and shaking his head. There was a desperation on his face that she had not seen before; his anger and antagonism had vanished to be replaced by a childlike West that pleaded to any empathy that Tarley held.

"I'm sorry I couldn't tell you before," whispered Lenna, looking a little sheepish.

"Anyway," said Penn, "this is why the Bureau wants to pin the disappearances on us. We know about Sovrans and, for some reason, they don't want the public to know about them. Although, given the information you told me yesterday it seems highly likely that a Sovran, or at least *something* with supernatural abilities, is involved in the abduction of the guards."

"What do you mean 'something'? Surely it's a person or a group of people behind the attacks?" asked Tarley, feeling slightly exasperated already.

Penn shook his head, "You have a lot to learn. *Anything* has the potential to have supernatural powers. For years

Sovrans have placed their powers in inanimate objects to hide who they really are. There's nothing to say that a huge tree containing thousands of Sovrans' powers isn't behind the abductions."

Tarley furrowed her brow; she usually knew when she was being made fun of but on this occasion she couldn't really tell. A lot of information was being thrown at her in a short space of time and she felt as if she was struggling to keep up with the pace.

"But if we have Sovrans on our side, Tarley, it means that our small army becomes much larger and we can take on Henya Quinn and whatever it is she's hiding," said Penn. "Which leads me on to, hopefully, our final mission."

He placed four pale blue crystals, each with one long sharp edge, on each corner of the table and pointed them inwards. A holographic map of the bridge instantly appeared with the academy's logo spinning in the bottom right hand corner.

"We intend to attack the bridge in two days' time and finally find out what it's guarding," said Penn. "As you know there is the main gate with one guard and then there are five gates, each manned by two guards-"

"-it's five guards now," shouted West.

"Five? Are you sure?" said Penn.

"Yes, Darvin increased the number of guards because of the disappearances."

"Makes sense. Anyway, as you're all aware the bridge has an extremely rare identity crystal and seeing as the majority of us are on the dangerous persons' list, there's no way we're getting past that thing, even with enchantments."

A hum of laughter went around the room but Tarley was the only one who remained stoic. There were only two people in that group who could easily gain access to the bridge without too many questions and she was certain that Penn had already made up his mind.

"Tarley, you're going to gain entry to the bridge and then knock out the guard, okay?"

No!

"Yes," muttered Tarley.

"Good, everyone else will have to move quickly as those cadets from the first gate are alert little fuckers," said Penn, causing a few chuckles in the room.

"Now we're going to get to the bridge for ten o'clock because that's when the Cloaks access the building at the end," Penn continued and Tarley found herself biting her lip to stop herself from shouting out.

I should be stopping this, she thought.

Civilians weren't meant to know anything about the Cloaks, let alone what time they accessed the bridge. It frightened Tarley just how much The Inquiry knew about the bridge's protocol and how long they had known it for. They were clearly taking their time in gathering their information before attacking the bridge, something that none of the guards or commanders would have expected. They all assumed that one day they would go into work and suddenly be faced with a hundred raging Inquiry members with no solid plan of attack.

"Once we're all in, we'll let off dormid gas to knock the guards out. Of course, the gas doesn't work on everyone so be prepared to fight."

"Can't the Sovrans knock out the remaining guards?" asked Tarley.

"Do you have any idea how much power that would take?" said a short man at the front.

Penn ignored their exchange and continued to talk, "As the dormid gas will obviously alert the commanders on the bridge, we'll need our best fighters to go up against them as we battle towards the end of the bridge. Lenna, Hart, Brecon, Ash and I will aim for the building while everyone else helps to hold off the commanders. Would anyone like to propose an alternative plan?"

When he asked the question to the group there was no condescending manner to his voice, he seemed genuinely interested in what everybody else had to say. Tarley wanted to say that it would never work, that the guards were too strong but those days were over. She knew how exhausted they all were and if the cadets were now working it was quite likely that they would flee at the first sign of trouble.

Besides, if Darvin really was losing his grip on the bridge then there was no way that he would be able to face a mass attack.

"How come it's you five going for the building?" asked Tarley. She wasn't certain but she thought that she could see Brecon smirking out of the corner of her eye.

"Because we're the most competent fighters and can take down most of the commanders before the rest of you get there. Obviously we're going to let everyone see what we discover. Is there a problem?" asked Penn.

"No," said Tarley quietly and feeling like a fool.

"Although I think that this plan is great, Penn," said Lenna, "I do think that Tarley should be on the bridge with us. She's the best swordswoman I've ever known."

"I agree," said Brecon.

"Me too," grumbled Ash.

Tarley had to stop herself from gaping at him but all he did was shrug in response. She didn't even want to think about when he might have seen her handling a sword and she even wondered if he was only recommending her because he thought she might fail.

Penn sighed, "Okay, Tarley, if you want to be on the bridge with us then you can."

"Yes," Tarley said, firmly. She thought it best not to elaborate for fear of embarrassing herself, again.

"Good," said Penn before explaining how they would get to Miraylia and meet at the bridge. "Before we all disperse I just want to reiterate that The Inquiry *does not* kill for the sake for it. But when you're on that bridge you must remember that you'll likely be in a situation where it's kill or be killed. Please be prepared for that."

111

CHAPTER ELEVEN

The day before The Inquiry was due to attack the bridge Tarley and Lenna had been tasked with travelling into the nearest town to secure more weapons for the group while Rhoswen and West went in search of food supplies. The four of them walked the two miles it took to the town in almost silence but Tarley appreciated the quiet. Although she had never seen the appeal of the countryside, the constant noise that came from the house meant that she had an almost permanent headache. Growing up with two older brothers she thought that she knew the definitions of loud and hectic very well but living in an average sized house with almost forty other people was making her look back on her childhood moans and laugh. Baodor and Macklyn were as quiet as a soft wind compared to The Inquiry.

Rhoswen flashed her another smile and Tarley happily returned it. Whenever she looked at Ash's mum she always appeared to be staring at Tarley with a welcoming face and none of the sourness that Ash projected on to her. Tarley would never say it out loud but being around Rhoswen only reminded her of her own mother and she felt an ache over her chest that she was not used to. Even through her years at the academy she had not pined for her family much and it had been an expectation that family visits would be rare. But the way she was now forced to sever ties with her family left her feeling more lost than she had anticipated.

West, however, seemed to be fixated on the grass beneath him and only gave short replies when Lenna tried to engage him in conversation. Tarley had been desperate to talk to him alone ever since the meeting the night before but he always seemed to be surrounded by people.

Once they reached the town Lenna and Tarley left Rhoswen and West to explore by themselves, agreeing to meet in the centre in two hours. There was a narrow high street lined with shops, all of which were made of different coloured bricks and in Tarley's mind were the epitome of quaint. They had to pass several clothes shops, bakeries and cafes before they found a three -story, red-bricked building that sold weapons.

The display in the window was centered on a large sword that Tarley was certain weighed more than her entire body. The golden hilt had a single jade stone laid into the metal and was surrounded by an intertwining thorn design. Despite its simplicity Tarley could tell by its shape and the way the metal shone that hundreds of hours' worth of work had gone into its creation. Surrounding the sword were various knives and throwing stars that all followed the same design but none of them had the same magnificence as the sword. Tarley didn't even look at the price; she preferred to imagine that one day she could afford to buy it and display it in her front room for all her guests to admire.

"You're like a magpie," said Lenna.

"What?" said Tarley, managing to look away from the sword.

"If you see something shiny you can't help but stop. I hope you don't get distracted on the bridge tomorrow."

Tarley shrugged her shoulders and walked past Lenna into the shop. She had been trying not to think about the upcoming attack, if she did get distracted she knew it would more than likely be because of her own conscience and not because of the beautiful swords. Every time she pictured herself running down the bridge, fighting to protect Penn and The Inquiry, all she could see was her locking swords with Macklyn. If Penn saw her faltering tomorrow she would never find the answers she was looking for and Darvin would have every right to exert the most brutal of punishments.

As much as she hated to admit it, Tarley quickly realised that Lenna's words were true. Once she had entered the shop she couldn't help but examine every knife and sword that was lined up before her.

Even in the country they know how to make a blade, she thought.

"Come on," said Lenna, walking up the stairs. "We have to think cheap."

Tarley reluctantly followed her cousin to the third floor where the cheaper priced swords, bows and other weapons were placed. They both immediately began to pick up knives and inspect their quality, even if they needed to think cheaply they didn't want weapons that were going to snap halfway through the attack.

"So what's going on between you and Brecon?" asked Lenna, twisting a small knife through her fingers.

"I told you, we used to live together. He graduated the year above me and I moved into the house he was in about eighteen months ago," replied Tarley.

Lenna spun around and pointed the tip of the knife towards Tarley's throat, playfully smirking. "And?"

Tarley laughed. "Okay, we had a one night…*thing* but then he disappeared so that was the end of that."

"What a dick," said Lenna, removing the knife from Tarley's throat.

"It's fine, he wasn't that good anyway," said Tarley with a wicked smile, causing Lenna to laugh. "But I get it now."

Lenna sighed and returned to inspecting the plethora of weapons that surrounded her. She wasn't an expert in bows and throwing stars, she had spent all of her life studying swords, but Ash had taught her how to look for nicks in the wood and how the string should feel as you pull it back so she felt confident enough in the task at hand. Penn knew her worth.

"And what about you and Ash?" asked Tarley.

"We've been together about a year," said Lenna before cheerfully adding; "he's really sweet when he's not being passive aggressive!"

"Well I look forward to seeing that rare break in his personality."

Lenna giggled quietly and turned to look at her cousin. They had always told their friends they were sisters when they were younger because Lenna was an only child and Tarley had said that she had two brothers; they didn't need her as well. Tarley could be Lenna's sister and they'd protect their kingdom together.

Without warning Lenna marched over to Tarley and wrapped her arms around her. Neither of them smelled particularly alluring but Lenna didn't care, it was something you just got used to being in The Inquiry.

"I did miss you," whispered Lenna. "And mum and dad, even if I've acted like I didn't."

"I know," said Tarley, "we all miss you, too." She pulled free from Lenna's arms for a moment. "I am sorry about what I said before you left. You're not a traitor or any of those awful words I used. I understand why you had to do this."

Lenna smiled, "If anyone would, I knew it would be you."

"Right, enough of this. We need to choose what we want."

They filled their bags with weapons and when they went to the sales assistant to pay, he simply lifted an eyebrow at them and counted their money. Tarley had been ready to say that they were buying them for their new training academy but Lenna had remained silent throughout so Tarley had done the same.

Rhoswen and West were already waiting for them once they had left the shop, their bags filled with food. As they walked back to the house Tarley wondered what kind of mood Penn was going to be in when they got there. Everyone in The Inquiry seemed to look upon him with amazement and from what she had seen so far Tarley had to admit that he seemed like a fair leader. However, he only ever greeted Tarley with a disdain and resentment that she couldn't help but feel went deeper than simply loathing her job. On the rare occasions that he did look her in the eyes all she could see was an intense anger that made her want to reach for her sword.

"So why does Penn hate the bridge so much?" asked Tarley, "I mean; I know everyone in The Inquiry does but…I don't know; I feel like it's more personal for him."
Lenna and Rhoswen exchanged an uncomfortable look as they trudged through the field.

"She should probably know," said Lenna, "everybody else does."

Rhoswen nodded, she didn't like talking about people behind their backs but she had felt a surprising need to protect Tarley from the moment she had first seen her. Despite her attempt to act strong she could see the confusion and unease of a scared young woman and knew that no one else in The Inquiry would try to make her feel welcome. After all, she had been there from the beginning and seen every power play and betrayal that humans were capable of making and none of them had had a happy ending. In the end, she thought, things would be a lot easier if they all just respected each other.

"Penn adored his wife," Rhoswen began, "I think it's important that you know that. He and Viv worked together in the police before The Inquiry was deemed criminal, which is where Penn's obsession with Sovrans began."

Rather than express her shock at Penn being in the police, Tarley remained quiet and allowed Rhoswen to continue. Now was not the time to be gasping like a gossip fueled teen.

"Investigations with Sovranic activity were hushed up pretty quickly and it didn't take Penn long to connect the dots. As you can imagine, he's not a big fan of being kept in the dark," said Rhoswen. "Anyway, they both joined The Inquiry and given their backgrounds they were a great asset to the cause. Viv was excellent at hiding and observing people, so a couple of years ago we all agreed that she would watch the bridge from afar to see who was coming and going. We just wanted to know how often the Cloaks were going there, really, and if we could see any of their faces."

"And did you?" asked Tarley, suddenly worried

"No," said Rhoswen, "in fact we didn't gain any useful information. The whole plan was futile. But one night Viv didn't come home and so the next morning we all went searching for her. My poor Ash found her lying in an alley, her clothes stained with blood. Someone had obviously mugged her; all her jewellery was taken and her knives. But Penn is *still* convinced that someone from the bridge had something to do with it."

Rhoswen looked at Tarley almost apologetically, as if it were her fault that Penn resented Tarley so much. After all, she had been the one to tell Tarley the truth.

"Maybe they did," said Tarley, forlornly. "We're trained to protect the bridge and stop its enemies from infiltrating it."

Her stomach tightened, Tarley had never thought that she would ever speak badly of the bridge, even if she was speaking plainly. She doubted that she could have killed someone for spying on the bridge but maybe one of the commanders got worried, they were always wound more tightly than the guards. It wasn't hard to imagine one of them finding Viv one night, following her home and, thinking that they were doing right by the bridge, push their sword into her chest.

The four of them spent the rest of the journey in complete silence, preferring to concentrate on carrying their heavy loads than think of something trivial to say. Once they got back to the house Rhoswen began handing out snacks and Penn inspected the weapons that Lenna and Tarley had bought, stating that they would be fine for their purposes. Tarley wondered if he would have called them phenomenal weapons had she not been there.

Penn dragged Lenna away to talk to her by herself but Tarley wasn't bothered in the slightest; she could see West disappearing into the throng of people in the house and she wanted to catch up with him before he was commandeered by an Inquiry member. She followed him up the stairs, shouting his name, but he continued to ignore her until she pushed in front of him and blocked him from walking any further down the corridor.

"Not here," he said and turned on his heel, leading Tarley through the house and out through the front door.

They kept walking through the fields until the house was barely visible and all they could hear were the nearby cows. Tarley could see that West was sweating all over and the arrogance she had come to associate with him had seemingly vanished.

"Why don't they know you're a Sovran?" asked Tarley.

"I could ask you the same question," said West.

"What? I think you're confused."

West smirked, "There's no point in playing dumb, Tarley. I might not be the strongest Sovran in the world but I can still sense when others have power within them."

Tarley shook her head, "No, you've got that wrong."

"Don't lie!" shouted West. "I understand. It's a disease and you're already the outsider. My guess is you don't want Penn to hate you even more when you can't perform glorious enchantments at will."

West was glaring at her now as if she had committed some terrible act against him. Tarley could see his chest rising and falling so fast that he looked as though he might be having a panic attack. She saw the pain in his face and suddenly realised that she had seen that same look before as he was fleeing the academy. She walked a little closer and was surprised when he didn't immediately back away.

"West, I promise you, I'm *not* a Sovran. I'm just a guard. Maybe your powers are off or something?"

"If you say so. I won't force you to admit it."

Tarley sighed; she could already sense that his attempts to project his own issues on to her were going to be exhausting. One of the many things that the bridge had taught her was not to continue with the same strategy when it clearly wasn't going to work.

"What happened that night at the academy?" Tarley asked and West's eyes instantly began to water but he quickly wiped away the incoming tears.

"It was an accident. Two of the cadets spotted me leaving and I panicked," said West. "Flames started coming out of my hands and I couldn't stop them, all I could think to do was run."

He averted his eyes away from Tarley so that he was staring into nothingness. Every night he heard their screams and their desperate shouts for him to come back and help them.

"Being a Sovran is a curse, Tarley. My parents were killed because my mother was a Sovran. No good ever truly comes of it."

He wiped his eyes one last time and began hurriedly walking back towards the house, leaving Tarley alone in the middle of the field with a growing sense of nausea in her stomach.

She spent the rest of the evening alone in the garden swiping a rusty sword through the air. Lenna called her in for dinner but she said she wasn't hungry; she still hadn't decided how she should act around West. Instead, she lunged and twisted the sword in her hands for hours in an attempt to clear her head. She had always found it strange how a sword, something that was used in battle to end a life, could have a wonderfully calming effect on her at times. Gripping the hilt, understanding its weight as she sliced it through the air made her mind focus and block out what was bothering her. She still ached to go home and turn her back on these people but she wanted to see her father again even more so, but would breaking into that building tomorrow solve anything? For years she, like everyone else in the world, had speculated over what it housed. A poisonous crystal, a dragon, a map, a sword, absolutely anything that would have the potential to cause harm but everything she had ever thought of she had been trained against to a high level. After all, what weapon could be there that she had not seen before? Tarley could feel her hands start to shake as she twisted the sword, for she knew the answer. Whatever it was that The Arben Bridge protected it would be the last thing that anyone could ever think of.

* * *

Penn had secured several trucks for them to travel to the edge of the city in the following night and Tarley had refrained from asking where he had got them from. She had a short sword in her scabbard and several knives hidden in her jacket as well as a set of throwing stars, even though she had never been very talented with them but Penn had insisted.

She was waiting outside the house with Hart, a man not much taller than her but so broad that he had a naturally imposing presence. He did not say much to Tarley; he merely introduced himself the night before and then left to do push-ups.

"So have you been a member long?" Tarley asked him.

Hart let out a low groan. "Five years," he said and Tarley had a feeling that the conversation had now come to an end.

Soon everyone was pouring out of the house and she spotted Lenna and Ash holding hands as they left, the former looking a little nervous. Ash gave her a soft kiss and Tarley looked away, turning her gaze to her shoes. It felt odd to see Ash being so affectionate, even if Lenna had said that he had the tendency.

Penn soon emerged and split everyone into their teams, ordering them to get into the same vans. Tarley followed him towards a blue one with no seats or windows in the back. She sat in the corner at the furthest end of the van so that she wasn't directly behind Penn in the driving seat, she could handle his digs and jibes but she still didn't want to encourage them. Ash and Lenna sat opposite her, their hands firmly intertwined. Lenna, seeming a little more relaxed, gave her cousin a smile and Tarley returned it, although her heart beat was starting to steadily increase. Brecon was the last to get in and the only space left was next to Tarley but he happily took it.

"Buckle up!" shouted Penn and a ripple of low laughter echoed back. The van lurched forward and soon Tarley could hear the swish of the air below them as they glided over the ground.

No one spoke for the first hour; Lenna rested her head on Ash's shoulder, Hart played with one of his knives and Tarley tried not to think about the possibility of fighting her brother or any of the people she had ever worked with.

"You okay?" Brecon whispered to Tarley.

"Yeah, fantastic," she snapped.

The rest of the journey was spent in silence and Tarley was certain that she'd fallen asleep for twenty minutes but no one had seemed to notice. The only time any of them spoke was when Penn passed around the antidote for the dormid gas, they would have to take it at least two hours in advance for it to be effective.

They got out of the van a mile outside of Miraylia where they met up with the other groups. The plan was to approach the city from different directions with strict instructions to keep to the side streets and alleyways. Tarley could hear the familiar sounds of the city and its distinctive smells as they advanced. The floral scent from the parks mixed with the dirty rubbish left on its side streets made for an odd combination but it had always comforted her; it meant that she was home and home meant safety.

Not tonight, she thought.

Penn gestured for them to gather in an alleyway in a quiet, southern part of the city that was half a mile from Victory Road.

"This is where we split. Stick to the plan and we'll rendezvous on Delyth Avenue," Penn instructed.

They all nodded before Lenna and Ash left the alley and joined the few people that were enjoying the evening. Brecon and Tarley waited five minutes before she grabbed his hand and dragged him into the street.

Brecon laughed, "You might want to look a little happier."

"What?" said Tarley.

"You look like you're going to drag me all the way to the bridge. We're meant to be a couple, not a prisoner and his handler."

"Maybe we've had a fight," said Tarley, slowing down her pace before kissing Brecon's cheek just to prove that she could play the loving girlfriend.

"Now, *that's* more like it," Brecon replied.

Tarley rolled her eyes as they both turned right without even consulting the other. Tarley was confident that she could guide anyone anywhere in the city but that was because she had grown up there, it was easy to forget that Brecon had not as they headed towards the bridge. They seemed to both be following the exact same route without any discussion.

"So are you ready for this?" asked Brecon as they neared Delyth Avenue.

"No, are you?"

Brecon shook his head. "Who knows what we're going to do to the city tonight."

Tarley didn't reply, whatever the outcome was she was sworn to protect Miraylia. If she was going to be part of something that changed the city forever, then it was her duty to keep it safe afterwards. She only hoped that Brecon still held a vague sense of responsibility towards his adopted home.

Tarley looked around her; those that dared venture out into the streets as the sun was setting all possessed looks of unease as if they were ready to explode at the slightest touch. She noticed a young man walking side by side with an older woman, giving her a subdued smile that Tarley was sure was meant to be reassuring but the sadness that tinged it was easy to spot.

"Oh shit," said Tarley under her breath, only just recognising Macklyn's short, golden brown hair.

She quickly turned to face Brecon and pushed him against the nearest building, pressing her body up against his and burying her face in the crook of his neck.

"Can you see my brother?" she whispered into his ear before kissing his neck. She had forgotten how rough his skin felt.

Brecon leaned down and wrapped his arms around Tarley's waist. "Yes," he whispered, "he's okay and so is your mum."

A homeless man walked past them and made exaggerated kissing noises but neither of them took any notice. Brecon pressed his lips against Tarley's, the motion feeling almost automatic, and pulled her closer.

"Ow!" shouted Tarley. "Your sword's digging into me." Brecon lifted his eyebrows at her. "No, literally your sword is digging into me. Your scabbard's shit. Have they gone?"

Brecon forgot where he was for a moment and found himself staring idly at Tarley until she gently hit the side of his arm. He scanned the street behind her to see only an elderly man walking along the cobbles.

"We're fine. Let's go."

Tarley linked her arm through his and they carried on walking down the road. It wasn't long before they reached Delyth Avenue and could see Penn and the others hiding in a side street. The bridge was merely a two-minute walk away and looked as beautiful as ever. The flames in the lamps had been lit, giving it both a foreboding and wondrous atmosphere that she adored.

"Everyone else is in position and the Cloak has just entered the bridge," said Penn as Tarley and Brecon approached. "Tarley, I want you to take this just in case."

He reached into his pocket and handed her a minor explosion crystal. She was already carrying a small arsenal of weapons and wondered just how prepared she really needed to be. Was she even going to make it through the night?

"Do you know how it works?" Penn asked and Tarley nodded. "Okay, good. Only use it if you need to but that guard looks like he'll only need one punch to the head."

Tarley's stomach tightened. The idea of hurting Ryder and actually doing it were two situations that had not yet collided in her head. She took a deep breath and walked out of Delyth Avenue and towards the bridge. The cadets and Junior Guards were lining the gate as always and when Tarley showed them her pass all their eyebrows seemed to collectively shoot up. She could see Ryder looking at her, trying to work out who she was but she kept her head low until she drew closer.

"Tarley?!" said Ryder, taking a step forward.

"Hi Ryder," said Tarley, stopping by the identity crystal.

"Are you okay? Where have you been?" asked Ryder.

"It's a bit of a long story," she replied, placing her hand on the crystal. It immediately began to change colour and the guilt started to converge on Tarley. The crystal never lied about who it was in contact with but it couldn't reveal their intentions. Part of her wished it could so that Ryder could stop her before she even had the chance to enter the bridge.

"We thought you had gone missing! Carida's been so ill!"

Tarley's leg started to shake. Why couldn't this just be over? Ryder was babbling about every single person in her family and how emaciated they all looked these days. Eventually the crystal turned clear and her name and age appeared before her. She didn't pause to read it and began hastily walking towards Ryder, who was quickly opening the gate. He turned towards her with his arms open and a grin on his face.

Tarley clenched her fist and silently cursed herself over and over again. Penn had been right; it only took one punch to knock Ryder out.

Tarley immediately grabbed Ryder's arms and dragged him further into the shadows. She could hear The Inquiry members already flooding on to the bridge and taking out the guards with the dormid gas. Those that weren't immune were knocked out in seconds.

"Nice work, Tarley," said Penn as he walked past her.

She didn't have time to reflect on the compliment she had just been paid as the adrenaline rushed through her body, making her feel like she would never stop shaking.

The rest of the group was soon by her side, followed by several loud bangs. Tarley looked towards the gates to see that a purple smoke was quickly travelling across the ground. Technically, it was an illegal substance and so Tarley had only ever seen it once, and that was when she was at the academy, but everyone in the world knew how it worked. If you didn't take enough of the antidote in advance you would become unconscious as soon as it came into contact with your skin. The main reason it was illegal was because there was also a thirty percent chance it could kill you without the antidote.

"Come on, we need to get to the gate before they send reinforcements," said Penn and immediately all six of them ran towards The Queen's Gate.

Tarley withdrew her sword from its scabbard, she could hear the sound of metal clashing as she ran but didn't want to turn around to see her fellow guards fighting against her new comrades. The smoke was growing thicker the longer it lurked around, which made it difficult to see. Tarley quickly lost sight of Lenna and the rest of her group as she raced down the bridge.

"Lenna! I can't see you!" yelled Tarley.

"Just keep running forward!" Lenna shouted back.

Before Tarley could answer she felt a hard hit to the

stomach before she fell backwards on to the ground. She was gasping for breath and at the same time choking on the smoke. She looked up through watery eyes to see a figure approaching her, a sword pointed at her throat. As Tarley looked up she could see Ainsley standing in front of her with curled lips and anger streaked across his eyes. He moved forward and Tarley scrambled backwards before sweeping her legs under his and sending him towards the ground. Tarley quickly got on to her feet and gripped her sword tightly as Ainsley followed suit; throwing all his weight behind the first throw of his sword. Tarley easily pushed him away but he was faster than she had anticipated, moving his sword with such eloquence and speed that it was impossible not to class him as a guard of the bridge.

"Argh!" screamed Ainsley as Tarley blocked another of his jabs, "come here you little bitch."

Tarley growled as she twisted her body and sliced her sword through the top of Ainsley's arm. He moaned as his free arm instinctively moved to cradle the wound allowing Tarley just enough time to kick him hard in the stomach and sprint further down the bridge.

When she reached The Queen's Gate all the guards were lying in front of it, two of them bleeding profusely while the other two had minor cuts. Tarley recognised all of them but wouldn't grant herself the indulgence of staying to help. Instead, she ran through the gate into the thick smoke and was immediately overwhelmed by pained cries and feral growls of people fighting for their lives. As she ran two more guards attacked her but she could barely make out their faces due to the smoke. The ease with which she defeated them, however, made her think that they must have been cadets.

"Tarley!" yelled Ash from further down the bridge.

Tarley ran towards his voice, unable to find his face among the fighting and the mist.

Several Inquiry members had now burst through the gates and were taking on the commanders. Even though the commanders were outnumbered they easily matched The Inquiry's skill and each fight was longer and more strenuous than any of them had anticipated.

Tarley kept running. The torches were always dimmer on the bridge and so it was difficult to see but she soon came across Ash who was being pushed to the edge of the bridge by a commander twice his size. The commander knocked the sword out of Ash's hand and grabbed his neck, shoving him against the side of the bridge. Ash scrambled to hold on to the wall as the commander pushed harder against him, almost snapping Ash's back in half as he bent over the wall.

Tarley reached into her jacket and pulled out one of the throwing stars. She threw it hard at the commander's arm but it only managed to nick his shoulder before falling to the ground. He turned around and his eyes flashed with recognition as he saw Tarley. Her sword was outstretched, waiting for him to approach and he happily swiped his towards her but she was too quick and jumped to the right, swinging her sword around her as she did so. The sound of the commander's blade hitting hers was lost amidst the sound of the battle but she felt the force of the hit travel down the metal and into her hands. He pushed her away and aimed the sword at her stomach but she dropped to the floor and rolled to the side before jumping back to her feet and finding herself smiling. She had loved sparring in the academy, the feeling of the adrenaline pumping through her body was unlike anything else she had ever experienced but *this* was different. This was exciting. One of them could die and fighting for her life seemed to give her a chilling thrill that she had not expected.

Suddenly, a blue light from the end of the bridge burst out across the sky and this time several guards and Inquiry members had to shield their eyes from it but Tarley felt fine, she only felt the warmth that the light emitted and took her opportunity to stamp down hard on the commander's foot. He instantly dropped his sword and Tarley swooped down to grab it as it fell but before she could do anything else the commander fell to his knees, choking. Blood started pouring out of his mouth and as he fell forward on to the ground Tarley could see Ash withdrawing his sword from the commander's back. She felt cold for a moment, her eyes flitting between Ash and the dead commander, his dark blue uniform now stained with blood.

"You okay?" said Ash.

Tarley nodded but could feel something crawling up her throat and ran to the side of the bridge to be sick. Ash was soon by her side, pulling her away. They couldn't run for too long before another set of guards and commanders were upon them. The whole fight had quickly turned into a free for all and everyone was storming the bridge no matter what their rank.

One of the commanders suddenly threw their body on to Tarley's; pushing them both on to the ground. Tarley used whatever energy she had to push her body on to the commander's and use her arms to pin down his chest. She could see that he was gasping for air but in that moment the only thought going through her mind was which knife she should use to pierce his heart. She went to grab a knife from inside of her jacket but before she could she had been pushed off the commander's body and found herself lying flat on the bridge. Without hesitation she jumped back on to her feet and raised her sword towards a furious Mabli.

"You can stop this, Tarley," said Mabli, blocking Tarley's first lunge. "No one else has to die."

Tarley had only ever seen Mabli sparring in a training room and even then she had tried her best to avoid her but it didn't come as a shock to her that they were so well matched. They were both quick and neither showed any signs of relenting as they twisted and jabbed the metal blades in their hands. Mabli nicked the side of Tarley's abdomen as she swung round but Tarley didn't falter, she only put more strength and effort behind each movement until Mabli managed to knock the sword out of Tarley's hand. Mabli dived for the sword and hurled it over the side of the bridge.

"I don't want to hurt you, Tarley," said Mabli, turning back towards her opponent. "Let's just go back-"

Mabli couldn't finish her sentence because Tarley had pushed her hard against the wall and slammed her sword arm so that Mabli's grip loosened, causing her to drop the sword. Mabli stamped on Tarley's foot and in the few seconds that Tarley's strength had weakened Mabli pushed her away so that they were standing opposite each other, seemingly weaponless. Tarley began to reach into her jacket for her throwing stars but found that she only had one remaining. The others must have fallen out as she was running.

"Don't do that," said Mabli. "Let's settle this the old way."

"Fine," said Tarley and the two women instantly broke out into a run towards each other.

Mabli got the first punch in; sending her fist straight into the side of Tarley's jaw but Tarley quickly retaliated by hitting Mabli in the stomach. With every punch, kick and throw they both grew more tired and more determined in equal measure. They had both given up on words; Mabli knew that Tarley was well past the stage of listening to what she had to say and so the only way to stop her harming Miraylia anymore was to take her out. Besides, Darvin wasn't around to tell her otherwise.

Tarley aimed to kick Mabli hard in the chest but her supporting leg wavered and instead her boot landed straight on Mabli's shoulder. The crunching sound that followed was audible even over the din of the attack and Tarley had never heard Mabli yell so loudly before. Tarley took her chance and ran as fast as she could straight down the bridge. She could hear Mabli screaming after her, begging her not to go into the building.

She had never been this side of the gates before and so she did not realise just how close she was to the end. She could see Lenna, Ash, Penn, Brecon and Hart slowly coming into view, standing over the body of the Cloak outside the building.

"What's going on?" asked Tarley, "why aren't you inside?"

"The stupid prick swallowed the key," said Ash, kicking the Cloak.

"I don't see why we can't just cut it out of him," said Hart but, to Tarley's surprise, everyone shot him a look of disgust. He simply shrugged in response.

Tarley looked down on the man; she had never seen a Cloak's face before. He had a receding hair line and crow's feet like any other middle-aged man; there was nothing scary or imposing about him in the slightest.

"Shit!" said Tarley, "I know him! He was at the pub a few weeks ago…he wanted to give me money for a taxi."

"That's a great help, Tarley. Thank you very much," said Penn.

Tarley stood up and looked at the building, they weren't even given permission to see pictures of it in the academy; you had to at least be a Junior Commander before you were given that privilege. It was only a small circular building made of thick rocks that had been chiseled so much that they were perfectly even. The roof was flat stone and there were no windows at all, if it wasn't for the door at the front it would simply look like a large podium.

The door was wide and made of dark, thick wood, Tarley could tell by the depth of the carvings. The design was exactly the same as The Queen's Gate but without the jewels that Tarley so admired.

"I think someone's coming," said Brecon. "It looks like Darvin!"

Lenna threw Tarley a spare sword and joined the rest of the group in forming a line in front of the Cloak with their swords pointed outwards. There was an eerie quiet on the bridge now that had not seemed possible forty-five minutes ago when the screams and cries were so deafening. However, Tarley remained still as she stared at the Cloak's face.

"Tarley, we need you here," said Penn but Tarley shook

her head.

"What good is it going to do?!" she screamed, "we've caused all of this hurt for nothing! We can't get into this stupid fucking building and I am *not* helping you kill Darvin just for the sake of it!"

She kicked the door in frustration but it only caused pain to her foot.

"All of this!" she screamed, hitting the door with her sword. "Leaving my family, risking my life, it's been for nothing!" She was hacking away at the door, making small cuts into the wood and disfiguring the Queen's face. The anger was becoming its own entity, taking over her body and acting out as it saw fit.

"Tarley!" yelled Lenna and marched over to her cousin, trying to wrestle the sword from her.

"Get off me!" screamed Tarley, her voice felt raw and strained. She pushed Lenna so hard that she fell to the ground on her side, hitting her arm on the concrete. "This is your fault," spat Tarley, pointing her sword at Lenna, "making me think I could solve this. And I'm still trapped!"

"Trapped?" said Lenna.

"Yes, trapped! And you're going to pay for betraying me!" Tarley kicked Lenna's sword aside and raised her sword over Lenna, who looked up at Tarley like a terrified animal waiting to be slaughtered.

A blue light burst from the building; rays seeping out through the tiniest of gaps in the stones and the side of the door. Everyone's eyes shifted from Lenna to the building as the door began to creak open of its own accord. Tarley absentmindedly dropped the sword and gravitated towards the building, transfixed by its light.

"Tarley!" yelled a voice from behind her. She turned around to see Darvin being held back by Hart and Brecon. "Please don't go in there. Please." There was a pleading in his eyes but Tarley chose to ignore it, she was the one in control now.

Mabli and Macklyn appeared with a group of exhausted

looking guards but Darvin told them not to go forward. Mabli was staring at Tarley with pure venom while Macklyn was a mixture of disgust and longing. Tarley could read her brother's eyes like no one else could.

"Please, Tarley," repeated Darvin. "I'll explain everything. Once you go in there you won't be able to undo what might happen."

Tarley turned around and stepped inside the building, its coolness coming as a shock to her skin. The light instantly faded and condensed itself into an oval shape that hung in the air. And at the centre of the light was a body, suspended in the middle of the room, with skin so pale that it looked like a corpse. It was the body of a woman who wore a simple cream night gown that had not been in fashion for centuries. She had dark red hair that fell to her shoulders and when Tarley looked at her face the only reaction she had was to scream.

She screamed a distressing, unearthly scream because she recognised the woman's face all too well. It was the face that Tarley saw every day when she looked in the mirror and the face that the rest of the world saw when they looked at her.

CHAPTER TWELVE

Tarley didn't move, even when Lenna and the others came rushing in, each of them trying to pile into the small, circular building.

"Oh my…," said Lenna once she saw the woman and turned to look at Tarley. "Do you know who this is?"

Tarley shook her head and moved closer to what looked like her twin. The woman's face wasn't the scariest part of the picture for Tarley; it was the complete lack of life that she held. Her chest did not rise and fall like it should have and her skin was an unnatural colour, there seemed to be no pigmentation to it resulting in a grey, almost transparent skin tone.

This is what I would look like if I was dead, thought Tarley.

"Don't touch her," said Darvin, pushing past the small crowd to stand next to Tarley. "We don't know what will happen."

"Is she dead?" asked Tarley, her voice soft. All the anger that had overtaken her like a virus had now vanished and she was left feeling simply hollow.

"No," said Darvin. "It's complicated to explain but if you come with me to the tower, I will try my best." He placed his arm on Tarley's but she shook him away.

"No, explain it now. I won't be tricked and locked away without any answers."

Darvin sighed, it had been a torturous night and he knew Tarley well enough to know that it was best to relent now before things turned even uglier. He ordered Mabli and the guards to wait outside and prevent anyone from coming in but allowed everyone else to stay, he was certain that this was the beginning of the end, anyway.

"That woman is called Nyra," began Darvin, "and she is four hundred and fifty years old. When she was truly alive and not a captive like she is now, she was the most powerful person the city had ever seen. She was born to an ordinary enough couple who were carpenters by trade and was named Atella Carden but she was no ordinary baby. She was born a Sovran and, as I'm sure you all know, they were a lot more common in those days but still rare enough that people revered those that possessed supernatural abilities. When she was just one-year-old she was able to manipulate water, making it triple in size or take the form of anything she wanted. Her parents thought it was incredible and as she grew older encouraged her to train with the local Mystic."

"What's a Mystic?" asked Macklyn.

"Someone who trains Sovrans," said Penn.

Darvin nodded before continuing, "She did well under his guidance and it soon became clear that she was more powerful than any other Sovran the Mystic had encountered. He worried that he would no longer be able to help her contain her powers, and he was right, but when he told Nyra's parents they told him he was jealous and stopped the lessons, which meant that Nyra could do whatever she wanted. She would often perform for the city, showing off her skills, and soon gathered a very loyal following. She was convinced that Miraylia would thrive under her rule and as nobody was as powerful as her she took the city for herself.

Her younger sister, Delyth, had been born without powers and had tried to reason with Nyra but she refused to listen.

She wanted Delyth to reign by her side but, instead, Delyth turned her back on her sister and went into hiding, but not before she renamed Atella 'Nyra'; an old word for evil woman.

During her reign Nyra forced the people of the city to pledge their allegiance to her and if they didn't they would be publicly tortured and executed. She could create terrifying monsters that you would only think possible in your nightmares. Many fled the city but she was slowly starting to take over the south of Liliath. Hundreds tried to kill her but no one succeeded; her powers were so strong that she may as well have been immortal.

While she was in hiding Delyth married a very talented Mystic who came up with a power source that could suppress Nyra's powers, the idea being that once she was in a state of limbo they could work out a way to finally kill her. The plan worked and they hid her in here, building the bridge and its fortress around her.

Together they founded Nyra's Patrol, which everyone now refers to as the Cloaks. Originally they were the most powerful Sovrans that Delyth and her husband could find so that they could perform experiments on Nyra to see if there was a way to kill her. But as there has been a decline in Sovrans over the centuries our progress has stagnated, which is why Nyra is still not dead."

"If this is true why doesn't every person in the city know about this? Surely it's our right to know who our greatest enemy is?" asked Brecon.

"Once Nyra was captured it was agreed that only the Patrol would know the full details and it was decreed that no one would ever be allowed to discuss or record what had happened under Nyra's rule. Do you have any idea the kind of cults and followings that would occur if the city knew about Nyra? In the early days there were several attempts to break her free; no one wanted to risk that continuing."

"It can't be true," said Macklyn, looking from Tarley to Nyra. "It's just a story."

Darvin shook his head, "I wish it were but I promise you I'm not lying. Think about it, Macklyn, the whole city is an ode to her defeat. *The Songs of Night*, the gates on the bridge, even our street names! The people of the city didn't, couldn't, speak about what she had done so they built her story into Miraylia."

Tarley looked at Nyra again and still saw her own face frozen like a picture. This woman did not look evil, she looked eerie but there was a peacefulness to her that did not suggest she once had the power that Darvin spoke of.

"Are Macklyn and I her descendants?" asked Tarley.

"Not quite," said Darvin, shifting uncomfortably. "I think perhaps now is the time that you and I talk alone, Tarley."

Macklyn looked at his sister, worry etched across his face, before moving away from Darvin and standing by Tarley's side. He held her hand and for the first time all evening Tarley was momentarily relieved of her anxieties.

"Whatever it is, you say it now," said Macklyn.

"If that's what you want." Darvin paused for Tarley to give a small nod before continuing. "Five years after Nyra was captured Delyth came across a little girl who was about three years old and looked exactly how Nyra had at that age. However, she was no relation to Delyth whatsoever. She and the Patrol kept track of the girl her whole life, she seemed completely normal until the day she was found dead, aged thirty. She was lying in what used to be a very deep river, except that it was bone dry and her clothes were soaked through. She had obviously drowned, unable to control her powers. Two years later, one of the Patrol heard of a toddler who could produce fire from their hands. Again, the Patrol monitored her and she grew up to look just like Nyra but only managed to produce flames once more when she was an adult."

Macklyn could feel Tarley's hand shaking within his and squeezed tight, despite feeling just as edgy as she did.

"Ever since these children were discovered the Patrol has monitored every female birth in Miraylia and kept track of them until they find one who has special powers or looks like Nyra," Darvin continued. "So far no one has been deemed powerful enough for us to bring them in and thus expose who they are, it's clear that Nyra has the power to be reborn as another life form even while she's in this suspended state. But we thought it would be another hundred years or so before she regained her full powers. However, we are confident that she's behind the disappearances of the guards, the people who keep her trapped from her city, and such a task requires *a lot* of power."

"Wh…what does this mean for me?" asked Tarley, although she was pretty certain of the answer before it left Darvin's lips.

"*You* are the one who can help Nyra return; she has been exerting her power through you for months. You are behind the disappearances, whether you've known it or not."

Tarley felt the same way she had when Ainsley had kicked her in the stomach. All the air had been sucked out of her body and she wanted to curl up on the floor, crying out in pain.

Her father. Her loving and beautiful father was nowhere to be seen because of her and she had no idea where he was or even how to get him back. There was pure evil built into her bones and she had never known it.

"We can't let her come back. We have to kill her!" shouted Hart and withdrew his sword but Darvin was surprisingly swift and pushed Tarley to the floor before blocking Hart from moving any further forward.

Hart's blade was pointed at Darvin's throat but he didn't flinch. "You can't kill her," said Darvin, "we don't know what it will do to Nyra."

Hart grunted and placed his sword in his scabbard, backing away from Tarley and Darvin. He looked towards Penn for some sort of reassurance but was only greeted with a blank face.

Tarley began to sob and hated herself for it, crying in front of so many people made her feel foolish. Lenna helped her to her feet as she wiped her eyes; there was so much fury in her veins right now. She couldn't even say that if they had left the bridge alone that they would be safe, Nyra was still on her path to awaken and cause destruction. She had been helpless from the day she was born, just a vessel to carry another person's soul.

The light that surrounded Nyra blazed out and enveloped the room in blue, making everyone jump and reach for their weapons.

"Tarley!" shouted Darvin, "I need you to try and calm down, every time you get angry or upset it makes you vulnerable to Nyra's powers."

"Calm down?!" shouted Tarley, the light intensifying around her. "I can't fucking calm down!"

"Then I need you to come outside. Please, you took an oath to protect this city, remember. You owe it to them to walk out of this room and keep her locked away."

Tarley obeyed and walked out into the cool night, grateful for the cold breeze that grazed her skin. She could feel the light dimming behind her as everyone left and Darvin locked the door.

Mabli and the guards looked to Darvin for orders.

"I'm afraid that I'm going to have to detain you, Tarley," said Darvin. "None of us know how this news is going to affect you. Mabli, I've got a truck waiting by the gate."

Mabli nodded and proceeded to clamp Tarley's hands into shackles. Tarley was still reeling from the news and so didn't even try to resist what Mabli was doing.

"You can't do this! She's not going to hurt anyone!" shouted Macklyn.

"I'm afraid we don't know that, Macklyn," said Darvin.

Tarley could only hear fragments of the conversation as Mabli marched her down the bridge. Uninjured guards were seeing to those that were hurt or, worse, lying dead on the ground and were so caught up in their work that they barely glanced at Tarley.

"You knew, didn't you?" said Tarley, "you've been monitoring me the whole time we've known each other."

"Yep; being paid was the only way I could put up with your sulking."

CHAPTER THIRTEEN

Tarley laid on the bed and stared at the ceiling. She was positive that she had been staring at it for hours but without a clock she couldn't be sure. Her sense of time had all but disappeared; she knew it was day time when light seeped through the barred windows and she knew it was night when the guards lit the lamps outside her cell.

The only thing she did know was that two nights had passed since she'd been taken to her prison and no one had been to visit her. The only people she had seen were the burly guards, armed with every weapon she could think of, and not one of them had uttered a single word to her.

She was also positive that she was the only inmate in the entire prison. All day and all night the only thing she heard were the guards walking around.

Her cell contained one single, uncomfortable bed, a toilet and a sink. The bars that trapped her in the room were made of nerth, the strongest crystal in the world, and would take hours of sawing just to make a single dent.

Tarley, inevitably, had had a lot of time to think about what had occurred on the bridge two days previously but she still felt like she had been watching somebody else's world fall apart and not her own. How could she have lived so many lives and not remember any of them? All those women who were meant to be Nyra reborn had powers that they couldn't control, they had families and jobs and Tarley didn't feel a connection to one of them. There was no extraordinary power in her family; she believed it had existed once, but no one in her world was special enough to possess it. She sometimes heard of a child on the other side of the world who could perform unthinkable acts of wonder but after the media frenzy died down she often forgot about them. Baodor had once said that those who expose their powers are nearly always killed, whether it's jealousy, fear or because a cult thinks that they can harvest that person's power.

She thought of her mother after Gwyl went missing and the paleness of her face when she suggested that a Sovran could be behind the attacks. Ivy had managed to calm Carida but Tarley doubted the idea had ever gone away, she just wondered how Carida would feel when she realised that her own daughter apparently possessed such a power. And had caused the same heartache to hundreds of people.

The ceiling remained unchanged, despite Tarley's constant surveillance.

She pondered over what plan Darvin had for her. Mabli had shoved her in the truck, driven her to the other side of the city and left her in the cell with only the hint of a vengeful glare as a form of conversation. Tarley guessed that they couldn't kill her, not yet, anyway, not until they knew for definite what would happen to Nyra. Maybe they would experiment on her first, torturing her with illegal crystals and tonics until she had nothing left to show them.

Tarley closed her eyes and turned on to her side, clutching at the sheets. If she was so powerful surely she could break out of the cell? She didn't dare to try, perhaps it was best for everyone if she stayed locked up. She didn't want to explore who she was meant to be, who was really hidden underneath the persona she had been presenting to the world. When she was on the verge of killing Lenna she could feel another soul taking over hers, shattering its being and quickly replacing it with a love of evil. She had *wanted* to hurt Lenna and remembered truly believing that Lenna was the one standing in her way from claiming what was hers but she didn't know why.

No, Tarley did not want to be that person.

She heard two sets of footsteps growing louder and sat up. She had become accustomed to the sound of the guards now and instantly recognised the loud thuds with which they walked but the other tread was undoubtedly softer. Neb Figmore soon appeared on the other side of the bars, accompanied by a guard who unlocked the door for him. Neb walked in and the guard quickly locked the door again.

"Hello, Tarley," said Neb, lingering by the door with a smirk. He wore a dark suit under a bulky black coat and removed the hat which had been worn so low that Tarley could only just decipher his features.

"Delegate Figmore," said Tarley.

"I have to be honest, I thought there would have been *something* different about you but you look exactly the same."

He walked towards Tarley, looking her up and down, before stopping just inches away from the bed.

"Are you disappointed?" asked Tarley.

Neb smirked again. "Perhaps."

"What are you going to do with me?"

"We're not sure, yet. Thankfully, the public still knows nothing about you, they just know that The Inquiry attacked the bridge and killed fifteen innocent guards."

Tarley gripped the bed sheet, she had been speculating for days how many had died. The image of Ash killing a commander seemed to be on a loop every time she closed her eyes.

"Are my family okay?"

"I'm sure they're fine, after all, who wouldn't want an evil Sovran in the family? I imagine that they're very proud." He took another step forward and bent down so that he could look into Tarley's eyes. "Can you do a trick for me? Just a little one, I won't tell."

"Fuck off."

Neb roared with laughter and clapped his hands together. "You are a feisty one! Come on, just one little enchantment, I don't believe that you've been hiding your powers all these years."

If I had a weapon you would see just how powerful I am, thought Tarley.

She wanted to launch herself towards him and beat the smug look off his face but instead she chose to avert her eyes to the barred window in the corner of the room. She could only see the colour of the sky but it was a far nicer and calmer view than Neb Figmore's face.

Tarley could hear footsteps again and as she turned her head back around she could see Henya Quinn standing on the other side of the nerth bars with one of the more imposing guards.

"Hello, Neb," said Henya as the guard opened the gate. "I didn't realise you were scheduled for a visit."

The smirk on Neb's face soon vanished and was replaced by a clear annoyance that seemed a little too comical to Tarley. She swore she could see his hand tighten around the rim of the hat he was holding.

"I hope you don't mind but I'd rather like to speak to Haf Hillis alone," Henya continued.

"Of course, Premier," said Neb and gave Tarley one last look of disdain as he stepped through the gate.

Henya gestured for the guard to follow Neb out of the building before sitting down on the bed next to Tarley, who was instantly shocked by the change in Henya's appearance. Tarley never thought of the Premier as being a glamorous woman but she always looked presentable and was never seen in public in anything other than perfectly ironed clothes and a neat hairstyle. And although there were still traces of that same woman sitting before Tarley there was a redness around her eyes and her face was hollow. The smile she was giving Tarley looked as though it required so much effort that it could never be a symbol of empathy or support.

"I don't have long," said Henya, "I've disabled the listening crystals but they'll be back on, soon. I want you to know that I'm on your side, Tarley."

"Then why am I locked up in here?" said Tarley.

"Because things are changing and no one can predict what will happen next," Henya replied, placing her hand on Tarley's. "I have a whole country to think about and I fear that they won't understand how important you will be to them. I know how powerful you could be, Tarley. Don't be scared of it and trust Darvin and Yvette implicitly, they're true warriors."

"Who's Yvette?"

Henya stood up and pulled her hood over her head, "You'll find out soon enough, I promise I'm not being cryptic just to infuriate you."

Tarley surprised herself as she chuckled in response.

"I'm sorry I can't stay any longer," said Henya. "I just want you to know that whatever is done and said in public is all in aid of you."

Before Tarley could question Henya further she had summoned a guard and was leaving the cell as quickly as she had entered it.

Tarley looked out of the window one last time before curling up into a ball on the bed and silently crying into the decrepit, dusty pillow.

As the days went by she was granted two hours outside in a concrete courtyard to exercise but wasn't allowed to do anything that might be seen as combat training. She didn't mind, though, she was just glad to breathe fresh air into her lungs and see the vastness of the sky. She longed to look at the city and its jagged sky line but the whole prison was surrounded by a twenty-foot-high wall.

In the academy the cadets had had a module in their

second year about surviving in unknown places, including prison cells, but the psychological tricks that they had learnt were of no use to Tarley. Not one lecture had mentioned how to cope in a prison by yourself when you might be the key to helping an evil sorceress conquer the world.

On her sixth night a guard arrived as usual with her dinner but told her that she was to eat quickly because she was being moved, a truck was outside and ready to go.

Tarley asked why she had to leave but the guard just snarled at her and told her to shut up and eat her dinner.

Tarley quickly ate the tasteless mush that had been handed to her before tapping the guard on the shoulder to let him know she'd finished. With an annoyed look on his face he walked into the cell where he pulled Tarley's hands behind her back and placed them in shackles. He marched her down several narrow corridors with dim flames before they reached a padlocked door, the guard unlocked it and pushed Tarley outside where she could see the truck waiting for her. The guard opened the back doors and carelessly threw her in. The doors shut and Tarley was left in complete darkness. There were no windows and no way of seeing who was driving, which made Tarley feel more scared than when she had been in the cell.

The van began to move at speed but she couldn't guess in which direction they were going. She knew that they were on the Eastern side of Miraylia but she couldn't work out if they were travelling into or away from the city.

"She's in there!" someone shouted from outside, "stop that van!"

The van lurched to the side, causing Tarley to fall hard on to her side. Pain shot up and down her arm, making her wince and as she tried to sit back up the van began to shake more violently.

She could hear shouts and screams from outside; people demanding that she be released, that she was brought to justice. She even heard somebody scream that they would cut Tarley's throat themselves. She could feel the van come to a stop but the banging and yelling continued.

"Kill the bitch."

"She'll burn down the city."

"We should find and kill all the Sovrans."

"Lock her up and throw away the key."

"She should have been drowned at birth."

The truck eventually began to move again but the vitriolic words did not subside as it moved along its path. There was less noise as the journey went on but the calls for Tarley's execution remained.

Although Tarley had stayed silent the entire time her face was wet with tears and her skin felt clammy. She remembered what Darvin had said about what happened when she got angry or upset but she couldn't stop it, never in her life had so many people said so many horrid things about her. They spoke about her the way people spoke about mass murderers or terrorists; full of hate and poison that seemed to not only be accepted but expected in those kinds of conversations.

Tarley couldn't help but ponder what it was they knew. Had Nyra escaped at last? Or had someone simply leaked the information to the press? Either way, the public knew that Tarley had the potential to hurt them and, as much as she now resented and feared them, she couldn't really blame them. Her face had probably been on every news channel a hundred times by now, almost sanctioning whatever treatment their viewers wanted to inflict upon her.

Her family.

Fucking hell! Tarley thought and whacked the side of the van in frustration.

All Tarley could see were explosion crystals bursting through her mother's window or Baodor's house alight with flames or Macklyn being attacked as he walked down the street. And their only crime would have been being related to Tarley.

The sounds of jeering rose again as the truck began to slow down. The doors burst open and Tarley was pulled out of the darkness by one of the guards. She climbed down into a courtyard and looked up to see a tall rectangular building made of dark brick. She was, once again, surrounded by a high wall but she could clearly see the barred metal gate that they had driven through and behind it stood a crowd of people, yelling at her to do terrible things to herself.

She could see several image-caption crystals and reporters standing in front of them, their arms moving around, wildly. How had this happened? When did she become one of *those* people? The people whose stories you hear about, talk about and dissect but forget about ten minutes later.

"Keep walking," the guard spat and pushed Tarley forwards into the building.

The temperature dropped considerably as soon as they entered the building and as Tarley was led down several flights of stairs she could feel herself start to shiver but the guard took no notice.

They eventually came to a door made of nerth that had several locks down its right hand side and took the guard at least five minutes to unlock them all. The door opened to a dimly lit corridor and at the bottom was a large cell similar to the one that Tarley had left just hours ago. She was promptly pushed into it before another three guards walked down the corridor and stood at measured intervals along it. Not one of them said a single word.

Tarley was still shivering as she got into the bed and the itchy, fake woolen blanket did nothing to help. She spent the entire night drifting in and out of sleep, thinking about her family, The Inquiry and even Darvin. By the time she was being shouted at to eat her breakfast there were dark circles under her eyes and she was on the verge of asking if she could be handed over to the angry mob outside.

* * *

Three days later and the number of death threats had

subsided somewhat; Tarley had assumed that only those who would be happy enough to execute her themselves were still stood outside the prison. She wondered how many had fled the city in terror over the past few days.

She curled up on the side of her bed, closed her eyes and tried to imagine Miraylia without a single soul to inhabit it. Just the image made her feel uneasy. Miraylia was infamous worldwide for its busy and chaotic lifestyle, only people who thrived in the pandemonium could live there and be happy. And Tarley had been so happy there. Where would everyone go? Tarley was a city girl through and through, like so many who called Miraylia their home, and the idea of staying in the country for more than a week seemed absurd to her. It had been different with The Inquiry, she knew she was there to serve a greater purpose, but trying to set up a life there just seemed surreal.

There would be no point in fleeing, though, Tarley thought. If Nyra would one day be as powerful as she was then nowhere would be safe. In fact, Tarley was fairly certain that the countryside would be easier to take hold of than the city. There were less people, less of a military presence and less monuments that the government would want to protect.

How cynical you are, she thought.

"Is she asleep?" a male guard whispered and Tarley could hear another one shifting slightly as they checked on her.

The guards never spoke in front of her, only to tell her to eat her food or to stop looking so miserable, so she remained still in the hope that they would continue their conversation.

"Looks like it," said a female guard.

"I've been thinking about it," said the male guard, "and I think we should make a run for it. Being around her freaks me out."

"We can't do that!" hissed the female guard.

"Why not? You've seen what the news is saying about her, she's the biggest terrorist threat to the city that we've ever had!"

"Yeah, the way she eats her food and does nothing for days on end is really something that we should worry about."

Tarley couldn't help but smirk at the guard's sarcasm.

"Well, she's not going to do anything yet, is she? She's just biding her time, waiting for the right moment to strike."

"That's enough!" said another guard. "You know the rules. No talking in front of the prisoner."

The guard mumbled something under his breath but Tarley couldn't hear. Part of her wanted to jump out of the bed and pretend to cast an enchantment on the guard in a bid to unnerve him just to see if he would run away like a scared child. The thought almost made Tarley laugh and she had to push her head into the hard pillow so that the guards couldn't see her face. She wondered if she would ever be given permission to laugh again or if this would be her life from now on. She would just be moved from prison to prison until Darvin and his group could figure out a way to kill her and Nyra. Perhaps they would experiment on her; no one from the public would object. She wasn't even sure if her mother would have an issue with it, how could she possibly love Tarley now that she knew who she really was? She had never really been her daughter, just a dummy lying dormant until it was brought to life and utilised.

Tarley thought about the daughter that her parents should have had; the perfect mix of both of them in every way. She would have light hair and blue eyes and be as daring as her father whilst retaining her mother's elegance. She wouldn't be snappy like Tarley or as keen to throw herself into a fight. Instead, she would fit in perfectly as the third child that completed the Hillis family. Tarley felt sick at the thought; she had robbed her parents of their rightful daughter and an innocent girl of the life she deserved. She was nothing more than a cuckoo, feeding on a life that was never really her own and remaining completely unaware.

As she was in the depths of sleep Tarley dreamt of her

mother; she was being handed a small bundle of blankets from Gwyl. An overwhelming sense of exasperation haunted the scene, seemingly tinting it with grey and dark blue tones.

Gwyl sighed as he handed the blankets over to the smiling Carida. Tarley's mother looked down to see a dark haired baby with strikingly chocolate coloured eyes staring back up at her.

"Oh. She'll do, I suppose," said Carida.

Gwyl put his arms around his wife and kissed the top of her head. "We can make her a Hillis somehow," he said.

"Wake up!" a voice suddenly hissed into Tarley's ear. "Come on, Tarley, wake up!"

Tarley slowly opened her eyes, unsure of how long she had been asleep for. She looked up to see Lenna and Darvin standing over her and the door to her cell was wide open.

"Lenna!" shouted Tarley once her mind had fully awoken. "I thought I'd never see you again!" Tarley got out of the bed and wrapped her arms tightly around Lenna, who responded in the same way. "What time is it? Isn't it late to be visiting?"

"We're not visiting," said Lenna, pulling away and thrusting a short sword into Tarley's right hand. "We're breaking you out."

"What?!" said Tarley, her head snapping around to look at Darvin.

"It's true and we don't have much time so get moving!" said Darvin, marching out of the door.

Lenna threw a jacket at Tarley and instructed her to put it on and keep the hood up before walking off in the same direction as Darvin.

Tarley almost gasped when she saw the guards lying on the floor, motionless. They all looked dead but when she looked closer she could see that their chests were still rising, Lenna must have used the dormid gas. Tarley didn't even want to think about why it had not affected her in the slightest.

"I'm guessing this isn't a government sanctioned escape, then," said Tarley as she followed Darvin around various corners and past more sleeping guards. She didn't realise just how many people had been keeping watch over her.

"Actually it is. Except that Henya can't lose face with the public on the eve of a war so strictly speaking she doesn't know anything," said Darvin.

Tarley's eyebrows shot up as she exchanged a shocked look with Lenna.

"I know, kind of makes me feel bad that I never voted for her," said Lenna.

"So who's arranged this?" asked Tarley, stepping over a small guard, "Nyra's Patrol?"

"Sort of," said Darvin. "I'll explain everything later."

They reached a door with several locks on it and Darvin reached into his pocket to produce a small lime-green coloured crystal that Tarley had never even seen a picture of before. He ran it down the locks and they instantly melted, causing the door to open slightly. Darvin kicked it open and the three of them walked out into the cool air and across the courtyard behind the prison.

In the wall was an opening just large enough for the three of them to bend through and had obviously been created by Darvin's crystal. Tarley wondered why it wasn't burning through his pocket.

They ran down to the end of the street and turned right where a small grey car was parked. Darvin got in the driver's seat, Lenna sat next to him and Tarley got in the back.

"I suggest you keep your head down," said Darvin before exiting the curb.

Tarley slunk down in her seat but as they passed the prison she could hear the shouts and screams as relentlessly as ever. She sat up ever so slightly to try and catch a glimpse and saw at least fifty people outside the gate, some with banners and all of them with weapons.

"Don't look at them, Tarley," said Lenna, softly. "They're idiots."

Tarley didn't reply as she pulled her hood lower and sunk back below the window.

* * *

Nyra could sense them watching her, more so now than ever before. They were closer, as if they could make her feel more trapped than she was but they were wrong. Everything they had done was wrong and it was only luck that had kept her sedated for so long.

They had no idea just how powerful she was or how powerful she could become. They had stopped her just before her peak and it was only right that she would be allowed to flourish once more and become their Queen. Liliath had never had a queen but they would. A queen to fear and admire in equal measure.

For centuries she could only sense the world around her and barely feel the air kissing her skin but recently she had become more aware. Her body knew the prison it was trapped in, she could, somehow, see the cracks in the bricks and she always knew when one of her sister's cohorts came to experiment on her. She longed to rip them apart and send their souls into the ether but she had been weak and knowing it was almost worse than feeling it. She had never been weak and she would never resign herself to that fate again. She could feel the energy coming back to her and she would protect it with all the power she commanded.

Her heart. She could feel her heartbeat! The sound of it against her chest was getting louder and its pace was quickening. What a lovely sound it was; what a *powerful* sound it was.

Her eyes shot open and she could see a single man looking up at her, his sword raised and terror in his eyes. Upon closer inspection she noted that he was not a man at all but a boy, someone far too young to be given such a hard job.

She lowered her arms and as she did so her whole body descended until her feet landed softly on the floor below.

Her body felt heavier than she remembered but she supposed that it would take time for her powers to fully take hold of her once more.

"Get back!" the boy shouted but his hand was shaking. "I mean it! Do not come any closer or I'll kill you." His free hand was on the door handle behind him.

Nyra smiled. Oh, it felt good to smile again, she thought. There were so many meanings behind just one smile and she had almost forgotten how unnerving that could be to such idiotic creatures.

"My dear boy, no one has managed to kill me for over four-hundred and fifty years. What makes you think that you'll be any different?"

Before he could answer he rose into the air and was flung across the room until he hit one of its walls. He slid down it slowly, blood instantly beginning to trickle from his head.

Nyra looked at the door before her and it flew open, revealing the bridge and the night sky that she had waited so long to see. She walked out on to the bridge and saw her city in front of her; she had sensed its changes over the years but even with new buildings and a new skyline she still thought it was beautiful. Her Miraylia was still there, waiting for her to take it back.

When she turned her attention back to the bridge she found herself surrounded by twenty or so guards, each of them pointing a sword at her and readying themselves to attack. She looked at all their terrified faces and smiled once more. Yes, it felt very good to smile again.

CHAPTER FOURTEEN

Tarley stepped out of the car to find herself in the countryside once again. They had driven an hour out of the city and even though it was still visible in the distance all Tarley could see in her immediate vicinity was hills and fields.

She had seen plenty of pictures of Forstelle so the vast greenness of it didn't come as a shock but, even so, the lack of life did not comfort her. She was used to constant noise, even if it was only a gentle hum of old cars passing by when she opened her window, and complete silence always unnerved her. Even her time in prison had been scored by the shuffle of the guards' feet or the crackling of fire in the lamps.

Darvin had parked the car near a small, quiet pub that had a dim light coming from one of the upstairs windows and told Lenna and Tarley to get out.

"It's not too far by foot," he said and handed each of them

a set of light crystals.

They rubbed the two crystals together and a soft glow instantly appeared in their hands. Darvin proceeded to walk along a stone path that led away from the pub and towards what looked to Tarley like a small mountain.

"What's not too far?" Tarley asked, "where are we going?"

Tarley looked at Lenna but she just shrugged in response.

"We're going somewhere safe," said Darvin, "now stop talking and concentrate on where you're putting your feet. These light crystals aren't very powerful."

Slowly, Tarley and Lenna followed Darvin along the path as it wound its way up the hill. The stones soon disappeared into the dirt but Darvin continued to head for the summit as if he had walked the route a thousand times.

The air grew colder the higher they climbed but the light crystals provided a small amount of heat that stopped Tarley from shivering. One of the biggest shocks to Tarley since leaving the city, aside from the lack of noise, had been how different the air was outside of Miraylia; she could feel it entering her lungs and bringing its freshness with it. She felt more alert, somehow, even though her body and her mind were functioning at their absolute limit. If she were back in Miraylia she would definitely be feeling a lot more lethargic.

Once they reached the top of the hill Tarley could see the ruins of an old castle. There were stone staircases that lead to nowhere, rooms that had been half knocked down and a tall tower without a roof. Weeds grew and poked through the stones, claiming the derelict building as their own and the lack of light seemed to mock the lifelessness of the place.

A tall figure in a dark cloak walked across the ruins towards them, their hood pulled down low over their face. Tarley immediately recognised the cloak as being the same design as the ones that Nyra's Patrol would wear when entering the bridge.

"Hello, Darvin. Lenna," said the figure as they pulled down their hood to reveal a woman with the lightest of blonde hair that was cut so short she had tufts across her head rather than locks. She had a long, angular face and Tarley guessed that she was probably only a little younger than Darvin.

"Hello, Yvette," said Darvin. "Tarley, this is Yvette Treelor, the Head of Nyra's Patrol."

"Hello," said Tarley, softly. She looked at Yvette and felt like a coil was being tightened in her stomach. There was something in the assured way that Yvette stood or the relaxedness in her face that made Tarley feel uneasy towards her. Except that it wasn't unease that Tarley was feeling; it was more than that. She seemed to have an innate hatred towards this woman whom she had only known for five seconds, a hatred that made her want to abandon all her politeness and morals and raise her sword to her throat.

Yvette gave Tarley a small smile that made the latter absentmindedly reach for the short sword in her scabbard.

"It's natural that you should loathe me, Tarley," said Yvette. "After all, I am head of the organisation that seeks to kill Nyra. But the feeling should pass soon; Nyra's hold on you does not last for long."

"Sorry," was all Tarley could think to say. She let go of the hilt on her sword and felt her desire to harm seemingly fade from her body and into the ground. Tarley didn't even know how to comprehend how she had felt such extremes within the space of a few seconds. She looked at Yvette sheepishly but Yvette simply gave a slight shake of her head as if to say 'don't worry.'

"Have the others arrived?" Lenna asked.

"Not yet," Yvette replied, "but Penn sent a message about two hours ago to say that they were leaving so I'm sure they'll be here soon. If you'd all like to follow me."

Yvette led the three of them through the ruins until they reached a smaller building just behind it that had one of its walls missing and only a few stones to show for what would have been the entrance.

"Darvin thinks this is where they kept the dogs," Yvette said with a light chuckle and pressed her hand against the side of one of the remaining walls. The grass inside began to shift sideways as the ground opened up to reveal a stone staircase that appeared to go deep under the earth.

Yvette began to walk down the stairs and the others followed her into the darkness. She held out her light crystals but their energy was fading and only the dimmest of light was pouring out of them. However, within seconds the space was flooded with an orange glow as Tarley could see a corridor lined with torches, each of them seemingly bursting into flames by themselves.

"Welcome to Bray," said Yvette. "This is the largest of the Patrol's bases and I promise that you'll be safe here until we decide on our next move. No one outside of the Patrol or Henya Quinn knows where we are."

The corridor that they were marching down was so long that Tarley couldn't see what lay at the end of it but the walls on either side of her were covered in old paintings and tapestries. She walked closer to look at them properly and an overwhelming feeling of sickness suddenly engulfed her. Each of them depicted her performing acts of evil on the city and its people. The artists had captured her features perfectly as flames came out of her hands and down on to the houses of the innocent. Another painting saw her standing on the back of a two headed monster as it flew over the city, its eyes gleaming with pleasure as blood dripped from its mouth.

I could never do this, thought Tarley.

A hand was placed on Tarley's shoulder, which made her jump and break her gaze away from the wall. Yvette was standing next to her with a soft smile.

"I'm sorry, I should have warned you," said Yvette. "Perhaps we should go into one of the reception rooms and have something to eat?"

"That sounds bloody amazing, I'm starving," said Lenna.

"Is there more to see?" Tarley asked Yvette.

The Sovran smiled; she didn't expect anything less. "Yes, are you sure you want to see it?"

"Absolutely."

Yvette gestured for everyone to follow her down the corridor and as they did so Lenna shot Tarley a glare so vicious that she momentarily contemplated reaching for her sword again.

For someone so fragile looking Yvette moved very swiftly and Tarley was almost struggling to keep up with her as they strode down the corridor. As it neared its end there were several doors and a winding staircase that went even deeper underground, making Tarley feel like she was in some sort of rabbit warren. Yvette pushed open one of the doors, which opened out into a large room outlined by filing cabinets and wooden desks. In the centre of the room was a line of glass cabinets that Tarley headed towards straight away.

In the first cabinet there was a mixture of sharp teeth with an illustration of a wolf-like creature underneath it labelled 'Blaid canine teeth.' Next to the teeth was an animal that appeared to be a stuffed bat but it was a deep purple colour and its feet were green with deadly claws, not the small creatures that Tarley sometimes saw lurking around the bridge.

Tarley moved through the room, examining each of the cabinets that were filled with various parts of animals that she had never seen or heard of, each with an unusual name and a description that set them out as animals of the supernatural. The one that stood out the most to Tarley was a lynx that could change its size to be as small as a cat or larger than a lion and even more aggressive.

As she reached the end of the room she could see nine pictures hung on the wall, each in an ornate golden frame and above them were golden letters that read 'The Heirs.' At the top was Nyra, recognisable by her red hair and the nastiness that seemed ingrained in her expression. Below her picture were another eight portraits, each of them with the same face and build as Nyra but with varying colours of hair and styles depending on the era. And at the bottom of the wall was Tarley, painted sitting down as if she were purposely posing for the portrait.

Tarley stepped back and looked at the women; they looked like ten identical sisters staring back at her and yet she felt no connection to them. There was a year between the previous woman's death and the birth of the next that saddened Tarley, somehow, as if she wished that they had got the chance to meet the one that came before. They were not family and they were; sharing not familial blood but an uncontrollable power that ran through all their veins, binding them together across history.

Tarley could hear Lenna rifling through the filing cabinets and picking out pieces of paper to read. She finally tore her eyes away from the portraits and crossed the room towards her cousin.

"What have you got there, Lenna?" said Tarley.

"Lyrics. I didn't realise how many poems and songs were written about you!" Lenna saw the flash of hurt across Tarley's face and quickly tried to put the paper back in the filing cabinet. "Not you. Nyra."

"It's fine," said Tarley, although she didn't believe her own words. "What else is in these cabinets?"

"Reports, mainly," said Yvette. "Eye witness accounts of Nyra's reign as well as those of The Heirs over the years." She walked over to a cabinet on the furthest end of the room and tapped it. "This one contains the majority of information about you, Tarley, if you want to look at it."

Tarley's curiosity, as always, won out over her fear of delving further into this dark world. She marched over to the filing cabinet and opened the first drawer, taking out one of the many files. She opened it to find a copy of her birth certificate and medical information, including dates of vaccinations and visits to the doctor. There were also pictures of her as a toddler and pinned behind them were pictures of the same girl at the same age except that her clothes were from another era. If Tarley didn't know the truth she would have assumed that it was the same little girl dressed up in different costumes.

"I'm afraid it's all rather boring in your case," said Yvette. "You didn't show any signs of possessing powers until six months ago. To anyone else you would have appeared to have been very normal throughout your life."

Tarley wanted to say that she *was* normal but she was certain that those days were gone. Within the space of a month she had gone from being a guard to a fugitive and then to a prisoner infamous all over the country. Part of her felt like adding supernatural powers into the mix would be the least of her problems.

Tarley continued to flip through the file until she came upon a selection of family photographs throughout the ages. She saw herself in the middle of large families, cradling a newborn baby and kissing a woman she had never met. She even found several pictures that hinted at what she might look like in her later years but she was in no mood to find the lightness in the situation.

She finally pulled out a photograph of her, Macklyn and Baodor as children leaving school with their mother and in that moment wished she could remember that day. All she could see was a scene from any other day in her childhood and yet it had been perfectly captured without any of them realising, as if it was somehow special. Tarley immediately hated the intrusion and felt furious that her six-year-old self had no idea that she was being watched so closely.

"Has Nyra's Patrol ever interfered with my life?" Tarley asked Yvette.

"Only in small ways. For example, if we thought you might have been on the verge of starting a riot in a pub," said Yvette.

Tarley immediately felt her cheeks turn red but was more frustrated with herself than with Yvette. She had nothing to be sorry for. Not in that instance, anyway.

"We've never drastically altered your life path if that's what you're wondering," continued Yvette. "It's always been our policy to observe from afar as much as we can."

"Guess you all slipped up when I joined The Inquiry, then."

"Yes, we did send Henya into a bit of a spiral over that."

Lenna guffawed from across the room as she flicked through more files.

Tarley placed all the photographs back in the folder and put it in the filing cabinet. How could she not have noticed these people following her every day? Even if they had refrained from meddling in her life she still felt like a science experiment that was waiting to explode.

"What theories do you have so far about killing Nyra?" said Tarley.

Darvin and Yvette exchanged equal looks of trepidation.

"The important thing to remember is that *all* we have is theories," said Darvin, "we won't really know what will happen until the time comes."

"Don't be a politician, Darvin, spit it out," said Lenna.

Yvette couldn't help but smirk. "Powers are peculiar things, there are no definite laws as to how they work," she said. "They cannot be made or broken. They can be displaced but the only way for a Sovran's powers to fade back into the ether is for them die *with* the Sovran. Nyra's Patrol has been trying for centuries to separate Nyra from her powers and to destroy them but she's too weak. Frustratingly, she needs to be her whole self but that will mean she will also be at her most powerful again."

"But am I right in thinking that Tarley is a part of her powers?" asked Lenna.

"In a way. A Sovran's powers must be displaced in their entirety and Nyra only has a fraction of hers at the moment," said Yvette.

"So how do we get her to her full strength again?" asked Tarley.

"*That* is the question we've been asking ourselves for centuries and we've still yet to find an answer, I'm afraid," Yvette replied.

Lenna groaned, "The fucking bitch is basically immortal."

Yvette gave a light chuckle, which irritated Lenna. "It may seem that way but I'm not convinced that anyone is immortal."

Tarley put her head in her hands and sighed. She longed for answers to all her questions but she also craved a bed and a pillow. Yvette glided out of the room while Lenna wrapped an arm around Tarley. Neither of them knew what to say; they had been transported into another world where they didn't know the rules or who was in charge. Words were just a distraction.

"Tarley!" a voice screeched from behind them.

Lenna and Tarley both looked up to see Carida with dark circles under her eyes, running towards Tarley. She almost knocked her daughter over as she enveloped her into her arms and sobbed into Tarley's shoulder. Tarley squeezed tightly, burying her head under her mother's. Of all the people she was desperate to see her mother had been top of the list and yet at that moment Tarley wished she never had to speak to her again.

"I thought I'd lost you," said Carida.

Tarley pulled away from her and lightly kissed her cheek. "I'm sorry."

Macklyn, Baodor and Ivy soon appeared, as did most of The Inquiry, and some other faces that Tarley didn't recognise. While everyone was busy reuniting Yvette moved through the crowd and climbed on top of one of the wooden desks.

"Hello everyone," she shouted, which managed to silence the room. "Seeing as it's been a very long day for all of us, I suggest that I show you all to your rooms and we can have a meeting first thing in the morning. After all, there is a lot to discuss."

Yvette looked down at Tarley and felt her heart sink deep into her chest. She had known this girl all her life, even though Tarley did not know it, and now Yvette was looking at her wondering if she would be the one that ended it.

* * *

Nyra had spent the rest of the night walking through the city and trying to avoid the guards. Nearly all the roads were different so she had to use what little power she had to conceal herself.

She had dealt with the guards on the bridge easily enough but as soon as she was through the gates the empty streets became flooded with guards and the police. It was quite funny, really, because even if they did catch her what were they possibly going to do to her? The power they used to suppress her gifts wouldn't work this time, she was not strong enough, and they couldn't kill her because she was not in her true form. Of course, even if she were reunited with her latest shadow her sister's disciples still wouldn't be able to figure it out. There had never been a Sovran like her before and there hadn't been one since they locked her up either. Their centuries' worth of work would be for nothing. She walked through Gracefalls Park as the sun began to rise and stopped in front of its fountain. She knew that the girl liked to come here but she couldn't see why; there was nothing overtly special about it. Nyra stared at the fountain and laughed softly to herself. She vividly remembered the warriors that had been immortalised in the stone, one of them had been her sister's husband, and the overwhelming sense of self-importance that they had possessed. They had led the city in its fight against her and adored the praise they received once she had seemingly been defeated.

She remembered the sleeping gas filling the room and all her guards choking as they fell to the floor, she had been quite impressed that they had invented such a concoction. Of course, it would never work on Nyra, the gas simply made her feel a little woozy, which had given them just enough time to place the glowing, jagged edged object on the floor and run. She had never seen anything like it before; a soft pink, crystal-like creation that looked like it was made of glass rather than crystal. Even now she could remember the intense heat that it radiated right before it exploded and threw her against the wall. She was paralyzed and yet her mind still vaguely understood what was happening around her. She could still sense movement and voices as they collected her. They knew she wasn't dead but she remembered the cries of happiness she heard. As the weeks went on she began to regain some of her sensing powers and could *feel* the joy that the city now reveled in. To them Nyra was dead and they no longer had to live in fear.

Her powers remained stagnated for centuries but she never forgot the people who had put her in her prison and she certainly never forgot her plan. First she would take over the city, it would be easy enough once she felt stronger, and then once she had the girl Miraylia and the rest of Liliath would have no choice but to bow down to her forever. One day they would see that she was their rightful queen and that her power was a gift for them all if they only respected her.

She knew she shouldn't, it would be such a waste of what resources she did have, but it was her first night back in the city and she was entitled to enjoy it. Besides, once she was in the mountains she would be able to revive herself. Smirking, she stared at the fountain once more and caused all the warriors' heads to crumble into the water below.

There, she thought, *now you all look wonderful.*

She left the park and walked ten minutes down the road until she came to a small cul-de-sac. It had once been a burial ground for those who had committed crimes against the city and even though it was now surrounded by houses she knew that the souls she would need would be most attracted to this area. After all, their remains were deep below the ground.

She closed her eyes, there was a time when she could sense anyone in the world with little effort but right now her powers required hard concentration. She pictured Glyn, who had been a young boy when she had met him but had quickly become infatuated by Nyra and her power and became one of her most loyal followers. She thought of

Zelene, the best warrior she knew and the only person she had allowed to be almost as close as a friend, and she thought of Turner, a Sovran who had sought Nyra out as her rise to power began. These were the only people whom she had placed a small amount of trust in and had stayed with her until the very end. She had sensed the day of their executions and she had only felt pride as they refused to betray her secrets. They had waited long enough for this day.

Finally, she could hear them. She could hear their souls speaking out to her, amazed simply by her presence.

Find a vessel, instructed Nyra, *choose whoever you want from the city and come back to me.*

When she opened her eyes she saw three young and strong figures kneeling before her, their heads bowed. She was not surprised at how quickly the takeover had occurred; time moved differently in their realm and fresh corpses were easy enough to take hold of.

"My Queen," they said in unison.

"It is good to have you back, old friends," said Nyra. "Arise; we have much work to do."

PART TWO

CHAPTER FIFTEEN

T he hall was silent as Yvette stepped on to the stage and looked at the many faces staring back at her. Each of them was pained and she could feel it all. She had learnt over the years how to block out other people's emotions but sometimes their feelings were too strong and she would have to endure every part of their hurt. There were times, however, when she felt obliged to attune herself to other people in order to remind herself that her powers could help people; she could sense things within people that they themselves had not yet addressed. On that evening Yvette chose to embrace the fear and loss that these people were feeling. Her whole body felt overwhelmed with grief and a pining for everything to end that she could easily relate to but would never admit. Darvin was by her side as ever but he had chosen not to lead the memorial; he'd always maintained that Yvette came across as more empathetic than he did. She'd never once told him that she knew it was because every loss hit him harder than he would say.

"Yesterday thirty people travelled into Miraylia to fight two vicious beasts that Nyra had unleashed on the city. But only twenty-four returned," began Yvette. She could see

Tarley towards the back of the room, huddled between Brecon and Carida as she closed her eyes.

Tarley could see the monsters that Yvette spoke of; the image of them had not left her since the day before. Known as cennogs, they were dog-like creatures the size of small buildings, covered in black scales and possessed the pointiest of teeth. The image crystals had shown them tearing through the city with blood dripping from their mouths and their faces were alight with unrestricted pleasure. Tarley had seen hundreds of pictures of them during her time at Bray; they were one of Nyra's favourite creations and their sole purpose was to destroy. Once Nyra had created them she only needed to use a little of her power to control them and they had no way of disobeying her.

Brecon squeezed Tarley's hand, causing her to open her eyes. She looked at his bruised face and the small smile that he was wearing and felt a tight pang across her chest.

Yvette and Darvin had not let her leave Bray since she had arrived three months ago, despite her constant begging. She had wanted to help fight the cennogs, to do something useful, but she was met with the same answer as always: it's not safe. She never pushed them to say who exactly it wasn't safe for.

"Their families have chosen not to speak this evening," Yvette continued, "but I know that everyone in this room can feel their loss. They were extremely brave men and women who did not deserve to leave this plain in such a way. They will be missed and we shall honour them forevermore."

Yvette walked across the stage and lit six candles; each of them a different colour and shape but all held upright by the same style of brass candleholder. As she lit each candle she spoke the name of one of the dead before standing back and bowing her head.

"May the next life be free," said Yvette and the words were instantly echoed by everyone else in the room.

Once the memorial was over the crowd began to disperse

to various rooms across the base. Tarley was still surprised at how large the place was; everyone was able to have their own room and there were plenty of lounges and meeting rooms so that its inhabitants were able to feel as free as they could whilst living underground. Yvette had told Tarley that when the five bases had first been built after Nyra's defeat the Patrol placed extremely powerful enchantments on them all so that they would expand as more people sought refuge.

"I need a drink," said Carida.

"I can help with that," Brecon replied as they left the hall.

He led them down a corridor towards the nearest reception room where they had all spent many nights worrying and waiting for news. Lenna, Tulis and Emlyn were already sitting in the corner with half-filled glasses in their hands.

The room slowly began to fill up and Tarley found herself staring at the image crystals in the centre of the room. No matter what channel they were switched to the only picture they broadcasted was a black square that hung in the air. Nevertheless, none of the image crystals in the base were allowed to be turned off in case Nyra decided to deliver one of her special messages to the country. Brecon was soon by Tarley's side and placing a glass of pale purple liquid in her hand.

"What's this?" she asked.

"It's best you don't know. Just drink," he said.

Tarley knocked it back and her mouth instantly felt like it was on fire but in a way that made her feel slightly more alert. She didn't particularly like the bitter taste but it wasn't entirely unpleasant.

"Did you give this to my mother?!"

"Uh, yeah, she loved it."

Tarley scanned the room until her eyes fell on Carida who was filling her glass back up with the purple drink and offering it to Rhoswen. The latter grinned and gladly accepted.

Tarley giggled as she sat down in one of the nearby armchairs, "Not sure how I feel about you leading my mum astray."

"Trust me, she didn't need a lot of encouragement," said Brecon, sitting down in the chair next to her. "So am I allowed to ask you how you're feeling?"

Tarley gave a small smile as her eyes fell downwards towards her feet. She understood that people cared about her but whenever she was asked about herself all she felt was guilt. How could she be granted the luxury of feeling sad and hopeless when she had been the one to start the chain of chaos? She finally looked back up and towards Brecon, who hadn't broken his gaze from her, and sighed.

"I'm feeling like a word that I don't think has even been created yet. There are just too many emotions to quantify or even label and none of them seem to be completely… present. I know that sounds mad," said Tarley.

"I think I've heard madder things recently," said Brecon.

The black square in the middle of the room suddenly disappeared and was replaced by the disheveled image of Henya Quinn. She had dyed her hair black and cut it much shorter but she was still recognisable, even with the cuts and dirt marks that decorated her face.

"She's back!" shouted Lenna and soon the whole room gathered around the holograph.

"Good evening, Liliath," said Henya. "As always, I must keep this message short. I would like to send my condolences to the families of those killed by those horrid creatures that tore through Miraylia last night. I only wish I could offer my sympathies in person."

The holograph was surprisingly clear for once; Henya's previous transmissions were usually broken and crackly. Tarley wondered how many people actually saw Henya's messages, she doubted it was that many but she still hoped that the Premier's words were a comfort to them.

"But it is now more vital than ever that we must all prepare to fight Nyra and her so called 'Devoted' followers when the time comes," Henya continued. "She refuses to believe that Tarley Hillis is dead and there are no longer any guards or police to protect us. I cannot reveal the work that we are doing or where we are but I can assure you that what is left of the Bureau is fatigued by the effort its making. We *will* be with you when we defeat that evil woman."

Henya disappeared and was replaced by the black square once more. Macklyn leapt towards the control and started punching in various channel numbers but the image remained the same.

"Len, when was the last time you heard from Ash?" Tarley asked.

"A few days ago; they were just leaving Hopperly and heading to Jobern. Fuck knows if that's where they are now," Lenna said.

Lenna picked up a bottle of cerise, a dark pink and very sweet drink, and poured it into Tarley's glass. They clinked their glasses and knocked it back before sitting down on one of the many sofas.

Rhoswen, Tulis and Carida had gathered on the other side of the room and looked like they were in deep conversation. Their friendship had formed almost instantaneously and for some reason Tarley found it strangely comforting. There was an obvious connection between Rhoswen and Carida; the loss of a partner, and although neither of them discussed the topic it was clear that they could see their pain reflected in the other. Tulis, however, always tried to revert the conversation back to Ash and Lenna, which infuriated her daughter. As far as Lenna was concerned Tulis was just trying to worm her way back into Lenna's life without apologising. Thankfully, Rhoswen knew Lenna well enough not to push her on the subject.

"So do you think that will be us one day?" Lenna asked, nodding towards the group of middle-aged women. "Old gossips."

"Don't let Rhos hear you calling her old; she'll kill you!" said Tarley.

Lenna chuckled and rested her head on Tarley's shoulder. Her cousin wished that she could say that they would both live until they were one hundred and have thousands of crazy stories to tell their great-grandchildren. She wanted to say that they would never lose each other again and they were a team until they died but the words only existed in her head. The truth was that Tarley felt certain that she would be dead before her next birthday.

* * *

Nyra, naturally, sat at the head of the beautifully carved table while her advisors sat on either side of her, each with varying looks of unease. Even in someone else's body Glyn was so desperate to please Nyra that he looked like he might cry with overwhelming adoration for her. She would have found it pathetic had she not enjoyed it so much.

Meanwhile Hart, despite being the most recent recruit to her inner circle, looked completely at ease. She knew that he was constantly on the hunt for a fix of violence and she admired that about him. As soon as Nyra had announced that anyone was free to join her ranks he had almost run into her arms as he praised her power. He had proven himself to be very valuable over the last few months, not just because of his intel on the girl but he also had a tactical mind and knew the modern Miraylia far better than her other companions did.

"So Henya is still alive," Nyra began. "Do we have an update on her location?" No one answered; the table in front of them suddenly seemed to be incredibly interesting. "I hope I don't need to remind you how important it is that she's found. Once I've wiped out the Bureau, Liliath will have no choice but to accept me as their Queen."

"I can assure you that I've got people scouring the country for her. They've got orders to kill those who don't co-operate," said Zelene.

Nyra nodded. "And the girl?"

"Your sister's cretins have done a very good job of hiding her," said Turner. "I've had every Sovran I can try to sense her and the Patrol but as soon as they find one they lose them."

"So there still hasn't been a sighting of her?" Nyra asked and Turner shook his head.

"Maybe she *is* dead?" suggested Glyn.

"No, I can still vaguely sense her power in the ether," said Nyra. "It's like a shadow of a feeling that fades in and out."

She stood up and glared at them all. "I know you've all worked hard but it's nowhere near good enough. We need to make preparations for a great enchantment, even if it weakens me. I cannot afford to wait for her any longer."

CHAPTER SIXTEEN

Tarley hardly slept that night so when it came to breakfast the following morning she made sure to take a large pot of coffee back to her and Lenna's table. They were always the first people to enter the dining hall in the morning and tried to leave before the flood of people came pouring in.

Tarley was finding it increasingly difficult to walk anywhere in the base without someone wanting to talk to her, whether she knew them or not. A lot of Bray's current residents thought that she had more information than she did and Tarley always felt guilty when she had to reiterate that she had no idea where their loved ones were or how they were going to defeat Nyra. All she could say was that they were in the safest place in Liliath and that they should trust Yvette and Darvin.

Lenna and Tarley quickly finished their food before returning the dishes to the people on kitchen duty and fleeing the hall. They both walked in silence as they sped along the many corridors. They eventually reached the largest training room which had an 'Occupied' sign hanging on the door. Tarley pushed it open to find that Yvette was already in the room pushing several mats together.

When they had first started their sessions Yvette had asked Lenna not to attend but Tarley was adamant that she stay, even though she had grown closer to Yvette over the months in the beginning she had only really felt truly safe when Lenna was around. Besides, Tarley knew that Lenna would be able to defend herself if something went wrong; she always had several weapons concealed in her clothes.

"Good morning," said Yvette. "Are you ready?"

Tarley groaned and walked over to her supposed Mystic while Lenna sat on the floor near the door and started twirling a small knife in her hands. Tarley didn't blame Lenna; her training had been incredibly boring. She'd managed a few extremely minor jinxes and to levitate a few inches off the ground one month previously but she wasn't convinced that made her a Sovran. Tarley wouldn't have been surprised if Lenna thought about it hard enough she, too, would have managed to achieve the feat. After all, there was a time in Miraylia's history when thousands of people were able to perform even the smallest of enchantments. Tarley just still wasn't convinced she would be joining their ranks any time soon.

Tarley had asked Yvette hundreds of times why she insisted on these sessions when she had shown minimal improvement but Yvette was adamant that Tarley would have huge power at some point and she needed to be able to control it. Yvette handed Tarley a glass of water as she always did and asked her to concentrate on the liquid. Increasing the volume was meant to be one of the easiest enchantments and Tarley had pulled it off momentarily two days ago but now Yvette wanted her to produce a full glass of water.

"Concentrate on how still the water is but also how it moves so fluidly when you move your hand. *Really* imagine that you're a part of it," Yvette instructed.

Tarley looked at the water but all she saw was the same crystal clear liquid that used to come out of her tap at home. She felt as connected to it as she did to the moon.

"Yvette this isn't working. Again," said Tarley after a minute or so.

"You're not giving up. You need to try harder," Yvette replied.

Tarley looked at the glass once more and imagined it overflowing with water, so much so that the entire room soon turned into a swimming pool. She could see Lenna, Yvette and herself swimming through it and doing somersaults under the water before the water slowly disappeared back into the glass.

Nothing happened. The water in the glass was as still as ever.

"Argh!" Tarley screamed and threw the glass on the floor, smashing it into tiny fragments. "When are you going to accept that I don't have any powers?! The only way I'm going to be of any use in fighting Nyra is if I have a sword in my hand!"

Rather than waiting for a reply Tarley immediately marched out of the room, nicking Lenna with her heels as she fled past.

"That was a good forty seconds worth of extra effort today, Tarl!" Lenna shouted after her.

Tarley groaned and continued to head straight towards the armory. The Patrol had collected and created some of the finest weapons ever made over the centuries and they were available to anyone who stayed at one of their bases. Tarley and Lenna had both spent days soaking up the detail and craftsmanship of some of the more beautiful swords; neither of them had seen so many from so many different countries. Tarley grabbed one of the newer swords that Lenna had forged since she had arrived and sliced it through the air a few times. Even though she adored the older swords she still wasn't completely confident in handling them and Lenna's just felt more balanced in her hand, especially when she was in no mood to hang around. She left the armory as quickly as she had entered it and headed to one of the training rooms where a handful of people were already sparring, lifting weights or running circuits.

Mabli was throwing punches and kicks with a friend that Tarley had seen at various meetings but never said more than 'Hello' to. Tarley could see Penn hitting a punch bag in the corner but his eyes were more focused on Mabli than the bag.

She'll eat you alive, thought Tarley.

"You look pissed off," said Macklyn as he sauntered towards his sister.

"Training," said Tarley, to which Macklyn simply responded with a knowing nod.

He then raised his sword and gave a playful smirk that Tarley had seen a thousand times. She placed her blade against his and they were soon leaping backwards and forwards as their swords beautifully clashed. Thankfully, the training room was huge and fairly empty so they could run and jump as much as they wanted. The adrenaline was soon rushing around their bodies as they tried to disarm the other but continued to fail. Tarley could usually tell what Macklyn's next move would be by the position of his feet but that day she was struggling to guess what he would do before she retaliated. Nevertheless, he was an excellent training partner and Tarley could not care less that she was grinning and laughing as if she had nothing to worry about.

"Tarley! Macklyn!" a voice yelled and the two instantly stopped as they turned their heads to see Darvin standing by the door. "We need everyone in my office; Henya and the others have returned."

Penn almost ran out the door after Darvin while Mabli, Tarley and Macklyn were close behind.

"I thought they were going to Jobern," said Tarley as they raced through the base and down two flights of stairs.

"Henya wanted to check in after the attack," said Darvin. As they entered Darvin's office Tarley could see that it was already filled with bodies. Lenna had immediately cornered Ash and felt no shame in kissing every part of his face, not that he seemed bothered. However, as soon as Rhoswen walked in he tilted his head away from Lenna's and gave his mother an embarrassed smile.

Penn and Brecon both headed towards West, pulling him into a hug as they patted his back. All three of them were grinning but West looked to Tarley as if he had aged five years since he'd been away. She caught West's eye but he quickly turned his head back to his friends who were keen to know the story behind every new mark that was visible on his skin.

"Hello, Tarley," said Henya. "How are you?"

"As you'd imagine," Tarley replied.

The bags under Henya's eyes had not disappeared from the last time Tarley had seen her but there did seem to be more resilience in her face. She had always come across as an intense woman to Tarley but the way she was looking at her in that moment made Tarley feel like Henya was ready to jump into a fight at any moment. She wasn't sure why that warmed her so much towards Henya but it did.

"So what's new? Do people genuinely think I'm dead?" asked Tarley.

"Some do, some don't. But their hate is towards Nyra, not you, so I suppose the plan *has* worked," said Henya.

"Where are the Councillors?"

"I've sent them to Moorland; Jobern is going to be too dangerous after the cennog attack."

After everyone had given West, Ash and Henya their obligatory hugs and hellos they all found somewhere to sit while Darvin updated them on the attack and everything else that had happened in their absence, which was mainly Nyra executing those who opposed her but that was hardly news.

"How are the other bases doing?" Darvin asked.

"Fine," said Henya. "They all have enough supplies, including weapons. A few Patrol members are still requesting that we open the doors to the public but we just can't."

Everyone in the room nodded; the same argument had been circulating through Bray ever since Nyra's Patrol and The Inquiry had arrived with their families.

"West and Ash have been instrumental in helping me to move what Delegates and Councillors we have left to the bases," Henya continued, which caused Lenna to plant a kiss on Ash's cheek.

"And how is your family?" Rhoswen asked Henya.

"Safe. I just wish I could get them out of the country."

"Well thank the sunset they're underground."

Henya nodded before clapping her hands together and getting to her feet. "Right, if I could trouble you for some food and a shower then I'll be on my way."

"You're not staying?" said Brecon.

"No, I just wanted to make sure that everyone here was okay and that West and Ash got back in one piece! They're a lot more delicate than you think." A ripple of laughter went around the room. "Besides, I've heard rumours that Neb is in Jobern and I think it's best if I go alone; we still don't know what he's up to."

"That's if he's alive," said Tarley, not feeling guilty that she wouldn't mind if he was actually dead. Their last encounter still played over in her mind on a regular basis.

The group began to slowly disperse into various corners of the base with Macklyn stating that West looked like he needed a stiff drink, despite it being the middle of the day, and Lenna was virtually dragging Ash towards her room. Tarley had wanted to go back to the training room but her energy levels were starting to dip and she had little motivation to exert herself.

"Where are you going, now?" Brecon asked as they left.

"Not sure," Tarley replied. "I might go hang out in the library; there's still about two million enchantments that I don't understand."

"Only two million? Wow, you're coming along brilliantly."

* * *

Nyra had eleven Sovrans in her ranks; they were from all over the country and were keen to join her as soon as she declared that it was time for Sovrans to come out of hiding. Once she was Queen they would all be treated with the respect they had been denied for centuries; people would be envious of their powers rather than fearful.

The twelve of them stood in a circle with their arms raised so that their palms could rest on the person's next to them. Nyra had demanded that the room be silent and that they closed their eyes in order to fully concentrate on the energy they needed to create.

They all pictured Tarley in their minds but it was only Nyra who could sense her. Since she had awoken it had been near enough impossible to control her like she once had but Nyra had expected that; their powers would be too similar in this realm. Therefore, she could only get the vaguest of feelings from Tarley. Once in a while she would sense her tears or her anger but the sensation lasted for a fraction of a second. But now she could feel her allies' strength building within her and slowly every emotion that Tarley was feeling was being replicated within Nyra. The guilt and the fear felt wonderful to Nyra's heart; it had been so long since she had had even a trace of those sensations.

"I can feel her. She's breaking free," said Nyra.

* * *

"Fuck!" screamed Tarley and threw her heavy book down on to the floor. Her hands flew to her head as the pain seared across it.

"Tarley, what's wrong?" said Brecon, leaping out of his chair towards her.

All she could do was groan; her head felt like it was being squeezed in a vice. She hadn't had a migraine for months and none of them had been as bad as this one. Before she knew it she found herself willing the pain away; there was a mightiness taking over every part of her body that she couldn't stop but didn't want to, anyway.

The headache began to fade and as she looked upon Brecon all she could see was a weakling that had no right to look at her the way that he did. He was nothing but dirt compared to her. She lightly pushed him out of the way but he hit the floor with a loud thud, nevertheless. She strode through the library and out the door towards the end of the corridor where there was a flight of stairs.

As she reached them Yvette, Darvin and Henya were walking towards her and the latter two were each acknowledging her in their own inane way. Yvette, however, looked horrified as she approached but before she could act Tarley had thrown her against the wall with a swift flick of her hand.

"Tarley-" Henya began but she couldn't finish her sentence because she and Darvin both fell to the floor in silence.

Tarley walked up the stairs and within five minutes she was breathing the fresh air of Forstelle.

CHAPTER SEVENTEEN

vening was finally starting to encroach on Liliath as Tarley pulled up at the foot of the Dyffiniad Mountains in a small blue car. She had stolen it from the pub that stood just outside of Bray and had not stopped driving until she reached the mountains. She could see Zelene leaning against a rock as she got out of the car and thought her nonchalance to be extremely rude. Zelene gave Tarley a nod before she began to walk up into the mountains. Tarley followed and they both walked in silence until they came upon a large wooden door that sat seamlessly within the rock. Two guards stood outside but neither acknowledged the women as Zelene ran a black and yellow crystal down the side of the door. They walked through and Tarley couldn't help but be surprised at how similar the long hallway was to the ones at Bray. Tapestries and paintings of Nyra's most famous battles lined the walls and they all looked so beautiful to Tarley.

Zelene led Tarley into the largest hall that was housed within the mountain. Nyra had thrown many victory parties and feasts in there when she was younger; each one had been more extravagant and raucous than the last. Once her plan was complete she had no doubt that she would throw the biggest celebration that Miraylia had ever seen.

All the Sovrans were sat in plush chairs while Hart, Turner and Glyn stood either side of Nyra. As Tarley walked towards her she had an overwhelming desire to kneel before this woman. She had never seen someone with so much terrifying grace before.

Nyra smiled at Tarley and with one twist of her hand the trance was lifted. Tarley's mouth dropped open as she looked around her; she felt like she was in a dream but she could remember everything. She hadn't fought the journey or her yearning for violence and the idea of being in the presence of Nyra had been an honour. But now she felt sick.

"Do not worry," said Nyra. "It will all be over soon and you'll be nothing more than another corpse."

Tarley knew it was futile but she turned to run, anyway. Within seconds she was falling on to the floor and the door was being slammed shut. Zelene grabbed Tarley by her collar and pulled her on to her feet before shoving her towards Nyra.

The infamous Sovran slowly walked towards Tarley and only stopped when their toes were almost touching. Tarley could smell the faint scent of blood mixed with sweet smelling herbs from Nyra's skin and it only added to her nausea.

"I've never had the chance to get so close to one of my shadows before," said Nyra. "Do you ever wonder why I chose you? Even in my subdued state I could sense new energies forming and *you* shouted louder than them all. You were the natural choice to house my powers."

"Do you want me to say thank you? Because you're going to be really fucking disappointed," said Tarley.

Nyra chuckled, "*There it is!* The spark that got you into this! I have no doubt that you would have done great things but your time has come."

"I don't care if you kill me. But someone *will* stop you. It's happened before."

"And I came back!" snapped Nyra, her voice loud and

distorted as if she was possessed by a lion. "And I will keep coming back until all of humanity realises that the only way to save themselves is to serve me!"

Tarley took a step forwards, ready to push Nyra to the ground but before she could lift another foot she was thrown against the cave wall. The uneven texture of the wall pierced into her back as she tried to move away but she felt an invisible tie around her body that prevented her from moving.

Nyra signalled for Turner to fetch Tarley and bring her back to the centre of the room. Tarley squirmed in his grip but he had placed an enchantment on her that prevented her from moving too much. Nyra held out her hand and Turner forced Tarley's to rest on top of Nyra's as he took a step back. He began to circle his hands around the women's and as he did so a faint grey energy began to form that almost looked like smoke. There was an instant sting that hit Tarley's hand and quickly travelled up through her arm, over her shoulder and down her back. She suppressed a scream and tried to break her hand free from Nyra's but it felt like a weight was pressing their hands closer together.

She tried to visualise her hand moving away from Nyra's, hoping that something from Yvette's lessons had stuck in her mind, but all she felt was an ever-growing agony.

Don't you dare die looking like a fragile animal, thought Tarley.

The pain was now a strong ache rather than a stinging sensation and she could feel the heat from the energy source getting closer to her. She tried to imagine that it was the sun beckoning her into the next world. She was seven again and playing in Gracefalls Park with Lenna and her brothers. Her parents watched on as they ran away from Macklyn, the monster that had to catch all three of them to join his army. Tarley could feel the warmth on her face as she howled with laughter. Lenna was excellent at taunting Macklyn and running away before he could catch her.

The heat hit Tarley's body and her eyes involuntarily flung open to see Nyra standing in front of her as the grey smoke ebbed away from their hands and glued itself on to Tarley. She felt like her whole body was burning as she slowly fell to the floor. Tarley refused to scream but grimaced loudly as her skin itched and her heart tightened. She felt like a thousand hands were pulling at her hair and scolding her body with boiling water.

Nyra's smile widened as Tarley's body began to give into the power that was devouring her. Nyra reveled in her muted screams and flailing limbs, not once wishing that the torment would end quickly. This girl had tried to hide from her and now she would fulfil her true purpose in the most painful way possible. The smoke enveloping Tarley slowly began to disperse and her screams quietened.

Tarley looked at her hands; they were completely normal. There were no burns or melting flesh from her body. She quickly touched her face to find no difference and leapt on to her feet, her hands clenched into fists. She thought she would be dead by now but she didn't even feel weak. She had no weapon but she had felt a change in her body, a change that made her feel like she could defeat Nyra with one small punch. Nyra looked at the unharmed Tarley and shrieked as she ran towards her with her arms ready to strangle her but flames burst from Tarley's hands as she threw her first punch. Tarley screamed at the sight before her but Zelene was already withdrawing her sword and marching towards Tarley. Glyn and Turner followed suit, backing Tarley into the corner of the room. The flames from Tarley's hands would not subside, despite her willing them to, so she ran towards her opponents, hoping that simply touching them would cause them enough pain that they would back away. But as she moved her left arm a fire as tall as the room erupted from her hand. Zelene began to scream as the flames covered her, crying out for Nyra or Turner to help her. In the brief moment it took for everyone's eyes to fall upon Zelene, Tarley charged through Turner and Glyn and ran out of the door.

She ran down a dimly lit narrow corridor and could hear

footsteps following her. The fire from her hands died as she took left and right turns but as she sprinted through the cave a green light began to emit from them. The footsteps were getting closer and she had finally reached a dead end. She looked at her hands in disgust, the green light was fading in and out and she had no idea how to stop it.

"I've found her!" Turner yelled as he spotted her at the end of the tunnel.

Tarley began to hyperventilate as he came closer, knowing that the only way she could escape was to run down the corridor towards him. She looked at the wall to her right and as Turner approached a hole unexpectedly blasted itself into the wall. Tarley looked down to see that her arms were raised in the direction of the wall and the green light was shining through the hole. The only view from where Tarley was standing was blue sky. She looked down to see the mountain side below and Miraylia as only a speck in the distance.

Turner was now inches away from her. She turned to face him and pushed her hand towards him; a shot of green light flew from her hand and into his head. He hit the floor immediately. Tarley could still hear footsteps and voices calling out to each other, asking if anyone had seen her. She took a step towards the hole and stood on its edge. She guessed that she was twenty storeys higher than the rocks below. She took a deep breath and clenched her fists.

And then she jumped.

* * *

Brecon had no idea how long he'd been unconscious for as he woke up but he didn't want to waste time debating it. Once his vision was back to normal he was on his feet and on his way to Darvin's office. However, his path was blocked by Penn, Ash and Lenna kneeling next to three sleeping bodies.

"Darvin! Wake up!" Lenna shouted as she gave him a

nudge.

"What's happened?" said Brecon, "has anyone seen Tarley?"

They all shook their heads as Yvette began to slowly open her eyes. She quickly sat up, looked at Darvin and Henya and within seconds they were both awake and climbing on to their feet.

"Yvette, do you know where Tarley is?" Brecon asked, "we were in the library and then all of a sudden she got this headache or something and knocked me out!"

Yvette exchanged a grave look with Darvin. "She did the same to us before she left. I think Nyra has taken over her," she said.

"WHAT?!" Lenna shouted, "I thought you said this place is protected!"

"It is but we don't know what kind of power Nyra is messing with, she did use to be pretty indestructible, remember!"

Lenna was taken aback by Yvette's sudden surge in abruptness but rather than respond she just pursed her lips in frustration.

"We haven't got time for this. We need to act now," said Darvin. "Henya, you need to leave as soon as you can; you can't get caught up in this. The rest of you have ten minutes to round everyone up into the main hall."

All seven of them immediately headed off in different directions with Yvette leading Henya towards her office. She didn't care how rushed they were she still didn't want Henya to leave without a new set of crystals and as much food as she could carry.

Once everyone was assembled in the hall, Darvin and Yvette climbed on to the stage to explain what they knew. Somehow Nyra had got into Tarley's head and they could only assume that she was heading to the mountains.

Darvin was doing his best to avoid looking at Carida as her two sons gripped her hands but her weeping was impossible to ignore. Amongst the stoic mass she was the only one who dared cut the silence.

"We need to get Tarley back as soon as we can," said Darvin. "Which means that we need volunteers to possibly face Nyra and a shit load of enchantments. I know it's a big ask which is why I'm begging any Sovrans we have to come forward and help."

"We leave in half an hour; make sure you have everything you need," said Yvette, glancing at West as she left the stage.

* * *

Tarley hobbled into a small alcove and sat down on the nearest rock. She had hit the ground as hard as she had expected but the only pain she felt was in her left leg. She was sure she had fractured it but given that she was still very much alive she decided not to feel sorry for herself. Whatever Nyra had done to her she didn't want to spend time pondering its effects in that moment. She was still far too close to Nyra's base and she needed to get back to Forstelle. With a good leg she was certain that she could be in Miraylia in just under four hours and then she could perhaps steal a car or contact Yvette somehow.

She gave herself five minutes to think of an alternative plan before standing up and hobbling out of the alcove and beginning her descent down the mountain. There was only one way she was going to reach Miraylia and she could only hope that she didn't pass out from the pain before she got there. However, twenty minutes into her walk and Tarley couldn't help but wince every time she placed her foot on the ground. The weather was mild but she had not had a drink for hours. Her throat felt dry and her mind quickly began to fantasize about water.

She had expected to see some of Nyra's followers by now, she was sure that she had not travelled far but perhaps her jump out of the cave had given her a head start. Even so, they were bound to catch up to her soon and she doubted she'd be able to fight any of them with the zest that she would need.

She could feel the tears welling in her eyes and, for once, she didn't want to resist them. If Darvin had been there she would have bit her lip and pretended to be fine but he wasn't so she let the tears flow down her clammy face.

She debated trying to fix her foot, she had seen Yvette mend broken bones just by staring at a person's arm but she had been a Sovran her entire life. She knew exactly how to control her powers. Tarley was still terrified that she might accidentally set herself on fire.

She came across a mound of rocks and allowed herself two minutes to sit on them just to rest her foot. If she had been on the bridge she would have had a doctor on site within minutes and been taken to the hospital straight away. Brecon had always been great when someone became injured on the bridge. His cocky demeanor instantly vanished and everyone would look to him for direction, even the commanders at times.

Tarley silently scolded herself for thinking of Brecon when she should be thinking about how she was going to get down the mountain. But the thought of him brought her comfort. She had missed him so much that weeks after his apparent disappearance she had promised herself that she could not think about him more than once a week. It was the only way she could see herself going to work with a clear head.

She started to feel woozy again and all she wanted was for someone to be next to her so that she could hold their hand until the feeling passed. She placed her head in her hands and wept, wishing that she could be with someone for just a few minutes.

* * *

Nyra splashed her face with the purifying leat water for the final time and looked at herself in the mirror. She would not be able to hide the burns until she had all her powers but the water would lessen their appearance for now. Thankfully, her skin didn't react the same way that non-Sovrans' did so she only looked like she had a minor scratch across her face. Poor Zelene would remain scarred forever if Nyra decided not to help her.

Nyra returned to the meeting chamber where Glyn, Hart and Turner were already sat around the table, eager to hear their commands. She'd sent Zelene to her room with one of the medics; Nyra still hadn't decided what she would do with her.

"Glyn, I want you to lead a group to find that stupid girl," said Nyra. "And take Hart with you, he has some experience with her. He might be able to help identify where she would go."

"As you wish," said Glyn, ignoring Hart.

"You must both leave at once," said Nyra, "Turner is to accompany me to the Revival Chamber. I need to recuperate."

Hart and Glyn immediately left the room while Turner stood and took Nyra's hand in his own. He loved being the only Sovran in her inner circle; it was a claim that Glyn could never make and Turner was convinced that when the time came Nyra would name him her deputy if she ever chose to have one. He did not feel he was being a fantasist when he thought of their bond as being so much stronger than everyone else's. Their abilities to manipulate the world around them gave them a deeper connection to the universe and, ultimately, to each other. Turner had always been in awe of Nyra's talents and he only hoped that at the very least she respected his.

He walked her down the many tunnels that led to the Revival Chamber and opened the door to reveal a small room with tiny light crystals ingrained into the jagged walls. At its centre was a wooden throne that had flowers and thorns carved into it that led to a perfect crown at its top. Turner had created it centuries ago and placed an enchantment upon it so that the wood would never age. He led Nyra towards the throne before crossing to the other side of the cold room.

The whole experience had now become like a ritual and it felt so sacred that neither of them spoke. Nyra sat still as Turner pulled on his gloves and glasses, as gifted as he was even he couldn't withstand the power of the tanith. He opened a small metal door that he had built into the cave wall and carefully picked up the rectangular-like crystal that few in history had ever seen. It was lilac in colour with a blue strip down its centre and light flashed within it that could blind a person with a single glance.

Nyra held out her hands and Turner slowly placed the tanith within them. She wrapped her fingers around it and soon the whole room was ablaze with purple and blue lights. The reaction only lasted for a second before the lights disappeared and the room returned to its dark hue.

Turner quickly removed the crystal from Nyra's grip and even after performing this task hundreds of times over the previous months, he was still amazed by the results.

The paleness of Nyra's skin was replaced with her natural colour and her thinning hair looked shiny and thick once again. The outward effects were minimal but it was easy to see in her eyes just how revitalised she felt. Any weakness she possessed had disappeared to be replaced by the power of a Queen.

* * *

"We're never going to find her!" a voice growled as Tarley attempted once more to walk down the mountain.

She frantically looked for its source but couldn't see anyone. She saw a high pile of rocks and quickly squatted down behind them. They just about covered her body and a simple flinch would have easily exposed her.

"We'll find her," said another voice. "We have to."

Tarley didn't have to wait long before she heard the thud of boots close by, growing louder as they neared her. Her whole body tightened as she tried to remain as still as possible, thinking about what would happen to her if she was found rather than the agony she was in.

"There's a trace of blood down there," a woman shouted and Tarley could hear all the footsteps stop. "I'm going to take a look."

Tarley could hear many people yelling at the woman that no one was there but she marched on, nevertheless. A rock flew past Tarley's leg as the woman walked further down the ledge and Tarley found herself clenching her fists as the woman drew closer.

Please don't find me, thought Tarley.

More rocks fell as Tarley listened to the nearing footsteps. Her whole body was wet with sweat and full of cramp as she tensed every muscle she possessed.

The footsteps stopped and Tarley looked up to see a broad woman holding a sword leaning over the rocks above her. Neither woman spoke as they gazed upon the other.

Tarley wanted to beg for her life and at the same time ready herself to fight this foreboding woman. She felt terrified and brave all at once but she did not act on either emotion, instead she remained still and waited for the woman to speak.

She looked directly at Tarley, blank faced, and sighed. "You're right, there's no one here," she said and walked away to re-join her companions.

Tarley slowly grabbed the nearest rock she could find and gripped it, waiting for someone else to come and seize her. She knew she wouldn't be able to fight them all but perhaps if she could just knock one of them out she would gain a head start.

She heard their footsteps again as they moved away and soon saw a line of them walking down the mountain besides her with their heads held low.

She wondered what their plan was, confused as to why they were leaving her alone. That woman had looked straight at her and then pretended that she had not seen her.

Tarley very much doubted that anyone in Nyra's ranks held an ounce of compassion so what were they planning? Were they trying to lure Tarley away of her own accord and then jump her when she least expected it?

Whatever they were planning she was sure that it would be sadistic and grotesque. Every message they sent to Miraylia via image crystals was filled with blood and torment just for the sake of it. They would take over every channel on Miraylia's frequency and recite their manifesto while torturing random members of the public.

But it could all be stopped, they would say, if everyone simply accepted Nyra for the queen that she is and live in peace under her rule. All she wanted was to be loved by her city and its people.

Tarley looked at them as they walked away, wondering how they could succumb to the lure of power so easily. If they defeated Nyra Tarley hoped that whoever was in charge of their punishments took great pleasure in deciding their fates.

A second passed and the Devoted fell to the floor at the exact same time as if they had been shot dead by an arrow. Tarley looked around but could not see an archer or anyone else. Tarley stared at them, twenty or so all lying on the ground in a mangle of limbs. Nobody's chest seemed to be rising and falling and not a single arm or leg flinched.

Tarley used the pile of rocks she was hiding under to help push herself up and slowly stepped over them, feeling like her left foot was about to snap as she did so. She hobbled down the path the Devoted had followed, trying to be silent but failing terribly. When she reached the first body she was surprised by how pale he looked and the limpness of his frame. If she had not known any better she would have sworn that he had been dead for hours.

She bent down and checked his pulse, surprised to find that it was still there, albeit faintly. She examined more of them and found the same; they all looked dead but their hearts were beating. Once she was satisfied that they were all in the same state she grabbed one of their bags and began collecting weapons and canteens filled with water. They could all be awake in seconds and even if she was a broken mess at least some of them would be without their swords.

It took her several minutes to step over them all as they had left limited space on the ground but eventually she had passed them all and could begin the long journey into Miraylia.

* * *

They had been driving for about half an hour before Yvette felt even the faintest connection to Tarley. She was surprised at how quickly the strength of the bond grew between them; she had never sensed Tarley quite like this before.

"She's heading to Miraylia," said Yvette to Darvin. "We don't need to head to the mountains."

"Are you sure?" said Darvin.

Yvette nodded, "I think something's happened to her powers. I can feel a stronger tie to her."

"Can you sense the power in all Sovrans, Yvette?" West asked.

Yvette turned so that she could see West sitting in the seat behind her. "Not all, no, but most." She smiled at him and then turned back to face the windscreen of the van.

Within the hour they had arrived at the outskirts of Miraylia followed by several other cars and vans. Everyone who had volunteered climbed out and surrounded Yvette and Darvin. They promptly split everyone into groups and told them their only purpose was to bring back Tarley. They were to return within four hours with or without Tarley in order to reassess their plan. Yvette was praying that they had enough time.

* * *

The sun had finally set and the whole city was in darkness. Tarley had lost track of how long she had been walking for but at some point her foot had stopped hurting and she could walk normally. She felt both grateful and unnerved by its transformation.

She knew she was on the outskirts of Miraylia but there was so much rubble in place of buildings that Tarley could not decipher exactly where she was. She very rarely ventured to the edges of the city but, even so, after twenty-five years of living there she still felt like she had a vague idea of where certain roads and pathways should have been.

Tarley only saw a handful of people as she navigated the bricks and debris around her. Every person she encountered completely ignored her and kept their heads down, moving along the street as quickly as they could. Miraylia had never been known for being a particularly friendly city but Tarley had never known its people to be quite so insular. No one automatically trusted a stranger on the street but these days there was an instant dislike towards anyone that they didn't know.

Tarley sat down on what remained of a wooden bench and drank the rest of her water. The only way she could safely get back to Forstelle was to walk but that would take another day and she was exhausted. She didn't even have a home to go to; as soon as her family had evacuated the city Nyra made a point of destroying every house that Tarley and her family had ever lived in.

I could build some sort of shelter, she thought. She had been trained how to at the academy but she had not practiced since her final exam.

"Excuse me," said a teenage boy as he walked closer to Tarley. She had not even noticed that he was there. "I don't suppose you have any food going begging, do you?"

"Not much," said Tarley, "but you can have this." She reached into her rucksack and pulled out a small pie that was slightly crumbling. It looked pitiful but she only had a small supply herself and she was reluctant to give anything else

away.

"Thank you so much!" said the boy, snatching the pie out of her hands and eating the whole thing in two bites. "Where'd you get that from, anyway? No one's trading this side of the city."

"Does it matter?"

"I suppose not. Thanks anyway," he said and began to walk away. He stopped just a few steps away from Tarley and turned back to look at her. "Do I know you from somewhere?"

"I don't think so," said Tarley, standing up and slowly moving her hand closer to her scabbard.

He can't recognise me, there's only one light on this entire street!

The boy was now inches away and glaring at her as he studied her features. Tarley tried to walk past him but he quickly blocked her path.

"I know exactly who you are!" he roared.

Tarley swiftly removed her sword from its scabbard but she was not used to its weight or shape. She pointed it at him but with one kick he had knocked it out of her hands. She tried to run but he had already grabbed her arm and twisted it behind her back. He looked so young and weak and yet there was so much power behind his grip that Tarley wondered if he was a Sovran.

"My mother was one of the first to go missing from the bridge!" he spat into her ear.

"I'm sorry!" said Tarley. "That wasn't me! It was Nyra!"

"What's the difference?!" he twisted her arm even further, causing her to wince. "It was only her and me. I was at the academy until it burned down and now I'm left begging alone on the streets like a tramp!"

Tarley stamped on his foot and his grip instantly loosened. She began to run but he launched into a sprint and soon caught up with her. He threw his body towards Tarley's and pushed her on to the ground, completely ignoring her scream as her chest met stone. She managed to messily hit him in the face, which gave her a few seconds to twist her body, but his guard training shone as he swiftly pinned her back against the ground.

"I bet you don't even remember her, do you?" he said, pushing his left arm against Tarley's throat and using his right to pin down her arms. "Moira Kenning."

"I knew her!" choked Tarley, "you're…Clyde. She always…always spoke-"

"-shut up!" Clyde shouted. "I know what you're doing and it won't work. I've had the same training as you, remember."

He reached into his jacket and pulled out a knife before placing it against Tarley's throat. "Now get up. Slowly." Clyde jumped off her and she did as she was told, raising her arms in the air. He placed his arm around her neck again and pointed his knife into her back.

"Walk," he commanded.

They began to walk through the rubble and Tarley soon realised that he was taking her back in the direction she had just come from. She wondered if she should bite down on his arm and make a run for it; there was a chance that he would slice his knife through her back but he wasn't pointing it at any major organs.

"Hey! What are you doing?" someone shouted from across the street. Tarley turned her head to see two burly men striding towards them.

Clyde jumped slightly causing his knife to nick Tarley's back but he didn't remove his arm or remain still. Instead, he squeezed harder against Tarley's chest and began to pick up the pace.

"She's a criminal, I'm handing her in," said Clyde.

The taller of the two men grabbed Clyde's arm from around Tarley's chest and effortlessly removed it.

"To whom? There's no one protecting the city anymore," he said before turning his attention back to Tarley. "Shit! You're that Hillis girl!"

Tarley immediately broke into a sprint, jumping and leaping over areas of rubble that had not been cleared. She could hear the three of them behind her, shouting at each other to grab her. She darted down what she thought was a side street only to find that it opened on to a large park that was now nothing more than dirt and mud. Every part of her ached but she kept pushing her legs forward, hoping that she had enough energy to wear the men out before they reached her. But she soon felt a hand latching on to her arm and pulling her towards the ground. She tried to get up again but Clyde had appeared and was now kicking her in the stomach. She curled into a ball as she clutched at her abdomen, wishing that she knew how to make the pain disappear again.

Clyde and the men began arguing over what they should do with her; Clyde wanted to take Tarley to Nyra but the other two thought they should kidnap her and demand a ransom.

Tarley made it on to her knees but Clyde had already seen her and kicked her back down to the ground. She howled as she fell, frustrated that she did not have the energy to punch him in the face.

As she lay on the ground she imagined withdrawing her sword and plunging it into each of them. She wouldn't torment them or do it slowly, she would be so quick that they would be lying on the floor before they would even have a chance to run. She was certain she could do it if she was well.

Tarley understood that people were scared; should they join Nyra or fight her when it looked like she was going to rule over them, anyway? But until a few months ago Tarley had been like any other young guard on the bridge and she could never have imagined someone being so willing to trade her life for any sum of money.

Clyde hit the ground, followed by the other two so that they were a mangle of bodies.

Tarley waited a few seconds before she got up and walked over to them, worried that they would wake up and attack her again. She bent down and took their pulses, they were still alive and she had no idea how she had managed to do this again.

She grabbed Clyde's knife and hobbled out of the park. She desperately wanted to run but she was in too much pain. She could feel trickles of blood running down her back and wondered if she could stop it. She focused on the image of the wound healing and of Ash applying ointment to it but nothing happened. She could still feel its stickiness against her skin and she wanted to scream louder than she ever had.

As she turned on to a wide street the tears began to stream down her face and her rage was encasing her body. Every part of her wanted to roar and thrash against the city, to take out its people one by one. The street was quiet but she wanted it to erupt into life. She wanted to make so much noise and so much mayhem that they would hear her in Rhedos.

"Here I am!" she bellowed. "What's taking you so long, Nyra?!"

She felt drunk and angry all at the same time. She felt every emotion pumping through her body but her vision was starting to blur and the street ahead was dipping in and out of focus. She stumbled along, screaming out for someone to fight her and throwing rocks in any direction she wanted. She had destroyed the city and now it was time to revel in its remains.

Tarley picked up another brick and saw that her hand was covered in a golden light with white flecks, causing her to immediately release it. She looked at the rest of her body and could see the light growing in brightness as it began to cover every inch of her.

Tarley laughed louder and higher than she had ever laughed before. She was finally turning into a monster and she loved it. She felt woozy and powerful all at the same time. How had she gone her entire life without feeling like this? Yvette and her people had tried to stop this from happening but it was impossible to stop nature. After all, *this* is what she was always meant to be and there was something beautiful about finally embracing it.

She stumbled against the remains of a pub and could see a single bottle of cerise buried amongst the bricks that had somehow survived the turmoil of the city. Tarley grinned and dug through the stones, triumphantly pulling out the bottle. It was only then that she realised that she was not covered in light but golden flames.

* * *

Yvette and Darvin were halfway down one of the hills that led into Miraylia when Yvette suddenly stopped upon seeing the city below her.

"Shit!" she shouted.

The flames were growing and rampaging through the city; turning it into a cluster of bold white and golden light against the black sky.

"Only Nyra can produce those flames," said Darvin.

"Or Tarley," said Yvette.

"We need to hurry."

The two of them began racing down the hill, desperate to get into the heart of the city before more damage was done. Darvin thought of the few remaining buildings that had not been destroyed by Nyra's attacks and silently hoped that just a few bricks would not succumb to whatever this new attack was.

* * *

Tarley tried to lose herself in the rabble of people that had now converged on the streets. The fire had spread in an instant and any structure it touched seemed to crumble within minutes. People had begun throwing water over the flames but it made no difference; the fire seemed impossible to extinguish.

Tarley wished that she had a hood to cover her face as her attempt to hide under her collar only made her feel ridiculous and more exposed. The light coming off the blaze meant that the whole street was illuminated and so she could not simply disappear into the darkness.

She began to feel faint again and momentarily leant on a nearby wall before she thought she saw someone staring at her and quickly walked off. Everyone around her was screaming and shouting but she remained silent, trying her best to move through the crowd without drawing attention to herself but she could only take a few steps before she fell to her knees and then on to her side. She tried to place her weight on to her arm but her whole body felt lethargic and double its usual weight. She wanted to call out for help but every time she tried to form a word no sound came out of her mouth as if she had forgotten how to speak.

"Come on, Tarley," said a soft voice above her. "Let's get you out of here."

Tarley looked up to see what she thought was Penn pulling her to her feet. Someone lifted her other arm and she turned to see Ash supporting her other side but her vision was so blurry that she couldn't be sure.

"Shit, she looks terrible," said Lenna but Tarley couldn't see her.

Tarley wanted to protest and thrash about in their arms until she was certain that they really were who she thought they were. She didn't trust her mind at all and could easily be carried away by complete strangers who wanted to hold her hostage or worse.

But as much as she tried to shout and kick her movements were minimal. She could barely stand and so Penn had no choice but to throw her over his shoulder and run towards the outskirts of the city before the rabble behind them noticed who Tarley was.

* * *

Ash, Penn and Lenna reached the van just after Macklyn and West had returned feeling nothing less than futile. As soon as Macklyn saw his sister hanging over Penn's shoulder he ran towards them both, shouting out for Tarley.

"She's out cold," said Penn, slowly lying Tarley down on the grass.

"Ash!" shouted Macklyn. "Have you checked her over?"

Ash was on the verge of snapping at Macklyn, of course he hadn't checked her over, they'd been too busy running for their lives! Nevertheless, he knelt down next to Tarley and placed his hand over her wrist whilst calling out her name but she didn't even stir.

"She seems physically fine; I don't know what's caused her to fall unconscious. I don't think any doctor who isn't a Sovran could know," said Ash.

Brecon and Rhoswen soon came into view as they walked down the hill towards the group, quickly followed by Mabli and Netta, another member of the Patrol. As soon as Brecon spotted Tarley lying on the ground he ran over and knelt down beside her.

"She's just sleeping," said Lenna, placing her hand on Brecon's shoulder. "Yvette will sort her out once she's here."

Brecon lifted Tarley's hand towards his lips but was met with a static shock that forced him to drop it. Tarley's eyes suddenly burst open and with a kick of her legs she was standing on her feet, glaring at the stunned faces around her.

"Tarley, are you-" began Brecon but he was silenced by the green flames that shot out of Tarley's hands.

He quickly ducked and narrowly missed the fireball before rolling on to the ground and jumping back on to his feet. Tarley snarled at him and threw another fireball in his direction but he had already jumped out of the way.

Mabli charged towards Tarley and pushed her to the ground but as she did so Tarley's entire body seemed to set itself alight. Mabli screamed as she rolled off Tarley and withdrew her sword before she was even on her knees.

"Tarley, I think you need to calm down," said Macklyn.

"Do not tell me what to do!" roared Tarley. "I am no one's slave!"

Mabli ran at Tarley but the latter only had to glance at Mabli's sword before it flew out of her hand and into Tarley's. The flames that covered her body suddenly disappeared and Mabli became a most lucrative target.

"I'll make this fairer," said Tarley and held the sword in both her hands before bending it in half and snapping it as if she were holding a piece of card.

She dropped the sword on the ground and punched Mabli in the jaw, feeling a thrill all over her body as she withdrew her fist. Mabli's rage replaced any regard for technique as she threw her body towards Tarley and clawed at her face. Both women fell to the ground, screaming as they messily punched and kicked whenever they could. Brecon and Macklyn tried to separate them but all Tarley had to do was imagine them being thrown on to the ground and seconds later they were on their backs in agonising pain.

Mabli pushed all her weight on to Tarley and tried to place her arm against Tarley's neck but a burning sensation quickly shot up her arm. She jerked it back to find a faint scar line had appeared on her forearm.

"You fucking bitch," Mabli growled.

Tarley smirked and swiftly kicked Mabli off her before jumping back on to her feet. Penn ran towards her but within a few steps he was lifted up into the air and thrown against a nearby tree.

Mabli joined the rest of the group as they backed away from Tarley, wanting to fight her but feeling a mixture of guilt and unpreparedness that they didn't usually encounter. Brecon looked at the mighty, volatile young woman before him and could not see any trace of the Tarley that he knew but the thought of hurting her still didn't sit well in his head.

Tarley looked at them all and thought of the many ways she could stop their hearts in the most painful way possible. These powers were still new and just the thought of them sent an excited chill all over her body. She wanted to test herself and now was the perfect opportunity. She locked her eyes on to Rhoswen and imagined squeezing her throat. As soon as she did Rhoswen's eyes widened in terror as she began sputtering and reaching out for Ash's arm.

"Tarley, stop it!" yelled Ash. "Please!"

Suddenly Tarley was thrown thirty feet into the air and fell back to the ground as quickly as she had left it. A collective gasp went around the group as the sound of Tarley's back hitting the earth seemed to echo across the hill.

As they looked around to find out who was responsible they could see West standing over Tarley's limp body with his right arm outstretched.

CHAPTER EIGHTEEN

Nyra had allowed Zelene one night's rest before she summoned her to the main meeting room. Most of her body and face were covered in bandages; the Sovrans had only been able to heal so much of her wounds.

Hart, Turner and Glyn each sat along the table in silence as they waited for Zelene to enter the room. Nyra had instructed them to remain plain faced.

"Zelene, thank you for coming," said Nyra, standing up. "I want you to know that you have been a most loyal servant and once I am Queen, the whole of Liliath will know your name."

"Thank you," said Zelene.

"I hope you are proud of everything we have achieved thus far. Watching you fight with such determination and passion; killing so eloquently has only reaffirmed that I was wise to have you by my side. Wherever you go, never forget that."

Zelene's gaze shifted from Nyra to those sat along the table but everyone continued to remain silent.

"But unfortunately in this body you are now weak," continued Nyra, "and I cannot have weaklings in my ranks. It is time for your soul to return to the ether. Thank you,

Zelene."

Zelene opened her mouth to plead but before a sound left her body she was lying on the floor dead. Nyra gestured for one of the guards on the door to take her away and minutes later Nyra was sitting at the head of the table as if she had only just entered the room.

Despite her anger at the failure to retrieve Tarley, Nyra found herself feeling somewhat more relaxed since she had been revived, despite having to kill Zelene. She was confident that her former ally would be in another plain and understanding of Nyra's decision. She could feel her lungs taking in the air around her and her whole body felt more awake than ever. Every time she absorbed energy from the tanith it was like she was being awoken from her centuries of sleep all over again.

She didn't like to think how little life the tanith had left; she had sent several of her followers into the country to find it knowing that their only hope would be to dig deep underground for the crystal. She doubted that more than two or three would return but it was no matter as long as they were successful. What she really needed was for her powers to be restored and then there would be no need for revival crystals or tonics for hundreds of years.

"My Queen, I'm so sorry," said Turner, trying to speak as quickly as he could. "I had practiced the enchantment many times before on the low lives of the city and-"

Nyra raised her hand and immediately silenced him. "Do not apologise, Turner, we are dealing with power far greater than any we have ever experienced. I did not anticipate that the girl's powers would need to be awakened before the ceremony. Enchantments have their own processes in place; we should have been more respectful of this."

Nyra shifted slightly in her chair and sipped from her glass while the rest of the room remained completely silent.

"The good news is that I am still in possession of my powers; Turner only awakened my replicate's dormant powers," Nyra continued, "which still proves problematic as it will now be harder to capture her and return her powers to me."

Hart bowed his head, "Nyra, may I speak openly?"

Nyra grinned. "Of course."

Hart raised his head and looked her straight in the eyes. "Tarley may be more powerful now but I have no doubt that she's terrified about what is happening to her. She's far more emotional than she tries to let on. We need to find her before she learns to control her gifts and take them from her."

"I agree," said Turner. "That stupid little bitch set half of Miraylia on fire last night."

Nyra nodded, "Are we any closer to finding out where Delyth's people are hiding?"

Before Turner could answer there was a loud and continuous knock on the door, which caused Nyra to scowl. Glyn immediately got out of his chair and marched over to the door where the guard whispered something in his ear. Glyn nodded and returned to Nyra, quietly relaying the information to her.

"Bring him in," she said.

The guard left the door for a few moments before walking back into the room, dragging Neb Figmore along with him. The guard pushed him in front of Nyra before returning to his post outside the door.

Neb's clothes were creased and the hem of his trousers were covered in mud but he had managed to scrape back what little hair he had and held himself as if he were addressing the Bureau once more. The black and grey stubble on his chin was an unusual sight for anyone who knew him but Nyra couldn't help but feel warmth towards his transformation.

"Nyra, it is a pleasure to meet you," said Neb, giving her a low bow.

"I'm certain. Would you care to tell me what it is you want?" asked Nyra.

"I want to rule with you," said Neb, oblivious to the

sniggers from everyone in the room. "I've been thinking about it ever since I knew you were on the path to awakening and seeing the destruction you caused last night with that incredible fire was truly breathtaking. I want to help you take Miraylia. Henya has no idea what true ambition is but you do."

Nyra laughed, his words were flattery personified and she adored them but he did not know her at all if he thought ambition was her true motivation in this life.

"You will definitely be of use. But you are a fool if you believe that you can rule alongside me. And I do not tolerate fools."

Neb smirked, "Fair enough, it was at least worth a try. But I don't want to be one of your slaves, I've worked my way to the top of this city and I want to stay there."

"If you can prove your loyalty to me I promise you will be fairly rewarded. Although I do wonder why it has taken you so long to pay me a visit?"

"Well, I didn't want to come empty handed," said Neb and gestured towards the large window on the opposite side of the room.

Nyra stood up and crossed over to the window, which overlooked the bottom of the mountains. She couldn't tell how many there were exactly but there appeared to be hundreds of people, all standing in lines waiting for her.

* * *

Tarley woke up screaming. She felt like she had been set alight and the flames were quickly swallowing up her body. The heat and the pain were relentless, only growing in power and intensity. She thrashed around in her bed, kicking off the sheets that were covering her. She fell on to the wooden floor below and it was only then that her body began to cool. She lifted her hand to see that it was not covered in fire but perfectly normal except for a few bruises.

Ash ran into the small room and upon seeing Tarley

crouched down next to her.

"Come on, let's get you back in bed," he said, gently grabbing Tarley's arms and pulling her to her feet.

Tarley lay down on the bed and allowed Ash to pull the covers up over her legs. He pressed his hand against her forehead but promptly removed it, stating that her temperature was fine.

"How are you feeling?" he asked.

"Fucking shit," said Tarley. "Am I okay?"

"Well, every bone in your body should be broken but that's not the case."

"What happened after West knocked me out? Did I go crazy again?"

Ash shook his head, "Yvette did some Sovran stuff on you and then when we got back pumped you with every sedative we have. Both natural and…not so natural."

Tarley shivered; she wasn't sure she wanted to know the exact details.

"Nice to see you're a little calmer," said Brecon as he leaned against the door and gave her a cocky grin.

"I'm sure it won't last," said Ash, which Tarley begrudgingly smirked at. "I'll go and let Yvette know that you're awake."

Brecon ambled into the room and sat in the chair next to Tarley. She could see that his arms were covered in bruises and he had a small cut on his chin.

"Did I hurt you?" Tarley asked.

"No, these were courtesy of a homeless man in Miraylia. You did, however, give Penn the largest bruise I've ever seen across his back," said Brecon.

"Fuck," said Tarley, dropping her head into her hands.

"I wouldn't worry; he seems to enjoy showing it off to Mabli."

Brecon got out of the chair and sat on the edge of the bed, wrapping his arms around Tarley. She instinctively nuzzled her head into his shoulder and just let him hold her for what felt like hours. Was this cruel? To allow him this intimacy when she felt in her heart that she might not live for much longer? She finally lifted her head and looked into his eyes, wishing that they would tell her to stop. She wanted to see a change in them that would make her snap out of her selfish desire but nothing came. Instead, they looked at her with the same intensity she had seen for months.

She placed her lips on his and he took no time in pressing his hard against hers, kissing her as if this was his one and last chance to be with her. He moved his arms down to her waist and pulled her close, wishing that they were in his bedroom and not the clinical room of the infirmary.

"It's about bloody time," said Ash as he returned.

Tarley laughed as she drew away but Brecon was noticeably less jovial as he turned to face Ash.

"Seeing as you're feeling so much better, Yvette wants everyone in her office. Come on, Brecon; leave the lady to get dressed."

As they left Tarley could hear Brecon mumbling something about Ash being an idiot that only caused her to giggle to herself. She quickly pulled on the clothes that had been left by the side of her bed and raced towards Yvette's office. She was the last to arrive and could see everyone huddled around the image crystals where a holograph of Henya appeared.

"The flames that brought yet more destruction and death to Miraylia last night were caused by Nyra," said Henya. "If any of are you are still under the impression that she will be a loving and generous leader YOU ARE WRONG. She kills and feels nothing. If you do not want to fight, *please* leave the city. There is nothing left for you there."

Tarley began to feel queasy; for once it wasn't Nyra who was responsible for so much pain but her. Families had lost loved ones because Tarley couldn't control the power inside her and she had never hated herself more.

"How many died?" Tarley asked, softly.

Every head in the room snapped towards her but Yvette was the first one on her feet.

"We don't know," she said as she took Tarley's hand. "We think just under twenty but this isn't your fault."

Tarley snatched her hand away. "Yes, it is."

"Please, Tarley, it's more important now than ever that you remain calm."

Tarley scowled and sat down in the empty chair next to West. Macklyn was close by and Tarley couldn't fail to see the look of concern on his face.

"Did I hurt you?" West asked Tarley, his voice sounding as though it might crack.

"No, I'm fine," said Tarley, attempting to smile. "You saved everyone."

The whole room agreed and praised him for his quick thinking; no one else could have done what he did.

"You know what I'm going to ask, West," said Penn. "Why did you keep this a secret?"

West looked around the room and all the concerned faces made his leg start to shake. Tarley placed her hand on his knee to calm him and nodded.

He sighed and finally began to speak, "My mother was a Sovran and she always told me that it was a disease. She'd seen some of her family killed for using their powers so she never spoke about them, my dad didn't even know until they were married."

"Your parents were in The Inquiry for years and we never knew…," said Rhoswen.

"I think mum was always scared that someone would turn on her. And they did. You all thought that they were killed by anti-Inquiryists but that's not what happened. We went camping and mum got scared by a bird or something and accidentally caused the campfire to explode. A mob was soon on us and we had to run but…they just didn't get away quickly enough."

Rhoswen refused to cry; she didn't want to demean West with her own anxieties but she still felt awful. She never forgot the day that a ten-year-old boy called her in tears because he was alone in the woods and he was certain that his parents were dead.

"I'm not looking for sympathy," West continued, "I just want you all to understand. I know how much admiration you have for Sovrans and I'm a pathetic excuse for one; I didn't want you to know how useless I am."

Yvette sighed, "West, I have never met a useless Sovran in my life and don't for one moment flatter yourself by thinking you will be the first. You and Tarley will be training together from now on, agreed?"

West was so taken aback by her words that he couldn't think of anything else to do other than nod.

"Good. Now, Tarley. What can you remember from last night?"

She began by telling them how she could remember reading in the library with Brecon but out of nowhere she had this incredible anger take hold of her body. There was a small fraction of her brain that was telling her to stop but the rest had a compulsion to leave Bray and head towards the Dyffiniad Mountains. Once she arrived she was desperate to see Nyra; it wasn't until she was standing before her and the trance had been lifted had she realised the horrendous situation she had marched into.

She then relayed how Turner had tried to perform an enchantment on herself and Nyra before she escaped into the city, despite her supposedly injured leg, and avoided capture by setting the city alight.

"I'm terrified it's going to happen again and I'll end up going on some sort of killing spree," said Tarley.

"*If* that happens," said Yvette, "everyone in the room will take her out, won't you?"

Tarley looked around to see everyone nodding and noticed that Mabli seemed to be showing more delight in the prospect of clobbering Tarley than anyone else.

"You have to do more than that, you have to swear to kill me," said Tarley.

"I don't think anyone is going to agree to that," said Darvin. "Besides, we don't even know if it *is* possible to kill you."

"For fuck's sake, you guards are all about the death, aren't you?!" said Lenna, shaking her head.

Everyone laughed, despite feeling guilty for it, except for Tarley. There was still queasiness in her stomach that refused to subside.

"Yvette, what enchantment was Turner trying to perform?" asked Tarley.

Every set of eyes fell upon the Mystic.

"It was a conjoining ceremony, Darvin and I kept it from you because we've never really entertained the possibility and we didn't want to scare you," said Yvette.

Tarley looked from Yvette to Darvin, growing increasingly frustrated that there were still more secrets she had left to unearth.

"About two hundred years ago someone from Nyra's Patrol suggested that Nyra would try to conjoin with an Heir in order to take on her powers," said Darvin. "But there are so few cases of Sovrans conducting that kind of enchantment that we couldn't be convinced that they were real."

"And what would have happened to Tarley if Turner had succeeded?" said Lenna.

"We can't say for certain," Yvette replied. "Tarley would presumably be a lot weaker...perhaps even suffer permanent brain damage."

"You had no right to keep that from her!" Brecon yelled, immediately jumping to his feet and beginning a tirade into Yvette and Darvin's obsession with secrecy. Even now, when The Inquiry had decided to be absorbed by the Patrol, they were not full members who could be trusted.

"Brecon, just calm-"

"-no!" shouted Brecon, "I came here expecting answers and an end to all of this but the less you tell us the more at risk we are!"

Brecon didn't wait for a response; he stormed out of the room and slammed the door behind him. No one spoke or even moved for a moment.

"He has a point," said Rhoswen.

"Yes," said Yvette, "we didn't keep this from you out of spite, it's genuinely something we haven't considered. We obviously have some more digging to do."

"So are we done? I'm starving," said Ash and even with Lenna hitting him on the arm he still looked eagerly at Yvette.

"Unless anyone else has something they'd like to say, I'll see you all tomorrow."

No one responded; the only sound was of chairs moving and feet hurriedly walking out of the room.

Tarley didn't head straight to the dining hall with the others, instead she headed to her room so that she could shower and attempt to feel more like herself, although she wasn't sure if that would ever happen again. As she pulled on her clothes, her stomach rumbled and she begrudgingly made her way back downstairs wondering how much more efficient humans would be without the need to eat.

As soon as Carida spotted Tarley entering the hall she was smothering her with kisses and telling her how worried she had been. Yvette had only allowed her to visit for an hour this morning and no one had told her that Tarley was finally awake.

"Come and sit down," said Carida. "Baodor, fetch your sister some food, please."

Tarley was pushed into a chair between Ivy and Carida and told to stay put otherwise she would get a clip round the ear. Rather than agitate her mother Tarley duly obliged and allowed her family to inundate with questions about her health.

Macklyn, however, stayed quiet for the entire conversation and simply stuffed mashed potato into his mouth. There had been a lot of talking that day and not enough eating.

Tarley could see Brecon placing his empty tray on a stack by the serving counter and so quickly made her excuses to leave. Carida was desperate to know the full story of what had happened, Yvette only knew so much, but Tarley was too tired and too scared to reveal the truth.

"I don't want you to hate me," said Tarley as she kissed her mother's cheek.

"Tarley, I'm incapable of hating you," said Carida and Tarley knew that if she didn't leave then she would end up crying in front of the whole dining hall.

She couldn't see which way Brecon had gone but anyone could have guessed that he would either be in his room or training. Tarley opened the door to the training room to find that Brecon was alone, hurling throwing stars from one end of the room to the other. He looked like he was putting little effort behind his throws but the stars were flying across the room and falling several metres away from him.

"I wish I could throw like that," said Tarley.

"Well maybe if you weren't so obsessed with the sword you could," Brecon replied, walking towards her. He took her hands in his and kissed the top of her head.

"So now you know everything."

"And you're worried that it changes how I feel about you."

Brecon wrapped his arms around her waist, making Tarley feel like she was untouchable. There were drops of sweat on his skin but she didn't care, the feeling of his flesh against hers was more revitalising than it had ever been before.

"I could kill you and everyone here just by sneezing and I have no idea how to stop it," said Tarley.

"Maybe," said Brecon.

"You have no idea how terrifying it is wondering if you're going to turn into a monster at any second."

"So what's the solution? Spend all of your time worrying when you could be helping to finally beat Nyra?"

Tarley's glare seemed to change in a second. Brecon could still see the rage and fright across her face but she was also looking at him with a sense of surprise. Neither of them spoke for a moment, they simply observed the other.

Brecon wanted to lock the door and never let her leave.

He was prepared to fight anyone who would dare try to take her from him, even though he knew that Tarley wouldn't exactly be passive in that situation. In that moment he had never seen her look so fragile but he knew better than to acknowledge it, he just felt privileged that he was allowed to see her like this.

Tarley placed her head against his chest. His heart was beating just as fast as hers and she found it oddly comforting.

"I don't want anyone to die protecting me. And I don't want to lose control so much that I kill someone I love," said Tarley.

Brecon rested his head on top of hers. "No one has been forced to fight. We all want the same thing and that's for Nyra to be gone for good." Tarley's arms tightened around his waist. "And despite what Darvin said I'm sure Mabli will be happy to kill you if you become too much of a problem. You really do seem to have it in for her."

Tarley laughed, she didn't feel any less worried but she knew that if her mind fell into a dark place again there was someone to pull her back into the light.

She placed her lips against his and began to kiss, slowly and softly. She was soon desperate for her whole body to be against his. She didn't anticipate how different she would feel towards him this time; their one night in his shabby room a year ago had simply been the result of months of lust and hours of alcohol. But this time she felt like she would never want to be away from him. She felt like she could never want anyone else.

"You haven't seen my room yet, have you?" she whispered in his ear.

"Are you sure?" asked Brecon.

"Definitely," she said.

CHAPTER NINETEEN

Huge piles of jewels, gold and rare crystals filled one of the many caverns that Nyra had claimed in the mountains. Her recruits had all reverted to children as they scrapped over who had lay claim to what first and imagined just how rich they would be under Nyra's reign.

Music roared throughout the room and those that were not fighting for an ancient necklace were drinking the best wine in the country and dancing as if they had already conquered the world.

Hedonism had never been frowned upon in Miraylia but this was a freedom that none of them had ever experienced before. All they had to do was ask for another expensive bottle of cerise or another pig to be slaughtered and it was in front of them in seconds. And this was only a taste of what Nyra could offer them.

"I suppose you're going to kill them all once they've

served their purpose," said Neb, entering the room and standing next to Nyra.

"Perhaps. But they do provide incredible entertainment," said Nyra.

Neb sniggered as he looked on; there was no gold or wine and the room was completely silent save for the shuffling of drunken feet. He had to agree with his latest ally, her followers were very entertaining and he didn't even pity their stupidity. He would never have joined Nyra just to serve; he would rather have been killed in that ghastly fire than become one of her servants. He may not be next in line to rule over Miraylia but he knew where the power in the city lay and he would do whatever it took to be a part of it. He had no issues with playing the long game, after all, Nyra had survived for centuries and if he could just gain her trust he couldn't see why she would not do the same for him.

"Are you happy with the plan?" Nyra asked.

"Unequivocally," said Neb.

"Good because I no longer have time for failure."

"Do not fear; I know exactly what I'm doing."

* * *

Brecon's heart was still beating in time to Tarley's, albeit at a slower pace than before. She had her head rested against his chest and both were perfectly comfortable to remain in silence.

Tarley felt incredibly selfish; there was a large chance that she could be dead soon and all she could think about right then was how much she wanted to be with Brecon. She wasn't arrogant enough to think that she could break his heart but it was a possibility that she had given little thought to until then.

Brecon moved his arms so that Tarley was forced to move closer to him. He would never be scared of her but he knew that the idea worried her and for some reason he thought that the closer they were the more likely she would be to fully accept him. He wanted nothing more than to be lying in that bed with a Tarley that was at peace.

"You fucking bitch!" a voice bellowed from the other side of the door. "You complete fucking bitch!"

Tarley's head shot up as she tried to figure out where the voice had come from and who it belonged to. She looked at Brecon, who was secretly furious that their calm had been broken so dramatically.

"I think that's Penn," said Brecon. "Come on."

They both leapt out of the bed and hurriedly pulled on their clothes before running into the hallway. They found Penn pulling Mabli's hair so tightly behind her head that she was bending backwards and hopelessly trying to escape his grip.

"What the fuck are you doing?!" Tarley shouted.

"She killed my wife! I heard her talking with Darvin after dinner," said Penn.

Penn threw Mabli on to the floor and kicked her hard in her side before producing a knife from his jacket. Tarley ran towards him but Penn pushed her away so that she fell back against Brecon.

Mabli was on her feet with her fists raised but there was no anger in her face. Instead, she looked exactly how she always did before she readied herself for a fight. Tarley had seen that expression a thousand times across the guards; it was a result of every trainer at the academy telling them to clear their minds of everything other than what their next move would be.

"I was just following orders," said Mabli, seemingly ignoring the blade that was being pointed at her. "We had to stop people infiltrating the bridge."

Penn launched at Mabli but she quickly side stepped to dodge the knife before kicking Penn in the back. Brecon grabbed Mabli and pushed her to the ground, forcing himself between her and Penn.

"Don't do this, Penn," said Brecon.

"It's nothing more than she deserves! Viv was a beautiful

and kind woman; she didn't deserve to die!"

Penn tried to push Brecon out of the way but the latter punched Penn in the jaw, causing him to pause for a moment in shock. Penn shoved Brecon against the wall and Tarley winced at the sound of his bones hitting the bricks. Penn was a lot bulkier than Brecon and Tarley was sure that it would only take one light punch to his head from Penn to knock him out.

"Stop this!" shouted Tarley. "Give me the knife or I'll use my powers on you!"

Penn let go of Brecon and turned to Tarley, "Don't make threats you can't keep. You don't even know how to control them."

"Exactly. Who knows what I could do?"

Penn glared at Tarley in a way that she had not seen since she first joined The Inquiry. Over the past few months they had not become friends but a mutual respect had grown between them and with that had come a sense of trust that they had both appreciated. But Tarley was now looking at him and within seconds it felt like all that trust and respect had vanished.

"You're going to get us all killed! I hope you know that!" said Penn and stomped down the hallway.

Brecon immediately ran after him, asking him what he was going to do next, and soon the two of them were out of sight and earshot.

Tarley offered Mabli her hand but Mabli just raised an eyebrow at her as she got to her feet.

"I was handling it," said Mabli.

"I know, how's your head?" asked Tarley.

Mabli shrugged and began to retie her hair into a high ponytail. "I suppose we had better tell Darvin and Yvette."

Before waiting for a reply Mabli began marching down the corridor without looking behind to see if Tarley was with her. They raced down two floors where they found Brecon running towards them in the opposite direction.

"Penn's gone. He just walked out the door muttering

something about joining Nyra," said Brecon.

Mabli rolled her eyes. "What a drama queen. He would never join Nyra."

"I wouldn't be so sure, he said he liked that she was open about who she kills."

"Great," said Mabli, pushing past them both. "Darvin and Yvette are going to fucking love this."

* * *

The next morning Tarley walked down to the dining hall to find Lenna sitting by herself. She queued up, grabbed a bowl of porridge and joined her cousin on the small table.

"Darvin told me everything," said Lenna as Tarley sat down.

Tarley was grateful that she didn't have to talk about yet another incident over and over again. As soon as Mabli, Tarley and Brecon had reached Darvin's office the night before they not only had to relay everything to him before he found Yvette but they also had to go over the story many times once Yvette was in the room. Apparently it was for 'absolute clarity' but Tarley was convinced that somehow Yvette knew that she just wanted to get back into bed with Brecon and pretend to be normal.

Brecon wanted to send a search party out for Penn but that idea was shot down straight away as it was the middle of the night and Penn was not deemed important enough to risk a trip into Miraylia.

Mabli had asked if Darvin wanted her to move to another base but both he and Yvette were adamant that she remained; the other bases were too far and they needed their best fighters in Bray. Tarley was certain that she saw the briefest of smiles come across Mabli's face when she heard that.

"Do you think Penn will come back?" Tarley asked Lenna.

"I have no idea. Could you live with the person who killed the love of your life?"

Tarley sighed and continued to eat her porridge. The answer was a resounding 'no.'

"From what Darvin told me, it also sounded like a Hyd Caydell was in your room late last night…," said Lenna, smirking.

Before Tarley could reply Carida appeared with a tray and sat down in between the two. Lenna immediately began to laugh, to which Carida burrowed her brows.

"What's so funny?" said Carida.

"Nothing, Lenna is just easily amused. Did you hear about Penn, mum?" said Tarley.

Carida nodded, "It's so awful, can you…"

But she did not finish her question as her gaze had fallen upon Mabli as she walked into the hall. The silence quickly spread and every set of eyes were soon following Mabli as she approached the food counter. However, she appeared to be oblivious to the stares and whispers she was causing as she queued up for her breakfast. Tarley couldn't believe how so many people already knew what had happened, she doubted that Darvin and Yvette had told anyone but she supposed that all they had to do was tell one person and Mabli's secret was no longer a secret.

Tarley knew that Darvin had teenage daughters; perhaps they stayed awake last night and listened to their parents' conversation when Darvin finally returned to their quarters. But Penn had hardly been quiet as he dragged Mabli through the corridor; anyone could have heard his shouts and screams.

Mabli collected a piece of toast and joined some of her old friends from Nyra's Patrol on a table in the corner. As soon as she sat down they all began talking as if it was any other morning.

Tarley wondered what other secrets they shared and how they kept them quiet for so long. Tarley had lived with Mabli for months and never thought of her as anything other than annoying, the idea that she was an elite killer had never even been a prospect. The bridge had always brought secrets but, for most of the guards, it was nothing more than keeping the details of a shift to themselves. They didn't have to change persona once they stepped back on to Victory Road.

"Well she certainly doesn't seem bothered," said Lenna.

"Good for her," said Carida. "I thought we might have finally got away from all of the gossips but obviously not."

Lenna and Tarley exchanged a bemused look but remained quiet; neither of them wanted Carida to begin a lecture on privacy.

"Anyway," Carida continued, "I was speaking to Yvette before breakfast and she said now that you have your powers maybe you'll be able to locate those who have gone missing. Your dad could be back in a few weeks if all goes to plan!"

Tarley smiled at her beaming mother; she didn't want to be the one to send her back into fits of tears. Tarley knew that Yvette didn't have any time for such an endeavour; her only priority was to kill Nyra. She may have been a powerful Sovran but Yvette was essentially a spy and had been for a long time; wasting resources on collateral damage was never going to be a part of her plan.

All Tarley had ever hoped was that once Nyra was defeated *someone* could find a way to bring back the guards who had gone missing but she was doubtful. Even Yvette, who had studied Nyra and The Heirs for most of her life, still didn't fully understand how Nyra's powers worked.

"That would be great," said Tarley, placing her hand on Carida's. "Right, I have to get to training or Yvette will lose it."

Lenna left with Tarley and as they walked down the corridor they could see Macklyn leaving the armory with two swords in his scabbard and hurriedly placing a knife inside his jacket pocket.

"Whoa! Where are you going with all of that?" said Tarley.

"We're going to look for Penn in Miraylia. But Darvin doesn't know so we need to leave right now!" said Macklyn.

"Who else is going?"

"Ash, Brecon and some other Inquiry people."

"Do not leave!" Lenna demanded, "I'm going to get Rhos, we'll meet you outside in ten."

Macklyn nodded and soon Tarley was left standing by herself in the middle of the corridor. She sighed and walked into the training room, hoping that Yvette couldn't sense her brother's secret mission.

Yvette and West were already in the room and chatting but their talk soon faded once Tarley walked into the room. West gave her a nervous smile, which she returned, and stood next to him.

"Right, let's crack on, then," said Yvette. "We'll start with the basics; a jinx. They're only meant to last a few seconds so I'm sure you can both manage that. If you could face each other, please."

Tarley and West obliged but were unsure of where to look. Neither of them wanted to show how worried they were and yet they were still both grateful for the fact that they weren't alone.

"Tarley, concentrate on West's hair and turn it blue," ordered Yvette.

Tarley was about to object when Yvette shook her head and gestured towards West's head.

Fucking Sovrans, thought Tarley.

She looked at West's hair and pictured the shade turning from dark brown to bright blue but it stayed the same colour as it had always been. Tarley wasn't surprised.

"In the beginning it can sometimes help to use your hands to channel your powers," said Yvette. "Imagine the colour blue flowing through your arms, towards your hands and out on to his head."

Tarley lifted her arms and tried to picture the blood running through her veins as a blue dye that only she could release. She told herself she was the most powerful person in the room and could control whatever she wanted; the colour of West's hair was entirely her choice. She aimed her hands at West's head and pointed her fingers as she imagined shots of blue firing out of them. His hair remained unchanged but the sense of power she had felt in Miraylia was hinting at a return, as if it was revving inside of her. She decided to focus her eyes on a single strand of his hair; she was certain she could feel enough power within her to change just one hair on his head. Her eyes narrowed and once again she pictured a blue dye racing within her body, desperate to escape.

The space around her seemed to erupt into life as it vibrated around her body, making her feel like the only truly solid thing in the room. Even Yvette and West felt like whispers in the ether.

She curled up her fingers, sensing that the movement would whip up an energy within the room, and released them so that her fingers were splayed. For two seconds West's hair was the brightest shade of blue she had ever seen.

"Well done, Tarley!" Yvette shouted.

Tarley stood in front of West open mouthed. The room felt still again and any energy she had managed to conjure had dispersed into nothingness. She could feel a clear shift in the vibrations of her surroundings and she had been the one to create it. However, her pride only lasted for a moment. She had to remind herself that it was only a jinx and jinxes wouldn't kill Nyra.

Yvette asked West to do the same thing to Tarley but with more shades and for a longer period of time. He did this effortlessly and Tarley wondered if he felt like he had been pushed back several years in school; he could easily have his own, more advanced training session.

They spent the rest of the morning experimenting with more jinxes and Tarley found herself being in complete awe of West. He could change the colour of everything in the room as well as its size and shape for minutes at a time.

Tarley found herself enjoying the training a lot more than she thought she would; having the ability to alter an object at will felt as fun as it did powerful. As the hours went on the struggle to tap into the atmosphere around her lessened and a quiet confidence grew. She even managed to cause Yvette's hair to grow past her knees, which she thought was hilarious but Yvette only cracked half a smile.

"Okay, try this," said Yvette and handed Tarley a glass of water. "Try not to flood the room."

Tarley knew that wouldn't happen but part of her hoped it would. She didn't want to be seen as a show off but she was impatient and wanted to be the master of her powers as soon as she could.

She held the glass in her left hand and pressed the index finger of her right hand against it level with the water line. As she moved her finger up the glass the water began to increase until she was holding a mini waterfall in her hands. The jinx only lasted for a minute but the feeling of satisfaction would remain all afternoon.

"Very good," said Yvette, and almost snatched the glass back from Tarley. "Now I want you both to go and rest. I know you want to push yourselves but you can't do that without letting your bodies recover. So, no swords! Understood?"

They both nodded and made their way back towards their bedrooms. Tarley looked at West and felt that there was a lightness about him; a sense of peace. She wondered if it was intuition or if she was starting to sense other people the way that Yvette did.

As if you're that advanced!

"So, do you still think being a Sovran is a disease?" Tarley asked.

West shrugged, "I don't know; I'm still reticent. I can hear my parents chastising me."

"They were just scared, if they knew that Yvette was your Mystic I bet they'd be over the moon." West smirked but offered no reply. "Besides, Macklyn has always been attracted to powerful men."

West laughed so loudly that even Tarley was caught off guard; she'd never heard a sound like that come out of him before. As they went in their separate directions West's anxiety began to hint at a return. He knew his parents loved him, whatever realm they were in now, but he still couldn't shake the feeling that every time he cast an enchantment he was adding another betrayal to the list.

* * *

Yvette knocked on the door to Darvin's office despite being fully aware that he was in there alone. Although her strong sensing powers had saved her life more times than she could remember she still felt like they made her a traitor to her friends at times. She tried to pull back on them as much as she could but when emotions were running so high it was impossible not to feel every mood and temperament that passed by her.

Darvin called for her to enter so she pushed open the door, locked it behind her and took a seat in front of his desk. He was worrying about his daughters again; there was a distinctive essence to his anxiety that Yvette had learnt over the years was directly related to them. The pain was overtly present but so was the incredible amount of love, which affected Yvette more than she would ever let on.

"What's the verdict?" said Darvin.

"Well they both show huge potential, they could be very powerful Sovrans one day," Yvette replied.

Darvin put down his pen and raised an eyebrow. She knew that's not what he meant.

"Tarley is undoubtedly the strongest of The Heirs," Yvette continued. "I'm continuing to downplay how quickly she's advancing so that she doesn't get scared. That being said; I'm going to increase the enchantments on the base, just in case she starts experimenting…,"

"Yvette," said Darvin, his voice soft and his eyes boring into hers. "You know what I'm getting at."

Yvette nodded, "She's going to be an incredible Sovran one day but I don't know if it will make a difference. I think we're still on the right track; they'll need to conjoin if we're going to defeat Nyra."

Darvin nodded, "When should we tell her?"

"I know we agreed to wait six months but now that she has her powers I think we can afford to wait a little longer if needed."

He couldn't deny that he was relieved; for twenty-five years he had been wondering if Tarley would be the one that finally ended the saga and the more he got to know her the more worried he was that she would be.

He had been against her joining the bridge from the start but Henya and Yvette had been adamant that they couldn't alter her life too much. She was from a very old guard family; it would raise too many questions if she was refused entry to the academy, especially as she was so brilliant. He had tried to treat her like everyone else but there were many times when he had wondered whether he was being too hard or too soft on her. Either way, he felt that he knew her and had been secretly holding the executioner's axe in his hand for decades. What terrified him more than dropping it too soon or too late was being unable to drop it at all.

"Do you know that a group has gone after Penn?" Yvette asked.

"It was fairly obvious when I couldn't find any of them after an hour of searching," said Darvin. "Can you sense them?"

Yvette shook her head. "I only hope that he hasn't gone after Nyra. A pain like that can drive someone to do foolish things."

* * *

Tarley slept for most of the afternoon; she didn't know why she was so surprised that Yvette had been right about needing to rest but, even so, she didn't realise quite how exhausted she was. She felt like her mind hadn't stopped whirring since her training session. Nerves, excitement and intrigue were all bubbling away within her as she tried to fathom how she had joined the ranks of history's Sovrans. Such power could bring so much goodness into the world but also destroy it with a single thought.

When she woke up she headed towards the kitchen in the hope of alleviating her hunger to find that Ivy was helping to prepare dinner. Without saying a word Ivy threw a potato at Tarley and pointed towards a set of knives. Tarley chuckled and immediately began to peel and chop the large pile of potatoes that were sitting on the counter.

Even Sovrans aren't beyond chipping in, I suppose.

"I feel like I never see you," said Ivy.

"I know. Sorry, I promise it's not intentional," said Tarley.

Ivy giggled, "I should hope not. I still find it strange living here; can you imagine how confined it would feel if we couldn't go outside?"

"I wish we didn't have to be here. I wish I could just cast an enchantment and everything would go back to the way it was."

"But then we'd still be waiting for Nyra to break free. Things would be the same but they wouldn't be moving forward."

Tarley didn't respond; she partly agreed but she still wished that she could clap her hands and the mess that was her life would be clean and tidy. But if that couldn't happen she was grateful that her brother would be spending the rest of his life with someone who not only loved him but was quietly wise.

Tarley thought about the life they would have; the nieces and nephews she would be an aunty to and all she felt was love. She could see Baodor and Ivy bringing their hoard of children to her parents' house, Macklyn sweeping them up and Carida kissing them all so much that they squirmed in her arms. But she couldn't see herself. She would just be a ghost; a picture on the wall or a candle on her birthday. If Baodor and Ivy were to have this life Nyra would have to be dead and Tarley was certain that she would take her duplicate with her in the process.

"There you are!" shouted Lenna as she marched through the kitchen. "They've got Penn!"

Tarley immediately put down the knife in her hand and began to follow her cousin out through the dining hall and into the corridor.

"Where is he? Is he okay?" asked Tarley as they sped through the base.

"He's in one of the reception rooms, he seems fine. They found him passed out in front of a pub in Tophill."

They walked into one of the smaller reception rooms to find Darvin sat opposite Penn with the rest of the search group lounging around them. Nobody even acknowledged that Lenna and Tarley had entered the room.

Tarley immediately began to question Lenna's definition of 'fine' because Penn's bloodshot eyes and dirt-covered body almost made Tarley recoil. He looked more like a tramp than a member of the Patrol.

Darvin was looking at him intently but Penn was fixated on a spot in the corner of the room. He reminded Tarley of Macklyn when he was a boy and Carida was scolding him for doing something a little too adventurous. For the first time since she had met him Tarley felt a little sorry for Penn.

"Did you seek out Nyra?" Darvin asked.

"No!" Penn snapped, "all I did was go to the pub and drink until I passed out." He stopped staring at the corner of the room and finally focused on Darvin, his eyes seeming heavy and haunted. "I hate Nyra just as much as anyone else here. She's destroyed my city and the thought of joining her makes me feel sick."

Darvin remained perfectly still as he studied Penn and the whole room became so quiet that Tarley was scared to breathe too loudly. She was certain that the former guards in the room were all too aware of how strict Darvin could be. Simply being ten minutes late for a shift could result in a mandatory extra session in the gym and Tarley had known several guards that had been dismissed during her time on the bridge for incompetency. And that was when Nyra was dormant.

"He's telling the truth," said Ash. "I know him. He wouldn't lie about that."

"You've been a huge asset to this fight, Penn, but I need you to tell me right now if working with Mabli is going to be an issue. If it is, I'm going to have to ask you to leave," said Darvin.

Ash opened his mouth to protest but Lenna could already sense what he was about to say and so shot him one of her deadliest looks.

"You seriously expect me to live and work with that bitch?" said Penn.

"She's one of our best. I can't lose her. But I don't want to lose you, either."

"Can't you give him some time to think about it?" suggested Brecon. "He's a mess. Let him get a shower and some sleep and then he can decide."

Tarley felt a strange pang of pride towards Brecon and was worried that her cheeks might have turned red. For all her life Lenna seemed to have been primed to spot Tarley when she was feeling embarrassed and so Tarley had to turn her head away in case her cousin caught her.

And I'm meant to be the one with the powers, thought Tarley.

"Not until he swears to me that he can work with Mabli, I won't have in-fighting," said Darvin.

"For fuck's sake! She *murdered* my wife. And don't think I don't know that you were involved, I bet you planned the whole thing!" Penn yelled, quickly getting to his feet.

Ash and Brecon jumped in front of him and although Penn refused to sit back down he did look a little less likely to punch the former Head Commander.

"How dare you-"

"-STOP!" Tarley shouted and the whole room fell silent. "Come on, Darvin, just give him the night to sort himself out and think it over. You are asking a lot."

"Fine! Everybody out! I've got nothing more to say on the

subject," said Darvin.

Everyone left in stunned silence and sloped off to their various corners of the base. Tarley saw Brecon walking after Penn but the latter was quick to get away and so Brecon was left standing in the corridor on his own.

Tarley slipped her hand into his and kissed him on the cheek. "You okay?" she asked.

"Yeah, I'm just worried about him," Brecon replied.

"I know," said Tarley before taking a tentative breath. "Did you go to Miraylia?"

"Yes, it's horrendous. I only saw a handful of people and those that I did see were just skin and bone, weeping in the streets."

Tarley felt woozy for a moment and was worried that she was going to start involuntarily shooting fire from her hands again but Brecon saw the fear creeping on to her face and pulled her close, kissing the top of her head as he did. He rested his head on top of hers so that he was almost smothering her with his arms.

"We're going to keep fighting until this is over and then I'll take you on a proper date," he said.

"You think a lot of yourself, don't you," said Tarley and was glad that Brecon couldn't see the hint of tears forming in her eyes.

Later that night Tarley slowly pulled back her bed sheet and quietly swung her legs out of the bed and on to the carpet. Thankfully, Brecon was sleeping on his side and so she didn't have to try and slither out from his embrace.

After she had very carefully put on some clothes she treaded across the room and out of the door, praying that Brecon wouldn't wake up. She didn't like lying to anyone but she especially loathed not being completely honest with him.

Yvette's bedroom was two floors below Tarley but before she even reached the door Yvette was walking down the corridor towards her.

"Do you know what I'm going to say, too?" whispered

Tarley.

"I'm a Sovran, not a mind-reader," Yvette replied with a teasing smirk. "Come on, let's go in here."

She pushed open the door to one of the reception rooms, which only had a few armchairs and a coffee table, and gestured for Tarley to sit.

"We can't take things slowly, anymore, I'm fed up of seeing everyone around me getting torn apart by this shitty situation." said Tarley. "I need to be as powerful as I can as soon as I can."

Yvette nodded, "I'm inclined to agree. I'll coach you separately to West from now on; he may be more powerful now but who knows what you'll be able to do once you're at your peak?"

Tarley agreed, after all, it was the same question that kept her awake at night.

CHAPTER TWENTY

Nyra looked down on the city and smiled. The destruction and ash were all because of her and she had never felt prouder. The people may have been scared but they would soon learn that they could all be content if they followed her. How else was she supposed to show them how powerful she was? She couldn't just threaten them; she had to prove her worth. One day they would be grateful to have a leader who could protect them so brilliantly.

She had wondered whether she would need an heir. Turner would be the only candidate she could think of who she could bear to share her body with, despite Glyn's constant infatuation. But Turner was a powerful Sovran and the idea of having a child that could possibly be more powerful than her was sickening. To be defeated by her shadow would be atrocious but to be overthrown by her own flesh and blood would simply be pitiful.

She had contemplated immortality enchantments in the past but had never gone through with them; they had always seemed so pathetic. Only Sovrans that had so little faith in themselves dabbled with that kind of power and, ironically, they nearly always ended up dead. Perhaps she would investigate it once the conjoining ceremony was over. The more she thought about it the more it seemed cruel to leave Miraylia without her as their Queen.

A loud knock on the door broke her thoughts. She yelled for whoever it was to come in, still feeling angry that her sensing powers had yet to return to her. There was a time when she would have known someone was walking down the hallway let alone lurking around her door.

Turner entered the room and gave her a smile that momentarily made her wonder if having an heir would be such a bad idea, after all. His new body was certainly an improvement on the shell that housed him before.

"Any news?" she asked.

"He's found her. He's going to monitor her for a little while longer and then bring her to you," said Turner.

"Let's just hope that he does not fail for all our sakes."

* * *

Tarley wasn't sure if she'd always got such a buzz from looking at Brecon's face but she had become increasingly aware of it over the past few days. As they both ate their breakfast she couldn't help but study his brown eyes or the stubble on his chin; she loved every part of him.

Do you love him? she thought.

She hated the idea of not being with him but she had grown to accept it. She would leave and he would move on; did her pragmatic approach to their relationship mean that she could never completely love him?

"They're looking smug," said Brecon, nodding towards the door.

West and Macklyn were both walking into the dining hall, seemingly unable to stop themselves from smiling at each other and causing Tarley's heart to flip.

"They're good for each other, I think West could be a calming force for Macklyn," said Tarley.

"Really?! There's a way to calm a Hillis?"

Tarley laughed and playfully kicked him under the table.

"Well, you seem to have your ways…," said Tarley with the hint of a smirk.

"Oh, is that the trick? I'm not sure I've got time to have sex twenty-four hours a day."

"Could be worth a try though?"

Brecon had made the mistake of taking a sip of tea as Tarley spoke and almost spat it back out when he heard her, much to her amusement. When she eventually managed to look away from Brecon she spotted Penn walking into the dining hall, scanning the room with a morose look on his face. She instantly lifted her arm and waved for him to come over. As he strode towards Tarley and Brecon, Penn felt like every set of eyes that he passed latched on to him but he chose to ignore it. He wouldn't ever call himself famous but he'd had enough encounters with people who were shocked to meet him that the attention didn't truly faze him. He pulled up a chair and planted himself next to Brecon, helping himself to a piece of his toast as he did so.

"You okay?" asked Brecon.

"Just been in with Darvin, Yvette and that bitch," said Penn through bites.

Tarley's brow furrowed but she remained silent.

"And?" said Brecon.

"As you'd expect, Darvin was adamant that we both stay, even though *she* offered to go to another base, but Darvin won't let her. I can't say I was exactly gracious in my behaviour."

"So what's happening?" said Tarley.

"Yvette made the very good point that we only have to put up with each other until Nyra is defeated and then after that I never have to speak to her again. So if you could hurry up and figure out how you're going to kill the red head, I'd be very grateful."

Tarley sighed and picked up her tray. "No problem, I'm off to training now so give me an hour and it should be sorted."

Once Tarley had cleared away what was left of her breakfast, she began to make her way towards the training room. She always felt more nervous the closer she got, which was guaranteed to make her feel foolish. It was only a training room; she had grown up sparring on mats and surrounded by training weapons but this one had an intimidating atmosphere. She wasn't sure if it was the idea of the unknown or being unable to control it. Either way, it scared her more than she liked to admit.

Yvette was already stood at the centre of the room with various objects flying around her as Tarley arrived. As soon as she spotted her student, she smiled and everything in the air above her quietly found a space on the floor.

"Morning," said Yvette.

"Hi," said Tarley, slowly making her way towards the Mystic. "Before we start, can I ask you a question? It's been bothering me for a while."

"Why hasn't Nyra tried to control you since you returned?" said Yvette.

Tarley let out an awkward laugh and nodded. "I still can't get used to you doing that."

"Sorry, bad habit," said Yvette. "I think that when Nyra awakened your powers her ability to control them weakened. Mind control is unachievable to almost all Sovrans, despite popular opinion, and only works on the weak minded. As you were created to act as a tool to enact Nyra's work it stands to reason that once Nyra was powerful enough she could control you and now that you're powerful she's going to find it more difficult, if not impossible." Yvette increased the brightness of the lights in the room with a swish of her hand, "but that's just a theory."

"And the disappearances? How did I do that? It's all I've thought about for months but…I've been too scared to find out."

"I can't say for certain but it's safe to assume that Nyra tapped into your dormant powers momentarily and sent the guards to who knows where. But I'm afraid I don't know for definite and we shouldn't waste any more time. Move back, please."

Tarley knew better than to argue with Yvette and so took three very large steps backwards. She had a feeling that she best get in the correct mind set for what could be a grueling training session.

"If you're serious about pushing yourself then I only have one rule; do exactly what I say, no matter what." Tarley nodded. "Good." Yvette immediately threw three fireballs in Tarley's direction that travelled at the speed of a galloping horse. Tarley dropped to the floor and rolled to the right to avoid them before jumping back on to her feet.

Yvette shook her head. "No, use your powers, not your guard training."

A wooden chair from across the room flew towards Tarley and she instinctively lifted her leg to kick against it, causing it to break in half.

"No!" shouted Yvette. "Do whatever it takes to tap into your powers. Remember how you felt when we first met, how much you hated me. Think about how much you wanted to kill Lenna on that bridge or hurt Mabli in Miraylia."

Tarley took a breath and imagined running down the bridge with Ash beside her. Realising that they could not get into the building that protected Nyra had sent her into a hysteria that she still dreamt about. The frustration had quickly infected her and killed any sense of understanding or reason. She didn't find it difficult to replicate the feeling; she had never felt so many negative moments in such a condensed period of time. She had given up her life for The Inquiry, she had committed treason and it was likely it would have all been for nothing.

And when she had tried to enter the building it had been Lenna who dared attempt to stop her. Within seconds Tarley had decided that she should kill Lenna for undermining her like that and neither did she know where that feeling had come from nor did she dislike it.

"Hold on to that," said Yvette. "Now try a charm."

"A charm?! I can just about do a jinx!" said Tarley.

"Just do it!"

Tarley turned her attention away from Yvette, who was starting to irritate her, and towards the weights in the corner of the room. She didn't know what kind of charm Yvette wanted her to do so she decided to try a levitation charm, even if it only lasted for five minutes Tarley hoped that it could still be classed as a charm.

"Don't lose focus, harness the energy around you" said Yvette. "Think about the cennogs. Didn't some part of you admire them? Didn't you revel in the destruction they caused?"

Tarley thought back to the images that everyone had huddled around weeks before. The scaly, blood thirsty creatures had such joy on their faces as they tore through Miraylia. Each house they flattened and resident they ripped apart caused their eyes to flare in delight and a guttural, jubilant roar to erupt from their bodies.

They were *beautiful*, thought Tarley.

They dominated the city with so little effort that Tarley felt like she could only ever dream of having power like that. If they were let loose on the world she was certain that they could destroy civilizations within days and how could anyone ever condemn that if it meant more power for her? And now she could *feel* the power that surrounded her; every part of the air she breathed held such potential that was just waiting to be utilised. She knew she could manipulate this realm to her advantage; it was what she had been born to do.

Several of the weights lifted into the air and hovered at varying heights. Tarley could sense the energy they exerted and every particle in the room seemed to be flocking towards them. The sensation was so beautiful and terrifying in equal measure that Tarley didn't know whether to cry or scream.

Another fireball appeared in Tarley's periphery but this

time she turned and waves of water flew out of her hands and hit the flames, turning them into smoke.

Tarley twisted her hands around each other until she, too, had a fireball hovering above her. She glared at Yvette before sending it towards her but rather than destroying it she increased the fireball so that huge flames were dancing around each other in the centre of the room. Tarley stared at the flames in front of her, they remained mid-air and she found herself admiring the way the orange and red bled into one beautifully destructive weapon. The flames began to grow and an aggressive crackling sound accompanied them. Tarley turned her hand towards Yvette and the flames shot across the room towards her tutor but before they could reach Yvette she forced them to disappear into nothingness.

Tarley glared at Yvette; what right did she have to stop her? She was just a lowly Sovran; she should be worshipping everything Tarley did even if it resulted in Yvette's death.

Yvette sent the levitating weights towards Tarley but within a second Tarley had turned them into dust. Yvette ran to the other side of the room but as she reached the opposite side Tarley had increased the volume of water from a bottle that had been left behind and created a wall of continual waves around Yvette. As Tarley walked towards the other end of the room she could see the waves regrouping into one large mass that was heading her way. She growled in frustration and the water froze creating a jagged ice sculpture that almost reached the ceiling of the training room.

Yvette sent the ice crashing to the floor in a thousand pieces before marching towards Tarley, reaching into her jacket pocket and throwing a small vial filled with glistening silver liquid towards her mentee. The vial smashed at Tarley's feet and soon she was surrounded by thin grey smoke. She felt like her mind was reverting to how it should be, as if a disease that she was not aware of was being removed from her brain. Her chest felt tight and her stomach twisted as her tears began to flow.

"I'm so sorry," Tarley choked. She began to hyperventilate and quickly sat down on the floor to steady herself.

Yvette sat down next to her and lifted Tarley's chin so that she could look at her. "That was brilliant."

"What?! I wanted to kill you, Yvette! Every time you threw something at me or countered my attack it just made me want to destroy you!"

"I know," said Yvette with a sigh. "It is a concern that your powers are so rooted in anger but you've never had that kind of strength before. You were in complete control of everything you did."

"I'm struggling to see the positives in this."

"I know but I'm sure we will find a way for you to control your powers without-"

"-turning into Nyra?"

"You are *not* Nyra. Why don't you go and get some rest? We can have a proper debrief tomorrow."

Tarley wasn't sure where to go, she had no desire to sleep or rest and yet there was nothing for her to do that day. She decided the best use of her time was to do more research on Nyra; perhaps there was still a book somewhere that could tell her how to be less like her creator. She went to the archive and headed towards the corner that was dedicated to The Heirs. She picked up one of the many files brimming with notes before lugging it towards the nearest desk. The loud thump it made when it hit the surface made one of the Patrol members jump slightly, giving Tarley a small feeling of sadistic triumph.

Tarley already knew that each of The Heirs was stronger than the last but she had never taken the time to research the individuals. She wasn't sure whether that was because she was too scared about what she might find or because she had been too obsessed with learning about Sovranic powers.

She took out the first page to see that it was a sketch of a woman named Opal Arlorn when she was aged twenty. She, of course, looked exactly like Tarley but the way her hair was curled and twisted on top of her head seemed to make her look even more youthful. Opal had lived two hundred years before Tarley was born and was one of the eldest Heirs, living until she was sixty-five.

Tarley took out the next page and began reading physical descriptions of Opal, although there was nothing of note. She had not sprouted horns from her head or developed scales over the years so Tarley had to wonder why Nyra's Patrol had been so bothered by her appearance.

Tarley settled down into a nearby armchair and began to devour all the information before her; Opal had shown great strength from the age of six when she could levitate not only objects around her but also people. She had been born not far from where Tarley had grown up but when her parents discovered that she was a Sovran they fled to a farm in the country. She had gone on to join the police and occasionally used her powers to stop criminals but was only caught once. It was noted that Nyra's Patrol had to step in so that she not only kept her job but her powers remained a secret. However, Opal never knew about this and her senior officer had simply told her that she was too good to be let go.

Her life appeared to be very ordinary, she married, had two children and remained in the police until she was sixty, reaching a very senior role. It wasn't until Tarley was halfway through the file that tears began to reappear in her eyes. On her husband's fifty-seventh birthday she apparently lost control of her powers, the details were sparse as only her husband was in the house, and her whole home was set alight. They both managed to escape but too much smoke had got into his lungs and he was dead within the hour.

Tarley immediately thought of the fire she caused in Miraylia and could see the flames before her. She had tried not to allow herself to think about those who had died but when she did all she could imagine was their bodies writhing in the heat. She wondered if Opal had ever thought about her husband in that way.

Tarley picked up a photograph of Opal with her family

when she was a teenager; just like Tarley's family, none of them looked anything like The Heir. Their only similarity had been their dark hair but Tarley knew that was just a coincidence.

In that moment Tarley was desperate to talk to Opal. She wanted to hear what she had feared and did she ever have a sense of who she really was? Nyra's Patrol never approached her but did she know on some level that she didn't really belong in this world?

Opal was a part of her, a part of her history, and until now Tarley hadn't realised she could feel so connected to someone she didn't know. It wasn't just that they shared the same face or were made for the same purpose but Tarley knew, somehow, that this woman had spent her whole life fighting and Tarley could profusely relate to that.

"Hey," said a voice from the other end of the room. Tarley turned to see West walking towards her with the faintest of smiles. "I've just finished with Yvette. She told me there's a book in here about perfecting charms that I should read."

"How'd it go?" Tarley asked.

"I nearly decapitated Yvette but I think I'm improving."

Tarley chuckled and reveled in the unusual calm of West's demeanor. He sauntered over to one of the book cases, scanned the titles and eventually removed a thick book which looked to be centuries old. He started flicking through the dark yellow pages as he sat down in an armchair opposite Tarley.

"I owe you an apology, Tarley," said West.

Tarley looked up her file with confusion. What had happened now?

"I know it's well overdue," West continued, "but I just want you to know that I realise I was a dick and…well, you'll always have an ally in me."

Tarley smiled. "In that case, pick up a bloody file and help me figure these women out."

West grinned, stood up and pulled out another of the large

files from the cabinet. "I don't know if you've noticed, Tarley, but women aren't really my specialty."

Tarley howled with laughter and decided that, perhaps against her better judgement, she would consider it to be a good day.

* * *

Nyra didn't particularly enjoy dining with her mass of followers but, nevertheless, she knew it was wise to allow them to see her from time to time. They had to believe that she was on their side for as long as possible and she knew she couldn't afford to lose them now.

The doors opened and Neb Figmore walked in, bypassing the tables surrounded by the foolish sheep, and headed straight towards Nyra's table. He bowed before she beckoned for him to come closer.

"We've got her. Where do you want the execution to take place?" asked Neb.

Nyra was above huge grins or celebratory cheering but this was the first time in weeks that she had felt truly jubilant. And it was thanks to Neb Figmore, no less.

"The centre of Miraylia," said Nyra, "it's where I used to draw in the biggest crowds."

PART THREE

CHAPTER TWENTY-ONE

The blaze of light that came out of the image crystals caused Darvin to wake up straight away. He slowly sat up in bed, careful not to disturb his wife, and saw Nyra and Neb Figmore standing on a wooden stage, surrounded by the ashes of Miraylia.

Darvin quietly got out of bed and picked up the control box, he didn't want to wake Isla, especially when it was a rarity for her to sleep at all these days. He walked down the corridor and into one of the nearest reception rooms where he laid the crystals down on the coffee table.

"The inevitable has happened," said Neb. "Miraylia and Liliath finally belong to Nyra and it is time that we bow down to our queen."

* * *

Nyra felt ambivalent towards Neb at the best of times but she did admire the way he could capture an audience and give her a suitable introduction. Once he had finished telling the country how powerful Nyra was and how she was the best person to protect them, she gestured for Glyn to bring forward the captives. He pushed Henya and the two other Councillors towards the stage and forced them on to their knees. Thankfully, none of them were crying or sniveling; she couldn't stand that.

"Hello," said Nyra, facing the caption crystals. "I am so sorry to wake you all at this hour but I didn't see the point in waiting. As you can see I have the Premier of Liliath and her remaining ouncillors and I think you will all agree that they should be admired for surviving this long. I'm going to give them one last chance to join me and if they decline I will send them on to the next plain."

She started with the Councillor for Defence; a middle-aged man who was often viewed as being too moody for the job. He instantly declined and begged the people of Liliath not to succumb to Nyra. The Sovran frowned and within seconds the Councillor was writhing on the floor as if he was choking before falling completely still.

Nyra continued down the line of Councillors and as each refused to join Nyra; Henya felt even prouder of them than she had done over the past few months. She was surprised that even at the end of her life it was still important to her that she had surrounded herself with the right people.

"And now for our Premier!" shouted Nyra. "Liliath's voice of reason and the woman who has been in hiding for months rather than supporting her people!" Nyra bent down so that her face was inches away from Henya's. "Tell me, Premier, will you join me?"

Henya remained stoic and silent until Nyra threw her head back in laughter. "It was worth a try," said Nyra.

"Tarley Hillis is still alive!" Henya yelled, staring at the caption crystals. "And she's on our side!"

Glyn was quick to hit Henya across her head but she continued to shout as blood spouted out of her. "Help her! She's…she's the only one who can kill Nyra."

Henya rose into the air as she tried to break her hands free from the rope. It appeared that she was choking but there was nothing around her neck preventing her from breathing. She thrashed around as she desperately tried to breathe in the air around her but her face was turning pale at a rapid rate and within a minute her whole body had become limp. Nyra lowered Henya's body back down to the ground where it lay in front of the three dead Councillors before turning to the caption crystals and smiling.

"From now on Miraylia will be the capital of Liliath and I'm going to tear down that horrendous bridge and replace it with a palace. I will be a fair queen but anyone who dares to defy me will join their *former* Premier in the next plain. Welcome to the new world."

* * *

Tarley's whole body felt cold as Darvin switched off the image crystals. He asked if they needed to see it again but nobody said yes. Brecon reached for Tarley's hand but she pulled it away. Every part of her felt numb.

"What are we going to do, Darvin?" asked Ash.

"We need to end this now," said Tarley. "We have to go up against her sooner rather than later."

"Don't be ridiculous! We still don't know how to kill her and you're not fully in control of your powers yet," shouted Lenna.

"I don't care! Yvette will come up with something!" said Tarley.

"Let's just all calm down," said Yvette. "This is a lot to take in; we can't rush into the first plan we think of."

Lenna gave Tarley a smug look but her cousin still scowled and began to pace the room. She could feel the anger spiraling inside of her; threatening to grow until her only outlet would be her powers.

"Yvette, we can't keep her in the dark any longer," said Darvin.

"What does that mean?" said Tarley and could see the

same look of confusion on every face in the room.

"Tarley, you might want to sit down," said Yvette.

Tarley returned to her seat next to Brecon and this time when he grabbed her hand she held on to it tight. Maybe her perception powers were increasing or maybe it was something else, but Tarley could tell that Yvette was about to stampede through her world once more.

"We've strongly believed for a long time that the only way to truly kill Nyra is for you to conjoin with her and during the enchantment there will be a brief period when you are both weak enough to be killed. But it will be impossible to kill just one of you and for the other to survive."

"What?!" shouted Lenna, "you said that you didn't know much about conjoining enchantments and now you're saying it's the only way to kill Nyra?! Why do you all keep lying to us?"

"We wanted to bide some time, we really hoped that there was another way," said Yvette.

Darvin crossed over to a cabinet with a lock on it. He removed the key from his pocket, unlocked the cabinet and pulled out a file with 'Conjoining' written across it. He handed it to Lenna and sat back down at his desk, his palms sweaty and his head feeling like it could explode at any minute.

Lenna read through the file, tears quickly forming in her eyes as she pulled out more and more pages. She screamed and threw it to the floor as Ash got up from his chair and wrapped his arms around her.

"No, no, no," she sobbed into his shoulder.

Every set of eyes appeared to be on Tarley as she picked up the papers and began to read. As she read, Lenna explained through sobs and stutters its content to the group. The papers documented several experiments that had taken place on Sovrans over the centuries and all over the world. Hundreds of people had tried to transfer a Sovran's power to a non-Sovran but none of them had been successful. Several had managed to conjoin the two bodies but never were they able to just transfer the powers. However, during all the experiments there had been a point when both people had not been bodies but what had been described as floating energies; smoke that seemed to swirl in the air. Some of the experimenters had manipulated their subjects when they were in this state and once the energies dispersed, their bodies returned. Lifeless.

As soon as Lenna had stopped speaking there was uproar in the room. Everyone seemed to be proposing an alternative plan but Tarley could see the holes in all of them. Nyra could not be defeated by a sword, she could not be defeated by the strongest of enchantments and the energy source that had been used to subdue her would only yield the same result.

Tarley silenced them all; everyone kept moving their mouths but no words were spoken.

"I said we have to end this and I meant it," said Tarley. "You have one week to come up with an alternative plan otherwise I'm going straight to Nyra and you kill us both."

* * *

Neb filled two glasses with the finest wine that Miraylia had to offer and handed one to Nyra.

"To Henya," said Neb, smirking, as he lifted his glass.

"To the Premier," said Nyra, clinking her glass against Neb's. "I must say Neb that you have proven to be very useful."

'Useful' wasn't exactly the kind of praise that he looked for but Neb wasn't going to argue with her. The more he was allowed to be in her presence the more he realised just how far her power could stretch. Liliath was hers now, even if Tarley remained alive, and no one had dared to challenge her.

Liliath wasn't the most powerful country in the world but it held enough gravitas that any other Premier would have to seriously consider the risk before attacking. After all, those that had tried to provide aid had disappeared halfway across the sea. Why bother, now? The people of Liliath would be happy now that they had Nyra to protect them.

"How are we going to kill the girl?" Neb asked.

"The plan remains unchanged. I will conjoin with her and her mortal body will die in the process."

"And now that your army is grown it should be easier to restrain her."

"Precisely."

They finished their wine in silence before Nyra told Neb to leave; she said she needed to rest but the truth was that she had grown bored of him.

She poured herself another glass of wine and thought about Delyth. Nyra was very tempted to resurrect her just long enough for her to see Nyra fully restored to her powers. But she doubted that her sister would accept the call. Nyra had offered Delyth the world and much more but she preferred to be among the masses, to be boring and plain. There had been nothing extraordinary about her sister, she had been the second daughter in every sense, and Nyra had tried her best to make their parents share their love but her attempts always failed. Delyth never seemed fazed by this and neither did she resent Nyra, which is why Nyra had been so hurt when Delyth had turned on her. That was the last time she had allowed herself to feel anything for a non-Sovran. They may have had the upper hand for centuries but it was now time for the scales to tilt back to where they belonged. Delyth's legacy would soon end.

* * *

Tarley had gone straight to her room and locked the door. Thankfully, no one had followed her. She wasn't ready to talk to anyone yet and she couldn't sleep. She thought she would be angrier with Yvette and Darvin for lying to her for so long but she understood and it seemed to make her more empathetic. She had longed for Darvin's job and knew that if she were in the same position she would have taken the same approach. You don't tell an unpredictable asset information that could endanger more people.

And now she was readying herself for death. Tarley highly doubted that this whole mess would end simply with Nyra dead and her able to live a carefree life as if nothing had ever happened. She had never been more grateful for her guard training than in that moment; dying on the bridge wasn't likely but if you lived without acknowledging its possibility you were a fool.

Tarley sat on the edge of her bed and looked around. She thought of all the space around her and her proximity to every object in the room. She focused on her wardrobe, the carpet, the bed side lamp and everything else, trying to sense their weight and the energy they exerted. She started to feel her own presence clashing against the atmosphere, fighting to take hold. There were powers hitting her from every angle, desperate to penetrate her skin as her mind glowed at the vitality of the room. There was so much *life* around her that she didn't know was there and it was all attempting to stay strong amongst the constant shift in the atmosphere. There was a continuous battle that she had suddenly found herself at the heart of and, despite her apprehension, she was amazed by its relentlessness. Tarley could see the brittle beauty in its unsettledness.

She focused on the wardrobe in front of her, its presence was domineering on her mind, and slowly managed to edge it forward so that it was in line with the bed before moving it back. As she did she could sense the shift in power in the room and the other objects and the air itself seemed to retract in response. Soon she was sending every entity in the room up into the air and twirling them around, delighting in the peaks and troughs of the energy changes.

Once she had finally grown bored she set everything back down and stood in the centre of the room. Her own energy was more commanding than she had ever experienced; she could feel her place in the ether much more strongly than anything else. She almost felt that she was swaying between two worlds; the one she lived in was pulling her back but the other promised power like no other.

She used the strength from this other world to push her further into her own plain and she could soon feel a slight tremble in her feet. The energies from the two realms felt like monsters as they grew and collided with each other, gently lifting her whole body into the air. The space below her felt like a powerful, silent wind that was forcing her further towards the sky. She reached up to touch the ceiling and giggled. She had never felt safer.

The room instantly turned to black and Tarley couldn't even see her own hands or feet. She could feel the ground beneath her but she had no recollection of lowering herself back down.

"Is someone there?" said a quivering voice, "can you help?"

Tarley's heart instantly began to race, she knew the voice all too well.

"Dad?! Dad, where are you?!" Tarley shouted.

She took a step forward but as she did she found herself back in her room in Bray, hurtling towards the ground.

She stood up straight away, ignoring the pain in her back, and tried to get back to Gwyl. She could feel his realm battling to get through to her but it was so much fainter than it had been before. The more she tried to contact him the weaker the connection became.

She threw herself on to the bed in tears and hugged her knees. She couldn't save him; she didn't have time. No one would see Gwyl Hillis again.

* * *

The next morning Tarley had never seen so many people in the archive at one time. Everyone who had been privy to her ultimatum in the early hours of the morning had decided to spend their day splitting their time between the library and researching every piece of information they had on Nyra.

Tarley was once again researching The Heirs in an attempt to forget about Gwyl. During her intermittent sleep the night before all she could hear was his voice, begging her to come back and save him.

She wasn't really looking for anything that could help stop Nyra; instead she just wanted to know everything she could about the lives of The Heirs. At times she felt like she was reading an elongated soap opera; there were lovers, affairs, children, crimes, spouses and every other aspect of life that makes a person who they are. Tarley was fascinated by all of them and how their powers worked. Only a couple of them fully embraced their gifts whereas the others chose to hide them as much as possible. Even so, Tarley could tell that they were formidable women who would rather die than not fight for something they believed in, even if it was just the chance for their child to go to the right school.

Brecon caught Tarley's eye but quickly returned to his book. Just as Tarley had managed to stop crying at about three in the morning, Brecon came into her room and shouted at her for an hour. He'd begged her to change her mind, telling her that he wasn't the only one who would be devastated if she went through with her plan.

"There's no guarantee it will work," he had said. "And Nyra will *still* be winning but we'd be left without you!"

"Far too many people have died, Brecon!" Tarley yelled, not caring who she woke up. "It's cowardice for me to stay hidden any longer!"

"You speak as if you *want* to die."

Tarley tried to stop them but the tears hit her eyes before she could even comprehend they were there. She took Brecon's hand in her own and when he didn't snatch it away she felt her chest tighten just a little more.

"Of course I don't want to die. I want to stay here with you and pretend that none of this is going on. But it is and I'm the only one who has a chance to end it."

"But you don't have to do that in a week's time!"

The argument had seemed endless; Tarley kept telling him that she didn't want any more death and Brecon would retaliate by saying that if Nyra regained all her powers then Liliath would be synonymous with death forever.

All she had wanted him to do was wrap his arms around her. She was worried that he had touched her for the last time and despite knowing that it would happen she had not embraced it as much as she should have.

Lenna and Macklyn hadn't been any less snappy towards her; they had both promised not to tell Carida, Baodor and Ivy but that didn't stop them yelling at Tarley. All she had heard all morning was how stupid and selfish she was being, were her family not worth enough that she was willing to fight for them? Eventually they gave up, fell silent and decided to shift their focus on to the many books that Bray housed.

Rhoswen came in with cups of tea for everyone, which they silently took and quietly thanked her for but their attention was firmly fixed on whatever book was in front of them. She sat down next to Tarley and placed a mug in front of her, ordering her to drink it.

"Tarley, I know you want it all to stop, for people not to die anymore, but-"

"-please, Rhos. Don't do this," said Tarley.

"Just think about it! If we take our time and plan this properly we'll save more lives than by rushing in. What if everything goes wrong?"

Tarley kissed her on the cheek, "Thanks for the tea."

Rhoswen sighed and joined Ash and Lenna in trawling through a high pile of books on enchantments. She could see the fear on everyone's faces, it was a look she was more than familiar with, but, for once, she couldn't see a way to stop it.

As the days raced forward more time was spent in the library, more questions were asked and more dead ends were met.

Tarley avoided her mother as much as she could, feeling a tight pang in her chest every time Carida asked her if she could spare her ten minutes of her time. Tarley was all too aware that these would be the last moments they would have together but she felt as if she would never be ready to face them.

Brecon and Lenna exchanged as little dialogue with her as they could and Tarley was both grateful and yet pined to be with them. She wanted to say goodbye but the words and feelings wouldn't fully form.

* * *

Darvin sat at his desk guzzling coffee as he read through the conjoining hex for the thousandth time. Hexes were permanent until a counter-hex was performed but he knew that this would be the one exception to the rule. There was no way that Tarley would be coming back from this.

The doubts were pickling his brain, again, but he was used to them by now. Should he be doing this? What kind of monster was he? How would he feel if it was one of his girls?

He had been honoured when he had been offered a job in Nyra's Patrol all those years ago but every birthday that Tarley reached had squeezed his heart a little tighter. He was meant to be prepared for her to be the one that stopped Nyra but he'd always hoped that her awakening wouldn't be in his lifetime. All he'd wanted was to die an old man, knowing that Tarley would also meet the same fate. The next Heir would be the one.

A fine guard you are, he had thought. The juniors would jump into a fight as soon as the order was given and keep going until they were either dead or told to stop. And here he was; the most senior guard on the bridge and he was worried that when the time came he wouldn't be able to pick up his sword.

There was a knock on the door and when he yelled for them to come in, Tarley walked into the room and sat down in one of the chairs opposite his desk. Seconds later Yvette floated in to be greeted by two confused faces.

"I sensed that this was a meeting I should be at," said Yvette, also detecting a huge increase in strength from Tarley. Yvette tried to remain expressionless but she wasn't sure she was successful; she couldn't remember a time when she had ever been in the presence of such power. Even during Nyra's surges she had never felt this overwhelmed.

"Tarley, what's going on?" asked Darvin.

"I don't want to wait another four days," said Tarley. "I want to do it tomorrow, is that possible?"

Darvin looked towards Yvette, who gave such a small nod that it was barely noticeable.

"Nyra will obviously welcome you with open arms but we need to make sure that we can contain the hex so that we can kill her," said Darvin.

"I can perform the hex but Nyra won't trust me to do it; she'll probably want Turner to try again. And you'll have to go alone," said Yvette.

The ease at which the words rolled off Yvette's tongue did nothing to comfort Tarley.

"We'll need to immobilise the Devoted during the hex, which means we need more people," continued Yvette. "We have seven Sovrans excluding you and I but convincing them all to help will be a task and I'm not entirely convinced they're powerful enough to restrain Nyra's inner circle. But they're all we have."

"They don't have a choice. Promise them titles or gold or whatever once it's over but they *must* do this and they *must* keep it to themselves," said Tarley.

"Agreed," said Darvin. "I'll send one of the senior members of the Patrol into Miraylia straight away to see if Nyra is still in the mountains and to see how big her army is."

"Now we just need to figure out how we kill this bitch," said Tarley.

* * *

Lenna was sat next to Ash and felt like she had read the same sentence about fifty times. There was a stack of books next to her and they all seemed to be full of gibberish rather than having anything useful to say. Words had somehow become a puzzle that she was struggling to work out.

"Ash," whispered Lenna, "have you found anything?"

She felt like she had asked him this question countless times but even so, she still hoped his answer would differ.

Ash shook his head. "I feel like I've looked through a million books on tonics and potions and none of them are any use."

"Do you think…," Lenna couldn't even finish her sentence; just the thought of what she was about to say made her hate herself.

"I don't know," said Ash, grabbing her hand. "But we're not going to stop looking for an alternative. We've still got time."

The truth was the more he read the more certain he was that the only way to kill Nyra was to kill Tarley, too. But how could he admit that to the person who loved her most?

* * *

Dinner that evening was a quieter affair than usual with the only conversation involving requests to pass the salt shaker. Tarley was surprised anyone had been happy to sit on the same table as her but she was grateful. She couldn't tell them but it meant a lot to her that they were all together for her last meal.

Tarley looked at Lenna; the bags under her eyes more prominent than ever, and felt her stomach turning over and over. They were so close now but Tarley still felt like she hadn't done enough to apologise to her cousin. Ever since they had been reunited the majority of their focus had been on Tarley. Lenna hadn't deserved any of this.

As Lenna stood up to leave Tarley gripped her fork, silently reiterating that she couldn't say goodbye. She had to act as if this was any other night. No tears, no goodbyes and no arguments.

Tarley soon made her own excuses and left the room, silently casting every enchantment she could so that Yvette couldn't sense what she was about to do.

* * *

Mabli knew how to appear calm in the gravest of situations but she was surprisingly worried that she was faltering. As Darvin explained what Tarley was intending to do the next day Mabli found her palms becoming increasingly sweaty. She was the first to admit that she would never be best friends with Tarley, she had enough bruises to remind her, and she always knew this day could come but now that it was here she felt like she was having some sort of out of body experience. She could hear what Darvin was saying but the words felt wrong somehow, as if he was speaking another language or talking to someone else.

But the orders were clear. She was finally going to do it. She was going to help kill Tarley Hillis.

"You need to take five of the best from the Patrol, go into Miraylia tonight and report back. And don't take any of the new members; they're too close to Tarley," said Darvin.

"Yes, hyd," said Mabli and left the room, hoping that the queasiness in her stomach would disappear before she reached Miraylia.

* * *

Tarley stood in the centre of the ruined castle and closed her eyes. This was a risk. If she died before tomorrow Liliath would have to wait decades for their chance again, and that's if it came at all.

Power. Energies. Enchantments. Tarley still didn't fully

understand them but she could feel them within her and somehow knew how to manipulate them. She felt like a sculptor looking for her masterpiece within the clay.

She found it easier to become attune to the world in the silence and this was the perfect place. The breeze made her face feel cold but she liked it; she felt closer to what was around her and what was not. She could slowly start to feel the separation between worlds and their differences seeped into every part of her. They were all vying for her attention; pulling her closer to them and away from what she knew was real. She allowed herself to float into this nothing-world that was still overcome with activity clashing against her. Across the noise she could feel them coming to her; they could hear her. She was yelling and they were joining the rally. Their realms were splitting and re-joining in all the wrong places but that's what they needed. They needed a shift and convergence all at the same time.

Tarley finally opened her eyes and gasped. It had worked.

* * *

Brecon was lying on his bed and staring at the ceiling. The book he held in his hand had proven to be just as futile as the last thirty-two. He was an intelligent man but he was no Sovran; even some of the simpler books were pure gibberish to him.

He was going to lose her.

She was the one leaving this time but she wouldn't be coming back. They would not find each other again in this world. Even so, he still couldn't imagine not seeing her every day, being made fun of for no reason or just catching a glimpse of her when she wasn't paying attention to him. She was infuriating and fascinating in equal measure.

The knock on the door broke him from his thoughts and if it hadn't been Tarley calling from the other side he probably would have pretended to be asleep. He was angry but she could always pull him back. He got up and unlocked the door to find her standing in the corridor looking more sheepish than he'd ever seen her.

"Are you going to invite me in?" said Tarley.

Brecon stepped back and gestured for her to enter before locking the door once more. It was unlikely but he wouldn't put it past Ash to come storming in right now.

"I know you're still mad at me," said Tarley.

"It's not that I'm mad, I-"

"-we don't need to go over it all again. I really am sorry for all of this." She moved closer to him and dared to wrap her arms around his waist whilst placing her head on his chest. She wished she could express how grateful she was that he hadn't backed away from her but the moment was too fragile. "Can we have one night without shouting and arguing? I just want to lie next to you and pretend everything is perfect."

"I can do that," said Brecon and led her towards the bed.

Tarley curled up next to him and placed her head once more on his chest in order to hear the rhythm of his heart; she didn't have anymore words for him. Their end was coming and she ached to not ruin it with triviality.

Brecon held her close as his head gently fell on to hers and nuzzled into her hair. She was all he wanted, now and always.

CHAPTER TWENTY-TWO

Tarley waited until Brecon was in a deep sleep before she left. She wanted to stay but she knew the longer she allowed herself to be curled up in his arms, the harder it would be to leave. As she made to leave she couldn't help but stare at him and the calmness of his breathing; even the way his chest rose and fell made her heart break just a little bit more. She crept back over to the bed and kissed his forehead one last time. He would never truly know what he had meant to her but it was less cruel that way.

"I love you," she whispered before returning to her room. She quickly changed into her fighting clothes and grabbed the bag she had already packed before heading to the training room.

You were always going to die in armour, weren't you?

Yvette, Darvin and two of the Patrol's Sovrans were already waiting for her, passing around weapons and checking for faults. Nobody spoke but Tarley could feel the anxiety pouring off them and it only made her more nervous.

Yvette gave her a slight nod before she busied herself with sealing her remaining tonics while Darvin ignored her completely. It seemed that every sword he had needed to be checked at least twenty times before he placed it in a scabbard.

The other Sovrans and senior Patrol members began to join them with West being the last to arrive. The hurt look he gave Tarley made her want to weep.

"Please, Tarley, don't do this," said West. "Your family will be heart broken."

"And they'll be dead if I don't. I understand if you don't want to help but I really want you there, West. It would make me feel safe in a weird way. You're the only family I'll have there when it happens," said Tarley.

"Families don't stand by and watch each other die!"

"No, they help save them. And this is the only way to save Macklyn and everyone else I love."

"You can't blackmail me like that."

Tarley sighed, "Fine, go back to bed. But I mean it; I want you by my side, West."

He scowled and headed over to Darvin to retrieve what weapons were left and hide them in his jacket. All he could think about was sneaking away from Macklyn as he lay in bed completely unaware.

"I think that's everyone," Yvette shouted. "Let's go over the plan once more."

Everyone in the room had relayed their role in the mission to themselves a thousand times during the course of the night but that didn't stop them listening to Yvette. Mabli had reported back a few hours ago that Nyra and her followers had moved away from the mountains and were situated in The Arben Tower. They'd already begun tearing down the gates.

Once everyone was laden with as many weapons as they could carry they left Bray and climbed into the Patrol's vans. Tarley couldn't bring herself to look back as they drove

away.

* * *

Nyra looked out of the tower as her workers began to dismantle The Fire Gate. She wanted to just wave her arm and cause the whole bridge to collapse but she wasn't strong enough for that just yet. And she wanted this fortress gone as quickly as possible.

Hart, Glyn, Turner and Neb began to filter into the room along with every Sovran that Nyra had in her ranks. She was starting to feel the girl getting restless, it was only slight but enough to know that the time would soon be upon them. Soon she would truly be a queen and she needed to ensure that her subjects would be grateful.

* * *

The nerves, fear and anticipation rioting through the van was threatening to send Tarley into a meltdown. She could feel everyone's anxieties beating down on her like a thunderstorm, pressuring her to send them back to Bray. This wasn't their fight. They could die and it would be in Tarley's name.

All she could hope for was that they managed to kill Nyra before she could turn on them. Their plan was precarious at best, which went against every piece of training that Tarley had ever had.

Being a guard felt like a dream that Tarley was slowly losing memory of. She knew that every guard and commander who had joined the Patrol felt the same way but doubted they felt it the way she did. Her blood was in the bridge more than she had ever known; she was tied to it in a way that no other guard ever was and now she was going to die there.

There would be no relatives paying their last respects or a husband's hand to hold as she drew her last breath. She didn't think she was scared of dying but she was scared of what could happen. She might turn into a floating nothingness that could still feel and think but would be unable to act. How would that even feel? To be present but not have a physical body? She wondered how Nyra coped for all those years, existing in a state of in-between with no way of breaking free. Tarley understood the anger and the fear and could only hope that she wasn't condemned to the same fate.

"There's still time to stop this," West whispered to Tarley.

"No," said Tarley. "Today's the day she dies for good. No matter what."

* * *

Mabli pulled her hood down even further as she crossed Victory Road; the city was near enough soulless but she still couldn't risk being spotted. She turned down a nearby alley and crouched down behind a group of bins that had rubbish pouring out of them. She'd spent all night observing the bridge and running across the city and she was tired. The job had always been draining but that night felt even more so; uncertainty had not been an emotion she often experienced and it was determined to catch up with her.

Mabli didn't know if she even *liked* Tarley. She supposed that she respected her but she didn't think that would ever be enough to make her doubt herself. And yet she'd spent all night being snappy with the Patrol, barking orders and doing her best to avoid making a decision.

Orders. Split second decisions. Protocol. That was her life and she'd loved it. And she knew that Tarley had, too.

She reached into her pocket and pulled out her calling crystals, placed them into their boxes and tapped in the number, unsure whether she wanted someone to answer.

* * *

A faint blue light burst into Lenna's room along with the loud buzzing that indicated someone was calling her. She groaned as she pushed Ash away from her and struggled out of bed.

The words 'Unknown' floated in the air but she placed a crystal in the 'Answer' box nonetheless. After all, no one outside of the Patrol had the number. Mabli soon appeared looking exhausted and nervous all at the same time as if she'd just been caught doing something she shouldn't have been.

"Lenna!" Mabli shouted, almost shocked.

By this point Ash was now firmly awake and sitting on the edge of the bed wondering why he wasn't being allowed to sleep.

"Yes, well done," said Lenna.

"We don't have time for sarcasm, Tarley's going after Nyra today!"

"WHAT?!" Lenna bellowed.

"All the Sovrans, Darvin and Yvette are with her. I don't know what you can do but…do something!"

"How long have you known about this?" Ash asked.

"That doesn't matter! You need to see if she's already left and if she has, go after her. They're heading for the bridge."

Lenna grabbed Ash to steady herself, she felt like she could throw up, pass out or enter hysterics at any moment. Within the space of a second a million different thoughts and scenarios had gone flying through her head and they all terrified her.

"I have to go; someone might see me. Call me back when you have a plan," said Mabli before disappearing.

"You check her bedroom and the training rooms, I'll do everything else," said Ash and before Lenna could comprehend what he was saying he was running out the door.

Lenna did as she was told and sprinted towards Tarley's room; she knew she wouldn't be there as soon as she saw the door was ajar. She'd never known Tarley to keep a door unlocked. She checked every reception room but they were empty; people were beginning to wake up but Lenna didn't know what she should say, or even if she should say anything at all. She needed Darvin or Yvette but they were too busy betraying her. She saw Ash running towards her but the small grain of hope she had vanished as soon as he shook his head.

"We need to get everyone into the main hall," said Lenna. "Fuck! Who's going to tell Aunty Carida? And Macklyn…and…and…,"

Ash pulled her close and kissed the top of her head. "Just get everyone into the hall. We're going to sort this."

* * *

Brecon was more concerned about his half empty bed than the commotion outside. The noise had caused him to stir but the silence of his room had woken him up. He couldn't hear her moving around or even the sound of her breathing.

He got dressed and stepped into the corridor to see crowds of people rushing towards the stairs and amongst them he could see Ash marching towards him.

"Why do I feel like something weird is going on?" Brecon asked.

"Because it is," said Ash. "Tarley's gone; we need to get to the main hall right now."

Despite his years of training Brecon's heart immediately began to sprint inside his chest as angry tears threatened to break through. He nodded at Ash before shutting the door and racing around the room searching for clothes and what little weapons he'd brought with him. His head couldn't keep pace with the amount of emotions surging through his body but if he knew one thing it was that he was about to throw himself into whatever battle was before him with everything he had.

* * *

Lenna wasn't a huge fan of public speaking but she had to remind herself that she never bit her tongue and if that character trait was ever needed, it was now. She climbed on to the stage and, somehow, managed to yell loud enough that the whole room fell silent.

"If you think that letting Tarley die is the only way to defeat Nyra then there's nothing I can say to convince you otherwise," Lenna shouted. "But if *anyone* in this room thinks she deserves more than this, more time to investigate and think rather than acting out of guilt and fear, you must arm yourselves and join me in stopping her."

Lenna felt like half the room cheered in agreement whereas the other half mumbled something and looked at the floor. She knew that having half the room on her side was better than nothing but when faced with Nyra's Sovrans Lenna wasn't sure how long they would all last.

"I'm not forcing anyone to come with me," Lenna continued. "But please just put yourself in my position for two minutes. Someone I love is going to die for the sake of some ridiculous notion of duty. She's going to die to save people who don't even like her! If that was someone close to you wouldn't you ask everyone you knew to help save them?"

Lenna could see various people in the crowd glancing over at their loved ones, exchanging longing looks or trying to grab their hands whereas others simply looked at their feet.

"Whether you joined The Inquiry or Nyra's Patrol you did so because you wanted to protect something. I need to protect Tarley and I am begging that even if you don't see enough value in her, you'll see enough value in that."

Lenna looked down at Carida, Macklyn and Baodor to see all three of them gripping each other's hands and staring back at her with such ferocity that she knew they approved. She tried hard not to get lost in the moment but for the first time in years she felt like she had her family back.

Lenna ordered those who were ready to fight to head straight to the armoury and within minutes there was chaos in the hallways. People were begging their families to fight, others were begging to stay, and amongst the furore Ash was doing his best to make it back to his room so he could alert the other bases.

He knew it would take them all at least three hours to reach Miraylia with those in Moorland perhaps taking twice as long. He was confident that they would join the fight but he didn't want to ponder if they'd make it there in time to stop Tarley. He managed to get through to them all on his first attempt and they assured him that they would bring every weapon and Sovran they could find.

"The chances are I won't be able to find you," Ash had said, "but DO NOT stop looking for Tarley until either myself, Lenna, Penn, Macklyn or Brecon tell you otherwise. We can't even trust Darvin and Yvette on this one."

Once he was finished he pushed his way back through the crowds towards the armoury to find several members debating over whether they would be allowed to take the ancient swords with them.

"Take it all!" Carida shouted, placing a rather sharp looking short sword in her scabbard. "We need to do whatever we can to get my daughter back."

Ash didn't hesitate in grabbing one of the heaviest, most bejewelled swords that had been hanging in the armoury. He'd been admiring it for months and if he didn't make it through this fight he would be happy knowing he had died with it in his hand.

"How are you with a sword?" Penn asked Carida.

"Don't even go there, Penn. I'm married to a commander and the mother to two of the best guards that bridge has ever seen. I know how to use a fucking sword."

As Carida marched out of the base, Penn quickly followed and was suddenly determined not to let her out of his sight.

* * *

Brecon and Lenna had settled into an efficient system of placing everyone in the small number of vans that they had. They split most of their strongest and mediocre fighters into the vans whereas the rest were instructed to walk into the nearest town and steal whatever cars they could. Each group was given a commander and a set of calling crystals. Once they were in Miraylia they were to head straight to the bridge and begin looking for Tarley. If they saw her the mission was to immobilise her and get her out of the city. Of course, the likelihood was that the Devoted would erupt into battle and the Patrol would have no choice but to fight.

"It's a very messy plan," said Macklyn as he watched the second van leave.

"We don't have time for anything better," said Lenna.

"I'm not disagreeing. Just saying."

"Well don't!"

Lenna scowled and walked off to yell at the Patrol members who still hadn't got into a vehicle. They quickly scurried into the nearest van and soon the only one left was her group's. She turned around to see Brecon, Macklyn, Penn and the rest of her group staring back at her. She wasn't sure if it was fear or uncertainty in their eyes but either way it made her feel lost. How could she tell them how to behave when she was so terrified herself? She was asking people to die for one person; when had her views changed so much?

"Right, let's go!" Lenna shouted.

"Our group doesn't have a commander," said Brecon as he climbed into the driver's seat.

"I didn't think we'd need one," said Lenna.

"We think we do and we want it to be you," said Carida.

Lenna looked at all their faces and no one seemed to be objecting. Baodor was even nodding his head towards her.

"Right. Okay. Well in that case I'm sitting in the front with Brecon," she said and promptly got in the van before slamming the door shut.

Once everyone was inside Brecon placed the crystals into their holes and the van began to chug forward. He knew he shouldn't have been the one driving but he needed something to distract him. For the last hour all he could see was a thousand different ways in which Tarley could die and he wasn't by her side when it happened.

She wasn't old or surrounded by her family like he would want. Instead, she was engulfed by flames or asphyxiated like Henya and all while Nyra looked on and smiled.

* * *

Tarley stayed towards the back of the group as they walked down the hill into Miraylia. No one was speaking but that didn't matter; their doubt was so entrenched in the atmosphere that Tarley wouldn't have been surprised if a non-Sovran had felt it.

She wished that she couldn't feel their torture all over her skin, not because it saddened her or made her feel guilty but because she didn't want the distraction. So much of their plan relied on luck and it would be easier if she couldn't feel anything at all. If she had to die she didn't want to enter the new realm thinking about strangers.

Was that selfish; to want her own death? To float into the ether without a thought for anything? She wasn't so sure.

The uneven rhythm of their boots on the grass became addictive the nearer to the city they got. The sound meant that they were moving, no one was stopping and everyone was okay. They were the only sounds Tarley could bear to hear in that moment. Once they reached the outskirts Yvette made everyone pause to drink their water and eat whatever snacks they had brought with them but only a couple of them could handle it. West tried to hand Tarley an oat bar but she just shook her head. They were soon on the cobbled streets of the city and any concerns they had about being spotted were soon lost; no one was on the streets.

But Tarley could still sense them.

They were hiding in the cracks of the bricks and cowering in poorly built shelters. She had felt fear so many times before but never with so much despair, too. Whenever Tarley felt frightened there had always been a sense of hope driving her forward but now she was struggling to find even a trace of it in the ashes of the city. There was a purity to their terror that horrified Tarley more than any fight ever could.

The group turned down several streets before stopping next to The Tulip where they had agreed to meet Mabli and the other Patrol members. The pub had a huge hole in the roof but the building had remained intact despite the many attacks its city had faced. The morning was heading towards noon and the sun seemed to be mocking every grey brick that was below it. The light shone down on the pub like a spotlight but it was no longer a trophy to be shown off. There was only an unnatural emptiness.

"They should be here," said Darvin. "Can you sense them, Yvette?"

"No. If they're not here in five minutes we're going to have to go," Yvette replied.

Tarley tried to sense Mabli; she thought about the striking glares that were as natural to her as a child smiling and she thought about the way she could knock over someone twice her size with half the effort. But there was nothing.

"Where do you think she is?" asked West.

"I have no idea, which is why I'm so worried. This isn't like her," said Darvin.

"Anyone could be along at any moment and ruin this," said Yvette. "I'm sorry, Darvin, but we *have* to go."

Darvin nodded and they all began to walk towards Victory Road, each of them silently reciting their various parts of the plan.

* * *

Nyra enjoyed the look on their faces as she spoke; they looked like attentive puppies eager to learn a new trick, especially Neb. His desperation for power made him valuable but Nyra knew that he had to be monitored more than most.

Turner's face suddenly changed; his interest had vanished to be replaced with a concern that transcended the room. Nyra could almost feel his heartbeat racing from across the table.

"Turner, what's wrong?" said Nyra.

"There are Sovrans approaching the bridge," said Turner. "Two of them are strong; very strong. They're readying themselves to fight."

"Get on the bridge now and tell everyone to arm themselves! *No one* is to refuse."

All three of the men stood up and rushed out of the room towards the armoury. Nyra crossed over to the window and could see a group of people seemingly armed with every weapon in Miraylia slowly walking into view. There was a woman with very short hair standing next to the cretin who had run the bridge and neither of them seemed daunted by the hundreds of workers in front of them. Behind them was a young woman who was gripping her sword so confidently it was as if it was a natural extension of her body.

Perhaps the waiting had finally become too much or, maybe, the death that surrounded her had played on her guilt in that insufferable way of humans. Either way, they both knew how this was going to end and neither of them liked putting off the inevitable.

It was finally time.

* * *

Mabli had never been a smoker but she suspected if she had been then this would be the moment where she ploughed through a pack of twenty cigarettes in less than ten minutes. She and the other Patrol members were waiting in an alleyway just a few minutes away from what remained of the academy. Random pieces of gym equipment and bed frames littered the yard and shone eerily in the sun. Everyone knew they were now from a part of history that would never be visited again.

Mabli supposed she was a traitor now, although the laws of Liliath seemed to disappear once Nyra had broken free. Her duty was to protect her country and its people but she was now potentially at the vanguard of its demise. If Tarley continued to live would they ever really find an alternative plan? She kept wondering if it was someone she didn't know in Tarley's position if she'd still try to stop them. Their death would save the country. One life in exchange for millions.

"They were faster than I expected," said Netta as she nodded down the road.

Mabli looked to see several black vans speeding into view and stopping abruptly outside the academy. As Lenna jumped out Mabli ran out of the alleyway to meet her, grateful that she now had allies to share her burden with.

"What's the latest?" said Lenna.

"We saw them about two miles from the bridge half an hour ago," said Mabli.

"Okay, everyone in the vans," ordered Lenna. "We can get there in less than ten minutes if we hurry."

* * *

Tarley stood behind Yvette and stared at Neb Figmore as he sloppily held his sword in front of him. He was hiding behind Turner and Glyn but there was no mistaking the malice in his eyes. He wanted Tarley's blood almost as much as he wanted to rule by Nyra's side.

"Have you come to hand yourself over?" Turner shouted at Tarley, ignoring the Sovrans that surrounded her.

"What do you think?" said Tarley, knocking the swords out of every pair of hands she could see.

Turner laughed as he threw a red ball of energy in Tarley's

direction but she quickly deflected it with her own enchantment, creating momentary flames that were over six-foot high. Once they had disappeared every Sovran in the Patrol began to use their powers in earnest; using the elements to create mini storms, hurling swords towards the nearest body and casting charms that paralysed people in seconds.

Tarley ran towards Turner, readying herself to unleash a great hex that would immobilise him instantly but as she raised her arms he turned and caught her in a binding charm. As she fell to the ground squirming she could see each of her companions slowly lowering their arms and allowing themselves to be captured by any of the Devoted who would have them.

CHAPTER TWENTY-THREE

Hart and Glyn stood either side of Tarley, squeezing her arms in their grip. They pushed her into the centre of the large circle that was made up of Nyra's followers and forced her on to her knees. Yvette and the rest of the Patrol had each been captured and had sharp knives held against their throats but they didn't need to speak for Tarley to know that they were okay. She could feel their energy whizzing around the circle; bouncing off every Sovran who had volunteered to help. Their power was building as she could see each of their captors ever so slowly lose the grip on their knives.

Tarley looked up to see a ripple through the crowds as they allowed Nyra to walk through. Her hair fell in shiny curls and she wore a navy-blue tunic and trousers that were considerably more understated compared to her usual attire.

Tarley could feel a spike in the atmosphere and her head jerked towards the crowd. Their animalistic desire to see her die was overwhelming but spotted amongst the hate was a growing sense of love and a need to protect. It felt maternal, familial and overpowering all at the same time.

"Slit her throat!"

"We're here for you, Tarley."

"I want to see her bleed."
"We can end this together."
"Today it ends."

Nyra gestured for Hart and Glyn to step back before she stopped just centimetres in front of Tarley. Turner stood by her side and glared at Tarley. She could feel his desire for her death permeating the air, cutting through everyone's emotions to make her feel sick at the sight of him.

"Stand up," Nyra ordered and Tarley obeyed. "You have become so powerful; I can feel it."

"Yes," said Tarley.

Nyra smirked.

Turner placed Tarley's hand on top of Nyra's and began to twist his own in an obscure pattern above, forming the grey smoke-like energy that Tarley had been studying for days. She had memorised the ceremony and its intricacies from every book she could get on the subject. She now knew that Turner was drawing on every element, no matter how big or small, from the atmosphere and twisting it into an energy source that could destroy even the strongest of Sovrans.

Tarley quickly glanced around her to see that Yvette, West and everyone else in an arm lock was staring back at her, unwilling to break their gaze. Tarley had never felt so much power readying to envelop her; it was both beautiful and terrifying. She felt like the whole world was coming for her to take her back to a realm where power ran freely with no rules.

So much power; too much to control.

A loud scream from the back of the crowd caused it to immediately disperse as the sound of blades and arrows tore through it. Tarley saw the shock on Yvette's face before she could fathom its source but when she looked she saw Penn and Macklyn racing through the horde of people, slashing their swords, quickly followed by what Tarley could only assume was the whole of Bray.

Rhoswen soon came into view battling a man a head taller

than her and double her weight. He was grinning every time he took a swipe at her but all she needed was to distract him with her own devilish smile before she plunged her sword into his abdomen.

"You get the fuck away from her!" roared Lenna as she sprinted towards Nyra, her sword outstretched.

Brecon and Macklyn each took one of Tarley's arms and began to drag her away while Lenna stood in front of them, slicing anyone who dared to push past her.

West threw back his captor with such force that he landed twenty feet away from him. He raced towards Lenna but Turner had already seen him and sent an offensive charm his way. West ducked, barely avoiding the energy, and retaliated with a jinx that sent Turner high into the air and brought him back down to the ground just as quickly.

Nyra screamed as she saw a pool of blood begin to form around his lifeless body. She raised her arm and sent a fireball towards West but he was already battling another of the Devoted and didn't notice until Penn had thrown himself on to West and forced him on to the ground. The fire quickly spread over Penn's body, causing him to writhe and cry out in agony. West scrambled to his side but within seconds the fire had turned to smoke and Penn lay still on the concrete, his eyes seemingly still resting on West.

Tarley continued to scream as she was dragged further away from the chaos. She tried to push the three of them away from her but even with her powers she was not strong enough. Their minds and energies were too determined and strong willed for her to take on all three.

"She killed Penn!" Tarley screamed. "You shouldn't have come here!"

"He came here to save you and we're going to honour his wish," said Brecon.

* * *

Glyn ordered a group of the Devoted to escort Nyra to the

tower while everyone else was instructed to bring back Tarley no matter what. However, Nyra's Patrol had formed a blockade the length of the bridge and, despite being extremely outnumbered, they were all fighting with all their force. Enchantments, both visible and invisible, were flying through the air while the sound of blades clashing continued to grow more violent. The fight had erupted into a battle within minutes and Glyn threw himself into it, slashing his sword through any of Delyth's scum that came his way. Their squeals and cries gave him an addictive chill through his body that drove him onwards. He didn't have powers but his life had been devoted to the sword and he would slice it through anyone who dared to defy his glorious Nyra. She was Liliath's true Queen and he would ensure that any disloyal subjects were finally eradicated.

* * *

Macklyn and Brecon finally let go of Tarley once they had reached an alleyway just off Delyth Avenue. She immediately tried to run back towards the bridge but Brecon blocked her path and pushed her back in to the alleyway.

"You're not going anywhere," he said.

"Arghh!" screamed Tarley. "Why couldn't West just keep his mouth shut?! I had a plan!"

"It wasn't West, it was Mabli," said Macklyn, to which Tarley screwed up her face in response. "I know," he said.

"I have to go back and finish this, people are dying for no reason! Penn was killed!" screeched Tarley.

"No, we're going back to Bray. You can call us selfish or stupid or whatever you want but we're not letting you kill yourself for this," said Lenna.

Tarley shook her head, "You don't understand. I had a plan. I *have* a plan where there's a chance I might live."

* * *

Darvin stabbed another of the Devoted and kicked him to the ground, desperately searching for the rest of the Patrol. He could see Yvette in his periphery throwing an enchantment every second but there was no sign of Mabli, West or anyone else he truly trusted. And he had no idea where Lenna had taken Tarley. He hoped his wife had the sense to stay at Bray with the girls.

He continued to fight as more and more of the Devoted tried to kill him; he had no doubt that being the murderer of the Head Commander would bring great riches from Nyra. He had been in fights and battles before but none that had escalated so quickly and involved just so many people.

And it was all for one woman.

He had not allowed himself time to consider the consequences, too many thoughts and concerns were rushing through his head for him to focus on just one. Even so, he knew that if either of his daughters were in Tarley's position he would have rallied the whole of Liliath to save them if he could. But all he could do now was fight until he had the chance to grab Yvette and run for the hills.

* * *

"Is it working?" Brecon asked.

Tarley had to keep her eyes closed; it was the only way to block out the background noise of the fight. She thought about their faces, about how they spoke to her and the love they had instantly shared. She thought about the lives they had led and the secrets they were a part of and soon, across the sea of angst and need to survive she felt the tiniest of connections. All of them were fighting, she could tell that, and it worried her for more than one reason. She needed them well; they couldn't end this if they weren't.

"I think so," said Tarley. "We just need to find the Patrol."

"Macklyn, let's go," said Lenna.

"I'm coming with you!" said Tarley.

"Tarley, if you step foot on that courtyard, *everyone* is going to turn on you, which means more concentrated fighting for the Patrol, which we don't have the manpower for. People will die," said Lenna and without waiting for a response she gestured for Macklyn to leave with her.

Tarley fell against the wall until she was sitting on the dirty pavement with her head in her hands. Brecon walked over to her and sat down next to her in silence.

"Why are you so determined to die, Tarley?" Brecon asked.

"I'm not. I've only ever wanted to help," said Tarley.

Brecon moved closer to her and was gratefully surprised when she didn't push his arm away.

"I wish you could see how important you are to people. No one wants this for you."

"*I* don't want this but I can't keep allowing people to die for me. Penn…"

Brecon lifted her chin towards him. "He knew what he was doing and he believed enough in you to come charging into Miraylia with the rest of us. Your plan will work."

She moved her lips towards his, feeling like this kiss was more than she deserved. Even if she did live she had never been certain that he would let her kiss him again.

"I love you," said Tarley. "I'm sorry; I had to say it once." Brecon kissed her again. "I love you, too," he said.

* * *

Neb pulled his knife out of the unknown Patrol member and wiped it on his jacket. Thankfully, this idiot had been carrying a sword so he quickly picked it up and gripped it tightly, albeit with a trembling hand. He decided to head for the tower, hoping that he could advise Nyra by her side, but he would have to wade through the hundreds of men and women who were currently crashing their blades against one another.

He hated fighting, always had, and he'd only managed to kill the Patrol member by pure luck. The stupid sod had lost his footing as he was taking his sword out of its scabbard. Darvin would have been appalled, he was sure.

He remained on the outskirts of the fight as he navigated his way through, trying hard to avoid anyone who looked like they were without an opponent. He reached the tower and was met by a large group of the Devoted who were too busy fighting members of the Patrol to notice Neb. He dodged through them and made his way inside, clamouring into one of the old lifts as quickly as he could. He stopped on the final floor and felt like he was breathing new air as he slumped out into the corridor. No one had brought the fighting in here yet so this would be as safe a place as any for now.

"Scared of the fight, Neb?" Nyra said, although Neb couldn't see her.

"Not at all, I came looking for you," said Neb.

He slowly walked down the corridor, checking every room to see where she was but all he could hear was her voice. Very little sunlight was streaming in and so all that was ahead of him was near darkness.

Nyra laughed. "Even a non-Sovran could tell you are lying."

His hand gripped the hilt of his sword just a little tighter as his pace slowed. He checked behind him again but the corridor was empty.

"I can assure you-"

"-enough!" she yelled, suddenly appearing out of the shadows. She was not a large woman but she seemed able to block Neb's pathway just by staring at him. "I know what you desire, Neb Figmore, and I have only kept you alive for this long because you have been useful but that time is quickly coming to an end."

"I don't know what you're talking about; my only desire is to serve you! To make Miraylia-"

"-quiet! What was your plan, exactly? Gain my trust and then try to kill me? Tell the whole world that it was your plan all along and then take your place as Premier?"

Neb yelled as he sloppily launched his blade towards her but her hands clamped down either side, stopping the metal from entering her stomach. She snapped it and threw the rest of the sword out of Neb's hands. He broke into a run but before he was halfway down the corridor Nyra had lifted him into the air and thrown him hard against the wall. She held him there as she approached and looked into his eyes as she drained the breath from him. The last thing he ever saw was Nyra's smile and her flaring eyes.

* * *

As Lenna and Macklyn walked back towards the bridge they could see a handful of the Devoted who had broken through the Patrol's blockade fleeing deeper into the city. Both Lenna and Macklyn wanted to go after every one of them but they knew it would be a waste of energy. As angry as Macklyn was with West he was still desperate to get to him and take him to safety; the thought of him lying on the ground with a sword in his chest made Macklyn's skin turn to ice.

He still couldn't understand how Yvette and Darvin had convinced West to join them. He was more than aware of the differences he had once had with Tarley but Macklyn was certain that was all behind them and, even so, was he really the type to lead an innocent person to their death?

"We stick together, okay? Don't lose sight," said Lenna.

"Don't worry, cous, we got this," said Macklyn.

They were soon on the edge of the bridge and within seconds one of the Devoted had pushed past the blockade and was charging towards Lenna with her sword leading the way. Lenna instantly raised her blade to block her opponent's attack and pushed her away. Lenna swept her legs and sent the woman on to her back before kicking her in the side.

"Let's head towards those enchantments, Yvette is bound to be nearby," said Macklyn.

Lenna nodded and they both pushed their way through their fellow Patrol members towards the various coloured energies that were darting between warriors. The whole scene reminded Lenna of a painting in Bray; Nyra was stood at its centre with her arms raised while streaks of colour surrounded her. The look of powerful determination on her face had been so alien to Lenna when she first saw it but as the months had gone on she could see the same expression appearing on Tarley's face.

"Lenna!" a voice shouted, followed by Ash wrapping his arms around her.

She pulled back to see a cut across his cheek but he was mostly unharmed. She pressed herself against him and kissed him quickly, not caring if it was practical.

"You need to get to Tarley," said Lenna, "she's in the alleyway near where the antiques market used to be."

"Okay, mum's just over there," said Ash, pointing towards Rhoswen who was just a few steps away and single-handedly fighting two monstrously muscular men.

"Okay, grab her and-"

Lenna's sentence remained unfinished as she found herself being lifted high off the ground. She looked down below to see a man covered in tattoos holding his hands above his head as he moved her through the air. She tried to call out for Ash but her chest was tightening and she was gasping for air. She could hear Macklyn shouting for West as Ash readied his knife but they all looked so small and futile from her elevated position.

Ash plunged his knife into the back of the Sovran, causing him to flinch and lose his concentration. Lenna immediately began to plummet towards the ground, screaming at the highest pitch she possessed. Seconds before she hit the ground West threw up his hands and suspended her before slowly lowering her to the ground. Her legs buckled beneath her but Ash grabbed her arms so that she didn't hit the floor too hard. She squeezed and kissed his hands, feeling like her heartbeat was never going to slow down. The Sovran lay next to her, clutching at his wound.

Lenna wanted to push her sword through his chest but that was too merciful; she wanted his last moments to be in pain, knowing there was nothing he could do to stop it.

"You all need to leave; go to Tarley," said Lenna, getting on to her feet.

"I'm staying, the Sovrans should leave last," said West.

"Fine," spat Lenna, "you can help us locate everyone."

Ash gave Lenna one last kiss before grabbing hold of his mum and dragging her towards what had been the entrance to the bridge, despite her eagerness to stay and fight.

"Come on, I just spotted Yvette," said West and the three of them fought their way further into the battle.

Lenna was shocked by how many people lay on the ground either dead or dying; she didn't know what she had expected when she asked the Patrol to help her rescue Tarley, but she hadn't anticipated this amount of violence. Did the Devoted even know why they were fighting or were they just scared of Nyra? Was the promise of riches and power really enough to drive them into battle? At least the members of the Patrol were given the option to fight or not. Lenna tried her best to push these thoughts out of her mind as she swung her blade and kicked, punched and pushed anyone who was blocking her.

"I can see my mum," yelled Macklyn and directed the other two towards Carida.

She was wedged between Ivy and Baodor who were each ducking and dodging several Devoted. Ivy had a tight grip on a pristine bow as she kicked another of the Devoted to the ground. A woman ran towards Ivy but she had already grabbed an arrow, loaded it and sent it in her opponent's direction. She turned back towards Baodor just in time to see a short, stocky man running towards him with a knife that was dripping in blood.

"Baodor!" Ivy screamed, the desperation in her voice breaking through all the surrounding noise.

Baodor jerked his body at the same time Carida sent her

fist into one of the Devoted's head, causing him to land on the ground with a loud thud.

"Mum!" shouted Macklyn, racing towards her.

Carida kissed the top of his head before pushing him out the way so she could clash steel with an incoming Devoted. West and Lenna soon caught up and the six of them were fighting off what felt like hundreds of Nyra's followers. Any hint of exhaustion was violently distinguished by the drive to survive; an impulse that had been ingrained in them all from a young age.

"The three of you need to get to Tarley," said Lenna as she ducked under a swinging sword. "She's in an alley just off Delyth Avenue!"

The woman Lenna was fighting smirked at her before turning to run but West swept her on to her back with a simple jerk of his hand.

"Go!" Macklyn shouted, "we can handle this!"

"Okay, make sure you do," said Baodor and slowly began to lead his fiancée and mother through the carnage and into the city.

* * *

Nyra continued to watch as more Patrol members filtered into the bridge and more bodies fell to the ground. Was anyone looking for the girl? For the last hour she could feel her power flickering between explosion and annihilation; she'd never experienced it before and didn't know how to stop it. She felt like she could bring down the entire world with just a thought and then seconds later it was as if she was back in her cell, praying that she had the strength to break free.

Her shadow was powerful now; much more than she had expected but she was still scared. Unlike Nyra she was worried about the people around her but that had been a foolish thought; they had still run towards death regardless.

This is why Liliath needed her; she would save them from

their own stupid humanity. There would be no need to worry about friends or family when they had such a powerful queen to serve. Their desire to love and fight would be inconsequential under Nyra's reign, which would mean no more battles and no more needless death. They would finally have a purpose to unite under. Once the fight was over they would be grateful.

* * *

Tarley was pacing the alleyway, she couldn't sense anyone yet and not knowing whether they were safe or not was just as frightening as if Nyra had killed them all.

"Come and sit down," said Brecon, tapping the dirty cobbles next to him.

"I can't, I need to be doing something. Anything," Tarley replied.

Brecon reached into his pocket and withdrew a knife with tiny rubies laid into its hilt. He threw it to Tarley who clumsily caught it before twirling it through her fingers.

"Thanks," she said, smiling. "Where did you-"

But Tarley didn't finish her sentence because she was so overcome with the feeling of power that she was rendered speechless for a moment. Every one of them was inside her head; telling her that they were coming, reassuring her that they were safe. They'd been fighting for hours but they weren't finished, yet. They were going to end this.

"They're almost here," said Tarley.

* * *

Mabli had managed to find her way towards Darvin and the two of them were as stealthy as ever, despite Darvin's body threatening to fail him. He envied Mabli's energy and resilience, he had no doubt that she could take on a whole army and still have enough energy to run the length of Liliath afterwards.

He could still see Yvette but whenever she tried to approach them another Sovran would engage in a battle of enchantments.

"Yvette, just take them out!" screamed Mabli but she wasn't sure if Yvette could even hear her.

Yvette grimaced before raising her arms and pushing them back down to her sides causing several Devoted to be blasted into the air like leaves being swept away by the wind. She made use of the gap in the battle and ran towards Mabli just as Lenna, Macklyn and West arrived.

"You need to come with us now, everyone else has gone," said Macklyn.

"Lead the way," said Yvette.

They all began to follow Macklyn, attempting to avoid whatever bodies lay on the ground and the fights that surrounded them. They were all beginning to fantasize about water and resting their bodies but they knew better than to indulge too much in the dream. Any guard would say that the moment your mind wanders, you're dead.

"YVETTE!" Darvin bellowed and all five heads turned in his direction to see his sword fly out of his hand and his body stiffen as if it had been bound by ropes.

A female Sovran with rips in her clothing and cuts across her body stood over Darvin, grinning as he struggled for breath.

Mabli was the nearest and ran straight towards them but found she couldn't get any closer; the Sovran had erected an invisible barrier. Mabli knocked and kicked what appeared to be nothing other than air but it felt like she was punching a brick wall. The Sovran laughed and stepped closer towards Darvin, clenching and unclenching her fists as she allowed him a few moments of breath.

"Yvette, do something!" said Macklyn.

"I'm trying!" shouted Yvette, "the force field is too strong!"

Yvette pushed her way towards Mabli and stood by her side as she cast every enchantment she knew to bring down the force field or immobilise the Sovran but she was stronger than she appeared. Yvette could feel her power and it was terrifying.

"You don't deserve a glorious death," said the Sovran and withdrew a small knife from her inside pocket.

"No, no, no!" screamed Mabli.

The Sovran crouched down next to Darvin, raised the knife and stabbed him in his chest. Darvin gasped as his eyes locked on to Yvette's and she could feel his last breaths leaving his body. An overwhelming sense of numbness enveloped her as Mabli howled and Darvin silently willed them to run.

Yvette had never been so in tune with him; he wanted them all to be safe, he wanted his wife and his daughters to flee, he didn't want to be forgotten and he wanted Tarley to live.

There was pain and relief exuding from him that only made Yvette feel even more helpless. He felt lucky to have been her friend for so long and in that moment she was worried that he would never know how much she valued him, too.

"Get back," Yvette ordered but Mabli remained next to her, still hitting the force field. "Mabli, get back *now* and get ready to run!"

Mabli glared at Yvette before obeying and running into Lenna's arms. She looked back at Darvin one last time to see his eyes closing as his soul finally entered the ether.

Yvette was overcome with rage and a sense of duty that seemed to fuel her powers. She took a deep breath and twisted her hands as she raised them above her head, creating a trail of pure red fire behind them. She pulled them down and soon the whole bridge was covered in a thick red smoke that made it impossible to see.

She shot a stream of white light from her hands and yelled at her allies to run, causing them to break into a sprint and follow the light away from the bridge.

As they ran, amongst the smoky haze, Yvette allowed

herself to shed a tear for the only friend she had ever lived in fear of losing.

CHAPTER TWENTY-FOUR

Nyra screamed at the sight of the smoke and immediately marched out of the tower and on to the forecourt of the bridge.

The smoke began to clear almost as quickly as it had appeared and as soon as a few Patrol members had seen Nyra they were running towards her. All it took was a simple thought and they were out cold on the concrete.

"This fight has gone on long enough," Nyra yelled, amplifying her voice so that everyone on the bridge could hear her. "I want that girl brought to me within the hour or you will ALL die, no matter what side you are on!"

* * *

Tarley poked her head out of the alleyway to see Ash leading a small group down Delyth Avenue with all of them looking down beaten and covered in grime.

"Ash!" Tarley yelled and waved for them to come closer.

The entire group broke into a run and turned into the alley. As soon as Carida spotted her daughter she pushed past everyone in her way and flung her arms around Tarley.

"You stupid, stupid girl," said Carida, sobbing into

Tarley's shoulder.

Tarley kissed the top of her mother's head and closed her eyes, allowing herself to listen to their heartbeats as they raced to match the other.

"Hold on, who are they?" asked Baodor, pointing his sword towards the back of the alley.

Everyone instantly raised their weapons in the same direction to where a group of women stood. Every single one of them was different but all shared the same look of determination that could easily be misconstrued as threatening. They either had a blade or a bow in their hands and each one held it with confidence.

"They're allies," said Brecon, "where is everyone else?"

"On their way, I think," said Baodor. "I hope."

"Has anyone got any water?" asked Tarley.

"I wish, I've got about two drops left in my canteen," said Ash.

"That'll do, give it here," ordered Tarley, holding out her hand.

Ash handed the water bottle over to Tarley who immediately ran her hands over the top and caused the container to brim over with water. Some of the group let out gasps of admiration but most were too desperate to get their hands on the canteen.

"Pass it round," said Tarley, handing it to Ash. "I can create more."

As everyone took several gulps of water Ash tried his best to see to everyone's wounds as best he could. He was certain they were all going to get infections but he tore off whatever pieces of material he could from everyone's clothing to create makeshift bandages. Tarley followed him, attempting to heal the injuries as much as she could but it wasn't an area of her powers that she had developed enough and fatigue was starting to set in.

Tarley could hear footsteps running towards them and gestured for Brecon to follow her into the street but all they could see was the rest of their cohort charging towards them.

"We need to move," said Lenna once they had reached the others. "The Devoted are on their way."

"Who the fuck are they?" said Mabli, pointing to the women at the back.

"Allies, apparently," said Rhoswen.

"We haven't got time for this. Let's *go*," said Yvette.

Everyone grabbed their weapons and ran further into the city, not knowing which direction they should be going in but following Lenna nonetheless. They swerved around several corners and jumped over endless amounts of rubble before finally slowing their pace down to a walk.

"The Finch has a cellar we can hide in," said West, pointing towards a pub on the corner that still had the majority of its bricks.

Lenna nodded and headed towards the pub, ordering everyone to climb down into the cellar, taking note of every cut and wound that infected her friends' bodies.

"Tarley, West, we need to create a protection," said Yvette.

Tarley looked at her Mystic with complete confusion but once Yvette had shown her how to create the energy with her hands Tarley had no trouble in erecting a suitable force field.

They made their way into the pub and joined the others in the cellar where the Patrol were sitting amongst barrels of beer while the women were standing in a corner, waiting for Tarley's command.

"Where's Darvin?" said Tarley.

The room fell silent.

Yvette placed her hand on Tarley's shoulder, already sensing that the young woman's heart was thumping against her chest.

"He didn't make it," said Yvette, softly. "One of Nyra's Sovrans."

Tarley pushed Yvette's hand away and stepped away from her, hoping that no one could see the tears forming in her eyes.

"He didn't deserve that," said Tarley.

"Nobody here deserves any of this but we don't have time to start placing blame," said Mabli. "Nyra wants you on the bridge in an hour or she's going to start killing *everyone* on both sides. So what's the plan, Tarley?"

Tarley gestured for the women at the back of the room to move forward.

"These women are the plan. I'd like you to meet The Heirs."

Yvette's hand flew to her mouth as she gasped. "Tarley, I knew you were powerful but...this is incredible."

"Don't praise me just yet; this plan could still go tits up."

* * *

Plenty of the Devoted had broken through the blockade but the Patrol remained strong; all the bases had arrived and almost equalled the Devoted in numbers. Arrows continued to soar followed by throwing stars and were shadowed by the colours of every offensive and defensive enchantment. Battles like this had not existed in Miraylia for decades.

Nyra was trying every visualisation she could to sense Tarley but all she could feel was the death and pain from below. She thought she would have found comfort in this but all she felt was frustration. She only needed one death, not hundreds.

* * *

Once everyone in the cellar had allowed the shock to set in they quickly began grilling Tarley and The Heirs, regardless of the bruises and possible broken bones they now possessed.

"Which one are you?"

"How did you do it Tarley?"

"This is incredible. This is going to work."

Tarley stood as bodies milled around, eager to chat but

her palms were growing sweaty and tears were threatening to break through again. She didn't have time to embrace all the emotions coursing through her.

"Guys, I'm really sorry," Tarley shouted. "But we don't have time. They have to go."

The noise stopped and everyone looked to Tarley, understanding the nerves and determination raging before them. None of them would dare to challenge her.

The Heirs immediately collected whatever weapons they could and said their bittersweet goodbyes to the rest of the group, pining for more time but also wishing that the end was near. As soon as they'd returned they could feel the centuries' worth of fighting and loss surrounding them at every corner.

Tarley hugged Opal last as The Heirs filtered out. All ten of them felt the pull and the innate need to protect each other. They no longer shared the same face but their souls were intertwined more than ever. Across all the realms and plains in existence they had been drawn to each other and returned together. However fleeting this moment would be, none of them could think of a time when they had felt so connected with another person.

"I really do wish we had time to talk or something," said Tarley.

"I know," said Opal, stroking the side of Tarley's face as if she were a daughter. "But time is not a luxury we have right now."

"I hope you know how grateful I am, I-"

"-we willingly accepted your call, we're happy to be reunited in the ether once more."

Tarley looked at all The Heirs as they nodded towards her, their energy making her feel almost invincible. They looked more like great statues than great women in that moment.

If this goes wrong, at least I'll be in good company, she thought.

"Good luck," Opal said to everyone in the cellar before the nine Heirs made their way out of the pub.

Tarley found herself pacing the small room for several

minutes before Mabli shouted at her to sit down; she was giving Mabli a headache. Tarley was too tired to be angry and just squeezed in between Brecon and Macklyn.

While they waited Ash continued to see to everyone's injuries as best he could while Yvette, West and Tarley refilled the canteens.

Even though it was only Darvin and Penn who were missing Tarley felt like half the room wasn't there. She wanted to go back to the bridge and collect their bodies but she knew she owed it to their memories to see the plan through properly. Even so, the scenes she was imagining of them lying maimed and lifeless amongst the fight refused to leave her.

West had been subdued ever since they had left the bridge and Tarley could see Macklyn staring at him with sadness but avoiding West's gaze any time he dared to look up. Tarley understood his anger but only hoped if they made it to the end of the night alive that anything before would be forgotten. She thought it would be too much to ask of the city but, hopefully, her brother would allow himself to be happy.

"Where's Darvin's family?" Tarley asked no one in particular.

"At Bray, thank the sunset," said Lenna.

Yvette started rambling on about giving him and Penn a proper goodbye but Tarley had stopped paying attention and instead chose to edge herself a little closer to Brecon. They both looked immaculate compared to the others and Tarley couldn't help but feel guilty; she should have been covered in blood and dirt just like everyone else.

There was relative silence for the next hour and Tarley was so glad that everyone she loved was safe and hidden that she wished they would all stay there. She could probably cast a locking charm on the door but she wasn't arrogant enough to think that she could face Nyra alone.

When the time came they gathered their now clean weapons and made their way back outside into the dimming light. Tarley had expected the whole mess to be over hours ago and she still had yet to put her plan into action. Everyone formed a close circle around Tarley with Yvette at the front and West at the back and began to make their way back towards the bridge. Tarley wasn't sure if she felt like royalty or a criminal being taken to their execution.

A handful of people stumbled in the streets but Yvette managed to avert their eyes with a perception jinx. Soon Tarley could hear the screams of the bridge and feel The Heirs hiding amongst it once more.

Tarley was surprised to see that the blockade wasn't as broken as she thought it would be. The Devoted were breaking through but, on the whole, the Patrol were remaining strong despite their fatigue.

"Call Nyra!" Yvette shouted as they reached the bridge. "We've come to surrender!"

Several of the Patrol shot Yvette looks of confusion but she simply nodded her head and begged everyone to put down their weapons. The battle was coming to an end.

The crowd began to part as Yvette led her companions through the furore and further on to the bridge. She could see Glyn running towards the tower only to return minutes later with Nyra. She almost floated towards them and the closer she got the more Tarley could sense her uncertainty, she'd never felt so unsure of herself or her cohorts.

"Let me see her," said Nyra and Tarley pushed her way out of the circle so that she was once again face to face with the would-be Queen. "How do I know that this isn't a trick?"

"Use your sensing powers," said Tarley, "can't you tell that I've had enough? Am I not ready to die to end all of this?"

Nyra did not need to be ordered to sense what Tarley was feeling; even in her weakened state the pain was radiating from the duplicate.

"You are the only one strong enough to conduct this ceremony," said Nyra, pointing towards Yvette. "And I want these removed straight away," she continued, gesturing towards Lenna and the others.

Glyn and Hart instantly grabbed Lenna and Macklyn, pulling them into arm locks while several of the Devoted did the same and dragged the Patrol back into the crowd.

As Yvette, Tarley and Nyra drew closer together Tarley caught a glimpse of Opal edging ever so slowly towards them and close to her was another of The Heirs. There were waves of power and protection floating above the three Sovrans and all of them could feel it lilting back and forth. Nyra and Tarley both felt their connection weaving around as if it wasn't quite sure where it belonged and how it should behave. But neither of them looked anything other than calm.

"Begin," ordered Nyra.

Yvette twisted her hands unnecessarily and began to walk around the two of them, glancing over the crowd.

"What are you doing? Begin!" shouted Nyra.

"I'm sorry," said Yvette, "I'm just cleansing the atmosphere; it's a modern practice, I doubt you're familiar with it."

Nyra's lips twitched as she glared at Yvette but the latter ignored her look and placed Nyra's hand on top of Tarley's.

"NOW!" Yvette yelled and within one swift movement Tarley had jumped back and thrown her arms towards Nyra as Yvette did the same.

The Heirs leapt forward, surrounding Nyra so that all eleven of them had her in a binding charm. Nyra's resistance was transcending the enchantment, causing all the women to put as much energy as they could into their powers.

The Devoted instantly began to run forward but Yvette had already erected a protection charm against them. Only those who truly wished to help Tarley were allowed to pass through.

The Heirs and Yvette began to close in on Nyra as she writhed against her invisible chains and screamed for Glyn to help. Each of The Heirs placed a hand against Nyra's body as Yvette began to circle them, twisting her hands to create a grey energy that grew so rapidly that it covered all ten of them within a minute.

Nyra's screams were guttural and chilling all at the same time but Tarley's attention was firmly on The Heirs as their bodies collectively faded into nothing more than golden energies, glowing in the night.

"No!" screamed Nyra. "Someone stop this! I demand that one of my Sovrans save me!"

Nyra's body finally began to ebb away into nothing more than a swirling light as gasps and cries echoed from the crowd behind. Glyn had let go of Lenna and had tears streaming down his face as he beat his hands against the protection charm.

Lenna grabbed the sword he had taken from her and threw it towards Tarley, who messily caught it. She lunged towards what once was Nyra and pushed the sword through what Tarley assumed was her chest.

A burst of energy shot through the sword, making Tarley scream as she dropped it on to the ground. The energies had now turned into one single blazing light that almost blinded everyone in its vicinity. But the brightness only lasted for a moment before its glow slowly began to diminish.

There was so much power before Tarley but now she could feel it falling through the air and back into the ground. Her whole body felt like it was being drained; the anger and the hate were fading but so was the love and the need to survive.

She stepped back and watched as the light disappeared; ten bodies lay on the ground, lifeless. Blood was pouring from Nyra's chest and her eyes were wide as if the last thing she had seen had been so terrifying that even she couldn't comprehend it.

Tarley crouched down next to her to take her pulse but she knew before her hands touched Nyra's neck that there would be no rhythm. Her skin was so cold it would have been easy to assume she'd died hours ago.

Yvette bent down next to her and wrapped her arms over Tarley's shoulders. Tarley stared at Yvette for a moment before she threw her head against her Mystic's chest and screamed as the tears erupted from her eyes.

CHAPTER TWENTY-FIVE

"Y ou ready for this?" West asked.

"Fuck knows," said Tarley.

West smirked and the two of them followed Yvette out on to the silent bridge.

The bodies had been removed but the blood stains and rubble remained; there still weren't enough people in Miraylia to help with the clean-up let alone tearing down the bridge. Only two weeks had passed since the city became quiet but it felt like so much longer to Tarley.

She had expected her powers to disappear as soon as the life had left Nyra but they had remained and she was as strong as she had ever been; the only difference was that everything came so much easier to her. Charms, jinxes and hexes could be achieved with nothing more than a thought and without reliance on anger. Yvette had surmised that Nyra had felt Tarley's potential the moment she was conceived and that's why she chose her. After all, it was incredibly rare for a Sovran to appear in a family line hundreds of years after the last.

"Where do you want to do this, Tarley?" said Yvette.

"I don't think it matters. Here's fine," said Tarley.

Yvette nodded and gestured for her and West to step

away.

Tarley closed her eyes and thought of Gwyl's voice; the only thing she had heard across the darkness. She thought of the way his voice changed when he laughed, when he was angry and how scared it had been the day she had accidentally entered his world.

"Is someone here? Can you help?"

She could feel the pull of the ether once more, taunting her with its proximity. The gateway was omnipresent and yet still out of grasp, as if it was floating by unable to be caught by anyone of that plain. She kept Gwyl at the fore of her mind, determined to wrap her arms around him once more and make fun of his thinning hair or how she could outrun him through the city.

Suddenly hundreds of voices were calling out to her, begging to be helped, begging to be taken home. There were so many that their voices turned into a haze of noise but the desperation pervaded any words that were spoken.

Tarley's eyes flew open but all she saw was black; she moved towards the ever- growing voices but she saw no one.

"Tarley! My Tarley," Gwyl cried.

"Dad! Where are you?" shouted Tarley.

"You shouldn't be here...you shouldn't be here..."

"Bollocks to that! I'm taking you home!"

She could feel herself slipping back towards the bridge but she kept her mind in the present; focusing on every part of the atmosphere around her. She felt so cold she thought she might be dying but the voices wouldn't quieten and she would hate herself if she left without them. She thought about the loss she had forced their families to go through and could feel each of their souls binding with hers. They were all part of the same realm now, tied to one another.

"Tarley, you have to go now or you'll stay forever," said Gwyl.

Tarley could *feel* the bridge; every man and woman that had ever walked it was waiting for her, demanding that she return. They needed her back and so did Miraylia.

She could hear Yvette and West calling out for her and their voices became her path, leading her back into the light. She could sense the atmosphere changing; they were passing through realms and plains at the speed of light, clinging on to the hope that this was it. After what felt like an eternity of teetering on the edge of one world and another, they could feel themselves smashing through every barrier that ever existed. It was as exhilarating as it was terrifying but still a vague feeling of hope began to course through them. They were either going home or they were moving on.

Tarley's eyes jolted open as she found herself back on the bridge, standing just as upright as she had been when she left. Yvette and West didn't even look at her; they were too busy taking in the sight before them. Every guard that had gone missing was now sitting on the bridge, looking from face to face and ever so slowly bringing themselves to their feet.

"Tarley...I can't believe you did it...," said West but Tarley wasn't listening as she was already racing down the bridge to the spot where Gwyl had gone missing.

She found him there, clinging to a high pile of broken bricks and shaking as if he were in the depths of an illness. She ran towards him and threw her arms around him, desperate to make sure that he was real but as soon as she touched him she felt like he wanted her to let go, to leave him be and not bother him again.

"Dad, are you okay?" she said as she withdrew her arms.

"It was just darkness, Tarley," said Gwyl. "All I've known is darkness without dying."

* * *

Miraylia's General Hospital was still a skeleton of what it once was but the Patrol had managed to bring all of their medical supplies into the city over the past two weeks and turned what remained of it into a makeshift infirmary. All the guards were now in beds but only a handful still had family to be reunited with; the rest were either dead or had fled the country. Some of those without families had even asked Tarley to send them to the next world but Yvette had pushed her out of the room before she erupted into tears.

All Gwyl had spoken about on their way to the hospital had been how much darkness he had been in; he could feel his family on the other side but he had no way of reaching out to them. He had been stuck between life and death with neither one claiming him. Tarley had made an excuse to leave his side an hour ago to help Brecon conduct a stock take of medicines but she'd found herself counting the same five bottles of tonic ten times over.

"Come here," said Brecon, putting down his clipboard and opening his arms.

Tarley walked into them and buried her head in his chest. Ever since Nyra's death they had only managed a few clandestine-like moments together. Each time they were left feeling like they should run away together but knew they would never succumb to the fantasy.

"I need to take you on that date I promised you," said Brecon.

Tarley smiled. "I don't think there's any restaurants left in the city."

"Can't you just swish your hand and make some?"

Tarley let out the lightest of laughs and tightened her hold on him. She wasn't sure how long they stood like that for but it felt like hours before Brecon pulled back and kissed the top of her head.

"Why don't you get out of here for a bit? I know being this close to the guards is upsetting you."

Tarley nodded. "Not a bad idea. Love you."

"Love you, too."

Tarley squeezed his hand and strolled through what was left of the corridors and out into the dilapidated gardens. She found a single bench hidden amongst the long grass and debris and sat down to take it all in.

Ada would have transformed this place, she thought. *There would be trees as tall as the hospital and flowers so bright that even the sickest of patients would feel happiness for a second.*

Tarley wondered if the city would ever rebuild itself to what it was.

"This isn't your fault," said Yvette, causing Tarley to jump.

"I didn't even see you," said Tarley.

Yvette giggled. "Even mighty Sovrans are victims to their own thoughts."

"Will the guards get better?"

"I honestly don't know; I've never dealt with this kind of power before."

"Do you think there's an enchantment? Like a way to bring them back to their old selves?"

"My dear, we may be powerful but there are some things that even we can't handle."

Tarley nodded, she had suspected as much.

"Lenna called; she wants you to meet her at her old shop." Tarley raised her eyebrows. "No idea but we can cope without you for a bit."

Tarley nodded and left the gardens, heading further into the city. She was still amazed that she could find her way around despite all the rubble.

She'd stopped visiting Lenna's old shop as soon as Lenna had joined The Inquiry but every now and then she would pop by to see what swords they had on offer. Every time she went in the owner used to shake his head as if he knew the real reason why she had come by. Now the shop was barely standing and as she stepped through the doorway all she could see was piles of bricks that had been cleared to the side.

"Lenna?!" Tarley shouted.

"I'm out the back!" came the reply.

Tarley made her way to where the workshop had once stood to see Lenna swishing a sword through the air.

As soon as she saw Tarley she stopped and smiled before handing it over.

"What's this for?" said Tarley.

"I promised you a new one so here it is."

Tarley stared at the hilt, which had several pieces of long silver intertwining around one another and had what appeared to be small rubies lain into them. But as Tarley brushed her thumb over the hilt she could feel that they were more like crystals.

"Are these rubies?" said Tarley.

"No," said Lenna, "they're actually tiny pieces of the identity crystal from the bridge. I don't want you to ever forget who you are."

"I'm sure plenty would."

"Well they're idiots. I don't know anyone else who would put their life on the line for this shitty city the way that you did."

"Thank you; it's beautiful."

"Ash asked me to marry him."

"Wow," said Tarley. "And what did you say?"

"I told him to stop being so fucking stupid and then went to help Baodor with dinner."

Tarley laughed so loudly that the sound of her own giggle almost shocked her.

Lenna sighed. "It's not that I don't want to it's just...it doesn't feel right at the moment with everything that's *just* happened."

"Come on, let's go for a walk. There must be a bottle of cerise somewhere in this rubble."

Lenna smiled, pulled on her jacket and followed her cousin back into the remains of Miraylia. The silence was still unnerving, even after months of life slowly leaving the city, but at least now there was a hope. Soon the people would return, the walls would be built and there would be noise once more.

ACKNOWLEDGEMENT

This is the first time I have ever written one of these things and it's possibly one of the most surreal writing experiences I've ever had. Nevertheless, people need to be thanked and thanked they shall!

Firstly, I would like to thank you, dear reader, for taking a chance on this book. I know how many authors are out there, especially indie authors, and the fact that you chose to read this story, which has been in my head for so long, is incredibly humbling.

A massive thank you must also go to Becky Sandy for creating the beautiful covers for this book and being the first person ever to read any version of this story. Becky, not only are you insanely talented but it is a complete pleasure to know you.

To everyone who read the book and gave me notes (Bex, Emily, Alex and Elen) you are all so brilliant and kind. Sending a piece of writing to people who know you is next level nerve wracking but you all gave me the confidence to finally publish this work and I know it's better for it.

Mark and Charlotte, you didn't know this at the time but it is thanks to working with you (albeit for a short period) that you gifted me with the lesson of 'put yourself out there and see what happens.' I have no doubt that this change in thinking is what led me to decide to finally publish this book.

Finally, I have to end this list by thanking my family. This book is dedicated to my grandparents; they helped to shale so much of who I am and I will miss them forever so I hope that this a worthy tribute. They are built into almost every page of this book.

To my parents and Ieuan, all I can say is thank for continuing to put up with my shit and supporting me in a way that is impossible to fully comprehend or explain. You are amazing.

ABOUT THE AUTHOR

Ellie Rees is a writer based in South Wales who hopes
she's as funny and witty as she thinks she is.
If you're so inclined you can find her on various social
media platforms attempting to flog more copies of this
book.

Facebook – Ellie Rees Likes to Write
Twitter & Instagram - @msellierees

Printed in Great Britain
by Amazon